That
Loving
Feeling

*By Carole Matthews and available
from Headline Review*

Let's Meet on Platform 8
A Whiff of Scandal
More to Life than This
For Better, For Worse
A Minor Indiscretion
A Compromising Position
The Sweetest Taboo
With or Without You
You Drive Me Crazy
Welcome to the Real World
The Chocolate Lovers' Club
The Chocolate Lovers' Diet
It's a Kind of Magic
All You Need is Love
The Difference a Day Makes
That Loving Feeling

CAROLE MATTHEWS

That Loving Feeling

headline
review

First published in 2009 by HEADLINE REVIEW
An imprint of HEADLINE PUBLISHING GROUP

1

Cataloguing in Publication Data is available from the British Library

Hardback ISBN 978 0 7553 5415 3
Trade paperback ISBN 978 0 7553 5416 0

Typeset in Bembo by Palimpsest Book Production Limited,
Grangemouth, Stirlingshire

Printed in Great Britain by
Clays Ltd, St Ives plc

Headline's policy is to use papers that are natural, renewable and
recyclable products and made from wood grown in sustainable forests.
The logging and manufacturing processes are expected to conform
to the environmental regulations of the country of origin.

HEADLINE PUBLISHING GROUP
An Hachette UK company
338 Euston Road
London NW1 3BH

www.headline.co.uk
www.hachette.co.uk

Acknowledgements

A big thank you to all the staff at Stony Stratford library for their generous help – Steve Grant, Viv Tole, Nicky Newlands, Christine Salles and Lynn Phillips. I was so excited to work there and they even let me stamp the books! (Before they went all new-fangled.) Needless to say, although the novel is based in a real library – and a very nice one too – all the events and characters are entirely fictitious. Oh yes they are!

For information and anecdotes about fishing, thanks to my uncle, David Coleman, and to top MX5 mates Craig 'The Hat' Hitchman and The Terrible Twosome – the fearless, the inimitable, the frequently very silly – Mr Richard Markus and Mr Owen Earl.

Thanks also to Jill and Simon at The Pudding Club, The Threeways Hotel in Mickleton for facilitating my research. Would heartily recommend one of their Pudding Club dinners – yum! Just leave the diet at home. For info go to www.thepuddingclub.com.

Chapter 1

Good morning, me. I smile at my reflection. Sometimes I don't think that I look too bad when I catch sight of myself in the mirror. Then I put my glasses on. When I'm no longer in flattering soft focus I can see all too clearly the fine lines that radiate from the corners of my eyes, the deepening tracks that score my once flawless skin from my nose to my mouth, the unwelcome puckering of my once full and pouting lips. Now that I know life begins at forty, my mouth is turning into a cat's bottom. I try to relax it and fail. I used to call them my laughter lines, but there's been precious little to laugh about recently – and still the lines deepen.

Pulling the skin taut, I see what I'd look like if ever I found the courage or the cash to have a facelift. A more surprised-looking me stares back and I let the skin fall into place again with an unhappy little huff.

I wish that I was one of those women that people describe as 'feisty'. But I'm not. I wish I had an edgy, swishy haircut that says I'm a woman with my own style, my own mind. But I don't have the nerve to go into the hairdresser's and ask for one of those either – all those stick-thin women in black scare the life out of me. Am I the only person who finds the very thought of Gok Wan getting me naked terrifying? I would rather saw off my own arms than let someone like him tell me all that's wrong with me. I'm forty-five years old, a mother, a wife and a librarian to boot. None of that really adds up to sex-on-legs, does it? Meet Juliet Joyce. Mrs Average.

'Breakfast's ready!' my husband shouts up the stairs. I'd already heard the steady clattering of breakfast preparation coming to a head in the kitchen, but I was ignoring it, putting off the moment when I'd have to face another day. Now I'm going to be late for work if I don't get a move on.

Rubbing foundation over my skin with a heavier hand than normal, I have a last glance in the mirror and sigh. Then, before I forget, I grab the pile of books from my bedside table that are due back at the library today. It wouldn't do for a librarian to be paying overdue fines, would it? The words of Tracy Chevalier, Philippa Gregory and Kate Atkinson have spent the last few weeks soothing me to sleep. Giving them a thankful pat, I tuck them under my arm, then snatch up my bag and head downstairs.

'Bit burned,' Rick says apologetically as I come into the kitchen.

My husband burns the toast every morning because our toaster is old and knackered and Rick is too tight to replace it. I see this as the most important meal of the day and don't appreciate the element of risk that our temperamental appliance brings to it. Rick doesn't share my concerns. He seems to think that, miraculously, one day our toaster will be restored to its former glory and will be able to produce crisp, golden toast once more and not charcoal frisbees. I think we should go to Argos and shell out twenty-odd quid for a new one, but I constantly lose that battle. We had the toaster as a wedding present nearly twenty-five years ago from Ricky's Aunty Gladys – the one who died of a heart attack on a Ryanair flight on her way to Dublin for a salsa-dancing weekend.

My husband insists that he's sentimentally attached to the toaster, whereas I am not. I would like a shiny new one, with variable toasting options and maybe a four-slice facility. Sometimes, in my bleaker moments, I fantasise about it. Rick seems to think that the toaster embodies all that our marriage is about – solid, steadfast, struggling on stoically, standing the test of time. I think it's just not working very well.

At least I don't have to make my own breakfast – Rick does that every morning, regular as clockwork. His intentions are very good. And I should be grateful. Instead, I am considering heart-lessly switching to Bran Flakes as a form of silent protest. See what my husband and our toaster would think of that.

I elbow my way in next to my dearly-beloved and, scraping lurid yellow I Can't Believe It's Not Butter over the blackened I Can't Believe It's Toast, I cast a sideways glance at my husband as he busies himself making tea. Rick looks as if he's permanently in soft focus these days. He's always been quirky-looking rather than classically handsome. A bit like Hugh Laurie, who used to be a geek but is now, mysteriously, a heart-throb. Rick's thatch of hair, which was always spiky long before spiky became trendy, is now thinning. His grey-green eyes are kind rather than smouldering and have soft folds of skin beneath them that make him look tired – the tribu-lations of family life having been stored there. The once chiselled jawline has slackened somewhat and is now threatening to turn into a duet. His tall, gangly frame was all angles and awkwardness when I first knew him. Now the six-pack he used to sport, although we didn't have a particular name for it way back then, has eased into the comfort zone and makes only a vague attempt at a two-pack. Though he's still in great shape for his forty-five years, he looks like he could do with a little tightening all over. But then who am I to talk? Cate Blanchett is never going to feel threatened by my presence on the planet, whereas I'm constantly concerned about hers.

'What?' he says, as he realises that I'm staring at him.

'Nothing.' I risk breaking my teeth on the toast. The dog sidles up to me. Buster doesn't care what state his food comes in as long as it's plentiful. In fact, as long as he gets toast at all, he doesn't care if it's blackened. He's a hound of indeterminate parentage, a black and white bundle of adoring faithfulness. I snap off a piece of toast for him and he chomps it with delight, his tail battering an ecstatic tattoo against the kitchen cupboards. If only I were so easily pleased.

'I thought we could go out tonight,' Rick suggests. 'There's that new film you said that you wanted to see.'

I can't even recall mentioning one.

3

'We could eat out afterwards.'

'How could I leave my mother alone for so long?' I ask. 'She'd probably burn the house down.'

'I heard that.' On cue, my aged parent arrives. She has pink curlers in her sparse hair – the hair that she's recently had dyed an alarming shade of red. I should sue her hairdresser for crime by Clairol for giving her locks the colour of a ginger biscuit. Her dressing-gown is buttoned up all wrong, but at least it's quilted and flowery, the sort of dressing-gown a mother past the age of seventy should wear. I've hidden her short, black silk kimono with the shocking pink dragon embroidered on the back. She had taken to wearing nothing underneath it and I just couldn't cope with that over breakfast.

'I told you when you invited me to live here that I didn't want to be under your feet, that I wouldn't be any trouble,' she says.

For the record, I didn't 'invite' my mother to live here. A couple of months ago, she decided that she'd had enough of my father and left him. She arrived at my door with a battered suitcase, all the gnomes from her garden in two carrier bags and tears in her eyes. What could I do? Rick said I should tell her not to be so stupid, turn her round and send her home again. But I didn't. I couldn't. She's been nothing but trouble ever since.

My mother sits down at the table and waits to be served. I wish she'd stay out of the way until we've left for work and then she could have the kitchen all to herself and we wouldn't have to make nice but, of course, I don't say that to her. She eyes my pile of books and wrinkles her nose.

'You read things that are too posh,' she says. 'Can you get me some of those romances? I like the racy ones. Plenty of sex.' Mum makes a leery face at me.

My mother's literary tastes have turned away from Rosamunde Pilcher and Maeve Binchy to embrace a more salacious, semi-pornographical read. Now she's left my father, she's decided she likes books that feature leather bondage wear on the covers. It's not a trend I'm keen to encourage. You don't want to think of your mother reading that kind of thing. 'I'll see what there is,' I promise, knowing that I'll come home with an armful of Rosamunde Pilcher and Maeve Binchy. People might see me stamping the other books out and think they are mine, for heaven's sake. If she wants to read smut, she can go and get it herself.

Rick pours out some more tea and places it in front of her.

'Bit strong.' She scowls at it in lieu of a thank you.

'Can you get babysitters for senile old bats?' my husband whispers in my ear. I smile.

'I'm not deaf,' my mother says. 'I know what you said.'

'Rita,' Rick cajoles. 'I'd just like a bit of time alone with my wife.'

'I'll go out,' she offers. 'I've just met a lovely lad on that interval.'

'Internet,' I correct automatically.

'He's twenty-nine. Says he likes older women. He says he'd like to meet me.'

'Have you told him you've turned seventy?'

My mother folds her arms across her bust defensively. 'I could pass for a much younger woman, I'll have you know.'

Last week I caught her pasting one of Chloe's more provocative photographs on her dating profile. I had to make her remove it. Part of me wishes she wouldn't spend so much time on the internet – heaven only knows what she gets up to – but if she wasn't on the computer half the night, then she'd be in the living room with us and that would be worse. She talks non-stop through all the television programmes. It drives Rick to distraction.

Anyway, I've stopped checking my mum's history on the net because I know she looks at porn sites. She goes online to chat at *saucysilversurfers.com*, where there seem to be a wide range of grey-haired gents making *very* saucy suggestions. We should make her keep the computer in the kitchen like we used to when the kids were younger. I shake my head. Pensioners surfing porn – whatever next!

'Seventy is the new fifty,' my mother informs me.

What can I say to that? Other than that on some days, I feel as if forty-five is the new ninety.

Chapter 2

Outside the house, an AA transporter van pulls up. From the kitchen, we all crane our necks to see what unfortunate household might be in need of its services.

Chadwick Close is a cosy little street of houses built in the 1970s. We've lived at this same address in Stony Stratford near Milton Keynes for years and, from our prime position, we can see all the comings and goings in the Close. And there have been a few over the years, I can tell you.

Most of our neighbours have lived here for ages too. Houses don't come up here very often and they're sought-after when they do. We often get those estate agent's leaflets posted through our door asking us if we're considering selling, as even in these difficult times they have buyers queuing up to part with their money to move here.

The houses may not be anything special, architecturally speaking, but they're sturdy, square homes with good-sized rooms and gardens big enough for a growing brood. Ideal family homes. In fact, number 10 seemed like our dream home when we moved in twenty years ago. OK, we could do with some modernisation now – the house as well as the people who own it. And its look isn't really enhanced by the group of grinning, fishing, foppish gnomes in the front garden that my mother has foisted on us. But one day Rick will get round to doing the list of jobs that keeps growing. I live in hope.

Then we hear Chloe's key in the lock. I didn't realise that she wasn't yet home. Has she been out all night? I need my car for work. How did she think I was going to get there? The deal is that she can borrow it, but has to be back in time for when I need it. The fact that she also uses it as an overflow shoe cupboard as she's run out of space in her wardrobe for her extensive collection is another contentious issue between us. I think it's a quiet protest as she's been ousted out of the biggest room to make way for her gran and is now relegated to the rather 'cosy' box room.

My daughter bursts in through the front door wearing a white crop-top that struggles to contain her breasts and a skirt that barely skims her bottom. Her legs are bare and she's wearing knee-high white boots. The young seem to have got the message 'less is more' somewhat confused.

'I've got some great news,' she says, grinning wildly as she bounces in. 'Your air bags work brilliantly, Mum.'

Ricky and I rush back to the kitchen window for a better view, and offer up a simultaneous gasp as we take in the crumpled front of what used to be my pride and joy atop the vehicle transporter. My little Corsa is the only new car I've ever owned and I chewed my fingernails to the quick before I reconciled myself to paying out all that money for it. I've always been used to making do, having second-hand. The kids' needs always came first – that's just what you did then.

Now I look at my cheerful daughter and wonder if I did the right thing. Chloe is home from university for the summer after finishing the second year of her Fashion and Media course. She's also nearly eight thousand pounds in debt and is showing no signs of getting a job for the holidays. Instead, she's been out every night partying and spending money that she doesn't have and lying in bed all day.

'What the hell happened?' Rick wants to know. His face is a shade of puce that can't be good for his blood pressure.

'Bit of a fight with a bollard.' My daughter shrugs. 'Got the pedal thingies mixed up. I hit go when I meant to hit stop.'

'Are you hurt?' Rick asks tightly. His tone implies that she might be very soon if she doesn't think to apologise.

'Right as rain,' she says, then flicks a thumb towards the front door. 'You need to see the bloke about the paperwork.'

Rick, fists in tight balls, goes out to see the man from the AA.

'All right, Gran?' Chloe flops down next to my mother. 'I'm shagged.'

'Language, Chloe.' My daughter has the mouth of a sewer rat.

'I love that outfit,' my mother says, eyeing the minuscule crop-top. 'Can I borrow it? I've got a date with a toy boy tonight.'

Chloe giggles. 'You crack me up, Gran.' They high-five each other. I shudder. If my mother's thinking about going out in that, I hope it's under the cover of darkness. I don't think that Chadwick Close is quite ready to be exposed to acres of crinkly flesh.

'I'm going to be late for work,' I say to no one in particular, which is just as well as no one's listening. Only Buster cocks an ear and that's simply because he lives in hope of hearing the word 'food'.

Rick comes back in carrying a bundle of paperwork, black cloud fully formed above his brow. 'He's taking it to Auto Repairs. I've just phoned them.' He shoots a glance at Chloe. 'This is going to be expensive.'

My daughter is blissfully unaware that the comment is aimed at her.

'Can you give me a lift to work?' I ask.

My husband nods. 'Give me five,' he says, and disappears upstairs.

Buster is crossing his legs because no one has had the time to walk him. I turn to Chloe. 'Can you take the dog out for us, please?'

'No way,' my daughter protests. 'I'm knackered.'

I think to argue, but can't summon the strength. 'Come on, Doggers,' I say with a tut. 'A quick run round the garden again.' I open the door and our aging mongrel bolts out and heads for his favourite tree.

Chloe is finishing the rest of my toast, oblivious to the disruption she's caused and the fact that I am seething quietly behind her.

My daughter is blonde, bubbly, bright and utterly self-centred.

Have I made her like that, I wonder as I pull on my jacket. Why does she think that she can treat me and her father with complete disregard and we'll still just be there to pick up the pieces? I've got a headache already and my day hasn't even begun. All I ever wanted was a family of my own. Now I can't imagine why.

Chapter 3

As Rick bounded up the stairs to the landing, his son's bedroom door opened and a tall man, naked apart from a dubiously small pair of underpants wandered out, scratching his personal places.

'Who the hell are you?' Rick said, recoiling from the sight.

The man yawned and stretched. 'Gabe.' He nodded languorously towards the door behind him. 'I'm with Tom.'

'Oh.' As if that explained everything. It wasn't the first time that a bloke he'd never seen before had come strolling out of his son's bedroom and he'd have to have words with Tom about it. Later. Something like this could give Juliet's mother a heart-attack. Hmm. Maybe it wasn't such a bad thing after all. 'I need to use the bathroom.'

'Five minutes, man,' Gabe said, as he slipped past and locked the bathroom door behind him.

Rick thought that 'Gabe' moved quite quickly for a man who radiated so much ennui. He tapped his watch impatiently. This morning he didn't have five minutes to spend waiting. He had to get to work and it would take him even longer now that he had to drop Juliet off at the library on his way. The few snatched minutes of peace he enjoyed with the newspaper on the loo every morning would have to be sacrificed. He felt there were very few pleasures left in his life. Privacy was a dirty word in this house and if his daily bathroom meditation was going to be curtailed, he didn't know how he'd survive. Sometimes he didn't even *need* to use the loo, but chose to. He just wanted to shut the door on everyone else and breathe quietly and steadily without worrying what else would come out of his mouth.

Picking up his watch and his wallet from the bedroom, Rick headed instead back down the stairs and to the front door. Juliet was waiting for him in the drive, standing by the door of his van. Well, the van that belonged to Walk All Over Me, flooring contractors to the stars – the company where he served as a much under-valued employee. In the back window of the van there was a sign which read: *The driver of this van carries no cash – he's married!* It was supposed to be a joke, but Rick knew from bitter experience that it wasn't.

He felt like giving his mother-in-law's gnomes a sly kick as he passed to make himself feel better, but resisted.

'Your daughter's going to have to pay for that car,' he told Juliet as she climbed into the van.

His wife clutched her pile of books and her handbag tightly. 'How, exactly?'

'She'll have to get a job.'

'You try telling *your* daughter that.'

'I will,' Rick said, as he reversed out of the drive. 'I don't care what she does or where she does it, but that girl's going to have to start bringing in some money pretty soon. She seems to think it grows on trees.' He glanced at Juliet, and when he realised that she was mouthing the words along with him, he shut up. Momentarily. Then: 'A naked man came out of Tom's room too.'

Juliet, he noted, had nothing to say about that either. Why did Tom keep bringing strange men home? What were they doing in there? He hoped it wasn't what he thought it might be. But then only weeks ago it had been a string of nameless young women who looked liked they had a deficit of morals whom Tom brought home to use their bathroom facilities. Either way, it was going to have to stop.

As Radio Two blared out, he swung the van into the road. He'd started listening to the 'old farts" station as Chloe called it when he once tuned in accidentally and they played the full, unexpurgated version of Led Zeppelin's 'Stairway to Heaven'. A radio station that did that couldn't be all bad. Today Westlife were blaring out. Rick sighed. It couldn't be wall-to-wall taste permanently, he guessed. They had to play something for the housewives too. At least he hadn't yet resorted to Radio Four. He had another five years before the dial needed to be moved again. Surely?

Chadwick Close was in the nicer end of Stony Stratford. Not perhaps as upmarket an address as the Victorian homes in the centre of the pretty market town – the places that bordered Horsefair Green – but a good second best. Now the kitchen needed replacing and the bathroom wanted a refit. Juliet nagged him about it constantly. But when he'd been working hard all week, the last thing he wanted to do was pick up his tools again at the weekend. Did no one in their household understand the term 'busman's holiday'?

Juliet wanted to get someone else in to do the work, but that would cost a fortune and they'd inevitably do a rubbish job. No, he wanted to do it himself. One day. Still, it would be nice if they could add an en-suite now that the kids were grown up. It had been bad enough only having one bathroom when Chloe and Tom were younger, but he and Juliet had never had the money to splash out on luxuries. He had thought it would get better, but now it was worse. An en-suite could be the answer to many of his prayers. No more sharing a bathroom with bare-chested, underpanted young men with more muscles and less flab than him. No more waiting in line for his mother-in-law to finish making her hair a heinous colour whilst getting dye on his grouting. No more going to use his Armani Code aftershave only to discover that Tom had nicked every last drop. No more finding that Chloe had used his razor to shave her legs or worse.

It was only a five-minute drive to the library in Stony Stratford. Juliet could have walked it quicker rather than sit in the traffic, but she loved her little car and the independence it gave her. Like his five minutes in the loo, it wasn't about necessity, it was about luxury

– and her drive to work was the only time she ever got to herself these days. He could see why she'd be reluctant to give it up. That would explain why she was so quiet this morning.

'I'll pick you up tonight,' he offered, as they pulled up outside the attractive building where the library was housed.

'I might call in on Dad,' Juliet said. 'See if he's doing OK without Mum.' If he was Frank Britten, Rick thought, he'd be delighted that his wife had left. But, by all accounts, Frank wasn't quite seeing it like that. 'Una will give me a lift.'

Una Crossley had recently started working at the library with Juliet and they'd become firm friends straight away. This was the woman Rick called 'the Desperate Divorcée'. He'd only met her a few times, but she had *man-eater* written all over her. The woman scared him to death – but then most women did.

'Thanks, love,' Juliet said. The kiss on his cheek that she gave him was perfunctory.

'I'll get everything sorted out,' he assured her. 'Don't you worry. Your car will be fixed in a few days, I'll murder your mother and bury her under the patio, turf the kids out on the street . . .'

She laughed at that and Rick realised that he hadn't heard her laugh for a very long time. He put his hand over hers. 'We really should take in that movie,' he said.

'I'll see what DVDs we've got in the library that we've missed.'

If they watched a DVD together, Rita would be right there beside them, chipping in with her comments and complaining that the sound was too low even though it was loud enough to make cracks appear in the ceiling.

He and Juliet hardly seemed to have half an hour to spend by themselves these days. Somehow he had thought it would get better when the kids were older but, like the bathroom situation, it only appeared to be getting worse. 'Don't forget your books.'

He handed the pile to her. Even though she worked with them all day long, Juliet very rarely had her nose out of a book, but Rick himself had never been much of a reader. Never had the time.

'Thanks.'

His wife jumped out of the car and he watched her as she crossed the pavement by the Market Square and went towards the library.

Juliet Joyce was still a very attractive woman. Not too fat, not too thin – though she always went on about how she needed to lose half a stone. She looked just fine to him. Her hair was straight with one of those bobby cuts that probably weren't that fashionable these days. Juliet hated her hair, but Rick rather liked it. It was sensible hair. She didn't dye it although there were a few grey hairs coming through its natural soft brown colour now, and she kept muttering that she was going to reach for the bleach before long. He hoped that she wouldn't, but he'd never tell her that.

Her legs were great – always had been. And she probably still looked younger than her forty-five years, though Rick wasn't much of a judge of that kind of thing. So why didn't he get that excited buzz any more when he looked at her? Where had the passion gone over the years? When had his fingers stopped tingling with electricity as he touched her? Oh, the pair of them were comfortable together, but was that enough? Or was that diminishing spark simply what happened when you'd been together for most of your adult life?

His wife turned back, somewhat half-heartedly, and gave him a careless wave to which Rick responded in kind, before slipping the van into gear once more. It wasn't many couples these days who made it to twenty-five years of marriage. That was something to be proud of, surely?

Chapter 4

Una is at the front desk as I swing through the library doors. She looks at her watch. I'm already taking my coat off. 'I know, I know.'

'It's not like you,' my friend says.

'Chloe crashed my car. I had to wait for Rick to bring me in.'

'Is she all right?'

'Oh, yes. My daughter is the picture of health.' Thankfully. 'I can't say the same for my car.'

'Oh, Juliet.'

'Don't.' I hold up my hand. 'I'm feeling very teary.'

'Make yourself a cup of tea. Put your feet up for five minutes. Don's at a meeting at the Central Library in Milton Keynes.'

Don is our library manager. He's a proper librarian with a degree in it and everything, but because he's the only man in a sea of women, we've made him an honorary girl.

'No one will be any the wiser,' Una continues. 'Then you can hide upstairs for the rest of the morning while you shelve these books.' She nods at the laden trolley waiting patiently by the lift.

'You're a pal,' I say with a sigh.

Una frowns. 'Is everything else OK?'

'Oh, you know . . .'

'Not sure that I do,' my friend admits. 'Want to talk about it over lunch?'

I nod, unsure of my voice.

'There's a packet of chocolate digestives in Don's desk that he's hiding from us. Help yourself to a couple. That'll make you feel better.'

'He's probably marked them.'

We both laugh at that.

I go through to the staff room which isn't the most salubrious place to spend any quality time. The carpet tiles are grey and stained. Damp patches seep through the dirty white walls, leaving yellow wiggly outlines. Overhead, a fluorescent strip-light tries to blind us all. In the middle of the room a chipped Formica table serves as our lunch venue.

I make a cup of tea and nick two of Don's biscuits which are secreted under a folder in his desk drawer; his own office has a leaky roof so he's having to camp out in the staff room until we can beg, steal or borrow the funds to fix it. Makes nicking his biscuits easier. I choose one of the rag-tag assortment of plastic bucket chairs around the table and sit down. We have a sofa, but it's way too skanky to sit on and normally houses a pile of books that one or other of the staff have set aside to read.

The library won a design award or two when it was built back in the seventies. Now it needs some money spending on it to drag it into the twenty-first century. It's not only me who could do with a facelift. The whole place is looking a bit shabby now and needs completely redecorating, particularly the upstairs. It's nice to have so much space in our library, but that also costs a lot of money to maintain. In these days of cutbacks we don't even have enough funding to buy the new books that we so desperately need, let alone the cash to lavish on creature comforts such as a posh carpet and comfy chairs for our dedicated band of book borrowers.

Downstairs there's a large counter that serves as our reception area where books are logged in and out. The ground floor also houses the children's section of the library and, thankfully, that's a brightly-painted area with a corner set aside for our Thursday-afternoon storytelling session. The job of entertaining our regular group of mums and toddlers has fallen to me since the last willing victim left. It is, however, one of my duties which I enjoy the most.

I like to think that I'm doing my little bit to create the next generation of avid readers, even though I realise I'm competing with the latest computer technology including the ubiquitous Wii.

Staring out of the big, airy window I let the hot, sweet tea soothe my jangled nerves. It's a good job that I don't like strong drink otherwise I'd definitely be one of those women who take a sly tipple of brandy or whisky with their beverages to calm them down. Instead, sugar has to do the job.

The library looks out over the Market Square in Stony Stratford – an attractive little town that has done its best over the years to retain its quaint character, although we do have our fair share of sixties' monstrosities that somehow managed to barge their way in. The exterior of the library is relatively modern, but the soft red brick and white render blend in quite well with its surroundings. Just as well, as we're right next to the ancient Church of St Mary and St Giles in the centre of the town.

I love this place and can't imagine living anywhere else. Its history stretches right back to Roman times and further. I like to think that I'm in a long line of people who have enjoyed life here. I was born in this town, brought up here, will more than likely die here. What a thought. I'm not one of those people who has ever hankered after the open sweeping plains of the Serengeti or the steamy forests of Sri Lanka. The sad truth is that I like to spend my holidays at home, tending my garden, curling up with a good book, walking in the gentle Buckinghamshire countryside. I've never had this modern urge to get away to the sun and bake myself to a crisp for four weeks every year. I'm rather happy just where I am. Plus we've never had the money to be able to consider such adventures. I think that's bothered Rick more than me. He would have liked to see New York, Sydney, Hong Kong and a long list of other places, whereas I can find enough joy in my own surroundings.

One of our regular customers jolts me from my reverie. Our Mr Hindle always parks by the staff-room window and revs the bollocks off his poor old car when he leaves. At least his engine abuse has stopped me from daydreaming the morning away. I should get out there and help my colleague. There are only the two of us in today, but then Thursday is often very quiet. Nothing much happens on a Thursday. Though Wednesday isn't that much more exciting, it has to be said.

Librarians may not live on the cutting edge of life – the world's financial markets don't rise and fall at our behest, our book-stock choices don't cure terminal diseases nor our late-night opening hours change lives – but we are not the dull people we are made out to be either. I don't come to work in a tweed suit and I never wear my hair in a bun. I have never needed horn-rimmed spectacles. Having said that, there are days when I wish that I could sweep away my staid image by running naked down the High Street with a rose between my teeth. That would make the populace of Stony Stratford sit up and take notice. Maybe that's why I haven't ever dared to do it. Or perhaps I'm simply closer to the prim librarian stereotype than I dare to admit.

Sweeping the crumbs off the table to destroy the evidence of my biscuit crime, I then head back out into the library to face the day.

'Better?' Una asks as I approach.

'Yes. Much.' Una and I haven't known each other for that long but we became close friends instantly, from the first day that she started at the library. I give her a hug. 'Thanks. You're such a good friend.'

Una Crossley is everything that I'm not. She *is* one of those women that you'd call feisty. There are women who dress way too young and still get away with it: Una is one of those. Next to her I'm Mrs Dowdy from Dowdy Town. She looks like she should be a celebrity on television, a presenter or a newsreader, not working full-time in Stony Stratford library. My friend is slender, favours skimpy clothing with designer labels, and is groomed within an inch of her life. There's never a hair out of place on her contemporary cropped style and she goes to the best hairdresser around here once a month for highlights in three different colours. Her nails are always beautifully manicured – those white ones with the square tips. And her earrings and bangles tinkle and chink whenever she moves. She also gets one of those Hollywood spray tans every single week, which makes her look healthy and glowing. I'm the colour of a bottle of milk and yet I've never dared go to one of those places in case I came out looking like a satsuma. Somehow being borderline orange suits Una, whereas I'd look like I had a deadly disease or a liver complaint.

My friend would be the first to admit that she always led a pretty pampered existence until she left her husband last year. Martin took her unexpected departure very badly, insisted he was the perfect husband and that one day she would wake up and realise it. They had an acrimonious divorce – McCartney and Mills could have learned a few tricks from them – and Martin somehow managed to hide most of the money stashed in his property business from the divorce lawyers. Una knows that her ex-spouse is seriously loaded – after all, he managed to keep her in the style she'd become accustomed to for their entire marriage. According to his books though, he wasn't worth a bean. My friend walked away from her cosy life with very little – if you don't count her amazing designer wardrobe and a wide selection of Jimmy Choos. Still, she can't exactly eat those.

Now she lives in a small terraced cottage on Horsefair Green in Stony – so not too downmarket, but certainly not what she is used to – and she's had to go out to work again for the first time in twenty-odd years. When you ask her why she left the handsome hubby, the big house, the current model of Merc, all she will say is that she was bored. I think I could stand a lot of boredom if my life was like that.

Una's a great hit with the customers. She adds a bit of glamour to our little library and we've had a lot more men as regulars since Una started to grace our counter. My friend is the Victoria Beckham of library assistants. The other staff aren't that keen on her though. They think she has ideas above her station. Lady Crossley, they call her behind her back. My husband Rick's terrified of her. I think she's too full on, too confident for him. He calls her the Desperate

Divorcée, even though he knows that I don't like it. She's been a good friend to me and I won't hear a word against her.

'It's as dead as a doornail here today,' Una complains now as she idly inspects a manicured finger. 'Where are they all? Is there something fantastic going on that we don't know about?'

'I doubt it.' My friend would seem more at home in Monaco or St Tropez or Puerto Banus. I don't think that the delights that Stony Stratford has to offer are exciting enough for her.

'Nothing ever happens here,' she tuts.

She's probably right. But I like it like that, whereas Una does not. I like the solid stability, the peace that the library has to offer in these changing times. It's a calm sanctuary amid the breakneck pace of life. Still, even in the gentle quiet of the library, I can't just stay here and daydream. Time to do some work.

'I'll go upstairs with the trolley,' I say.

'See you later.' Una heads to the magazine rack to find one to flick through.

Calling for the lift, I then push the heavy wooden trolley into it and go up to the first floor. The information desk is up here and the four computers that the public can come in and use for a small fee. Today one of our regulars is on PC number one but, other than that, this floor is deserted. Sometimes I've suggested to Don that we might have some gentle classical music playing up here to soften the cavernous space, but Don is younger and trendier than the rest of us and would want to play the Arctic Monkeys and The Feeling instead of a little Vivaldi – and I don't think that the good people of Stony Stratford are quite ready for that.

I set about sorting out the books. It's likely that I could do this job in my sleep. Instead of counting sheep when insomnia troubles me, I should shelve imaginary books by the Dewey Decimal System – that would send me off.

My life in the library started when I got a job as a Saturday girl at the tender age of sweet sixteen. While my friends were working on supermarket checkouts or sweeping hair off the floor in hairdressers', I was immersing myself in the calm, quiet world of books.

As an only child, reading has always been my solace, a novel my favourite companion. Without leaving my room, I've been all round the world, have been seduced by 100 different heroes, have soared to the moon and back on the wings of love. When a full-time position became available, I abandoned any thoughts of sixth form and A-level studies, got the job and have never left.

Apart from a few breaks for maternity leave and part-time hours when Chloe and Tom were small, I've been one of the fixtures here for nigh on thirty years – which is a terrifying thought. My presence is as unchanging as the worn dark wood shelves or the classic novels that grace them.

My favourite area is the general fiction one, arranged from A–Z by author's name. Pristine hardbacks on one stack of shelves, well-thumbed paperbacks on the next. This is where I choose most of my own books from. Thrillers with their high body counts and grisly descriptions of unspeakable acts aren't for me, and auto-biographies chronicling the tedious lives of C-list celebrities leave me cold. I like books that express the emotions that somehow I'm unable to reach these days. Storytellers who delve into the depths of human love and life are the ones I gravitate towards. Lovingly, I stroke the covers of the books. Even though I don't know the authors, have never met one, they feel like old friends to me because they know the things that I suffer from, the problems that keep me awake at night, the small hurts that are in my heart. Jodie Picoult, Anita Shreve, Rosie Thomas – you are my saviours, my solace, my escape. If I was a character in one of your books it would be the small, insignificant woman. The one who had achieved so little, who had dreamed so much. The one whose life hadn't quite turned out as she'd hoped, but who still had no idea how she might have preferred it to be. The one who wondered whether it was too late to change, and whether this was how it would be for the rest of her life.

I cradle a pile of novels in my arms like children. Then, shuffling the books on the shelf, I make space for Margaret Mitchell's classic novel, *Gone With the Wind*. Always a popular choice. I like the order of things in the library, and Margaret's natural home is sandwiched between Peter Mayle and his *Year in Provence* and Kate Mosse's *Labyrinth*.

'Isn't that one of your favourite books?'

I turn at the familiar yet strange sound of the voice behind me.

'Yes,' I say, and my reply sounds perfectly normal, even to my own ears. No nervous tremor, no sudden lump in the throat.

Perhaps I should gasp out loud and drop my pile of books, letting them clatter to the floor, spoiling the peace and tranquillity of this Thursday morning in the library – do all the things you're supposed to do when you've had a terrible shock. But I don't. The years fall away, my mind rushes back in time, but I stand stock still and just look at the man in front of me. And it's just a look. A normal one. I don't even stare with my mouth agape. Given the circumstances, perhaps I should.

Chapter 5

Rick thought about phoning his boss, Hal Bryson, but it would be quicker just to put his foot down and get to the job as soon as he could. Today they were laying a laminate floor for a big house on the outskirts of Buckingham. It was so unusual for Rick to be late for work that he knew Hal would forgive him.

They'd been firm friends before Rick had started working for Hal as they'd been in the same Sunday league football team for ages and, subsequently, drinking mates in the pub afterwards. Rick had toiled away in an office job for years, boring as hell, producing reams and reams of figures that no one ever took any notice of, but it had paid the bills. When he'd been made redundant it was a blessing. Rick had always been good with his hands and welcomed the chance to join Hal in his business – the result of a drunken conversation down at The Bull one night.

Ten years later and it now rankled slightly that Rick did all the work and Hal sat back on his laurels, enjoying the fruits that were largely of Rick's labours. Actually, it rankled quite a lot.

Rick checked the client's address and then picked his way through Buckingham until he found the right road. Outside the enormous house, Hal's big, shiny Mitsubishi Shogun was parked. At least his boss was here. Hal had recently left his wife, Melinda, and a messy divorce had made him even more unreliable than usual. Coupled with that – bad choice of words, perhaps – Hal had found himself a new, twenty-two-year-old girlfriend – shortly before leaving his wife, it had to be said – who was proving a little more exhausting in the bedroom than he had imagined.

Finding the back door unlocked, Rick went in and located Hal perched on the windowsill of a large conservatory, nursing a mug of tea. Despite the time, it was clear that no tools had yet been wielded in anger.

'Sorry I'm late, mate,' Rick offered. 'Chloe crashed Juliet's car and I had to sort it out, then take her to work.'

Hal raised bleary eyes. 'Is Chloe all right?'

'Yeah. But she won't be if she thinks I'm going to pick up the bill.'

'Kids, eh?' Hal said.

'Tell me about it.'

'Lady of the house has gone out. You'll have to make your own brew if you want one.'

'I'll get cracking,' Rick said. It was a big area that they had to cover and they'd only allowed two days for the job as they had so much other work on. 'I've got to go out and do an estimate later. Unless you want to do it?'

Hal shook his head. 'Might leave you to it today. Heavy night. Feeling a bit fragile.'

It wouldn't be the first time Hal had neglected his duties in recent months.

'Too much booze?' Rick enquired.

'Too much sex,' Hal confided. 'The girl's insatiable.' He might be complaining, but he did so with a glint in his eye. Then he gave a laugh. 'I'm going to need help from some little blue tablets if this carries on.'

It wouldn't. Surely Hal should know that from his own experience. While love was young they'd be at it like rabbits, but once they settled down – say, if you'd been married for twenty-odd years – then sometimes a whole month might slide by, or even two, before you realised that you hadn't actually slept with your wife. Or, more accurately, *sleeping* was *all* that you'd done with her.

'Has Shannon moved in with you now?'

Hal shrugged. 'There's more of her stuff at my place than there is at hers.' He drained his cup. 'I'm hardly going to be able to stay round there with her mam and dad in the next room. They might learn a bit more about their young daughter's proclivities than they want to.' That made him guffaw.

It made Rick wince. He could have been talking about Chloe. His daughter was only a year or so younger than Hal's new squeeze and he couldn't bear to think that she might get up to some of the stuff that Hal had told him he and Shannon did. Rick was forty-five, considered himself broadminded, and yet he'd never heard of half of the things that went on in their bedroom frolics.

When Hal had abandoned his wife, his two kids – Ashley, who was just eleven, and Lauren, who was fourteen – had both taken it badly. How would Hal feel if Lauren was a bit older and had shacked up with a divorced, forty-year-old bloke with a shaved head and a slender grasp of political correctness? He doubted whether he'd be too pleased, and, by all accounts, it sounded like Shannon's parents didn't approve of *her* taste in men.

'You want to try it, Ricky-Boy. There's nothing quite like young, firm flesh.'

It had certainly cost Hal enough to try it. By the time he and Melinda had split all their assets, Hal had been out of pocket to the tune of nigh on a million quid and was looking forward to paying substantial maintenance for the foreseeable future. Now he seemed to be bankrolling Shannon too. It was a good job that he seemed to feel he was getting value for money.

'You wouldn't believe what we did last night . . .' he went on.

Rick tuned out as Hal regaled him with another one of his tales of their sexual high-jinks. It made Rick tired just thinking about it. What would a twenty-two-year-old girl see in his friend anyway? Hal was a handsome enough man, if you went for the Vin Diesel type – but Rick was convinced that it was more to do with the fact that Hal had the urge to flash his cash about.

25

His friend wore a gold ring on every finger, a chain that would anchor a ship round his neck and a diamond stud in his ear. Was that right for a forty-year-old man who was a flooring fitter not a gangsta rapper? Rick sometimes wondered whether there wasn't a touch of jealousy lurking behind his disdain for Hal's bedroom adventures. His own sex-life wasn't exactly likely to scandalise the tabloids. Juliet was the only woman he'd ever had carnal knowledge of − something that wasn't all that strange in those far-off days. He was married with a child on the way by the time he was twenty − one of the main reasons they got married at all. How things change. Now there was no stigma in being an unmarried mother. Even twenty-five years ago, it was very different. And he didn't want to know how many sexual partners his own kids had had by the time they'd reached twenty. They'd certainly both outstripped their father's tally. His son in the last week alone, by Rick's reckoning.

But way back then you had to be able to buy your own house to find somewhere to have sex with any degree of comfort. Other than that you were confined to the back of Ford Escorts or the occasional *al fresco* fondle if the weather was kind. His parents would never have condoned him bringing home a different partner every week as Tom did. And it wasn't as if he and Juliet liked the parade of strangers who came to sleep at their house. They just put up with it. Rick wasn't even sure when it had started to happen but, if it continued like this, he'd have to put a stop to it.

Rick often worried that he and Juliet had married too young − even more so these days, for some reason. He never used to feel like this. It wasn't that he was unhappy with Juliet, it was more that he wondered if this was how it should be. How could you tell when you had nothing else to compare it to? At forty-five, should he have lost his love of life? Should he feel that his youth was a distant memory and that retirement was looming too large? Should he feel quite so grumpy at the irresponsible attitude of today's youth? Was it so long ago that he'd been young and reckless too? Was it possible to recapture those feelings at his age?

Perhaps their impending Silver Wedding had made him start thinking. Twenty-five years was quite a milestone in anyone's life. They should be planning some sort of celebration, but his wife hadn't suggested anything as yet. Perhaps she didn't think they had anything to sing and dance about either.

Rick sometimes thought that he'd missed out on some of the fun things in life. Would he be lighter in his heart if he could look back, smile and think that he had once sown his wild oats, had once been a crazy, carefree fool? He and Juliet had been saddled with debt and responsibility for the whole of their married life. Whoever said that kids kept you young clearly hadn't had any. Now they were caught in the generation of mid-lifers who were trapped between paying out to help their wastrel children at one end and shelling out to keep their own parents in some kind of comfort in their old age at the other. Although having Juliet's mother come and live with them was a step too far in his book – but then, no one ever asked *his* opinion.

He used to be the hub of his family, the one they all came to for advice – the patriarch – and he had held his position with pride. Now Rick wasn't sure where he fitted in, or whether he fitted in at all any more. He felt like one of those spacemen who go outside the main spaceship, floating in the universe, anchored only by the very slenderest of lines, detached, alone, outside of the main mission, the one who could tumble free at any moment and go spinning off into oblivion.

'I think I'll put the kettle on,' he said.

Hal stood up. 'I'll have another one too, mate. I've only just got here myself. Had an appointment with my life coach this morning.'

Rick didn't have a life coach and he wondered why Hal needed one if he was having such a great time.

'Bloody expensive,' Hal complained. 'A hundred and twenty notes a pop. But worth it.'

27

Hal slapped him on the back while Rick tried to find which cupboard contained the mugs and the teabags.

'You ought to try it, Ricky-Boy. You're looking very down in the mouth at the moment.'

It was true, he was. But Rick didn't need someone charging him £120 per hour to tell him that he was thoroughly and completely fed up.

Chapter 6

Steven Aubrey. I haven't seen this man in twenty-six years. I realise that I'm gripping *Gone With the Wind* tightly to my chest.

'Isn't that the story of a woman who spends her life in love with the wrong man?' The wicked twinkle that was always lurking in the depths of his brown eyes is still very much in evidence.

'Something like that,' I say.

'You could look surprised to see me, Juliet.' He sounds disappointed that I'm not. Perhaps Steven Aubrey had hoped to make more of an impact with his sudden reappearance after twenty-odd years. 'You haven't changed,' he goes on. 'Not a bit.'

I laugh at that. But I don't sound as if I find it funny. I'm so different from the person he once knew. Surely he can see that?

'You look just the same,' he continues, shaking his head as if astounded.

Just the same as the morning he jilted me? I do hope not. Goodness, that brings some unwanted memories flooding back. Without warning, I'm right back there, in my bedroom at my parents' house on the morning of our wedding.

When Steven came to my house and calmly announced that our marriage, so long in the planning and then just a few hours away, wouldn't go ahead, I was hysterical, red-eyed, white-faced, distraught. Now, despite my pounding heart, I'm the picture of cool, calm collectedness.

But then appearances can be deceptive.

29

Steven smiles at me. 'Aren't you even going to ask me why I'm back?'

'I heard that your mother was ill.' I'm assuming this is why my former love is visiting his home town.

Mrs Harriet Aubrey, Steven's mother, has been one of our regulars for many years. For the last nine months she's been unable to come into the library and has gone onto our Home Readers' Scheme. Once a month a volunteer takes books out to her and brings back the ones she's read. Mrs Aubrey likes historical fiction – Julia Quinn, Elizabeth Chadwick, Sarah Dunant. I always choose novels that I think she'll like, but I'm never the one who delivers them to her. 'I'm sorry that she's unwell. How's she doing?'

'Not great.' Steven shrugs the uneasy shrug of the concerned. 'I've moved into Watermill House in Old Stratford, the one by the waterside park. For the time being.' It's a beautiful home, well-known and much coveted in the area. 'I felt I should be near her.'

I slip Margaret Mitchell onto the shelf, making sure that she sits comfortably. Perhaps I should see Steven's mother, make my peace with her. I was never offhand with Mrs Aubrey, but to my eternal shame I was never very warm towards her either. Why? I don't know now. It was hardly her fault that her son left me in the lurch on the morning of our wedding. But when Steven high-tailed it, she was the one left behind, the one I had to see over and over again, bumping into her in the High Street and in the library. His mother never said she was sorry that we didn't marry, and never asked if her son had given me a reason why. I got the impression that she didn't think I was good enough for Steven – maybe he came to feel that too – but that may be down to my own insecurity rather than the reality of the situation. Still, it's all water under the bridge now, as they say.

'I never expected to find you still here,' Steven says. 'Not after all these years. My mother told me where you were.'

'Like you said, I guess nothing much has changed.'

'You could say that you're pleased to see me,' the man who used to be the love of my life prompts.

A smile comes uncertainly. 'Of course I am.'

'I didn't expect you to hurl yourself into my arms, but a hug for an old friend might be nice.'

Is this man an old friend? He's the only person who's ever ripped out my heart and stamped on it. Should I still hold that against him, or has time really been the healer that it's reputed to be?

Without the protection of my books, I step forward hesitantly. Steven wraps his arms round me while I stiffen at his touch. He's warm and holds me tightly, carefully. My legs don't want to support my weight. It feels so good to be in his arms once more. I close my eyes and I could be a teenager again. The feel of his heart beating against my breast scares me. The old connection between us is still very much there, hiding just below the surface, and it's taken so little to reawaken it.

The man who was once my fiancé, my love, hasn't changed at all either. On the surface. Yes, there's a smattering of grey at his temples, but his dark hair is as thick and wavy as it ever was and he's still wearing it swept back from his forehead in a style that's not so fashionable here now. The well-modulated English accent is now overlaid with something else – a hint of American, perhaps a slight South African twang . . . or is it Australian? Whatever it is, it makes him sound exotic and, dare I admit this, sexy?

Shaken, I step out of his embrace and he hangs his hands by his sides while I wring my fingers together.

'I've been living in South Africa for the last ten years,' he says, answering the question that I hadn't asked.

I find my voice. 'Are you back for good?'

'That depends,' he says, and gives me an enigmatic look. 'On a lot of things.'

'You'll not find Stony Stratford changed much.'

'That's what I like about it. I've travelled the world,' he says expansively, 'but there's no place like home.'

'So they say.'

Now we've run out of conversation that doesn't take us onto more tricky ground. Not only did Steven leave me on our wedding day, but he left town too. He came to tell me that he didn't think he loved me enough to marry me and then he went away. From that day to this, he's never once contacted me. I was left to deal with the aftermath and the gossip alone.

Over the years, I heard snippets of tittle-tattle about him – that he was in America, China, New Zealand, Australia. There had been a wife, maybe more than one. No children, as far as I know. But then my sources may not have been reliable. In fact, 'my sources' were mainly my mother.

'Have lunch with me?' Steven suggests. 'We've so much to talk about.'

I'm not sure that I have anything to say to Steven Aubrey at all. What could we possibly talk about that wouldn't be awkward or embarrassing? 'I can't,' I tell him. 'I'm busy.'

We both take in my trolley stuffed with books that aren't going anywhere in a rush and the nearly deserted library floor that doesn't need my attention.

A smile plays at his lips and my emotions tumble into free fall. 'Surely the readers of Stony Stratford could spare you for an hour?'

I shake my head. *Stay firm. Stay in control. That's how to do it.* 'Not today.'

He steps towards me again, even though we're already closer than I'd like us to be. *Ignore that fluttering in your stomach, Juliet,* I advise myself sternly. *It means nothing.*

Steven lowers his voice. 'I know that I did you a great harm,' he says softly. 'And you have no idea how much I've bitterly regretted it over the years.'

Not enough to send me an apology, make a phone call, write me an email, I think, but already my hardened heart is turning to mush.

'But I'm back now, Juliet, and I want to make things right between us.'

'There's no need for that,' I assure him. A bright laugh is required at this point, but I can't summon one. 'All's well that ends well.

I'm a happily married woman now. I have been for nearly twenty-five years.'

'To Ricky Joyce,' he says. 'I've had my spies on you.'

'He's been a good husband.'

'I wish I could be glad to hear that,' Steven says. Taking my hand in his he holds it tightly, lifting it to his lips. 'But I'm not.'

He gently kisses my fingertips and the shock of it sizzles like electricity in my veins. The breath goes from my body. I gasp for the air that tastes dusty from years of being filled with books.

Steven lets go of me. He meets my eyes and smiles just as he used to. And the memory of it almost breaks my heart. I see him as a boy again. The boy who broke my heart.

'You haven't heard the last of me, Juliet.' Steven sounds very determined. 'I'm going to come in here every day and pester you until you, at the very least, agree to have lunch with me. I was an absolute fool to let you go once. I won't do that again.'

He turns and walks away from me. I stand rooted to the spot. Frozen. Fixed. Flustered. When Steven reaches the stairs, I shout out. I don't know where it comes from. I think my subconscious must have wrested control of my brain because, believe me, this is a completely involuntary action.

'Tomorrow,' I tell him. There's a quaver in my voice. 'I'll have lunch with you tomorrow.'

Chapter 7

Five hundred and seventy-five pounds and forty-three pence. Rick snapped off his mobile phone and tossed it back onto the top of his toolbox. That's how much it was going to cost to repair Juliet's car. A tidy sum to pay for his youngest child not managing to remember which was the brake and which was the accelerator. He'd taught Chloe to drive – as he did Juliet and Tom – and he thought he'd done a damn good job. His daughter had passed her test first time. She should know better.

Rick wished he could console himself by thinking that at least no one was hurt – that's what his wife would do – but, currently, that was providing no comfort. He was going to make Chloe hurt. Preferably in her pocket. And he would ban her from using the car for the entire summer. Probably for the rest of her life.

He sighed out loud.

'Bad news?' Hal wanted to know.

Rick banged that bit harder with his hammer at the nail beneath it. 'The garage just phoned with the estimate for the car. Nearly six hundred quid.'

'Harsh.'

'I'll be after some overtime, mate.'

'No worries, Ricky-Boy,' Hal said. 'There's plenty of work about.'

Rick banged harder still. Did his darling daughter even appreciate just how long it took to earn that amount of money? How many acres of laminate that had to be laid? How many rolls of carpet that would need to be lugged? He wondered what they should do. If they claimed from the insurance company then they'd lose Juliet's no-claims bonus and next time round it would cost them a fortune to renew the policy. Even the excess was two hundred and fifty quid. It would be better to bite on it and settle the bill themselves. See how Chloe liked *that*.

More hammering. Where had the fresh-faced baby he'd brought up gone? When had his lovely little daughter turned into the demanding diva with the dress sense of a hooker? About the age of thirteen, if he remembered rightly. Rick had been so proud when both Tom and Chloe had gone to university – the first kids in their family to do that. Now, having graduated, Tom – who looked like he styled his hair with a firework – seemed to be terminally unemployed. He did nothing but spend his days locked in his bedroom drooling over what seemed to be primarily dodgy websites while pondering what he might or might not like to do with the rest of his life – which was getting shorter by the minute. At this rate, by the time Tom decided what he wanted to do, he was going to be drawing his pension.

At university, Chloe seemed only to be learning how to drink and skive. Wouldn't it have been better if he'd insisted they both go out into the cruel world of work at the age of sixteen instead of providing them with a ridiculously cosseted life well into adulthood in the name of further education? Rick had worked hard all his life to provide them with everything they needed; now it felt that he'd given them too much, too easily.

'I think that you and Uncle Hal need to go out on the town one night very soon,' his friend suggested. 'Bring some joy into your grey little life.'

Hal was always harping on about them going out together. In their divorce it seemed that Melinda had not only got the house and a sizeable amount of maintenance, but she'd also retained all of the friends. And, as much as Hal protested his happiness with the youthful Shannon, Rick couldn't imagine that a night out with her similarly-aged mates and their boyfriends would be Hal's idea of fun. Even the thought of hanging around with a bunch of people barely out of adolescence brought Rick out in hives.

That was the trouble with divorce. Friends were inevitably forced to take sides and that normally meant sympathising with the 'wronged' party. It was hard to stay impartial in these matters, even if you tried. Women, particularly, liked to gang together to support a friend whose husband had gone off with someone else. Were they likely to invite round the bloke and his new partner for dinner to get to know her? Were they heck. The poor sod would be ostracised whether he deserved it or not. Hence Hal finding himself out in the social cold.

'Yeah, yeah,' Rick said, when the last thing he wanted to do was socialise with Hal after he'd spent all day listening him talk about the wide and varied sexual positions he'd tried with Shannon.

He couldn't remember when he'd last had conjugal knowledge of Juliet. It was months ago, possibly before her mother moved in. Somehow it wasn't the same, knowing that Rita Britten, who despite her advanced years had better hearing than the Bionic Woman, was in the very next room. That was a passion-killer if ever there was one. Perhaps he should try buying some Rohypnol from the internet and slip it into her bedtime cocoa one night. That should ensure him and Juliet some privacy for a wild night of love. But then he wasn't entirely sure that Juliet was up for a wild night of love any more. He watched telly in bed – his most recent pleasure was having a 19-inch LCD television put in the bedroom – while Juliet had her nose stuck into one of her books. She didn't seem to miss the intimacy between them in the same way that he did. But wasn't it a myth that men had 'needs' while women were content to let that side of the relationship slide into oblivion with the passing of time?

He knew that Juliet was having trouble with her hormones. Once she used to be the world's chilliest creature, now the middle of the night would find her tossing and turning, flinging the covers off and complaining how hot it was. He should talk to her about it. But what the hell would he say? He was a bloke. What did he know about hormones? And perhaps it couldn't be blamed on that. Perhaps, after all this time together, she'd simply gone off him.

Chapter 8

'You lucky bitch!' Una declares as I tell her all about my history with Steven Aubrey and his invitation to lunch. There's a note of jealousy in her voice that worries me. 'How exciting.'

'It isn't really.'

She snorts at that.

We're both basking in the summer sunshine during our lunch-hour. 'And here's me complaining that this place is dull. While I was stamping out books, this smouldering drama was unfolding upstairs.'

'It's not a smouldering drama.'

More snorting from Una.

Horsefair Green is a pleasant patch of grass just off London Road and right near the library. When the weather's fine enough we escape here to eat our lunch. I have cheese and tomato sandwiches. Una has a range of vegetables, chopped into uniform sizes, and low-fat hummus. My friend is barely a size eight and yet is terri-fied of putting on an ounce of weight while I could do with losing a good half a stone, maybe more if I am honest.

This is where Una lives, so we could actually go to her house for lunch; sometimes we do in the winter. During the summer months her tiny courtyard garden is in deep shade in the middle of the day, so we prefer to sit out here on the grass not far from her front door. At the end of the Green there's a war memorial dedicated to the men of Stony Stratford who fell in the First

World War. This time of year, it's surrounded by a flurry of Busy Lizzies in clashing shades of red and pink.

Today, the canopy of old oak trees that line the edges of the Green provide some welcome cover from the sun. Una's wearing a slinky black designer sundress that skims her knees, strappy gold sandals and plenty of clanking ethnic jewellery. I have on something floral that's been in my wardrobe since time began and would suit a woman twice my age.

'So where are you going to go for lunch?'

'I wish I'd said no now,' I confess. 'I'm sure we've got nothing in common any more.'

'How come this is the first time I've heard about this Steven bloke?' My friend digs me in the ribs. 'You dark horse.'

'It's not something that I like to talk about. Steven was my first boyfriend. I adored him. He dumped me from a great height. I was devastated.' Part of me, I feel, has never quite recovered. 'He left me on the morning of our wedding, Una. No one wants to broadcast that.'

'What a bastard,' is Una's conclusion. 'And you never found out why?'

'We were young,' I say. 'We'd been going out together since we were fourteen. Everyone expected us to marry. That's what you did then. We were only nineteen. How crazy does that seem now?' I smile at my friend. 'Chloe's twenty, but I wouldn't trust her to boil an egg, let alone run her own household. Are the young now so much more incapable than we were, or does every generation think that of the one below them?'

'Danielle's the same age as Chloe and Kyle's just that bit older, but we still treat the pair of them like they're fifteen.' I've only met Una's kids a few times, but they do seem to be cut from the same cloth as mine. 'The minute anything goes wrong, they both run straight back to Mum and Dad. I do think that we were more self-sufficient at their age. I was married with my own home at twenty, like you, and two years later had Kyle.' She waves a hand dismissively. 'Money slips through their fingers. I've lost count of the number of times we've had to bail them out. They've got enough maxed-out credit cards between them to play a game of bridge. We've pampered them too much, I kept telling Martin, and now they're not interested in standing on their own two feet.'

'The pressure of the wedding was building up on us,' I continue with my own story. 'It was a huge do and it was all costing my mum and dad a fortune.' Money that they lost and which, to this day, my mum will occasionally remind me about. 'Relatives that neither Steven nor I had ever heard of were being dragged out of the woodwork. I think he just panicked.' Not that I want to excuse his behaviour. Even when I was married to Rick, people used to point at me in the street and say, 'That was the girl that Steven Aubrey jilted.' 'The thing is, Steven was such a catch. I'm sure most people thought that I didn't deserve him.'

'What nonsense.'

I shrug. I'm not sure that I thought that I deserved Steven either, to be truthful. He was the school heart-throb and had a string of eager girls just waiting to take my place. 'It was a long time ago.'

'Sounds like he still fancies you. How romantic!' Una bites into her celery and sighs. 'I wish someone would pop up from my past and whisk me off my feet.'

'He's not going to whisk me off my feet,' I laugh. 'I'm happy with Rick. We might be going through a bit of a rough patch, but we've been married for years. You don't give up on that lightly.'

Una bristles at that.

'Sorry,' I say. 'That was thoughtless of me.'

'You like being married,' Una says sniffily. 'I like being divorced. I'm having more fun than I've ever had before. Last night I was at one of those singles' supper clubs. I didn't get home until three o'clock. Mr Chang –' Una's Siamese cat '– was frantic.'

With my brood currently still in residence, would it seem strange coming back to a house that was empty but for a cat? 'Did you meet someone nice?'

'No,' she says shiftily. 'Not really. But there are plenty of great blokes out there.'

Una goes to a lot of dating events but, so far, doesn't seem to have come across any of these legions of 'great blokes'. Most of the guys she meets seem to be, excuse my language, complete wankers.

'And you met Rick just after Steven?' my friend says, deflecting the conversation back to me.

The six months after Steven left were terrible. I went what is commonly known as 'into a decline'. My mother, never the most patient of women, took me to the doctor for anti-depressants and then force-fed them to me on a daily basis. They made no difference at all. I lost interest in my appearance, started to drink gin when no one was watching, and thwarted all the attempts by my friends to 'bring me out of myself'. I didn't want to see anyone and didn't want anyone to see me.

'It was quite a while,' I say to Una in a modified version of the events. Those are details I'm happy to gloss over. It still hurts to talk about it even though all this time has passed. That's probably because I've never really opened up to anyone about how I felt. 'I went to pieces at first, hardly left the house. Then, after much cajoling, one of my friends persuaded me to go out to the pub one night. That's where I met Rick.'

'Love at first sight?'

I shake my head. 'Hardly.' I can remember him standing there all gangly and awkward in his drainpipe jeans and white shirt with a group of his friends. It was the first time I'd looked at anyone else since Steven had gone. And I liked what I saw. 'I went at it very slowly. Or so I thought. It took me a long time to relax with him, to even begin to trust him. All credit to Rick, he understood what I'd been through and was very sympathetic. He didn't rush me into anything at all.'

After a while I found that I was regaining my self-respect. I thought that I might be recovering enough to have real feelings for Rick. He made me laugh when I really didn't want to. I liked being with him, looked forward to the nights when he took me out. He held my hand, told me I was beautiful and made me think that there might well be a future for me without Steven in it.

'We'd been seeing each other for about six months – very tentatively. Then I had a wild night on the Cherry B.'

'You old slapper,' Una chortles.

'The first time we slept together I fell pregnant with Tom.' I give her a rueful smile. Just as I was beginning to relax back into being myself, ready to have a sensible and loving relationship with Rick, then that hit us. What a bombshell.

'Shortly after, we had the world's quietest shotgun wedding followed by the world's most miserable reception in a grotty pub.'

In those days, you still 'did the right thing'. I couldn't have faced the double scorn of being a jilted woman and then a single mum, so when Rick asked me to marry him, I readily agreed. What else could I do? When we finally plucked up the courage to tell our parents, they made it perfectly clear that there was no other option for us.

But did I love Rick? I liked him well enough at the time. As I said, he was fun to be with. He was handsome and witty, but I hardly knew him. Then again, I'd been with Steven for five years – and didn't know him at all, as it turned out.

We married hastily at the unprepossessing venue of Bletchley Register Office before my bump started to show too much. At the age of twenty, I had no idea how long forever might be. You don't, do you? It was a quiet affair, no years of planning and saving. No glorious swanning about in a gown fit for a princess. The bride wore the only dress in her wardrobe that would still accommodate her expanding waistline. The groom borrowed a suit from a friend and it very nearly fitted him. My parents attended, as did Rick's. That was it. Afterwards we went to the nearest pub for a modest lunch – a serve-yourself carvery on the A5. A meal which was eaten mainly in a tense silence interspersed with self-pitying sobs from my mother.

Less than four months later they were all grandparents to a bonny, bouncing baby called Thomas Richard Joyce and my life was never the same again.

'God, Una, it was truly awful.'

Una blurts out a laugh and, though there are tears pricking at my eyes, I join in. 'I can hardly believe it now. No one thought that Rick and I would last. Yet look at us.'

Despite the time lapse, there was even talk in the town at the time that Tom was really Steven's son, but we both knew that there was never any doubt about that. Steven and I had never slept together. It seems so old-fashioned now, but I wanted to save myself for my wedding night. That's not saying that Steven and I didn't get frisky on occasions – there was plenty of 'heavy petting' as it was called, nothing more – but it was so different back then. Very few of my friends had slept with their boyfriends and the ones who did were considered 'girls with easy morals'. I never wanted to be one of those.

'And are you really happy?' my friend asks. 'Sometimes I look at you . . .'

'I don't know, Una.' Suddenly, I'm perilously close to letting those tears flow. 'Just because you've spent twenty-five years with someone, does it mean that you're up for another twenty-five?' I pluck at the grass which is studded with daisies and stare at my feet. I need new sandals. 'Our anniversary is coming up and I just can't work up the necessary energy to organise a celebration. Rick's mentioned nothing about it either.'

'You need something to perk you up. This Steven Aubrey could be just the tonic.'

'You're not seriously suggesting what I think you are?'

'No one would need to know,' my friend whispers. 'Except for me, of course, who would need to know *all* the details.'

'I'm just having lunch with him,' I insist. 'I'm even thinking of cancelling that.'

'Don't you dare!' Una says. 'We both need a bit of excitement in our lives. And if I can't get any, then you damn well can.'

So that's it, really. Looks like I'm having lunch with Steven tomorrow.

Chapter 9

Rick pulled up outside number ten Chadwick Close. It was the end of a long, tiring day and all he was looking forward to now was a hot shower, a good dinner and a night in front of the telly.

Hal, on the other hand, was going home to a takeaway, Viagra for dessert and rampant sex all night. At this moment, Rick didn't feel jealous of his friend. The only action he wanted was with the remote control.

His first job though would be to walk Buster. Despite their aging mongrel supposedly being the family dog, Rick was the only one in the household that this onerous task fell to and he thought it was because he was the only one deemed uncool enough to carry around a bag of dog poo.

Rick put his tools in the garage. This might be a nice area, but it didn't stop yobs trying to break into the van with monotonous regularity. In the kitchen, Buster was delighted to see him, which was just as well as no one else at home was waving the welcome flag. 'Come on,' Rick said. 'Let's get this done, boy, then I can relax and put my feet up.'

Buster leaped for joy and happily submitted to the lead as Rick stuffed some of the requisite blue plastic bags into his pocket and they headed out of the house and into the Close.

As he reached the wide open space of Toombs Meadow where he took Buster for a walk nearly every night, he saw his neighbour, the voluptuous Stacey Lovejoy coming towards him walking her chihuahua, Britney, who sported a pink diamanté collar and barked constantly. Rick cast about him, but there was no hiding place. He was fully exposed with not even a friendly tree close at hand to dodge behind.

'Coo-ee, Mr Joyce! Ricky!'

Rick waved reluctantly. 'Mrs Lovejoy. Hello.'

She pushed him playfully as they met. 'Stacey,' she corrected. 'It's always Stacey to you. Shall we walk our doggies together, Ricky?'

'I thought you were on your way home?'

His neighbour changed direction as she linked her arm through his and steered him into the park. 'I've nothing to rush back for. No *man* to get home to.' She laughed uproariously at that.

Rick joined in though he wasn't sure why. 'Ha, ha, ha.'

Stacey Lovejoy's buxom busom moved all of its own accord. When its owner wiggled in one direction it seemed to set up a countermotion in the opposite direction. It was most disconcerting. Stacey was probably about thirty, maybe older, but dressed like Chloe, and her hair was a shade that Juliet called 'lesbian blonde'. But Rick was pretty certain that Stacey Lovejoy reserved her charms solely for the male sex. She'd moved into Chadwick Close about six months ago, just across the road from them, and Juliet said that she lowered the tone of the neighbourhood. Rick thought that his wife was probably right.

'No Juliet tonight?' Stacey tucked her arm in tighter.

'No, no.' Sometimes his wife came out to walk Buster with him. But he still had to pick up the poo.

He let the dog off the lead and Buster shot off into the bushes to have a good sniff around. Rick might be firmly anchored to Stacey Lovejoy, but there was no need for his trusty hound to suffer likewise.

'Juliet's going to see her dad on the way home,' he explained.

'That's lovely,' Stacey said. 'It must be nice to have a big family. I'm all alone.' She pouted at him. 'There's just me. And the kids, of course.'

45

Stacey Lovejoy had four children. All of them girls. All of them just like their mother.

'How are the girls?'

'I struggle, Ricky. They're all so wilful. Children don't want to be children any more.'

Stacey's kids all looked like they'd come straight off porn sets – alarmingly, even the seven year old. When Chloe was that age she'd been happy to wear frilly dresses and ankle socks. Now all the little girls you saw seemed to wear crop-tops and high-heeled shoes shortly after they got out of the pram. If things carried on like this they'd be knocking out push-up bras for babies.

'Ikea's the biggest worry to me,' Stacey confided. 'She's fourteen, Ricky. All she's interested in is boys.' His neighbour rolled can-you-imagine eyes at him.

Rick wondered if the child's mother had been the same. 'Ikea. That's an unusual name.'

'She wasn't conceived in Ikea, Ricky, if that's what you're thinking. What do you take me for? Shame on you!' Stacey nudged him in the ribs and then chortled while he grunted. 'It was on an Ikea sofa. A Plongstan, if I remember rightly.'

Seems as if the kid had got away quite lightly.

'I've got four children by four different men, Ricky, and I'm proud of all of them. I know that some people round here call me a "four by four", think I'm not good enough for Chadwick Close, but I loved every one of their fathers,' Stacey insisted. 'Well, for a time.'

'You don't have anything to do with them now?'

His neighbour shook her brassy hair. 'Levi, she's twelve. I just couldn't stop that man getting in my jeans!' She laughed at her own joke. 'Malibu – she's the cutest of the lot. That was a *very* memorable night. Everything apart from who the father was, of course. My resistance is very low after a few coconut-flavoured cocktails, Ricky!'

She dug him in the ribs again. You'd need danger money for living with a woman like Stacey Lovejoy, Rick thought, wincing.

'Becks's father isn't the real Beckham,' she continued without drawing breath, 'but a lookalike I met at a nightclub opening in Milton Keynes. Very good he was too. I probably loved him the most, Ricky. He left me after six months. Ran off with a new Posh lookalike who he'd been booked to do a gig with. I looked more like Posh than she did, if you ask me. He hasn't ever seen my lovely little Becks – bastard, that cuts me to the quick. A girl should know her daddy, shouldn't she?'

'Yeah,' he agreed too readily. Rick wasn't sure what he meant to his own daughter these days, other than being a constantly open wallet. Nevertheless, he was glad that he'd been around to see both of his children grow up.

They waited for Buster who was running round in circles by a park bench, tiring himself out for the night. Britney barked at Stacey's feet. His neighbour turned to him.

'I'm a polyamorist, Ricky,' she said, à propos of nothing.

'Really?'

Stacey stroked his arm gently while looking up into his eyes. He was transfixed. 'It means I believe in the power of unlimited love.'

He felt a gulp work its way down his throat. 'That's nice.'

'I've always found it difficult to operate within the constraints of a conventional marital arrangement, haven't you?'

'Yes. Well, no. No. Not really.' With his free hand he scratched his head.

Stacey lowered her voice. 'I like to share myself with many men.'

Juliet had told him as much. His wife even thought that Stacey Lovejoy had her beady eye on *him*. Every week it seemed that their new neighbour had a leaking tap or a blown fuse or some minor domestic crisis that required Rick to go across the road with his toolbox and help her out. Three times, already, he'd had to take his ladders over there and get in through her bedroom window as Stacey had locked herself out. Juliet said she did it all on purpose, for attention. He hadn't told his wife, but each time there'd been a different set of saucy lingerie displayed on a coathanger on the front of the wardrobe, some more draped on the bed, something frilly on the sofa. It was the sort of lingerie that never in a million years would he be able to persuade Juliet to wear. His wife, he thought, was allergic to lace in lurid colours. Whereas Rick quite liked it. Didn't all men?

'Is that the time?' When he looked at his wrist, he realised that he hadn't got his watch on. 'Dear me, dear me. I'd better get back,' he said. 'Juliet will wonder where I am. Buster! Buster! Come here, boy!'

Stacey laughed. 'Now I've made you blush. I like a man who blushes, Ricky Joyce.'

Rick scuttled back towards the park entrance. Blush? That wasn't all that Stacey Lovejoy made him do. The woman scared the living daylights out of him. He suspected that, like Hal's new girlfriend, Shannon, Stacey Lovejoy might well be a five times a night woman.

She tottered along after him in his wake. Stacey had to be the only woman in Chadwick Close who walked her dog while wearing leopardskin-print stilettos. 'I've bought a new plasma screen television and it needs connecting up. Any chance of you popping round sometime this week, Ricky?'

'I'll see what I can do.' He put a spurt on and waved over his shoulder. 'Catch you later.'

'There'll be a cup of tea waiting,' Stacey shouted after him. 'Or anything else you fancy.'

And that was the thing that worried him the most.

Chapter 10

Una drops me off outside my dad's house in her convertible Mercedes – a legacy from her married days. My hair is a tangled mess, but Una's blonde locks are somehow still sleek and untrammelled by the wind.

'Thanks,' I say, giving my friend a peck on the cheek as I try to flatten my hair down. 'See you tomorrow.'

'I want you in your best dress with plenty of slap on,' she instructs with a wag of her finger. 'You're going to knock that Steven's eyeballs out.'

I don't think I possess anything in my wardrobe that's capable of creating an ocular injury. Closing the car door, I watch as she drives away then turn to study the house.

My dad, Norman Francis Britten – or Frank to his friends and family – still lives in the small terraced house he and my mother had shared for over fifty years, the home where I was born and brought up.

Like a number of the houses in the street, it needs some work doing on it now. In the last ten years this has gone from a nice residential row of neatly-maintained Victorian terraces where all the neighbours knew each other to a slightly scruffy place where the majority of houses are now rental homes, snapped up by entrepreneurial landlords on buy-to-let mortgages as the elderly residents died off. Landlords who now don't care whether the gardens are tended or whether the windows are washed. It grieves my father to see its decline.

As if affected by the general malaise, my parents' home has started to blend in. The paint on the wooden windowframes is flaking badly and, in truth, they probably need replacing. The slates on the roof don't look all that much to me either. I'll have to ask Rick if we can afford to pay out for a gardener for Dad. Although he likes to look after it himself, it's clear from the state of the little patch at the front that he's struggling to keep on top of it. We must make some time at the weekend to come and give him a hand until we can get someone fixed up. Something else to worry about. Not only have we the kids to pay out for, but it's becoming increasingly clear that my parents' meagre pensions aren't managing to keep pace with inflation. We're caught in the middle trying to bankroll them all. Everything costs so much now that my modest wages seem to go nowhere.

Heavy of heart, I knock on the door. Dad's not managed very well since Mum left him. He's the sort of man who's never had to cook his own dinner and now seems to live on nothing but toast. Though, thoughtfully, she did buy him a recipe book called *Cooking for the Sad and Lonely*, or something equally depressing, with low-cost recipes for just one person before she walked out of the door.

I try to pop in once or twice a week and cook him something nutritious. On Sunday, I plate him up a roast dinner and bring it round for him to microwave. Just thinking about it breaks my heart. I don't know how my mother can do this to him at this stage in their lives. Mum's seventy and Dad's turned seventy-two. Wouldn't you think that they could have come to some sort of arrangement that allowed them to finish their years together in relative harmony? Mum says she's planning to live until she's at least ninety – another twenty years or so to 'suffer my father', in her words. I'm stunned that she still has the energy to want to break free at her age. Should I admire the fact that she's still so feisty, unlike me, and isn't just going to 'settle' in the twilight of her life? Perhaps I would be as dynamic as her, if being feisty also encompassed being independent and didn't involve her moving in with us and having me at her beck and call at all hours of the day and night.

Maybe if Rick and I sat my parents down and made them talk to each other like sensible adults then there could be a chance that they might get back together. My mother might be enjoying her newfound freedom, but I'm sure Dad's missing her madly.

I ring the doorbell, even though I've got a key. I've brought Dad a pile of books. Like me, reading is his favourite escape. He has a shed kitted out at the bottom of the garden expressly for that purpose, complete with old armchair, bottle of whisky that he hid from Mum and a pair of tartan slippers that he retrieved from the bin. He calls it his reading room. My dad likes the thrillers – Harlan Coben, John Grisham, Jeffery Deaver. He likes a good wartime story too – Len Deighton being his favourite – and pores over the books on local history that we have in the library as well.

Dad opens the door wearing one of Mum's frilly aprons and his best bow tie – the one he saves for New Year's Eve and wedding receptions. This is the man who's been shuffling around in a stained cardigan for the last few months. His cheeks are flushed and there's a twinkle in his eye that has been sadly missing. Inside, I hand over his books.

'Thanks, love,' he says, as he flicks through the titles. 'They look smashing. I've some to go back too.'

'Yes. Don't let me forget them.' I look my dad up and down. 'You're looking very perky,' I say, as I go into the small living room that's stuffed full of furniture and unnecessary knick-knacks. 'Everything OK?'

'Marvellous,' my dad says. 'Absolutely marvellous.'

The house is looking very spruce too, I have to admit. 'Been doing some housework?'

'Oh, you know.' My father looks all coy. He almost skips through to the kitchen and I follow him, puzzled. 'Thought it was about time.'

For years we've been trying to get them to refit the kitchen. It was last done up in the late sixties and it looks like it. There's a mish-mash of cupboards and worn lino on the floor. I keep asking Dad to come to MFI with me but he won't have it. At least we forced them to get a new cooker last year when theirs became a death trap.

On the hob a pan is boiling. 'What's cooking?' I ask. 'I was going to make you something for dinner.'

'All organised.' He stirs whatever it is in the pan.

'Smells great.' Dad has trouble boiling an egg. I flop down at the kitchen table.

'Jamie Oliver,' he informs me. 'Seems like a lovely chap. Saw him on the telly the other week. Thought I'd give his recipes a go.'

My father's watching Jamie Oliver?

Dad puts on his reading glasses and peers down at his book by the stove. 'Pasta with Parma ham, wild mushrooms and Parmesan.'

'And you got all that in the High Street?'

'No, love,' Dad admits. 'I took the bus into the city while the weather was nice.'

'What's all this in aid of?' I hope I don't offend anyone's sensibilities but my dad has spent the last forty-five years that I can remember calling pasta 'foreign muck'.

'Thought I'd be a bit more adventurous.' He fails to meet my eye. Even a jacket potato can be a bit exotic for his taste.

'There seems to be plenty in there. Have you cooked for me too? I've not organised anything for dinner at home.'

'Er, no,' my dad says. Then he turns to face me. 'The reason I'm cooking for two is that I'm having a guest for dinner.'

I try not to laugh. 'A guest?' That's a first. My parents were never the world's best at entertaining. Even the local vicar used to have trouble getting over the doorstep – particularly if he had a collecting tin in his hands. I can't remember them ever having friends round for dinner, but perhaps you didn't do that kind of thing then.

'Yes.' My dad stops stirring his sauce and looks me in the eye. 'This is a very hard thing for a father to say to his daughter,' he continues, 'but I've met someone.'

'You've met someone?'

'Yes,' my increasingly embarrassed parent confirms. 'Someone else. Someone who isn't your mother.'

Well, that was clear enough.

'Oh, Dad.' All thoughts of orchestrating a reconciliation between my parents has just flown out of the window. 'Are you sure you're doing the right thing?'

'The funny bit is, Juliet, that I never wanted your mother to go. But now that she has, I feel free to be my own person for the first time in my life.'

My mother can be very domineering, but I never knew that Dad felt like this. They might not have been love's young dream, but I thought they were OK together. There were certainly prolonged stony silences in the house when I was growing up, but they never rowed or anything like that. There were no plates thrown in anger.

'I just don't want you rushing into anything that you might regret,' I say cautiously. 'Who is this woman? How much do you know about her?' Though she's probably of pensionable age too with a racy line in cardigans — so, realistically, how much trouble is my old dad going to get into?

'The thing is, Juliet. Love. It isn't a woman I've met,' my dad says. 'It's a man.'

'A friend?'

My dad shifts from foot to foot. 'A bit more than that.'

I put my head in my hands. Quite a lot of trouble, it appears.

Chapter 11

When I get home, Rick is in the kitchen and he's ironing. Furiously. That must mean that he's feeling guilty about something, since my husband always does ironing in lieu of an apology.

'How's your dad?' he asks.

'Great.' I throw my bag down with a sigh. 'He has a gay lover.' Rick drops the iron.

'And his front lawn needs mowing. Other than that, everything's just fine and dandy.'

I pick up the iron and rub my foot over the resulting burn on the flooring while Rick closes the kitchen door and lowers his voice. That must mean my mother is watching *Emmerdale* in the lounge. 'He has *what?*'

'A gay lover. Called Samuel. He met him in one of the book-shops in Milton Keynes. He turned him on to Jamie Oliver.'

'And a lot more besides,' my husband notes.

'Oh, and Samuel Scott's forty-two.'

'Bloody hell,' Rick says.

'That's what I thought.' I sit down at the table because suddenly I feel very weary. 'Dad says that he's very nice.'

'I can't get my head round this,' my husband says, perplexed. 'Your dad, who thinks having half a bitter at the Conservative Club is a wild night out has, in the twilight of his years, come out of the closet?'

'So it would seem.'

'Has the world gone mad?'

'So it would seem,' I say again. 'Do you think it's because he's lonely?'

'I don't think you become gay because you're lonely. But then what would I know about it?'

'How am I going to tell Mum?'

'Why is it your job to tell your mother? Let Stony Stratford's answer to Dale Winton tell her himself.'

'He seems happier than I've seen him in years.'

'It doesn't bear thinking about.' Rick massages his temples. 'Perhaps it's just a phase that he'll grow out of.'

'He's seventy-two.'

Rick bangs the iron over one of his shirts. I can see his mind whirring, but he says nothing.

'We should support him in this,' I suggest.

'We should tell him not to be so damn stupid.'

'If Mum thinks there's someone else, then she might be tempted to go back to him. You know what she's like. She might not want Dad any more, but there's no way she'd want anyone else getting their claws into him.'

'Especially not someone called Samuel who's nearly half his age.' *And younger than you and me*, I add silently.

'I need to think about this a bit more.' I've got a stress headache coming on. I need a hot bath, a glass of wine and the soothing words of the new Adriana Trigiani novel that I picked up in the library today. 'Whatever happens, when Mum finds out she's not going to be happy.'

At that moment the kitchen door opens and Mum comes in. 'When Mum finds out what?'

Rick and I exchange a glance. I take a deep breath. 'Mum, sit down. There's no way to break this to you gently.'

My cowardly husband makes himself scarce at the far side of the kitchen.

Mum sits down next to me and I hold her hand. It's dry and papery to the touch and my heart goes out to her. She's wearing hot pink nail varnish on her fake nails. 'Why are you holding my hand?' she asks irritably.

I let go of it again. 'I've got some bad news for you.'

'Has your father died?'

'No.' I tut at her. 'But this *is* about Dad.' She waits impatiently while I find the right words. 'Dad has met someone else.'

'Has he now?' she bristles. 'It's nothing to do with me.'

'I think it is,' I say.

'Well, she won't treat him like I did.' My mum folds her arms in battle position. 'I don't care what the old fool's up to. It's none of my business.'

'Don't you want to see him, talk to him about it?'

'No.'

'You should. All this is silly.'

My mother puts her fingers in her ears. 'La, la, la, not listening,' she sings.

Now *that* is silly. So, coward that I am, I decide to leave it at that. She can't say that I didn't try. The rest can wait. Preferably until after one of them dies.

'I've come to a decision,' Mum then informs us.

'You're moving out?' There's too much hope in Rick's voice as he reappears from his fake task at the far reaches of the kitchen, and my mother scowls at him.

'I'm going to have a boob job,' she announces. 'I've got some money in the bank. I thought I might like to go for a 36 DD.'

'That's the silliest thing I've ever heard, Mum.' And, I'm sure you'll agree, there's been a lot of competition today.

'You don't have to have saggy tits these days.' She gives an accusing glance at mine and I sit up straighter. 'Just because I'm mature in years it doesn't mean I'm a has-been.'

'Yes, it does,' my husband chips in.

'I'm planning on growing old disgracefully.'

'Not in my house, you're not,' Rick mutters just loud enough for us to hear him.

'I'll put the kettle on, shall I?' I say, and my voice is shrill. And Jack Bauer thinks *he* has bad days.

Chloe's crashed my car, Tom has a naked man in his room, my dad's turned gay, my mother's planning surgical breast enhancement and my husband has done something to feel guilty about. And my old lover is stalking me. With everything else that's been going on, I've forgotten to tell Rick about Steven's reappearance and, suddenly, I feel quite grateful for that.

Chapter 12

Rick couldn't focus on the reality show on TV. Normally he liked watching *Cops and Criminals*, but tonight the crims seemed so stupid they deserved to be caught, and the police were just lucky. His attention wandered.

This was a comfortable lounge. Not trendy and the carpet needed replacing, a bit of updating – he wanted to put laminate down, but Juliet wouldn't let him. Still, he'd always felt it was a cosy room. With the three of them in here, however, it now seemed crowded. They'd been used to having it to themselves until Juliet's mum had moved in. Even when the kids were at home the pair of them just retreated to their bedrooms to watch their own televisions or spend hours doing something borderline illegal on the internet.

It was late. Rick checked the clock. Past eleven and still neither of the children were home. He had thought his days of anxiously waiting up for them would be long over by now. Had hoped they'd have moved out and started lives of their own, would be paying their own bills. Obviously he'd been way too optimistic on many fronts.

Juliet was reading, curled up in the armchair in the corner; she was never happier than when she had her nose in a book. Rick wasn't much of a reader; he didn't have the necessary attention span for novels and he wasn't interested in biographies of people who'd had more interesting lives than his own as it always made him depressed to read about them.

His mother-in-law, Rita, glass of gin at her side – *his* gin – was snoring gently on the sofa.

'The Exorcist's nodded off.' Rick glanced at Juliet's mother.

His wife tutted at him, barely looking up from her novel.

Rick could feel his blood pressure rising. Juliet didn't like it when he called her mother The Exorcist but she couldn't deny that spirits disappeared very quickly whenever Rita was around.

He picked up the local paper and leafed through it. Recently he'd taken to scanning the obituary column. More often than not, there was someone whom he knew in there, someone he'd been to school with, someone even younger than him, cruelly cut down in their prime. It made you think about your own mortality.

'What about this one?' Rick flicked the paper. He used suitably sombre tones. '"Life must go on, although you're gone. There isn't a day when I don't sigh or think of you and cry. Love you and miss you always". That's for Bob Stanway. The guy was only thirty-eight. That's too young. Way too young.'

Rita snorted from the sofa, but didn't wake up.

'Lovely,' Juliet said distractedly.

'You could say it as if you mean it.'

'It doesn't rhyme.'

'It does.'

'Does not.'

'They don't have to rhyme.'

'But they always do,' his wife pointed out.

Now it was Rick's turn to tut. '"You've left a place in my heart that no one else can fill. I loved you and I always will. In my heart you will ever stay. Loved, missed and remembered every day".'

'See?' Juliet said.

'That's for Charlie Canning. He was only our age. Forty-five. In the prime of his life.'

Another sleeping snort from his mother-in-law. Juliet lowered her glasses. 'Is there a particular reason why you've taken to reading the obituary column every night?'

'I just like to see who's in there,' Rick answered defensively. 'Pay my respects to the recently deceased.'

'Haven't we got enough to worry about?'

With that, the front door banged and the next minute Tom's head popped round the living-room door. 'Hi,' he said. ''Night. See you in the morning. Gabe's here.'

'Gabe?' Juliet said.

'The *naked* man,' Rick mouthed to her as Rita snorted herself awake.

'Who was that?' she wanted to know.

'Only Tom, Mum,' Juliet said softly.

Two pairs of heavy footsteps stomped up the stairs, accompanied by what sounded to Rick's ears like rather girlish laughter for two blokes. He couldn't think about that now.

'Has he brought *another* friend back?' Rita asked.

'Yes, Mum.' Juliet stifled a sigh.

'Quite the popular young man,' Rita noted.

Rick couldn't think about that now either. Tomorrow he'd speak to Tom about using this house like a hotel or the Stony Stratford branch of the YMCA. He returned to the newspaper. 'This is a nice one. "The love we shared is still the same. And I have a heartache that will always remain. Forever in my thoughts".'

'Shut up, Rick,' Juliet said.

The door went again. That would be Chloe this time. Sure enough, her head was the next to pop inside the living room. 'Hi.' She waved at them all. 'Wotcher, Gran. Can I borrow a tenner, Mum? I'm broke.'

'Chloe—' Juliet started.

'Get in here now, young lady,' Rick snapped. 'I want to talk to you about the bill to repair your mother's car.'

Chloe huffed and came into the room.

'Do you know that it's going to cost almost six hundred pounds to fix it?'

She shrugged. 'Can't you claim it on the insurance?'

'No, not this time. You're going to have to pay for it, lady.'

His daughter put her hands on her hips. 'How? I just told you I was skint.'

'You'll have to get a job.'

She looked horrified at that. 'This is supposed to be my holiday.'

'No one needs three months' holiday,' Rick shouted. 'I've worked for nearly thirty years and still only get four weeks a year.'

'Studying is much harder than working,' Chloe asserted.

'You've got a rude awakening coming to you, one day. Just you wait and see.' It seemed like he'd been having this conversation with Chloe for the whole of his life.

'What do you expect me to do?' his daughter retorted. 'All the summer jobs pay crap money.'

'Better to have crap money than sponge off your mother. Juliet, you are not to give her another penny.' His daughter's face blackened. 'I don't care what you do, Chloe, or where you do it. But get a job you will. The DIY sheds are crying out for staff.'

His daughter was outraged. 'Have you seen the uniforms?'

'I'll give you a week, otherwise I'll march you round all the shops, supermarkets and restaurants myself until you find something.'

'You are so sad!' Chloe pronounced and flounced out.

'You handled that very well,' Juliet said from the chair.

'What was I supposed to say? That girl has no idea of the value of money. We didn't teach her that. We've always had to scrimp and save and budget. She spends money like it's water. Where has she got that from? She thinks she's Paris Hilton.'

'Children can be such a terrible disappointment,' Rita said sagely. 'Mine were.'

'Mum, I'm your only child,' Juliet reminded her.

'Exactly.' Rita downed the rest of her gin and eased herself off the sofa. 'I'm off to bed. There's too much noise in this house.'

As she went out of the door, Rick muttered, 'You can leave whenever you like, Rita. Don't let me stop you.'

'I heard that,' came the reply.

He tried to settle back into his chair, but any chance of relaxation now eluded him. Flicking open the newspaper again, he started, "'A year has passed since you went from my side . . .'"

'No,' Juliet interrupted. 'I can't stand any more obituaries. I'm depressed enough as it is. I'm going to bed too. Why don't you do the same?'

'I won't be able to sleep now,' Rick complained. 'I'm too wound up.'

'Then do something useful.'

'I think I'll take a drive,' he said. 'See if it will calm me down.'

'You shouldn't drive if you're in a temper. You'll be an accident waiting to happen. I don't want another repair bill today.'

'I'll be fine,' he insisted. 'There's no one around at this time of night, anyway.'

'Do be careful,' Juliet said.

'If anything happened to me, you know . . . would you put an obituary like that in the paper for me?'

'Yes,' his wife said. 'Of course I would. "Here lies Rick, who always said, he'd want a poem like this if he was dead".'

'That's very amusing. And very heartfelt.'

Juliet laughed and grabbed hold of his hand. 'Come to bed.'

She might have meant, 'Come to bed, *come to bed*' – it was diffi-cult to read the signs even after all this time. But he wasn't in the mood. He was rarely in the mood these days. Perhaps he should get some little blue tablets off the internet, like Hal did. They might perk him up in that department.

Rick pulled away. 'I'm going out for an hour. I need some fresh air.'

But what he really wanted was some space to think about love, life and everything.

Chapter 13

I watch Rick out of the bedroom window as he roars off down Chadwick Close in his car and sigh to myself. He shouldn't be driving while he's in this mood. My husband doesn't seem to be quite himself at the moment, but we just haven't had the opportunity to sit down and talk about what's wrong. With Mum here and Chloe and Tom, and Buster to be walked and dinner to be cooked, we both fall into bed exhausted and then are scared to talk in case the Bionic Mother next door can hear us through the paper-thin walls. I always hoped against hope that she'd eventually tire of living here with us and would simply go home to Dad. Now that he's 'stepping out' with Samuel the gay bookseller, I have to accept that it might never happen. Then what will we do?

Sitting on the bed, I rub at my temples. This room is as tired as I feel. Perhaps I should get Una in to revamp it. She knows the right thing to do with cushions, how to co-ordinate soft furnishings, the correct way to place an accent vase. I'm hopeless with that sort of thing even though I could bring home a dozen different magazines every week from the library to help me with my lack of interior design skills. I can't match patterns, never have been able to, so consequently buy everything in varying shades of cream to cause the least offence. My friend would be horrified to learn that I've had the same duvet cover for the last ten years – possibly more. She'd faint at the fact that I don't have three different types of pillows that all complement each other and provide a splash of colour.

Crossing the room, I open the wardrobe door and try to pick out something suitable for tomorrow. I should have told Rick about the surprise reappearance of Steven Aubrey – I'm certain he'd have something to say about it – but I didn't. I kept the knowledge of my lunch date – I shouldn't really call it that, rather my lunch *appointment* – as a guilty secret. But then I think he's got more than enough to think about at the moment. I know he gets put upon by Hal, and Chloe crashing the car can't have helped. Better keep my old boyfriend out of the picture for the time being.

I flick through my clothes. Sure enough, there's nothing lurking in there that's suitable for knocking eyeballs out. The vast majority of my apparel appears to be beige. A quarter of my meagre wardrobe is made up of garments that I'm emotionally attached to but which no longer fit, so I'm keeping them purely for sentimental reasons – a new little black dress that I bought for our twentieth anniversary which showed off too much flesh but made me feel like a movie star for the night, a peacock-blue formal gown in a posh plastic dress carrier even though it's over ten years since we went to a ball and I'd never get the zip done up. If I remember rightly, it was a struggle then. Another quarter is taken up with clothes I bought and which have *never* actually fitted me, items I purchased with the sole intent of slimming into them. Why do women do that? Do men buy clothes a size too small and watch them hanging in the wardrobe reproachfully? The third section is stuff that I actively loathe – the scratchy, the ill-fitting, the over-exuberant patterns that were a big mistake, the clothes that should go to the charity shop as soon as I get time to sort them out. That leaves the final 25 per cent. These consist of the clothes I wear to work, a few pairs of well-cut trousers and some evening tops, a brownish wrap dress that I'm not sure suits me but which comes out every time I don't know what else to wear.

I sigh. The wrap dress it is then. Una will kill me.

Chloe pops her head round the door. 'Where's Dad off to?'

'He said he needed some fresh air.'

'He needs to take a chill pill,' my daughter advises.

'Dad's very cross about the car, Chloe,' I tell her.

'He's such a grumpy old git.'

'Don't talk about your father like that. You didn't even apologise.'

My child has the grace to hang her head. 'Sorry, Mum. I know how much that car means to you and I will pay it off. Honestly.'

'You do need to get a job. Dad's right.'

Chloe huffs. 'Neither of you seem to realise how hard it is at uni. Sometimes I have five lectures a week. Five!'

She waits for me to recoil in horror and is clearly disappointed when I don't. 'Do you want me to ask Don if you can come into the library for the rest of the summer?' I ask.

'No way.' Now she's the one who recoils in horror. 'No offence, Mum, but that sounds duller than dishwater. I'm looking for something a bit more exciting, more challenging.'

I should know by now that very few people regard being a librarian as a sexy career choice. How I would like to prove them wrong.

'Plus I want something that pays loads.'

That certainly wouldn't be a librarian then.

'You've only got about six weeks left until you go back to university. All the good jobs would have been snapped up months ago.' When we first advised you to start looking, I think. 'You might have to settle for something less.'

My daughter looks at me as if that's an alien concept.

Why do kids these days all have such high expectations? They all want to be pop stars, television presenters or c-list celebrities without having any appreciable talent. Chloe is bright but she doesn't realise that wanting something enough doesn't necessarily mean that you're good enough to do it. You only have to watch an episode of *Britain's Got Talent* to work that out. I hate to burst Chloe's bubble but I'm not sure what exactly a degree in Fashion and Media will qualify her to do and whether it's worth spending three years studying whilst amassing substantial debts in the process. Both Rick and I were so keen for the children to go on to higher education; now I wonder whether it was all worth it. Maybe Chloe would have been better off leaving school at sixteen and training to be a hairdresser or something.

Chloe slips her arm through mine. 'I came to see if I could cadge that twenty.'

I thought it was a tenner. That's inflation for you.

'I won't tell Dad.'

Me neither. I go to my handbag, pull out my last twenty-pound note and hand it over.

'Thanks, Mum.' My daughter pockets my hard-earned cash. Where will it go? On vodka? On cigarettes? A new skimpy top to cram into her overflowing wardrobe with all the others? 'I love you.'

'I love you too,' I say. And I do, despite her thoughtlessness and her feckless ways. She's my child and I'd lay down my life for her, as all parents would.

As my daughter turns to head back to her own bedroom and the delights of Bebo, Facebook and MySpace, I hold up the brownish wrap dress, moulding it round my contours. 'What do you think?'

Chloe screws up her nose. 'You're not planning to go out wearing that, are you?'

'Actually, I was.'

'Bin it,' Chloe tells me. 'It makes you look ten years older.'

'I'd better have that twenty pounds back then,' I tell her, 'if I need to buy something else.'

'It doesn't matter what you wear,' she says, as she blows me a little kiss, 'you'll look gorgeous. Where are you going, anyway?'

'Nowhere.'

'Don't tell me that Dad's taking you out. That would be a bloody miracle.'

'Don't swear, Chloe.'

She bangs the door behind her which will probably wake my mother up. And I think, No, your father isn't taking me out. Someone else is.

Chapter 14

Rick drove around the empty roads that were bathed in the orange glow of tungsten from the streetlights. He switched on the radio to listen to some late-night DJ spinning the discs – or did they not call it that these days in the age of downloads and virtual whatevers?

Milton Keynes was a young person's city – the average age of the population was under thirty-five. That made him ten years older than most people who lived here, which wasn't a statistic he wanted to dwell on. Every move he made now seemed to be accompanied by an age-related groan. Stand up, groan, sit down, another groan, bend to a lower cupboard, yet more groaning. In Stony Stratford – a place which was still managing to cling onto its own identity despite the encroaching urban sprawl – he was still considered a young whippersnapper. By some, at any rate.

He drove around aimlessly. Driving used to soothe his troubled mind, but it didn't any more. Rick remembered the hours he'd spent when the kids were babies with him and Juliet cruising the streets trying to get the little ones off to sleep so that they themselves could grab a few much-needed hours. Now the main trouble was actually getting the kids to wake up and get their lazy backsides out of bed. Rick had driven something vaguely sporty then, despite the children – trying desperately to hang onto his youth, he supposed. Now he drove a Vauxhall Cavalier Mid-Life Crisis because it was comfortable and reasonably cheap. And this from the man whose dream was to own an Aston Martin.

There was a waterside park at the top end of Stony Stratford – a lovely area with a bird sanctuary bordering the River Ouse. The area looked as if it hadn't changed in a hundred years. An ancient church stood guard over the fields and, if you wanted to walk that far, the Grand Union Canal crossed over the floodplain on an iron aqueduct which must have been quite a feat of engineering when it was built. When he had time – ha, ha – it was one of his favourite places to come and walk.

Now, at this late hour, he pulled into the car park with no intention of straying out in the surrounding countryside. All he wanted was to be alone for an hour. Nothing more. He was going to put his seat back, rest his head and look out at the stars. It was a reasonably clear night and, if he opened the sunroof, there should be a few celestial bodies to look at. Juliet had got him a book out of the library months ago, *The Encyclopaedia of Astronomy*, and he hadn't had a chance to get beyond looking at the title yet. She kept restamping it for him as no one else was waiting to borrow it, but still to no avail. His knowledge of the night sky remained somewhat limited. One day though, he might even treat himself to a telescope; he'd always fancied a bit of skywatching. No doubt it was something else – like brewing his own beer, taking up golf and walking the Pennine Way – that would have to wait until after he'd retired.

Surprisingly, the car park was quite busy for this late in the evening. Perhaps they were courting couples. Once upon a time he and Juliet had to do their smooching in the back of his car in places just like this. He smiled at the thought. Maybe it was something they could try again to add a little spice to their lives. But then, why would you want to bother having a cramped bonk on a cold back seat when you had a centrally heated house and a comfortable bed waiting for you?

He manoeuvred the car until he was tucked away in the corner. Not the prime position for stargazing, he realised as he cut the engine, since he was too far under the towering oak trees that bordered the gravel square, but it was the peace and quiet he craved as much as anything – time alone to think, contemplate his navel.

Rick reclined his seat until he was lying as flat as he could. That was better. Already he could feel some of the tension easing from his neck. Why did he find it so hard to relax? Hadn't he once been quite a content person with very little to complain about? Now, even by his own admission, he could be the winner of any International Indoor Moaning competition. Everything seemed to be piling up on him at the moment. He was at the behest of a Lothario boss who was supposed to be his friend but treated him like a lackey; he had acquired a live-in mother-in-law through no choice of his own who was like the love child of Dame Edna Everage and Attila the Hun; he had a daughter who seemed to be studying nothing at university but drinking games, and a twenty-four-year-old son who, despite having thirty grands' worth of student debt and a first-class degree in talking bollocks, was still unemployed. What he did in his room all day, goodness only knows – Rick certainly didn't. Every time he went in unannounced, Tom seemed to be clicking off dodgy websites. There had been no such temptation when Rick was his son's age and, sometimes, he was very grateful for that. When he was in his twenties he was too busy working and trying to provide for his young family to think about pornography. Now he was too old and busy to think about it. He knew though that in his next life he wanted to come back as one of his own children – no worries, no responsibility, everything laid on for you. That was the life.

And what about his wife? Juliet seemed so distant from him at the moment. Oh, they rubbed along well enough, and perhaps that was the best they could expect when they had so much else going on in their lives, but it wasn't exactly what he thought marriage would be at this stage in their lives. Free of responsibility, he thought they'd be eating out a couple of times a week, seeing friends, snatching quiet weekends in the country together, taking long romantic walks. Some hope. When had they last even gone for a night out together? He should sort that out, organise to take his wife somewhere nice. Rick did love her, it was just sometimes – too often – he seemed to lose sight of that.

A cloud floated across the sky, filling the sunroof and blotting out the few stars he could actually see. Rick sighed and folded his hands across his lap. Contentment started to return to his bones. The Cavalier might not be the car of his dreams, but it was comfortable and warm. He'd wait for the sky to clear. Shouldn't take long . . . But within minutes, he was studying the inside of his eyelids rather more than he was the sky anyway.

Chapter 15

A sharp rap on his car window woke Rick with a start. A bright light filled the car and he fumbled to find the switch for the window and wound it down. He struggled to open his eyes.

'Hello, sir,' a voice said. 'How are you?'

Rick blinked as the torch was shone in his face.

'Police?'

'That's right, sir. Win prizes for observation, do you?'

Could he find peace nowhere in this life? Rick had a much-needed stretch. Something clicked in his neck that shouldn't.

'Is this your vehicle?'

'Yes, yes.' Rick rubbed at his hair and yawned, trying to bring himself to full consciousness.

'Can I ask what you're doing here?'

'Watching the stars, Officer.'

'With your eyes closed?'

'I must have fallen asleep.' But he was waking up quickly now.

'Right.' The policeman glanced up. It was cloudy. 'Not much of a view there.'

'No. It was better when I arrived.' Though not much, Rick had to admit.

'I bet it was,' the policeman said.

'It's not the best place for stargazing . . .' The look on the policeman's face told him it would be better if he kept quiet.

'Any idea what *I'm* doing here?'

'No, Officer.'

'Do you come here – *stargazing*, did you call it – often?'

'No. Not really.'

'These friends of yours?' The office waved his riot baton round the car park.

For the first time Rick noticed that other drivers were standing at the side of their cars. Some were single drivers and some were couples. 'No,' he said. Clearly, this was some kind of raid he'd been caught up in. 'I've never seen them before.'

'Is that part of the attraction?'

'Pardon?' Rick said.

'That part of the attraction? Watching strangers?'

'I wasn't watching strangers. I was watching the stars.' This time they both looked up at the sky together. Still cloudy. 'Why would I want to watch strangers?'

'Takes all sorts, sir. Unfortunately, you're under arrest for it. Please get out of your vehicle.'

Rick opened the door and stepped onto the loose gravel of the car park.

'I'm arresting you on suspicion of Outraging Public Decency. Do you understand?'

'Yes.' Then, 'No!'

The officer clapped some cuffs on Rick's wrists, wresting his arms behind his back, which made him gasp. 'Why are you doing that?'

'Are you comfortable, sir?'

'Of course I'm not!'

'You do not have to say anything. But it may harm your defence if you do not mention, when questioned, something you may rely on in court. Whatever you do say will be given in evidence.'

'There must be some mistake.'

The policeman gave him a wry smile. 'That's what they all say.'

While Rick was wrestling against his handcuffs he noticed that another office was searching his car, opening the glovebox. 'What are you looking for?' Rick shouted to him. 'There's nothing of any interest in there.'

The second policeman held up a bag to the first, who asked, 'What have you got?'

'KY Jelly and a small packet of tissues.'

The first officer glared at him.

'It's not an offence to have KY Jelly,' Rick protested. 'Is it?' he added weakly.

'You're coming with me, sir.' The policeman pushed him towards the riot van. 'You can explain it down at the station.'

'Wait, wait,' Rick said. 'I haven't done anything. Why are you arresting me again? What the hell's Outraging Public Decency or whatever you said?'

'Let me make it easy for you. Dogging, sir. Ring a bell?'

'Dogging? But Buster's at home. He's already had his walk. I haven't got a dog with me.'

'Dogging,' the policeman repeated as if he was speaking to a small child. 'Watching other people perform sexual acts for your own personal gratification.'

Rick gasped again

'But you don't need me to tell me that, do you?'

'Really,' Rick insisted, open-mouthed. 'I had no idea.' This was the sort of thing that Hal would do, not him. 'I came here for half an hour's peace, to get away from an overbearing mother-in-law, a selfish daughter and life in general.'

'Everyone knows what this car park is used for.'

'I didn't. I've never heard of dogging.' Not in sleepy Stony Stratford, surely?

'Well, it's a criminal offence in this green and pleasant land.' The policeman banged Rick's head against the door as he pushed him into the riot van. 'And you're nicked.'

Chapter 16

Rick lay on the hard bunk in the cell at Milton Keynes Central Police Station, hands behind his head. It was a depressing little space in which to spend some time. It was his first visit to a police cell and he prayed that it would be his last. The cell was exactly how you imagined a police cell would be. It was predominantly grey and almost entirely bare, apart from a bed covered with an itchy-looking blanket and a metal toilet in the corner. He only hoped the person who'd been here before him hadn't got something contagious. Rick gave the blanket a wide berth just in case.

It had taken hours to process the paperwork for his arrest, presumably because they'd arrested everyone, no matter how innocent, who was in the car park. No wonder there weren't any policemen on the streets any more. Clearly they were all hanging around car parks in the dead of night and filling in forms.

Now it was three o'clock in the morning. Eventually, he'd been interviewed by the arresting officer and had simply told the man the same thing over and over again – that it was all a terrible mis-understanding and the only thing he was guilty of was being a miserable bastard who needed a good sulk every so often. It looked like the KY Jelly and the tissues were the sticking point, incriminating evidence. He had no idea how they'd got in his car. Rick only knew that he hadn't put them there and he hadn't intended to use them for something sleazy.

On the roof above him was a message stuck to the ceiling.

It said: *How did you get here? Was it through drink or drugs?* No option for being collared while innocently contemplating the complexity of one's life, then. Many successive prisoners, it seemed, had tried to pick at the letters to turn them into rude words, without much success.

He switched to the other end of the bed. There the message was: *Are you hanging out with the wrong mates? Interested in our clean slate programme?* Then it gave a phone number to call. Which wasn't much use as everything had been taken off him, his wallet, his belt, his shoes, all his worldly goods including his mobile phone.

He'd been allowed to speak to Juliet on the phone before they'd banged him up – if that was the right term. It must have been a terrible shock to her when the police called. She probably thought he'd had an accident or something, was lying crumpled by the kerb-side. Telling her that he'd only been arrested didn't seem to have done much to calm her down. Juliet would be on her way here now. Not that there was a lot of point. When they'd finished inter-viewing him, Rick was told that he was being bailed, then he'd been returned to the cells so that Prisoner 15473 Joyce could spend some time considering the error of his ways.

He'd been given a book called *Codes of Practice*, but it didn't look as interesting as some of the books that his wife read – very little sex and no gratuitous violence – and so he'd cast it to one side. Hopefully, they would realise that he wasn't in any way culpable and, in time, this would all become a distant nightmare.

An hour later, just when he thought the smell of other people's piss was going to make him pass out, they let him out. He was given all of his stuff and two officers escorted him back to the van dock door where he'd come in. 'Your wife's waiting in the main reception,' one said.

Rick walked round to the front of the building, glad to be breathing in the cool night air rather than the fug of the fetid cell. Juliet was standing in the reception area, white-faced. She looked like she'd been through the mill too. Her hair was untidy and, although she was wearing her jeans and a jacket, she still had her pyjama top on underneath it. For a moment, it seemed that she might be about to rush over and hug him, but she clearly thought better of it and didn't. Instead, she stood staring impassively, hands by her side.

'Sorry to drag you out of bed,' Rick said, pushing aside his need for a cuddle. 'Have you been here long?'

'Hours,' she replied. 'You look dreadful. What on earth have you been doing?'

'Nothing,' he said. 'But this lot won't believe me.' He flicked a thumb at the desk. 'They've arrested me for dogging.'

Juliet looked as puzzled as he had.

'Watching people having sex in their cars,' he explained. 'Apparently it's all the rage.' What sort of society were they living in, where people could do that kind of thing for entertainment? And to think that he was a man who was content with nothing more than some football on the telly or a DVD from Blockbusters and a couple of cans of Stella to keep him amused. The injustice of being tugged for something like this was too hard to bear.

Her eyebrows lifted at that. 'And were you?'

'How long have we been married?' he asked wearily. Now even his wife was doubting him. 'Does that sound like the sort of thing I'd do?'

Juliet failed to meet his eyes. So much for her vote of confidence.

'I'd parked up by the waterside park,' he continued. 'I wanted to watch the stars, but it was cloudy and I fell asleep. Next thing I knew, I was being dragged out of my car and herded down here. The police were having a clampdown. Apparently, it's a notorious area for it.' He shrugged his ignorance. 'I was just in the wrong place at the wrong time.'

Story of his life, actually.

'They found some KY Jelly and tissues in the glove compartment of the car. That, for some reason, makes me a villain.'

'Oh, I wondered what had happened to those.' Juliet's hand went to her mouth. 'I bought them in Boots a couple of weeks ago.'

'Well, now you know,' he said. And then: 'What the hell do you need KY Jelly for?'

'Buster's been scratching his itchy bottom on the hall carpet. I thought it might help.'

Marvellous. So there *was* a dog involved in it somewhere. 'I don't think they'd have believed me if I'd told them.'

'Is that the end of it?'

'No.' Rick shook his head. 'I've been charged with the offence of Outraging Public Decency. At least I've been bailed though. They're going to carry out more investigations and I've got to report back here in a month's time.' The date and time had been given to him on a sheet of paper.

'Oh, Rick.' There were tears in Juliet's eyes. In his own too. He didn't want his wife to 'Oh, Rick' him; he thought he might just break down and cry, and he couldn't remember crying since Chloe was born.

Now she did hug him.

'I'm fine. I'm fine,' he insisted, patting her back. 'Let's just get out of this place.'

'I ordered a taxi when they told me you could go home. It's waiting outside.' He'd forgotten that she wouldn't have her own car. 'Are you ready?'

Rick nodded. 'We'll ask him to take us to the waterside park then I can collect the Cavalier.' The thought of returning to the scene of his non-existent crime filled him with dread – he'd probably never walk Buster there again. But he couldn't leave the car there overnight or there'd be nothing left of it in the morning – if it was there at all. What he really wanted to do was go straight home, get into a hot shower and wash away the stink of the police station and crawl into his nice warm bed.

'I really didn't do this, Juliet. I promise you.'

She slipped her hand in his. 'I know,' she said.

But she didn't sound like she did.

Chapter 17

The next morning, Rick drops me off at the library. My eyelids feel like nails scraping over my eyeballs. After collecting the car and handing over the princely sum of seventy pounds to the taxi driver, we eventually fell into bed at about four o'clock this morning. Of course, I didn't sleep. I just lay awake, my mind in turmoil, and I know that Rick didn't manage to drop off either. Conversation was strained over breakfast mainly because the rest of the family don't know of our twilight trauma. I sneaked out of the house and didn't tell either my mother or the children where I was going, so at the moment, they're none the wiser.

'I'm sorry,' my husband says again as we sit in the car. He squeezes my hand. 'Next time I can't sleep, I'll take a Nytol.'

I manage a laugh at that.

'You look lovely today,' he says. 'I haven't seen that dress in ages.'

My cheeks flush. This would be an ideal time to tell him about my impending lunch with Steven, but I don't. 'I'll see you later,' I say, pecking his cheek. 'No need to pick me up. I'll walk home.'

I hear Rick drive away, but I don't turn round. He must be exhausted and I know that he's got a busy day.

In the library, Una tuts as she sees me. 'Ten out of ten for effort, but you haven't quite pulled it off. That colour makes you look very tired.'

'I *am* very tired,' I tell her. I'm worn out, in fact. Una is in a teal outfit today. A rich, jewel hue that brings out the colour of her eyes.

The sort of thing that I should really be wearing. The sort of thing that I don't possess. 'We've been up half of the night.' I make sure no one else is within earshot. 'Rick was arrested in the waterside park in the wee small hours.' I pause for effect. 'For dogging.'

There's a sharp intake of breath. I have no need to explain to my worldly wise little friend about this particular kind of sexual perversion.

'He wasn't, was he?'

Shaking my head, I say, 'I don't think so. He says he'd gone to watch the stars and had fallen asleep.'

Una laughs. 'That sounds more like Rick.'

'That's what I'm clinging to,' I admit. 'Nevertheless, it's a shock to find your husband accused of something like that. He's been acting a bit odd lately – distant. It makes you question what you really know about someone.' Who'd have thought that Steven Aubrey could leave me on the morning of our wedding, but he did. Who'd have thought that he'd turn up out of the blue at the library a quarter of a century later as if it had never happened between us – but he did that too. I thought I knew him inside out, and I never saw it coming. I could say the same thing about Rick.

'Come on,' Una says, steering me towards the staff room. 'Let me make you a cup of strong tea before the rabble arrive. Your date today could be just the pick-me-up you need.'

'I think I'm going to cancel.'

'No, you're not.'

I worry at my fingernail. 'I didn't mention it to Rick and that makes me feel bad. How can I complain about him sneaking around behind my back when I'm planning on doing it too?'

'It's hardly the same thing!' my friend protests. 'Rick was watching strangers get down to it in a car park. You're having a civilised pub lunch with an ex-boyfriend. You can't even begin to compare it.'

I sit at the table while she makes us both tea. Don, our library manager, comes in too and Una makes him a cup as well. 'Don,' she says as she puts it down, 'I'm not going to have a lunch-hour today, I'm giving it to Juliet. She's going out from twelve until two.'

'Una . . .' I widen my eyes at her.

'I'm not sure that's allowed,' Don says. 'It's probably against health and safety.'

'Well, we won't tell anyone if you don't,' she says, and flutters her eyelashes at Don. 'I'll buy you a new packet of digestives.'

Our manager pats his stomach. 'Having to watch the weight. I don't know where the last packet went. I can't even remember eating half of them.'

Una and I try not to giggle. Don takes his tea and, thankfully, retreats to his office which is in use again as his roof has been covered by a temporary tarpaulin.

'I'm going to nip home and get you some accessories to brighten you up.'

'I think it will take more than accessories.'

'You're a beautiful woman,' Una insists. 'You've just got a bit . . .' she searches for a word that won't reduce me to tears '. . . dowdy.'

'Dowdy' does fill my eyes with tears. Mrs Dowdy from Dowdy Town. Just like I told you.

'No crying,' she instructs. 'All you need is a bit of bling. You could think about Botox too.'

'Before lunch?'

'As a plan for the new you.'

'I hadn't planned on creating a new me.'

'Then perhaps you should,' Una suggests. My friend budges me up while she sits her tiny frame next to my rather more hefty one. 'I know that you're a wife and mother and all that kind of thing – and very wonderful you are at it – but first and foremost, you're a woman. You always put yourself last, Juliet Joyce. Maybe you should try being first for once.'

'And that includes skiving off work to have lunch with my old lover?'

'It's a start,' Una agrees. 'Now you'd better get moving as I want you working twice as hard this morning to make up for my generosity.'

'I've never had a good friend like you, Una. Thanks.'

80

'Now I'm going to shoot out before Don surfaces again and bring you back some of my killer heels. I want you walking all over that man!'

I thought I was just going to have lunch with my old flame; instead I find I'm going to poke Steven's eyeballs out with my dress, knock him dead with my charm and walk all over him in my killer heels. This feels more like a fight than a date. Poor Steven, I feel sorry for him already.

Chapter 18

'What were you thinking of, mate?' Hal laughed uproariously.

'I didn't know the place was a notorious hang-out for perverts,' Rick insisted with a frown. 'I just go there to mind my own business and walk Buster.'

'You have so much to learn, my friend.'

'So it seems.' Rick wasn't surprised that Hal knew all about the art of dogging or that it took place in car parks within their environs.

The two of them were still working in the conservatory and the sun was beating down on them. It was roasting in here, even with all the doors and windows open.

Rick had arrived late again this morning and Hal had been tetchy with him until he'd explained why.

'What did Juliet say?'

'Not much,' Rick shrugged. 'But I can tell that she isn't best pleased.'

'Melinda would have cut my bollocks off with a blunt knife or worse,' Hal decided. 'I'd have been joining the John Bobbitt Cruel Cut Club. Shannon would probably do the same thing too. Count yourself lucky, mate.'

Rick conceded that having Juliet looking reproachfully at him hadn't been too bad after all.

'We should go out on the town together, Ricky-Boy,' Hal said, clapping him on the back as he knelt on the floor trying to work out a pattern in the laminate planks. His eyes were gritty and his head thumped. 'Let our hair down a bit. Have a few bevies. Laugh about this.'

'I don't think that Juliet will let me out of her sight for the foreseeable future.'

'She won't mind you going for a little drinkie with your old pal.'

'I have to report back to the police station in a month's time. Supposing they press charges?'

'They won't,' Hal reassured him. 'There are rapists and murderers walking the streets. Being found guilty of being in possession of KY Jelly and a leery look won't get you a custodial sentence.' That started him off chuckling again. 'It'll just get you a slap on the wrist and an aversion to parking in lay-bys.' He gripped his sides as he laughed at Rick's expense.

'This isn't funny,' Rick reminded him.

'You are taking life far too seriously,' his friend pointed out. 'We need to kick back and have some fun.'

Rick thought it sounded like Hal needed a night away from Shannon.

'I'm not sure.'

'It could be just the two of us, or we could go out as a foursome. Juliet hasn't met Shannon yet, has she?'

No. And he wasn't sure how much his wife would have in common with Hal's new love interest. When Hal had been married to Melinda they'd often gone out for a meal together – sometimes they'd even thought about going on holiday together, but it had never happened. Juliet was very disapproving of the fact that Hal had left his wife and two children for a younger model. He didn't think it would be a good idea to get them together.

'I won't take no for an answer,' Hal warned.

Rick knew his friend only too well. Hal wasn't easily dissuaded once he'd set his mind on something; it was easier just to give in. 'We'll go out for a beer sometime,' Rick promised.

'I'll hold you to that,' Hal said.

'Yeah, yeah.' Rick sighed. Hal had been good to him in the past.

He'd been right there with a job offer when he'd been made redundant. Sometimes he took the piss, leaving Rick to work on jobs on his own while he skived off with Shannon, but then it was his company. On the whole, Hal was pretty sound.

'We need to get on with this,' Rick said, wanting to get his head down, 'otherwise we'll never finish it today.' He pulled a pile of planks towards him and set about laying them out.

He was allowed a few minutes of peace before his friend spoke again.

'Mate?' Hal tried to sound casual and failed. 'What time exactly did you say you'd turned up at that car park?'

Chapter 19

Steven Aubrey phoned me mid-morning at the library to arrange a time to pick me up. Even just hearing his voice made me feel all peculiar again in a way that I really can't describe. And here he is now, punctual on the dot of noon. Una, stamping books at the desk, gives him the once-over and makes it plain that she likes what she sees. She cups her face in her hands and stares at Steven in a very girly way. I study my feet.

'You look lovely,' Steven says to me, as I lurk in reception self-consciously.

This is down to Una. My plain brown-ish dress has been enhanced with a cream and teal scarf. I'm sporting ethnic bangles on my wrists and have dangly earrings swinging from my lobes. My size sixes are squashed into a pair of Una's glitzy sandals with heels two inches higher than I normally wear. Far from transforming me into a femme fatale I feel extremely uncomfortable to be dressed like this – a sheep in wolf's clothing, or mutton dressed as lamb as Rick would more likely say. Middle-aged mum dressed as glamorous divorcée.

Steven, on the other hand, looks very happy in his own skin. By some strange accident we're colour co-ordinated and he's wearing brown trousers, a coffee-coloured sweatshirt and a light cream jacket. They may not be the height of fashion here, but they all look like they're expensive. A hint of a tan makes him look healthy and relaxed – a complete contrast to my pale-faced, dark-shadowed countenance. But then Steven probably wasn't awake for the best part of the night wondering what on earth his other half was up to. It strikes me that I don't even know if Steven currently has another half.

'Don't stand around here dilly-dallying,' Una says, as she shoos us out of the door. 'You've only got two hours and there's twenty-five years to catch up on.'

Outside the library there's a flash car and Steven blips open the door.

'Nice,' I say. 'What is it?'

'Aston Martin DB9.'

This would be Rick's idea of heaven. I slide into its sleek interior feeling like one of those celebrities that you see in *Hello!* or *OK* magazines – the ones that Una pores over every day and the ones I flick through in the library when I think that no one's watching me.

'This feels very strange,' Steven says.

'Yes,' I agree. 'Very strange.'

'I've been told that the Paris House restaurant is the place to go, but I thought that as you'd only have an hour we'd just drive to Cosgrove and eat at the pub there.'

'That's fine.' I don't tell him that Una has inveighed on my behalf for me to have two hours. One may be more than I can endure.

'I could call Paris House, see if they have a table?'

'No, no,' I insist. 'That's way too posh for me.' I'm worried that I'll drop my cutlery as it is or somehow manage to pour wine over myself. 'Some pub grub is fine.' I wonder why neither of us has just thought to walk into the High Street and eat at one of the many fine places on offer there. Perhaps we both feared that we would be recognised by too many people who'd be wondering what we were doing together again. When you've lived here as long as I have, you know there are very few secrets.

Steven sets off, the car purring out of the town, and soon we're winding through lush green country lanes out to Cosgrove. I don't know what to do with myself or even how to start a conversation with Steven, so instead I stare out of the window and enjoy the scenery.

This is a beautiful part of the world. Even though we're on the border of a vast city, you can be out into the best of British countryside within minutes. The rolling fields which straddle the border of Buckinghamshire and Northamptonshire are spread out before us, and towering oaks line the road which is bordered by swathes of cow parsley swaying in the breeze. We fly past thatched cottages, tiny terraced houses and a stoic church before turning down towards Cosgrove.

'You can't believe how long I've waited to do this,' he says, eyes fixed on the road. His hand slides over to find mine which are folded anxiously on my lap. 'Feeling OK?'

I nod. 'Yes.'

But the truth of the matter is that I'm a seething mass of nerves. Why am I doing this? Steven is a part of my past and should have remained firmly there. I don't want to take a knife and start easing it slowly and painfully into old wounds. What's done is done and, after all this time, it should be left that way.

'I didn't think that you'd agree to see me.'

I should have said no. If I'd had any sense at all.

Steven smiles at me and it melts my heart. 'Not without lots of begging, anyway.'

Pushover, I think. Always have been, always will be.

Chapter 20

Arriving at the pub, I'm relieved to see that it's relatively quiet. The Barley Mow is nestled in the heart of the village, a popular haunt offering decent, home-cooked food. The front of the old stone pub is laden with hanging baskets which brim with blue lobelia, blowsy pink fuchsias and trailing ivy. The garden winds its way down to the side of the Grand Union Canal and there's a rash of play equipment for children dotted about the lawn. Today it's being well utilised. A group of mums with a generous handful of toddlers between them have set up camp here.

We decide that it's too breezy to sit outside and anyway, I'd feel conspicuous sitting out there with all the mums. So we go inside and in the cool, dark interior Steven chooses a table that's tucked away in the corner and that suits me just fine. It's not that I'm embarrassed to be with him but, well, you know. I don't really want to be seen out with him when I haven't told Rick where I am.

We order straightaway and I have just a diet cola as I don't want to be stamping books wonkily this afternoon. I'm at that age where one glass of wine is as good as a bottle and the conservative people of Stony Stratford would probably struggle with the concept of a drunk librarian. I sip my drink and try hard not to notice that Steven is looking at me somewhat longingly.

'So, what have you been doing for the last twenty-five years?' I say with a laugh that's intended to break the tension between us, but doesn't. Perhaps it would be better if the pub was busy then I wouldn't feel quite so self-conscious sitting here with Steven.

'I've been very successful in business,' he tells me earnestly. 'Not so lucky in love.'

'Just the opposite to me,' I quip.

Steven's face takes on a serious expression. 'I've been married four times.'

'That must have been very expensive for you.'

He shrugs. 'It's the price I've had to pay for letting my one true love slip through my fingers.'

Or I could have simply been number one of *five* Mrs Steven Aubreys, but I don't voice that out loud. Our lunch arrives which rescues me from having to reply.

'This looks very good.' I try to steer the conversation back to neutral ground and focus my attention on my Caesar salad. Una would pick off all the croutons and have the dressing on the side, but I don't. Before I tuck in, I untie her scarf and slip it off. Knowing me, I'd dip it in my dinner. Better safe than sorry.

'You still have a beautiful throat,' my companion says tenderly.

I didn't know that Steven ever thought my throat was beautiful. Putting my hand up to cover it, I give an involuntary cough.

'Now I've made you self-conscious.'

'No, no.'

'Have you thought of me at all over the years?' Clearly, Steven has other plans concerning the neutrality of our conversation.

'Of course I have, Steven. But not always kindly.' I smile to show him that despite the barb, I'm teasing him.

'Who could blame you?' my old flame says, cutting into the steak he's ordered. It's rare and oozes blood. 'I treated you despicably.'

'It was a pretty awful thing to do,' I agree without malice. I look at this boy now grown into a man who did me such great harm.

My mind goes back to that morning. I can still see it so clearly. The flowers had arrived and were waiting in the hall. My bouquet, resplendent with Singapore orchids and white roses, was all that I'd hoped it would be. The hairdresser had finished piling my hair into what I considered was a very sophisticated chignon, studded with pearls. I'd splashed out on a beautician to come and do my make-up, much to my mother's horror since she thought it was a terrible waste of money. The girl had painted what felt like a thick mask of foundation on me, but when I looked in the mirror I saw a woman lifted straight from the cover of a glossy magazine. I was wearing the most beautiful lingerie I'd ever worn under my old dressing-gown, and my gorgeous dress that had cost my dad nearly a month's salary was hanging on the back of my bedroom door. I knew I was going to drift down the aisle looking and feeling like a princess. My three bridesmaids were giggly with anticipation while I was feeling calm and collected, so ready to be flying the nest and starting out on my new life as a wife. This was the culmination of so much waiting and longing, I could hardly bear it. We'd bought a little terraced house that we'd be moving into as soon as we came back from our honeymoon which was to be two weeks in Cornwall and had seemed so extravagant at the time.

Then Steven had arrived. My mother hadn't wanted to show him up to my room, insisting it was very bad luck to see the bride before the wedding. Turns out she was right. It was very bad luck for me indeed. The hairdresser and beautician scuttled out, my bridesmaids, reluctant to leave, had to be forcibly dragged out by Mum who sadly had realised the bombshell that was about to be dropped on me. The minute I saw Steven's face, I knew that something terrible had happened. I thought his father had died, his mother had fallen under a bus, the wedding reception venue had burned down, the vicar had run off with one of his parishioners or someone had forgotten to get the correct paperwork. It never entered my head that Steven might simply announce that he didn't feel ready to marry me and that, instead of going to the church, he was heading to the airport. That was the last time I saw him – apart from yesterday.

Suddenly, I've lost my appetite and I push my salad away from me. My stomach is a knot of anxiety – probably a delayed reaction to the shock of last night's shenanigans. 'It's all water under the bridge now,' I say quietly.

Steven pushes his food away too and stares at me, eyes fixed on mine. 'I want you to know that I have regretted it every single day of my life.'

'Well,' I say, 'for a while I thought that I'd never recover. But I did. I'm happily married and have two lovely children. Things worked out just fine.'

'Are you sure about that?' Steven asks. 'Don't you ever wonder, what if . . . ?'

So many times, I think. When we've scrimped and saved to pay the mortgage, whenever Rick and I have had a row, when I've looked out of the library windows on a cold and rainy day, 'what if' has featured very large. But I'm not about to tell Steven that.

'I think I could have made you very happy,' he continues.

'I'm sure you could,' I concede. 'But none of that matters now. We made our choices. We've had different lives. Fate has been quite kind to both of us. It's nice that we can share a convivial lunch as friends.'

'But it's not enough, is it?' Steven says. His hand covers mine. I stare at our joined fingers for a moment then I gently ease my hand away.

'It is for me,' I tell him, even though my stomach's fluttering. 'I have a lovely husband and two great children. My life is just perfect.' And, while that might be slightly over-egging the pudding, Steven Aubrey doesn't need to know that either.

Chapter 21

Steven Aubrey drops me back at the library. He leans towards me in the posh car and I think that he might want to kiss me, but I duck away from him.

'Thanks,' I say briskly. 'Lunch was lovely. It was nice seeing you again.'

'Was it?' he asks with a sigh. 'I would have liked it better if you'd fallen into my arms again and told me that you couldn't live without me for another minute.'

I'm taken aback. 'You didn't really expect that, did you?'

Steven laughs. 'No,' he says. 'Despite what you think, I know you too well. I'm just teasing. We can do it again though?'

Now I'm all shy. 'I don't know, Steven. Perhaps it isn't a good idea.'

'I think it is,' he insists. 'I want to be back in your life.'

How can he be? We're different people now. Steven is a successful businessman who's travelled the world. I'm a staid mum who hasn't been anywhere or done anything. I'm one of Stony Stratford's fixtures and fittings.

'Same time next week?'

'I don't know . . .'

'I'll pop into the library before then.'

How can I stop him doing that? It's a public place. He could take some books for his mum who, Steven says, is becoming very frail.

'I have to go,' I say. 'Or I'll be late.' Not that it matters too much.

I can see from here that there are no customers waiting at the desk. Still, I shimmy out of the Aston Martin trying not to flash my knees before he can say anything else to delay me.

Steven was always a charmer, even as a teenager. He had an easy way with him that made people love him. My old flame hasn't lost that ability and now it's coupled with the confidence of maturity – a lethal combination, if you ask me.

I shoot into the library, seeking refuge. Una looks up as I bowl in. 'My, my,' she says. 'Someone's brought some colour to your cheeks.'

'The pub was hot and stuffy,' I tell her.

'A likely story.' My friend laughs. I've put Una's scarf back on so that she doesn't know I took it off.

'Have you been busy?'

'Don't worry about me. I managed to hold off the hordes of rampaging book borrowers all by myself.' When I look horrified, she tuts at me. 'Of course I haven't been busy. Chance would be a fine thing.'

Una finds the pace of life at the library stultifying while I like the calm, measured days, the subdued atmosphere. 'I'll go upstairs and shelve this trolley of books,' I say.

'You will not,' Una instructs. 'You'll stay here and pretend to be busy like me while you tell me all the gory details.'

From under the counter, I pull a box of books that are going back to other libraries towards me and make an attempt at looking like I'm sorting through it.

'So . . . ?' Una prompts.

'He's not changed much,' I tell her. 'More suave, more sophisticated than the teenage boy I knew and loved, but not so very different.'

'Was there still a spark there?'

'No,' I lie.

My friend looks disappointed. 'Not just a little one?'

'There's a lot of history there. It felt odd to be with him again. Very odd.'

'Odd can be very similar to excited, I think,' Una says. 'That's the bit I like best about being divorced. I like the feeling of going out with someone new, not knowing what they're going to be like, what they're going to say. Skin that you don't know against your skin, touching someone you've never touched before . . .'

I can feel myself going all warm and loosen Una's scarf.

'Sex with a stranger is very thrilling.'

I'll have to take Una's word for it. I've never had sex with a stranger. My husband has been my one and only lover. I know every inch of Rick's skin as he does mine. Isn't there a comfort in that? Do you have to have a long list of conquests before you feel that you're having great sex? Even if I had Una's allure, would I really want to be falling into bed with a different man every week at my age? I couldn't bear the thought of sharing my cellulite with strangers. And what would you talk about in the morning?

'Haven't you thought what it might be like with Steven?' She nudges me in the ribs.

'No.' I laugh at the very thought. 'That's the funny thing about him,' I say, and sound slightly wistful even to my own ears. 'He's a stranger and yet so familiar at the same time.'

'And still he hasn't turned your head?'

I think about how my pulse raced as I sat next to Steven, how my skin tingled when he touched me, how my throat tightened when he talked about the old times we'd shared – and the truth of the matter is, there were more good times than bad. 'Not a bit.' I wonder why I'm lying to my friend.

'You're not going to be rushing down to Doxley, Poxley and Roxley, solicitors to the mid-life crisis of the mid-life woman?'

'It hadn't crossed my mind.'

A customer comes to the desk with a book to take out. Ian McEwan – *Atonement*. One of my favourites. Una scowls at her as she's interrupting our conversation and swipes the bar code and stamps the book in a crisp manner.

94

'I thought he was hot,' Una says when she's gone.

'I can see why you'd say that,' I concede. 'Steven's a very attractive man.' But could I imagine myself in bed with him? Doing the things that lovers do? I push the thought away.

Una leans on the counter. 'Have you never thought about leaving Rick? Not even once?'

'Oh, sometimes when we've had a row, or when the kids were playing me up, I'd wonder what it would be like to be on my own. But I'm not like you, Una. I enjoy being married. Rick and I may not set the world alight,' especially not now, 'but we've always got along just fine. Mostly. I'm used to his funny little ways and he's used to mine.'

'And that's all there is to it?' My friend is open-mouthed. 'God, Juliet, you make it sound like a life sentence, not a vibrant relationship.'

I bristle slightly. 'I don't mean to.'

'This could be your big chance to escape, bring some excitement into your dreary little life.'

Is my life dreary and little? It shocks me to think that it might be. 'Why did you leave your husband?'

'I was bored,' Una tells me. 'Bored witless.'

'But you had everything that money could buy.' Una's family home was like a manor house. She drove me past it one day, stopping at the gates so that I could gasp in awe at it.

My friend shrugs. 'That isn't everything, is it? I wanted a man who was mad for my body, who wanted to do wild and crazy things. All Martin wanted to do was fall asleep in front of the television every night.'

'Isn't that what husbands do?'

'It doesn't have to be like that,' Una says, and she sounds irritated with me. 'Just because you've been married for twenty-five years, it doesn't mean that you still can't swing from the chandeliers.'

I don't point out to Una that now she's left her husband she doesn't actually have chandeliers any more.

'I just looked at my life one day, the kids are gone, busy with

95

their own lives, the years stretching ahead, and thought, I can't do this for another twenty-five years. Don't you ever think that?'

My mouth goes dry when I say, 'No.'

Una gives me a wry look. 'Then perhaps you should.'

'I'd better go and do those books before Don appears,' I say. Our manager thinks that the fabric of society will rip apart if books stay on the trolley for too long instead of being available for our browsing readers. At the moment I'm very glad of that.

And I take the trolley into the lift to go up to the first floor, seeking refuge in the books that I cherish so much, placing them lovingly, clearing my troubled mind, thinking of nothing else but where their rightful place is on the shelves – not Rick's arrest, not Steven's warm smile, not my twenty-five-year-old marriage which might win an accolade for longevity, but none for passion.

Chapter 22

When Rick got home his mother-in-law was reading the local paper at the kitchen table. He groaned simply because it was getting more and more difficult to find a space in the day when he could be alone with his thoughts. They'd shoehorned a small sofa into Rita's bedroom and had bought her a twenty-inch LCD television from Costco that he'd mounted on the wall, and he wondered why she didn't spend more time in there. But then if she was tucked away in her bedroom, she couldn't cause trouble and that was something Juliet's mother liked to do very much.

As he came into the kitchen, Rita flicked the paper pointedly and displayed the front page. Rick groaned even more. There in his full glory was a picture of Rick and several other men he'd never seen before with the headline CAR PARK PERVERTS ARRESTED.

'I'd better put the kettle on,' Rick said.

'You've got some explaining to do,' Rita barked.

'About what?' Juliet said as she came through the door behind him.

'This!' His mother-in-law gave the newspaper a good shake.

Why couldn't it have said LOCAL MAN IN MOTHER-IN-LAW MURDER PROBE, Rick pondered.

'I know all about it, Mum,' Juliet said wearily as she too pulled out a chair. His wife glanced at him. 'It's all a big mistake.'

'Then why is it in the local paper?'

If the *Stony Stratford Companion* said that aliens were about to land in Market Square then Rita Britten would believe it.

'All I was doing was trying to get some peace,' Rick said weakly. Something that was steadfastly eluding him.

His mother-in-law harrumphed, clearly more inclined to believe that he was a pervert because it said so in the local press. 'I don't know how I'll face the neighbours,' she said, putting a hand to her forehead.

'Perhaps you should move away,' Rick suggested, and received a black scowl in return.

'It's very worrying for us, Mum,' Juliet said calmly. 'Rick needs our support not our condemnation.'

More harrumphing. 'He's not the only one who needs support,' Rita declared. 'I'm going to be having that HRT. I'm not supposed to have any stress.'

'HRT? But, Mum, you don't need that.'

'I do if I want to have another baby.'

Juliet looked horrified. 'You don't mean HRT, you mean IVF!'

'That's the one.' Rita looked pleased with herself.

'But you're seventy years old – you can't have another baby.'

'Everyone's having late babies now. It's the trend.'

'Yes, but late as in late forties.'

Fifty if you're really pushing the envelope, Rick thought. The odd truly freakish one at sixty.

'Not seventy,' Juliet said.

'I can have one at ninety if I go to Russia.'

What a thought.

'I've money in my savings account.'

'I think she *should* go to Russia,' Rick chipped in.

'Mum, stop being silly. You can't possibly want another baby at your time of life. You're talking nonsense.'

'I want to do it all again and do it properly this time. I always wanted a boy.'

'Thanks,' Juliet muttered. 'Besides, I thought you were using that money for your boob job?'

'I'll still have a bit left,' Rita insisted, 'and anyway, I'll have to wait until after I've finished breastfeeding.'

Rick shuddered. 'Why don't you take your tea upstairs?' he said, resisting the urge to tip the contents over his mother-in-law and handing her the cup instead. 'Juliet and I have got things that we want to talk about.'

'I bet you have,' Rita grumbled, but to his relief, she stood up and shuffled out of the room, splashing her tea on the floor as she went.

'I think she's losing her mind,' Juliet said when her mother had gone. 'Do you think I should make her an appointment to see Doctor Kennett?'

'I think we should make arrangements to get her committed,' Rick suggested. He'd had enough of all this. All he wanted to do was get away for a couple of hours and not in a dark car park way. 'Why don't we go out tonight? Get out of the house?'

At that point, Tom swung through the door and flopped down at the table. 'I have something to tell you.'

'I hope it's good news,' Rick said, as he surreptitiously removed the newspaper from the table and slid it into one of the kitchen drawers.

His son took a deep breath. 'Gabe and I want to get married.'

'Who's Gabe?' Juliet wanted to know.

'My boyfriend,' Tom said. Then with a smile, added, 'My soulmate.'

Rick recoiled. 'You're gay?'

'Dad, are you blind?'

First, he was accused of being a car park pervert and now he was blind too.

'Is that the one I keep bumping into on the landing half-naked?' Rick wanted to know.

Tom nodded happily.

'I thought he was just a friend.' Rick rubbed a hand over his face. Did that seem possible? 'A *good* friend. You brought a girl home not that long ago. Who was she?'

Their son shrugged. Clearly the name of the young woman in question now escaped him. 'Times change.'

Too fast for Rick's liking. 'How long have you known this Gabe?'

'Not long.' Tom was now defensive. Weeks, Rick took that as. Days even. 'But then you and Mum hardly knew each other when you got married, and look how happy you are.'

Rick and Juliet exchanged a glance. They'd never told their oldest offspring of the embarrassing shortfall between the date of their hasty wedding and subsequent date of his birth. One day he'd work it out for himself if he ever took the time.

'We hardly know him,' Juliet intervened, putting her hands over her son's. Rick agreed silently. Seeing someone at your bathroom door in their pants didn't count as being acquainted. 'Why haven't you introduced him properly to the family?'

'You lot? I didn't want to put him off,' Tom laughed. Rick didn't think that was funny. 'We'd like to have a civil partnership and then Gabe would move in here while we save up for our own place.'

'No,' Rick said, holding up a hand. 'No moving in here.'

His son's face darkened. 'What are we supposed to do?'

'You're not using this place like a hotel.'

'I wouldn't *be* using it like a hotel – I use it like a hotel now,' Tom pointed out reasonably. 'This would be our home.'

'No,' Rick repeated. 'If you think you're old enough to get married, then you're old enough to find a job and pay for your own place.'

Tom looked as if that hadn't occurred to him. 'It's tough out there,' he said. 'Have you seen the price of houses?'

'Yes, that's why people study hard at university to get a good start. You seemed to have forgotten that bit.'

'I'm trying to make my mind up,' Tom shot back. 'Before committing myself to a career.'

'Care to share your current thoughts?'

'I'm thinking web designer, accountant or possibly landscape gardener.' This from a man who couldn't be persuaded to run the lawnmower over the family garden once in a blue moon. 'Or I might consider training to be a pilot.'

Was his son on the same planet as the rest of them? Before Rick could formulate a pithy reply, the front door opened and seconds later, Chloe burst into the kitchen. She threw her bag on the floor and then pulled out one of the chairs and sprawled over the table, resting her head on her arms. 'God, I'm knackered,' she said. 'Put the kettle on, Dad. I've had to walk all the way from the bus stop. When are you getting the car back, Mum?'

'Tomorrow,' Rick said over his shoulder as he headed to the kettle, 'and you're not going to be driving it.'

'I'll have to,' Chloe countered. 'I've got a job. How else am I going to get there?'

'That's your problem, lady.'

'The buses are rubbish round here.'

'Then you'll have to pay for a taxi out of your wages.'

'Rick . . .' Juliet started.

He held up his hand again – much good that it did. His wife was about to defend Chloe, he just knew. 'I'm sick of being taken for granted in this house.'

'I thought you'd be pleased that I'd got a job,' their daughter shouted. 'Everyone else's parents buys them a car, but not you. You don't do anything for me. How am I supposed to get around?'

'Chloe,' Juliet said reasonably, 'you know that we can't afford to do that. We'd have to buy a car for Tom too and we just don't have that money to spare. We do pay for your digs at uni.'

Chloe puffed unhappily at the injustice of it all.

'Where have you got a job?' Rick wanted to know.

'Don't pretend that you're interested now,' Chloe fumed. She collected her bag and slammed off her chair. 'I hate this family. No one cares.' Their daughter banged out of the kitchen.

Juliet stood up and went to go after her.

'Leave her,' Rick said. 'Spoiled madam. Let her stew for a while. One day she'll realise just how much we do for her.'

'What's for dinner?' Tom wanted to know. 'I've got to go and meet Gabe soon. When will it be ready?'

'Dinner is cancelled,' Rick said. 'You can all feed yourselves tonight. Grandma included. Me and your mother are on strike.'

'Chloe's right,' Tom complained as he stomped out. 'This family's well dysfunctional.'

Their son slammed the kitchen door behind him,

'If I wasn't so exhausted, I might well laugh,' Rick said, leaning against the kitchen cupboards and taking a deep breath. 'Can't we trade *them* in and get us a new family?'

'I don't think it works like that.'

Unfortunately.

Rick wound his arms round his wife's waist. Her skin held the lingering kiss of scent. It was a long time since he'd noticed that. 'What say you and I go out tonight and leave them all to it?'

'That sounds like a very good idea,' Juliet said, and she smiled at him for the first time in days.

Chapter 23

Rick and I drive into the centre of Milton Keynes and to the big multiplex cinema there. One time we used to like cuddling up in the flicks, snogging when we shouldn't, but now my husband isn't a big fan of the cinema. He doesn't like sharing his cinematic experiences with hundreds of other people. He'd rather be at home on his own sofa, with his own beer and his own popcorn, and not have to listen to people texting or talking when they've paid nearly a tenner to watch a film.

Rick wanted to take me to dinner in the High Street in Stony Stratford, but I told him that I didn't have much of an appetite. My husband thinks it's because I'm emotionally over-wrought due to our problems with the children and my mother. It's not – but how can I tell him, on top of everything else, that I had lunch with Steven Aubrey? That would be the straw that broke the camel's back and I can't do that to Rick.

My husband ran round the shower before we came out but, as I'm still wearing my posh brown-ish dress and Una's scarf, I don't bother to change. We queue up with a million other people as we didn't think to pre-book tickets. At this time in the evening it's a choice between *The Other Boleyn Girl*, which is based on one of my favourite author's books, or *The Cottage*, which appears to be a horror, slash-'em-up movie.

'You know I can't sit through a gory movie, Rick.'

'I don't care what I watch as long as it's about other people's misery and then I don't have to think about our own.'

'Come on.' I try to be encouraging. 'It's not that bad.'

'Did you think our life would be like this?' Rick wants to know. 'Is this what we signed up for?'

'Let's just enjoy the film,' I say. 'We never get time on our own. Which shall we plump for?'

The Other Boleyn Girl wins because Rick, along with most other males of the species, quite fancies Scarlett Johansson.

We queue up again to buy a hot dog and nachos in lieu of a proper dinner.

'Where did we go wrong?' Rick sighs as we wait for our plastic food. 'Tell me, why did we have children?'

'You know that you love them really.'

'Does that mean that I have to like them all the time?' My husband takes delivery of a gigantic bucket full of cola which will have him running to the loo at least twice during the film. I grab the hot dog and nachos. 'What about Tom?' he goes on. 'Did you know he was gay?'

Once, when I was hoovering in Tom's bedroom, I found some leopardskin-print underpants under his bed that I didn't think belonged to him. Should I have talked to him about his inclinations then? Or should I have done what I did and just ignore it and hope that it was a passing phase? There seem to have been plenty of girls gracing his sheets too. What does that mean?

You never really want to think about your children's sex-lives, do you? Chloe, I think, lost her virginity when she was fifteen. I have no concrete evidence to support this, just a vague feeling. I was horrified, of course, and tried to have meaningful conversations with her at the time about being 'responsible' and 'careful'. My daughter responded by avoiding talking to me at all until she was about eighteen, unless it was about the weather. 'I had my suspicions,' I confess as we join the line of people snaking into the cinema.

'Me too,' Rick admits, 'I just didn't want to face up to it. Is it politically incorrect to say that I wish the string of beauties he's had through his bedroom in the last year or so had been entirely female? I'm not trendy enough to have a gay son, Juliet. Really, I'm not.'

'Perhaps he's bi-sexual?'

My husband shudders. 'Is that better or worse? If he's bi, then why couldn't he have come down on the other side of the fence, then we wouldn't have to explain awkward things to the neighbours.'

Rick hands over the tickets to the uniformed and youthful member of staff and we go into screen fifteen.

'It's a shock,' I concede as we search for a suitable seat. Rick likes to go as near to the back as we can. I don't like to sit in the middle of a row, but prefer an aisle seat. Eventually we find two that suit us both. 'But we'll get used to it. He's still our baby. Worse things happen.'

'Like your seventy-year-old mother announcing that she wants another child?'

'Oh, Rick,' I say. 'What are we going to do with her?'

'Well, she can't go back to your dad now that *he's* got a boyfriend. Wait a minute! Do you think it's genetic, being gay? Perhaps Tom has inherited it from Frank. It's certainly not from *my* side of the family.'

'What about Uncle Henry?' I remind him. 'He always wore white suits and carried a handbag. We might not have thought it was suspicious at the time, but we also thought George Michael was as straight as a die back then.'

Rick laughs and I see some of the tension leave his face. It feels good to be out on our own – like real grown-ups – leaving all our troubles behind, if only for a few hours.

We settle into our seats and the cinema fills up around us as we watch the trailers for other films and the adverts for glossy products, most of them drink-related.

'We've always tried to do our best by them,' my husband says with a world-weary tone. 'We've done all we can to give them a good upbringing.' His eyes meet mine in the darkness. 'Sometimes at the detriment of our own relationship.'

'We do OK.'

'Is that enough?' Rick asks. 'Doing OK? I know there are times when I haven't paid you enough attention or said the right things. I forgot our last wedding anniversary.'

'We won't forget this one.'

'No,' Rick says. 'But we haven't talked about what we want to do, either. Shall the two of us just slope off together, or do you think we should have a big do?'

'I don't know . . .'

'Oh, dammit, I've dropped my sausage.'

'What?'

'It's fallen on the floor.' My husband starts to rummage around at my feet.

'You can't pick it up, Rick. You don't know what else is down there. Leave it. We'll get it when the lights go up again.'

'Bugger!' Rick exclaims. 'I was looking forward to that.'

'Do you want some of my nachos?'

'No. They smell funny.' He squashes himself down between the seats. 'Oh. Here it is.' He produces the sausage, now covered in fluff.

'You can't eat that now.'

He picks bits off it. 'It'll be fine. A bit of dirt never hurt anyone.'

I don't mention e.coli or typhoid. Instead, I say, 'Ssh. The film's about to start.'

And our discussion about our anniversary celebrations is forgotten as the opening sequence starts and my husband demolishes his fluffy hot dog, muttering all the while. I pick at the nachos, but the chips are stale and the cheese sauce tastes like cold custard. Somewhere we've lost the loving feelings that we used to have and I don't know where they've gone. Perhaps like Rick's sausage our love is still there, it's just been accidentally dropped in the dirt of daily living and is waiting for us to grope around and find it, dust it off and make it nice once more. I just wish it was within as easy reach as the sausage.

On the screen, Scarlett Johansson and Natalie Portman are looking particularly gorgeous as the sisters Boleyn. The film is rarely as good as the book in my mind, but in this case they make a damn good stab at it and bring out all the colour and drama of the Boleyns' time at the Tudor court. A story of another very dysfunctional family, I think. I slip my hand in Rick's. He always tries hard to do the right thing, but somehow, he never quite pulls it off. It makes my heart contract for him. As Anne Boleyn flutters her eyes at Henry VIII on the screen, I hear a gentle snuffling sound and turn to my husband. So much for our hot date. Despite the bosoms heaving majestically twenty feet high right in front of him, Rick is fast asleep.

Chapter 24

'We went to the cinema last night and Rick fell asleep,' I tell Una during a brief quiet moment in our morning. Today is always the busiest day in the library, with a constant stream of regular readers coming in to change their books. There's an excellent farmer's market in the square next to us which always brings people out, come rain or shine.

'I'd have got up and come home,' my friend says. 'Left him there.'

'I did think about it,' I admit. 'But I was enjoying the film and, well, there were extenuating circumstances. We had been up in the wee small hours the night before.'

'For Rick's dogging incident,' Una reminds me with a raised eyebrow. 'Now you're just making excuses for him.'

'I know. But I'm still cross with him. It just made me feel so frumpy, Una. We were supposed to be out on a date. The first time we've been alone together in weeks, possibly months.' I can't even remember the last time that Rick and I went out together it's so long ago – and clearly it wasn't marvellous enough to leave a lasting on my brain. 'And he had a lot to make up for too. You think that might have kept him on his toes a bit.' I sigh heartily. 'What's it coming to when my husband can't even stay awake in my scintillating company?'

'You were in the dark.'

'Are you taking his side now? Is this me being unreasonable? I didn't have an argument with Rick about him sleeping through all the lust, intrigue and beheadings, but I was a bit quiet with him. I don't think that he even noticed.'

'There's one man who seems keen to pay you a lot of attention.' Una raises her other eyebrow at me.

'When I was with Steven yesterday, I couldn't help thinking how good he looked. He'd hardly aged at all. Yet, look at me. I seem so old. Older than time itself. I'm forty-five, but that's not decrepit these days, is it? Forty's supposed to be the new thirty. And look at you – you're gorgeous. No one would think you're the same age as me. You're fit and trendy. Next to you I look like some charity shop reject.'

Una laughs at me, but not unkindly. 'Juliet, you're lovely,' she insists. 'But maybe you could do with a bit of help.'

'When a friend says that, then I really should take notice.'

'I go to a great little salon just off the High Street, tucked away in Swinfens Yard – Face Facts. Why don't I book you in there for a few little treatments to perk you up?'

'That sounds expensive.'

'It is, but it's also about time that you stopped spending all your money on your kids and did something for yourself.'

'You're right. Book me in. As soon as possible before I change my mind.'

'We'll do something to make that Rick sit up and take notice.' Una picks up the phone and punches in a number. I try not to listen as she lists all the areas of my face that need urgent attention before booking my appointment. When she hangs up, she says, 'One o'clock, today. Don's out this afternoon at the Central Library again so he won't know if you're a bit late back.'

'You're going to get me sacked at this rate. I'll come back looking beautiful but with no job.'

'I don't see a problem with that,' Una giggles.

The library door opens and my dad comes in with a dapper-looking man by his side. I take it this is Samuel Scott and that I'm about to be formally introduced.

'Hello, love,' Dad says. 'Not busy today?'

'We have been,' I tell him. 'Just a lull. Una and I are putting the world to rights.'

'That's a long job, these days,' he laughs.

My dad looks great. There's a spring in his step and a flush to his cheeks that was never there when he was with my mum – then he always looked like he had the weight of the world on his shoulders. He has on a smart white shirt and a red bow tie, and he's dug out his best tweed sports jacket. Whatever this Samuel's doing for him – and I don't even want to go there – then it's given Dad a new lease of life. No matter how much I might disapprove of his new choice of lifestyle, I can't deny that it's suiting him. My dad's walking taller than I've seen him in years and he looks a good ten years younger. Here I am putting my faith in beauty creams when all you need is to take a lover. Oh. Don't want to think about that.

'I wanted you to meet Samuel, love.' My dad looks bashful.

Samuel is clearly a lot younger than Dad. Nearly half his age, if I remember rightly. Younger than me, for sure. He's not a trendy young thing though. Samuel probably looks older than his years. He's cuddly around the middle with thinning hair, but he has a nice smile and kind eyes. My dad obviously thinks that he's love's young dream.

I hold out my hand and Samuel grasps it warmly, relief written large on his pleasant face. 'Delighted to meet you,' he breathes. 'Frank has told me so much about you.'

'Nice to meet you too, Samuel.' Una is giving us all a quizzical look, as well she might. With everything else that has happened, I've forgotten to tell her that both my father and my son came out as gay this week.

'This is my dad's . . .' Words fail me as I'm not quite sure how to describe Samuel. I'm picturing him as more of a companion for Dad in his old age rather than a . . .

'Boyfriend,' my dad supplies with a wide grin.

'It's been a very busy week at home,' I say as Una's jaw drops in surprise. 'Samuel works in the big bookstore in Milton Keynes.'

'I love my books,' Samuel says, giving himself a little hug.

Well, at least we'll have something in common.

'Why don't you join us for lunch?' Dad suggests. 'It would be nice for you two to get to know each other better. Now that we're family.'

'I can't, Dad,' I say. 'Una's just booked me a facial at one of the beauty salons. I'm hoping to turn back the clock.' About twenty-five years, I think.

'Oh, that's a shame.' My dad looks a little deflated. 'Another time.'

'Of course, of course. You must come round for Sunday lunch.' Then I recall that we have my mother living with us and think that might not be a good idea. I still haven't yet told her about Dad's newfound sexual status as I don't imagine that she'll take it well. 'Or we could go out. Rick's looking forward to meeting you too.'

Why did I say that? It's such a lie and they seem to be coming easier to my tongue at the moment.

'We'll just change our books while we're here then,' Dad says. He slips his arm through Samuel's and they both head up the stairs. I watch them, not knowing what to think.

'That's a bit of a turn up,' Una says.

'Tell me about it. He seems so happy though. That has to be a good thing.'

'No wonder you're feeling haggard, Juliet. I have no idea how you keep up with your lot. That's why I'm on my own. Apart from a rushed catch-up call to the kids once or twice a week to find out where they are and what they're up to, I've got no one else to worry about but me. I highly recommend it, my little friend. You should try it.'

And I wonder whether Una might be right.

Chapter 25

Rick couldn't stand listening to any more of Hal's stories. Normally, he had a quick sandwich for lunch and then just carried on – no hour-long break for him – but today he needed to get away completely.

They were only working five minutes away from home so it had been quick enough to nip back in the van. He was still dog tired this morning – perhaps a poor choice of words – even after his long and lovely sleep through the film, which Juliet hadn't been too pleased about. His wife had showed her displeasure by not making him his usual packed lunch, so he'd decided to pop home instead and take a breather, cheer himself up by reading the obituaries while no one was looking.

As he pulled into Chadwick Close he could see that Stacey Lovejoy was out and washing her car. Without having a discernible job, their jovial neighbour still managed to live in the biggest house in the street and drive a top-of-the-range Mercedes.

Stacey was wearing one of those vest-type tops that Juliet had stopped buying because she said they showed her bingo-wings – whatever *they* were – and a very short denim skirt. His neighbour was lying across her bonnet, elbow-deep in soap suds, stroking the car rhythmically with an over-sized sponge. Rick felt himself go hot. He was sure he'd seen Tom watching a music video just like that on MTV. It was an interesting technique, but Stacey'd never get the dead flies off the front if she didn't put a bit more effort into it.

Stacey waved at him as he passed and he knew that he'd have no chance of getting into the house without her accosting him.

He was still getting out of the van when she appeared next to him clutching her yellow sponge. The front of her T-shirt was wet and the absence of underwear apparent. Rick tried very hard not to look.

'Hello, Ricky,' she cooed. 'What are you doing home at this time of the day?'

'Just nipped back for lunch,' he said. 'Forgot my sandwiches.'

'Silly thing!' His neighbour punched him with her sponge, leaving a wet mark on his polo shirt. 'I'm just about finished here and I'm famished. I'll make us both something to eat.'

'No, no,' he said. 'That's very kind, but I've got a couple of things to do.'

'They can wait,' Stacey insisted, and steered him across to her house instead.

'Rita will wonder where I am if she sees the van.' In fact he'd forgotten that peace was difficult to come by these days, particularly at home.

'Your mother-in-law went out about half an hour ago. Walked into town, I should think. She had that purposeful look on her face. The one that makes her look like she's sucked a lemon.'

They both laughed at that. His neighbour really was quite likeable in a brash sort of way. Would it be so bad to spend what little was left of his lunch-hour with Stacey Lovejoy?

'It'll have to be a quick sandwich,' Rick said. 'I haven't got much time.'

'Oh, I like a quickie,' Stacey giggled as they went into her kitchen. 'I hope you like cheese, there's not much else in the fridge.'

'Cheese is fine,' he said, hoping that there was nothing else on the menu.

'I just need to get out of this wet top,' Stacey said.

'I'll go into the garden,' Rick said. 'Get a bit of fresh air while I can.' And he bolted for the back door.

★   ★   ★

Stacey's garden was immaculately maintained, as was the rest of the house. The neighbours might complain that she didn't fit into the Chadwick Close set, but they couldn't fault her for the way she kept her house and garden. It was quiet here, especially without her boisterous brood of children bringing the place down. Presumably they were all still at school today, though sometimes it appeared as if their attendance was rather sporadic.

He pulled up one of the padded recliner chairs and sat back in it, enjoying the feel of the sun on his face. Must be careful, wouldn't do to drop off here. Hal would never believe it was innocent if he did that. Neither would Juliet, come to that.

Minutes later, just as his eyes were starting to grow heavy, Stacey appeared in a black bikini top bearing a tray. He tried not to look at the bikini top or its burgeoning contents and focused on the tray below it instead. There was a pile of sandwiches heaped there, flanked by two tall glasses of lemonade.

'Lovely,' Rick said, as she handed him a glass. 'Is that home-made?'

'Ricky,' she laughed. 'What do you take me for? Do I look like a woman who has time to make her own lemonade? It's from Sainsbury's!'

His neighbour seemed to find everything he said hilarious and, although she scared him half to death, it was a refreshing change to be with someone who found him amusing company. After last night, he was sure that his wife didn't.

'This is very kind of you.' Rick tucked into his sandwich, trying to keep an eye on the clock.

Stacey sat down next to him and let her glossy white fingernails rest on his arm. 'You're a lovely man, Ricky,' she purred. 'Juliet is a very lucky woman.'

'I'm not sure she'd agree with you.'

'I saw what you'd been up to in the local paper. You naughty person!'

'That was a big misunderstanding,' he began.

His neighbour cackled and punched his arm. 'I didn't think you had it in you. I like a bad boy, Ricky. Always have. You've gone up in my estimation.'

If only Juliet had viewed it in the same way, perhaps there wouldn't be this underlying tension between them now.

He watched Stacey as she swigged her lemonade, her full red lips on the rim, licking them to catch every last drop as she swallowed. Condensation dripped from the glass onto her breast and ran in entrancing rivulets over their contours to disappear beneath the skimpy fabric of her bikini. A heart-shaped locket nestled in her cleavage and Rick couldn't tear his eyes away. It was time to go back to work.

Hastily he stood, brushing crumbs from his lap, grateful that there wasn't anything untoward going on down there. 'Thanks,' he said. 'Much appreciated.'

Stacey also rose and came towards him. 'The pleasure was all mine,' she told him and, pressing her body against his, she kissed him softly on the lips – the gentle urgency of her mouth at odds with her harsh persona.

'Lovely,' Rick said, backing away as fast as he could. 'Thanks for the lunch, Stacey.'

'We must do it again sometime.'

And, as he shot back towards the safety of his van, Rick thought that they definitely shouldn't.

Chapter 26

I look in the mirror at the Face Facts beauty salon. Has a decade been stripped away from my skin in the last hour? I prod about a bit. My face looks very red and a bit puffed up, but I'm not sure that I look thirty-five again – or ever will. My wrinkles are still firmly in place, if you ask me. The only thing that's missing is about a thousand quid from my bank account.

My mouth goes dry at the thought of what I've just spent on the foolish pursuit of youth. *A thousand pounds.* What else could I have spent a thousand pounds on? My dilapidated kitchen needs a facelift just as much, if not more, than me. A wave of nausea hits me. Have I ever done anything so selfish in my life? Rick would have a fit. I'm not sure that it was a wise move myself, but I got swept away with the moment. I came in here, Face Facts, prepared to be rejuvenated, and when Felicity, twenty-five, slim and extraordinarily pretty, recommended that I be peeled and plumped and injected, I went for it. Sucker that I am, I handed over my credit card and let myself fall into her hands and those of her colleagues.

Now, an hour later, I've had filler in my frown lines (and there are a lot of those), Botox in my brow, and my skin has been scoured with a mini-hoover that blasted me with crystals. My naso-labial folds – and I didn't even know I had them – have been plumped up with synthetic collagen or something. My crows' feet have been paralysed with dangerous chemicals and I can't believe that this all seemed like such a good idea even a short while ago.

116

'The Botox should last a couple of months before it needs doing again,' Felicity says.

I've paid all that money and it will only last for a couple of months? Well, they say that there's no fool like an old fool. 'Thank you,' I say politely.

'Shall I make another appointment for you? It would be a good idea to have another session of micro-dermabrasion next week.' I think that was the crystal thingy. 'Then one a week for another month.'

One a week? I'd have to sell my body to the highest bidder on eBay to fund that lot.

'I'll think about it,' I tell her and then I hurry out, eschewing the slew of products that my new best friend the beauty therapist has lined up for me as must-haves, fleeing back to the safety of the library.

Una is at the desk checking in some books when I return. She glances up. 'You look fabulous,' she says.

I don't. I can tell you that I categorically do not. I look like my face has been scrubbed with a Brillo pad.

Fussing at reception until all Una's readers have been dealt with, I wait to talk to my friend.

'How did it go?' she asks.

'It hurt,' I tell her. 'All of it. I was injected, pinched, scoured, electrocuted. But the most painful bit was the damage it did to my pocket.'

'Blimey,' Una says, surprise in her eyes when I tell her what I subjected myself to. 'I never thought that you'd have all that lot done.'

'Me neither,' I say miserably.

'Hasn't it made you feel any better?'

'Not at the moment,' I admit. 'If you don't mind, I think I'll go and hide upstairs for the afternoon. I feel a bit glowing.' And I've got a headache, but I don't tell Una that or she'll call me a wimp. However, it's fair to say that I'm currently not sharing her enthusiasm for extreme beauty procedures. I'm a woman who normally rubs round her face once a week with some Nivea, so I realise that I'm starting from a very low point.

'There's a trolley of books to shelve, why don't you do that?'

'I will.' I push the trolley into the lift and go upstairs, looking forward to losing myself for an hour with my pile of novels. What I need now is to curl up with a good book to recover from my beautifying trauma but, as I've been instructed and feeling like a twit, I keep clenching and relaxing my muscles to make sure the Botox works.

Much later, when I've just returned a teetering pile of novels to their home – Joanna Trollope, Tony Parsons, Fannie Flagg, Penny Vincenzi, Karin Slaughter, Thomas Harris, Lee Child – I hear foot-steps behind me and turn to see if it's a reader who needs help.

Steven Aubrey is standing there, just like when he first appeared, and my stomach and my heart flip at the same time again.

'Hello, Steven.'

'Oh. My. God.' Steven's hand flies to his mouth as he looks at me, horror in his eyes. 'What happened? Did Rick find out about us?'

'What?' I say, flustered. 'What? Rick? Us?' There is no us. Hasn't Steven realised that? Admittedly, I haven't quite told Rick about my lunch with him yet, but then there hasn't really been the oppor-tunity. Honestly.

'My poor darling.' Steven tries to gather me into his arms, but I push him away. There's no one else up here this afternoon, but that doesn't mean that I want to be cuddled in full view of the library. My old flame looks distraught. 'Did he hit you?'

'Rick?' I laugh out loud at the thought. 'What on earth are you talking about?'

Steven looks bemused. 'Your face,' he says. 'What happened to your face?'

'Dear God!' I feel my skin and it all seems to be in the right place . . . but clearly, something is seriously wrong. 'A mirror,' I say. 'I need a mirror.'

'Over here.' Steven ushers me to a full-length mirror that's between the audio-books and biographies.

118

I gasp when I see myself, and not in a good way. Along my naso-labial folds – the deep lines between my nose and mouth that are befitting of a forty-five-year-old woman – there are dark, black bruises where the filler has been pushed under my skin to give me that youthful fullness. I'm not sure there's anything remotely youthful about being black and blue.

Not only do I not look ten years younger, I look as if someone has drawn a Fu-Manchu Chinese moustache on my face. Round my eyes where the Botox was injected there are blue, bruised circles. I am half-woman, half-panda. My forehead might be less creased but there is now a series of navy tramlines in their place. Uncertainly, my fingers stroke my face as if it belongs to someone else. 'What am I going to do?'

'What on earth happened?' Steven asks for the third time.

I could tell him that I walked into a door, isn't that the standard reply for a woman who looks like she's been battered? Would he believe that this amount of bruising could be caused by something that's supposed to be a beauty treatment? Well, I certainly feel as if I'm paying for my vanity. 'I had a facial,' I admit.

'You look like you've done ten rounds with Amir Khan,' Steven tells me.

'I need to talk to Una,' I say. 'She'll sort it out.' Though quite how, I'm not entirely sure.

Steven takes my hand. 'You don't need beauty treatments,' he says, and he eases me towards him, into his arms. 'I love you just as you are.'

I flinch at that and our eyes meet. Did Steven really just say that he loves me? This is not the time or the place to pursue that further.

'I have to go.'

His voice is more urgent now. 'I wanted to see if you'd come out to lunch with me again. Or dinner. Anything.'

How can I go out looking like this? What will Rick say when he sees me? I'll have to confess how much money I've spent and he'll be furious.

'I want to spend some more time with you,' Steven says. 'We still have so much to talk about. There are so many things I want to say to you.'

'OK,' I agree, because my head's pounding and I just want to stop talking and see what Una can do to repair the damage. 'Next week. If I can get Una to do a bit extra for me then we can have lunch again next week.'

'Thank you,' Steven says. Then he hugs me tightly and I check over his shoulder to see if the coast is still clear. 'I look forward to it.'

Will I really see Steven for lunch next week? To be truthful, I don't know. I stare at my punch-bag face in the mirror again. At the moment I can't imagine going out of the house ever again.

Chapter 27

I'm making dinner when Rick arrives home. Call me manipulative, but I've cooked his favourite meal tonight. A nice bit of steak, some chips, mushrooms and a homemade apple pie with ice cream to follow. Rick is nothing if not a traditionalist. I hope that the way to his heart is still through his stomach. This would be so much nicer if it was just the two of us but, of course, we have a full house tonight. So my romantic dinner is for five. Six if you count the little bit of steak that I'll sneak to Buster.

My mother looks up when she sees Rick's van in the drive. 'He's in for a shock.'

'Yes, well, there's nothing you need to say on the matter.'

'I don't know what you were thinking of, wasting that money on beauty treatments.' I foolishly told my mother what I'd done and how much it had cost me to get in this state.

'Mum, you're the one talking about having a boob job.' At the ripe old age of seventy. If I think that I'm trying to dress mutton up as lamb then I only have to remember that. 'How much do you think *that's* going to cost? All I've had is a few injections.' And look at the state of me. There's a lot to be said for growing old gracefully. 'I don't think you can criticise me.' But she will. Why change the habit of a lifetime?

My mother harrumphs.

'I don't want you to say anything,' I warn her.

'Cooking him that won't make any difference.' She flicks a disdainful glance at my apple pie.

'Well, at least I can try.' I don't want to get into a discussion about the rights and wrongs of marital machinations with my mother – particularly when she has no idea what my father is currently up to. Perhaps if she'd looked after him a bit better then we wouldn't be in this mess now.

'Wow,' my husband says as he comes into the kitchen. 'Something smells good. What's cooking?' Then when I turn and face him he cries out in alarm, 'What happened to you?'

It's becoming a familiar refrain. Even though I tried to hide away from the general public in case I scared them, every reader who caught sight of me asked the same thing. Despite Una having applied a pound of make-up over my bruises they're still shining out lividly. They're going to take weeks to fade.

She says that I should go back to the beauty salon to complain. Frankly, I don't think I'll ever go near one again in my entire life.

Then my courage fails me. I can't tell Rick what I've done. He'll think I'm mad – *I* think I'm mad – and I'm feeling very tearful about this. Every time he sees someone on the telly with an immovable forehead or a bad facelift, he goes on and on about how stupid and gullible they are. How can I now admit to being exactly that sort of woman? So, instead of telling the truth, I blurt out, 'I had an accident at work.' I give my mother a warning glare. 'Someone came round the bookcases too quickly and banged into me.'

My husband's mouth is hanging slackly.

'It doesn't hurt,' I say self-consciously. 'It looks worse than it really is.'

'We'll sue,' Rick says, rubbing his hands together. 'This could be worth a fortune. I hope you took down their name and details.'

Behind my husband, my mother folds her arms and gives me a now-what-are-you-going-to-do look.

'It's nothing,' I say. 'Don't make a fuss.'

'Nothing?' Rick repeats. 'You look bloody terrible, woman. Have you seen your face? You look like you've been in a ten-car pile-up.'

At which point it all becomes too much and I promptly burst into tears.

Chapter 28

'I'm sorry,' Rick said, stroking his wife's hair. Another case of foot in mouth disease. Sometimes he could be such a thoughtless idiot. Women cared about their appearance. Too much in his opinion, but that was how it was. Juliet would worry about her face for weeks now. Although it did look a bit of a mess. Not exactly a ten-car pile-up, but certainly a significant skirmish.

She'd cooked his favourite dinner too – clearly meant to convey that she'd forgiven him for falling asleep in the cinema – and now he'd messed that up as well.

Juliet sat at the table, head in hands, while he finished off the steaks. He wasn't much of a cook but thanks to his training on the man-kitchen, or barbecue as some liked to call it, he could at least grill a bit of meat.

His daughter Chloe came in. She was wearing more make-up than Juliet and that was saying something, but nowhere near as much clothing.

'Dinner's ready,' Rick said. 'I was just about to shout you.'

'Can't stay,' Chloe said, nicking a chip from the dish on the side. 'Got to go to work.'

'There's a dinner here for you.'

'No time.' Another chip went.

'And what am I meant to do with this?' Rick showed her the piece of steak he was trying to cook to perfection.

Chloe shrugged. 'Buster.' She stole another chip. 'I'm dieting.'

The dog looked like he thought it was a good idea and wagged his tail enthusiastically in the hope that someone else would agree.

'Bloody hell,' Rick muttered through his teeth. He should make Tom and Chloe book for dinner and if they didn't turn up or eat it then he'd charge.

As his daughter helped herself to another chip, she suddenly spotted the elephant in the room. 'God, Mum, what happened to your face?'

Juliet put her hand over her bruised cheek. 'I walked into a bookcase at work.'

'Frig.'

'Language, Chloe,' Rick said. 'I thought you said someone bumped into you.'

'Yes,' Juliet said. 'That's what happened.'

'We're going to sue,' Rick said. 'Ha, ha. Take the bastard to the cleaners. We might get a holiday in the Bahamas out of it.' He laughed at that too, but Juliet just sobbed again.

'Can I take the car, Mum?'

'Yes,' Juliet said.

'No,' he said at the same time.

His daughter pouted. 'How am I supposed to get to work? It's my first night tonight. I can't be late.'

'Take a bus,' Rick advised.

'There aren't any.'

Juliet held out the keys. 'It's true, Rick. There's no public transport at this time of night. How will she get home?'

'That car only came back this afternoon, lady. If you put one mark on it . . .' Rick wagged a finger at her.

'You still haven't told us about your job,' Juliet said. 'Where are you working?'

'Gotta go,' his daughter said, snatching up the keys. 'Luv you. Laters!' And with that she flounced out of the door.

'That girl,' Rick complained, 'she doesn't think of anyone else but herself.'

'She's young,' Juliet said, and for some reason that made her start crying again.

'Look,' Rick said, 'I promised that I'd go out tonight with Hal for a few beers. I think he's got some teething problems with his new missus. I'll give him a call and put it off.'

'No, no. You go,' Juliet insisted. 'I think I might take a bottle of wine round to Una's tonight.'

'Is anyone bothered about what *I'm* doing?' his mother-in-law piped up.

'No,' they said in unison. They shared a smile at that – something that seemed far too rare at the moment.

'Well, I met a man in the Marks and Spencer Meals for One aisle,' Rita told them, unabashed. 'I'm going out with him tonight. He's taking me to that Pink Paradise place. It's supposed to be for gays, but Arnold says it's a good night out. I'm very broad-minded, as you know.'

That certainly managed to wipe the smile off Rick and Juliet's faces. Rita might be broad-minded when it came to other people, though there generally wasn't much evidence of it, but Rick wondered just how broad-minded she'd be if she bumped into her husband and his new boyfriend down there.

Chapter 29

'Tonight,' Hal sang in a tune that wasn't even remotely recognisable, as he parked up in the centre of Milton Keynes 'tonight, we're out on the town, bro. We're going to dance until dawn, bro.'

'Tonight's not good,' Rick tried again.

'Tonight's perfect,' Hal insisted. 'You, me, several beers.'

'I have already used up this year's supply of brownie points, mate, with the dogging thing,' Rick said. 'I don't think Juliet's that happy about me going out.' Though his wife was putting a brave – and rather bruised – face on it. He didn't tell Hal that he'd fallen asleep in the cinema last night or that would have assured him of an evening's ribbing that he could live without. 'I daren't be late. A few swift halves and we're done.'

'The night is young,' Hal assured him. 'By the end of it you'll be feeling the same too.'

Rick sighed. There was no stopping his friend when he was in this kind of mood. It could end with Hal in a fight or slumped by the side of the kerb or wrapped round his neck telling Rick that he loved him. Whichever way, Rick wasn't planning to be in the middle of it. He was in more than enough trouble as it was.

They started off at All Bar One. Even though it was a week night, it was still busy, everyone pushing and shoving to get a drink. Where did the kids get their money from these days to drink like that, Rick wondered. When he and Juliet were that age they'd had the responsibility of a mortgage and their first child on the way;

there was no going out on the town binge drinking for them. Were they any the worse off for that? Rick didn't think so. Fate might have thrown him and Juliet together in a slightly untidy way, but they'd made the best of it and had knuckled down to bring up the tight-knit family they were now so proud of. OK, so he might complain about Chloe and Tom – they had a different attitude to life, were a different generation – but, basically, they were good kids.

He couldn't really talk to Hal above the noise, but they still tried to hold a shouted conversation over the din. They downed two pints like that, being joggled back and forth.

'I've had enough of this, mate,' Rick said. There were times in your life when you realised that you were too old for your surroundings, and this was one of them. This was the sort of place that he expected to see Chloe and Tom in, not a couple of middle-aged geezers who should by rights be at home with their feet up in front of the telly with a nice cup of tea. 'I have to get out of here,' he yelled to Hal. 'I'm off home.'

'No,' Hal said, alarmed. 'Not yet. Let's go somewhere quieter. I know a little place.'

There were no 'little places' in Milton Keynes; they were all big chains, busy but ultimately soulless.

'It's not long opened,' his friend continued. 'We can leave the car here and walk.'

Rick glanced at his watch. It was only ten o'clock, a bit early for bailing out on what was supposed to be a big night. Juliet had said she wouldn't be late back from Una's, but he knew what those two were like when they got talking.

'Just one more,' Rick said.

Hal clapped him on the back and hustled his friend out of the bar and into the street. 'This way,' he said, throwing his arm around Rick's shoulders.

Hal was full of bonhomie tonight and it was nice to let a little steam off together. Sometimes when they worked in close proximity all day long, things could get somewhat tetchy. Rick thought that Hal used him, knowing that he wouldn't leave him in the doggie-doo, but sometimes he pushed Rick a bit too far. At the moment, Hal wasn't entirely concentrating on the flooring business; his mind was more on keeping Shannon sexually satisfied. Though, if Rick was right, Hal's attention might be waning in that department. Keeping up with a nubile twenty-two year old might not be all it was cracked up to be.

They'd been walking along Silbury Boulevard. It was a warm summer night but, due to the lateness of the hour, a chill had started to set in. More than anything else, Rick wanted to be at home in his own bed now. Perhaps he and Juliet could have a bit of a cuddle. That didn't happen too much any more − mainly due to having Attila the Hun in the next room. That would be a passion-killer for anyone.

Rick hadn't noticed where they were until Hal stopped outside double glass doors with a neon sign flashing above them.

'Hiya, mate.' Hal clasped the hand of the bouncer on the door. 'Good to see you.'

Rick vaguely recognised the guy. Was it someone they'd laid flooring for? Or was it someone's brother-in-law? He was useless with faces. Not much better with names.

Glancing up, he noticed that the sign flashed *The Happy Club*. And he instantly recognised from advertisements that he'd seen splashed all over the local paper − when his name wasn't in it, that is − that this was the new lapdancing place that had recently opened. 'No,' Rick said. 'Oh, no.'

Hal wheeled round. 'What?'

'I'm not going in there.'

'It's a great place,' Hal said.

Rick had managed to get to the grand age of forty-five without visiting a lapdancing club. Call him an old-fashioned fuddy duddy, but he didn't want to start now. 'Juliet would do her pieces if she found out I'd been here, mate.'

'She'd never know.'

'Women have a way of finding these things out.'

'It's only a bit of fun.'

Rick hadn't been to one of these fine establishments, but from what he imagined, he didn't think it would be his idea of fun. Would he really enjoy having women as young as Chloe waggle their boobs and bums in his face? Wouldn't it just be embarrassing? Hal was full of bravado – another word for bullshit – but was this really his blueprint for a good night out or did he do it just to prove that he was still one of the lads?

Rick knew that he wasn't one of the lads. He knew that he wanted to go home, put the kettle on, see if there was any bread left for some late-night toast. Holding up his hand, he said, 'I'm out of here, Hal. You go ahead, mate.'

Hal whispered to him, 'That's Bob. We did some flooring for him, over Willen way.' Hal had a better memory than he did. 'He's letting us in for nothing. The beer's really cheap here until eleven. We haven't had a chance for a proper natter yet.'

Rick didn't like to remind his friend that they could spend all day 'nattering'; even so, he could feel himself weakening.

'You don't have to look at the girls if you don't want to,' Hal said. 'Just keep your eyes closed.'

Rick laughed at that, although if Juliet found out, she'd kill him. This week had been bad enough without him giving his wife any more ammo.

'One little drink won't hurt,' Hal cajoled as he pulled Rick inside The Happy Club.

But a nagging little voice in the back of his mind told Rick that it probably would.

Chapter 30

I take a bottle of wine out of the fridge – Wolf Blass Yellow Label Chardonnay 2006. I don't know if it's a good vintage, but it will suit my purposes and it's already chilled to perfection. My mother is watching *Holby Blue* on the television and I haven't seen Tom all night, even though he said he'd be back for dinner. His meal is still plated up and waiting to be microwaved whenever he shows up.

'I'm going to Una's,' I tell my mother, poking my head around the living-room door. She barely tears her eyes away from the screen. Clearly, *Holby Blue* is riveting. 'I thought you were going out too?'

'Laters,' she says in the manner of my twenty-year-old daughter.

'Well, don't be out too late,' I say before I can stop myself.

'Take a chill pill,' my mother says, also in the manner of my twenty-year-old daughter. 'You're such a fusspot.'

If I could come up with a suitable retort I would, but I can't, so I leave, banging the door behind me.

Una doesn't live too far away, which is just as well as I've been stranded without transport again, my darling daughter having purloined my car on its first day back in my possession. I sigh to myself and set up a brisk walk along Chadwick Close and towards Una's house, bottle of wine in hand.

While I walk, I try to ring my dad on my mobile to warn him that Mum is planning to be at Pink Paradise tonight just in case he was also thinking of a trip there, but there's no answer from his home phone and my dad isn't technical enough to be able to handle a mobile. But with the lifestyle changes he's currently embracing maybe he'll suddenly find that he's not a technophone after all and will buy himself not only a mobile, but an iPod and a Wii too.

Fifteen minutes later, my friend opens her door and ushers me in. 'I'm on the internet,' she says excitedly. 'I'll grab you a glass and we'll go upstairs.'

She disappears into the kitchen and returns, as promised, with a large glass. 'I can't stay long,' I tell her.

'Why?' she asks. 'What have you got to rush back for? A big pile of ironing? Watching *The Bill* with your mum?'

'*Holby Blue*,' I correct.

'You already told me that Rick's out tonight, so there's no panic.'

'That's true,' I agree. 'What am I worrying about? Fill that glass up.'

I follow Una up her narrow staircase. Even though her Victorian terraced house is neatly proportioned – certainly compared to Una's previous mansion – it is like a show home inside. My friend is never knowingly under-cushioned. All her accessories match and I guess it's easier to keep a home-for-one much cleaner and tidier than our place, which is certainly well lived-in. Una's home smells of vanilla essence, honeysuckle and lily of the valley. My home smells of liberally squirted Cillit Bang.

Even Una's small box room is unspeakably tasteful: her computer is on a glass desk and there's a vase of calla lilies next to it that I know for a fact haven't just been put there for my benefit. The office chairs are made of stainless steel mesh, and her In and Out boxes are milky-coloured Perspex, all her papers neatly stacked.

Sitting down at the computer, Una pulls up a chair next to her and pats it so that I plonk myself down. 'Get a load of this.'

On the screen there's a hunky man – even my jaded eye is appreciative. He looks tall, tanned and is wearing a white open-necked shirt and jeans. 'He's American, from Texas, works for an oil company and is living in London.'

'Yum,' I say, and swig the wine that I've helped myself to.

'We've been emailing for a few days now and he's asked me out on a date. What do you think? Should I go?'

'Isn't the internet a bit dodgy? You could be talking to a wrinkly old grandad from Grimsby, for all you know.'

'Well, he thinks I'm a hot chick of thirty-five who owns her own company, so I guess we're all allowed a little leeway.' Una giggles as she twirls her hair girlishly round her finger.

'Be careful,' I warn. 'If you do decide to meet him, make sure that you tell me where you're going or, better still, drag me along with you.'

'A threesome,' she titters. 'He might be into that.'

'What's this guy's name?'

'Tex,' she tells me, tapping at the keyboard.

No one in real life is called Tex. 'That must be his internet nickname.'

'I don't know,' my friend admits. 'It's a bit sexy though, isn't it?' She giggles again.

'I admire you, Una,' I tell her truthfully. 'I don't know how you do this. I'd be terrified to be on my own now. I've been married for so long that I don't know if I could function independently any more.'

She swings round to face me. 'So you're prepared to put up with second-best?'

I shrug. 'It's not second-best. We're just going through an odd patch. All marriages have them. Don't they?'

'I found my marriage stultifying. This is so much more exciting.' My friend gives herself a thrilled little hug.

I think that dating strangers would scare the life out of me, but Una seems to thrive on it. Perhaps some people were meant to be independent and free of commitments while others were intended to be . . . like me.

'You can't tell me that you're not attracted to Steven.' My friend treats me to a probing gaze. 'I've seen how you are with him. Haven't you even thought what it might be like to run away with him?'

133

I laugh at that. 'Only in my darkest moments.'

'He's clearly mad about you,' Una notes. 'That's very head-turning stuff. I don't think I'd be fighting him off in your situation.'

'I love Rick,' I hear myself say. 'I promised forever.' I don't add that Steven had his chance at 'forever' with me and chose to high-tail it in the other direction.

'Your husband's acting very strangely at the moment. Sure he's not got a bit on the side?'

'You know,' I confide, 'I'm beginning to think that the male menopause is a very real thing. They might not get hot flushes, but there are certainly other symptoms.'

'Like the urge to buy a small sports cars and run away with a much younger woman?'

'Something like that.' Rick's definitely not himself. I don't know who he is, but he's not himself. I don't understand him any more. And not in the usual ways that women don't understand men, for instance why isn't the toilet roll ever changed when it's finished, why are empty cereal boxes put back in the cupboard, why is the bin never emptied even when it's overflowing? I didn't understand him on a level that I'd never previously experienced. Just when you think you know everything there is to know about someone, it's strange how life can throw a spanner in the works.

'Have you told him that Steven Aubrey is back on the scene again yet?'

'No.' I shake my head. 'It's not that I'm avoiding the subject.' Una looks like she doesn't believe that. 'But I haven't had a chance to talk to him properly yet.'

'So are you going to see lover boy again?'

'We're just friends, Una. There's nothing in it. Really.'

'I'm not sure who you're trying to fool, Juliet. Is it me or is it yourself?'

And, you know, that seems like a very good question.

Chapter 31

Inside The Happy Club, Rick seemed to be the only person who wasn't acting happy. Groups of men in business suits sat around the tables at the perimeter and guffawed loudly at each other, but it sounded forced as if they were pretending to have a really good time.

Sultry disco music pounded out. 'I thought this was supposed to be quieter than All Bar One?' he shouted at Hal.

'What?' his friend said.

This was his first time in this kind of establishment and Rick wasn't sure that he'd missed anything. The décor was as you would imagine. Leopardskin featured heavily: Stacey Lovejoy would be right at home here. There were clusters of chairs in animal print and black leather, purple velvet curtains screening private areas lush with gold tassels, and a curving bar along one wall which was bordered by a row of leopardskin stools.

Chandeliers hung from the ceiling – which seemed a bit pointless as none of the blokes in here were looking up, apart from him. It was all very plush but still somehow managed to seem seedy. Rick wished they'd stayed where they were. Frankly, he'd rather get an elbow in his eye than a nipple tassel.

'Let's get a drink at the bar,' Hal said, and proceeded to weave his way through the tables. Like a sheep, Rick followed.

There were six poles that Rick could see – if that was the correct term. Three just in front of the bar, three at the other end of the room.

On the poles by the bar, three women wheeled lazily. They were all dressed in what he'd call fetish wear – uninitiated as he was. One girl was in a red latex dress with thigh-high red boots, the other was in a black halter-neck dress slit to the thigh and then down to the waist, the third was wearing a shocking pink rubber basque and a very small g-string. Come to think of it, he wasn't the only one in here who didn't look happy. Without exception the girls looked bored to death as they gyrated in front of their audience. They twirled round on their poles, backs arched, breasts thrusting, legs outstretched. Rick had to admire their athleticism, but he really didn't want to see that much naked flesh so close up. There was no doubt that they were pretty too, but so young. These three looked barely out of their teens.

Over in the private area he could see a naked girl up on a small podium in front of a group of leery men. She was splaying her legs and showing them her nether regions while they laughed raucously. Why would anyone want to do that? And he meant both the dancing and the watching. Didn't either party find it demeaning? He'd never really been one for girly mags or porn to provide titillation. He'd only ever wanted Juliet, not to ogle other women. Trust Hal to bring him here. Rick knew before he walked through the door that it wouldn't be his cup of tea.

They sat at the bar on the leopardskin stools and ordered two beers from the scantily-clad barista. Hal lounged back on the bar, swigging his lager appreciatively and openly appraising the girls who danced just a few yards in front of them. Rick wasn't quite sure how to arrange himself casually – he felt all angles and awkwardness. He wondered how long the spectacle would go on and he suspected all night. One beer to appease Hal and then he was out of here.

Then the music changed and the three girls jumped down to much applause to be replaced by three new dancers at the other end of the room. These women were completely nude which, for some reason, took Rick aback. The disco beat struck up again and the women started to strut their stuff, sliding sexily up and down their poles while buck-naked.

Hal elbowed him. 'Fit, eh?'

'Very,' Rick agreed, as he tried not to focus on anything in particular. And then he spotted something at the far side of the club that chilled him to the core. Something that he really wished he hadn't seen.

'Oh, God,' Rick said. 'Oh, my good God.'

'What?' Hal dragged his attention away from the nude dancer in front of him.

Rick staggered off his bar stool. He could feel his blood rushing to his ears, his heart pounding. His legs seemed unable to support his own weight. Perhaps he was having a heart-attack. He bloody well should be, that was for sure.

He lurched forward as Hal, panic written on his face, said, 'Mate, what's wrong?'

'Chloe,' Rick said, and pointed to one of the poles at the other side of the room where his only daughter writhed completely unclothed. He hadn't seen her like that since she was about three years old and he certainly didn't want to see her like that now.

'Bloody hell,' Hal said. He didn't want his mate to see her either. Or anyone else for that matter. 'What's she doing here?' he wanted to know.

'What do you think she's doing!'

'Getting her kit off,' Hal conceded. 'She does it quite well.'

'Well, it will be the last time she does,' Rick said. A red mist was starting to descend in front of his eyes. How long had they scrimped and saved to pay her way through university – and this was how she thought to repay them?

'Chloe!' he shouted over the music, which brought his daughter up short. She stopped twirling and stared, horrified, at him. Rick stared, horrified, back.

Then he mobilised himself and launched himself across the room. He was going to get his daughter off that podium now before anyone else could get an eyeful and then he wasn't sure what he was going to do with her, but it wouldn't be nice. He'd have to ground her until she was about sixty-two for this. How could she do this? His only daughter stripping off and God knows what else for money? No wonder she hadn't told them what she was doing for a job. Juliet would be livid. How on earth was he going to break this to her?

Chloe tried valiantly to carry on her routine as he made his way towards her. He wanted to gouge out his own eyes so that he couldn't see her nakedness. On the back of a chair belonging to one of the businessmen was a jacket. Rick grabbed at it and lunged at Chloe's podium, the idea being to cover his daughter's embarrassment.

'Dad,' she hissed, as he tried to reach up to wrap her in the jacket. 'Get off. Leave me alone.'

'Mate!' a bloke shouted from behind him. 'You're blocking my view!'

Rick spun round, ready to give him a mouthful too. But in his quest to get to his daughter, Rick didn't realise that the dancers next to her were carrying on their routines despite the commotion. A tall blonde girl on the adjacent pole whirled round at a very unfortunate moment and caught him full-tilt in the face with one of her Perspex stilettos as she did.

Rick felt his nose explode, and blood splattered down his shirt and over the businessman's jacket and over the leopardskin seats.

'Ouch!' the lapdancer screamed. Letting go of her pole and clutching her ankle, she toppled from her podium.

Chloe, face thunderous, stomped off as Rick fell to his knees, pain bright in his head. This, he realised as he hit the floor, was going to take some explaining too.

Chapter 32

It's three o'clock in the morning when I hear the front door open. There are muttered voices in the hall, but it's clear that they're angry. I had three glasses of wine at Una's, one more than my usual quota, and now I've got a headache. The nearer I inch towards menopause the less I can handle my drink. Soon I'll have to go through life teetotal. How sad is that? Another one of my small pleasures out of reach. I've already had to abandon my daily bar of Dairy Milk for the sake of my waistline. With that depressing thought fixed in my mind, hauling myself out of bed, I pull on my dressing-gown and go downstairs to see what the fuss is all about.

In the hall, Rick and Chloe are bickering with each other in stage whispers.

'It's my life,' my daughter hisses.

'Not when I'm paying the bills, it's not,' my husband hisses back.

'You can't tell me what to do.'

'Yes, I can. I'm still your father, whether you like it or not.'

'I hate you.'

'Right now, I'm not that keen on you either.'

Both of them sound as if they're five years old. When they eventually realise that I'm standing there, arms folded, halfway down the stairs, they shut up instantly and look at me sheepishly.

I sweep down to where they are. 'Would you mind telling me exactly what this is all about?'

Then I do a double-take when I see that Rick has a big pink plaster over his nose and two burgeoning black eyes. There's blood splattered all over his shirt. He looks like he's been in a fight and Rick never fights. He also looks like he came off worse.

'Ask him,' Chloe says, throwing an accusatory finger in her father's direction. 'I'm going to bed.'

But, to her surprise, I block her attempt at climbing the stairs. 'No,' I say. '*You* can tell me.'

'He's ruining my life,' she spits.

'Tell your mother what your new job is,' Rick counters with much arm-waving. 'Then we'll see who's ruining whose life.'

Chloe pouts unattractively.

'What's your new job?' I ask.

'I haven't got a job now,' she retorts. 'I've been sacked.'

'What were you doing before you were sacked?' I'm trying to stay patient, the voice of calm.

'She's a lapdancer,' Rick shouts. 'And not even one of the ones who at least wear some clothes. She's a *nude* lapdancer. *Our daughter is a nude lapdancer!*'

'*Was* a nude dancer,' Chloe corrects. 'Thanks to you.'

'Oh, Chloe.' My heart sinks. Is this what my child thinks will look good on her CV? Have I brought her up to have so little morals or self-esteem?

'You were the ones that nagged me to get a job,' she reminds us. 'What did you think I was going to do? Stack shelves?'

'We didn't think for one minute that you'd cavort naked for seedy men for money.' Rick again.

'You're one of those "seedy" men,' Chloe shoots back at Rick. 'If you hadn't turned up at the club, you'd have been none the wiser.' My daughter turns to me. 'He *totally* embarrassed me.'

'*I* embarrassed *you*?' Rick looks as if his head is about to explode. 'You were the one shaking your breasts in blokes' faces.'

'I'm not ashamed of my body,' she screeches.

'Well, you should be,' Rick bellows back.

I've heard enough. 'Do you want to wake the entire street up?

Get to bed,' I say tightly to Chloe. 'Now. I'll talk to you in the morning.'

My daughter flounces past me. Only the two high spots of pink on her cheeks give any indication that she might think she's even slightly in the wrong here.

When she's gone, Rick sits on the bottom stairs and puts his head in his hands. 'I've got a headache.'

'Me too,' I snap. Sitting down beside him, I say, 'And what does the other bloke look like?'

'There was no other bloke.' Rick sighs deeply. 'I promise you I have never been anywhere like that before – not in twenty-five years of marriage. It's just not my thing.'

'But you did tonight?'

'It was Hal's idea,' he continues. 'Honestly. I agreed to go for one drink. We'd only been there half an hour, probably not even that long, when I saw Chloe on one of the podiums.' My husband squeezes his eyes tight as if trying to block out the image. 'I completely lost it. I dashed across the room, grabbed a bloke's jacket and tried to cover her up.' Rick turns his eyes to me and they're bleak, full of tears. 'No one should have to see their daughter doing that. Needless to say, Chloe isn't of the same opinion.'

'She knows that she's done wrong,' I say.

'Does she?'

'So how did you acquire the bruises?'

'Got kicked in the face by one of the other lapdancers as I went to the rescue. It was like walking into Bruce Lee in full flight. Hurt like hell. I've bust my nose.' My husband looks at me for sympathy.

But I can't find any. 'I don't know what's happening to you, Rick,' I tell him. 'First the dogging thing, which you tell me was all a big mistake – now this. What am I supposed to believe?'

'You're supposed to believe that I love you and that none of this is intentional. Do you really think that I went out with the express aim of finding my daughter like that?'

'You shouldn't have been there in the first place.'

'Neither should she!'

141

'Two wrongs don't make a right.'

'What can I do to apologise?' Rick asks. He searches for my hand and takes it, tucking it through his arm. 'I feel like our ordered little life is suddenly cracking apart. What do we say to Chloe? We can't condone what she's done.'

'I don't know.' Part of me feels so sad for her that she can think that demeaning herself like that is acceptable, and part of me thinks that she's a grown woman and just because I don't agree with it, should that mean that I stop her from doing it? Whichever way I view it, I'm still furious. 'I wanted my daughter to make something of her life,' I say, more to myself than Rick. 'To do the things that I didn't do.'

'Well, you certainly weren't a lapdancer, so she's achieved something.'

'That's not funny.'

'No,' he agrees.

'Let's go to bed and sleep on it,' is the best I can manage. Standing up, I stretch, stifling a yawn. I hope that my mother hasn't heard any of this tawdry exchange. Some hope. I have long since learned that my mother is only deaf when she wants to be. She's probably making notes right now. 'We've both got work in the morning.'

'There's no way I'll be able to sleep,' Rick says miserably. 'You didn't see her, Juliet. It was awful. I'm so ashamed.'

'Well, let's hope that she sees sense,' I try to reassure him even though I'm so cross with him for even being there, 'and that this is the end of it.'

'No, that's not the end of it,' Rick admits, looking utterly wretched. 'The lapdancer's suing me. She's broken her shoe and sprained her ankle, and is holding me responsible. The woman's going to take me to the cleaners.'

With that, I turn on my heel and go back to bed.

Chapter 33

Breakfast is proving to be a tense affair. Like Rick, I lay awake for the rest of the night. How could my daughter be so stupid? How could my husband – who ought to know better – be so stupid too?

To remind me of my own moment of stupidity, I put a thick layer of foundation on my face to cover the bruises from my 'reju-venation' programme. I don't look younger, I just look sillier.

'Has anyone walked Buster?' I ask.

'No,' both my daughter and my husband answer tersely.

Silly question. The dog is plaiting his legs and his eyes are nearly bulging. I open the back door and let Buster into the garden. 'Now I owe you three walks this week.'

If Buster could talk I'm sure he'd remind me that it was more.

Chloe is sitting at one end of the table. I'm surprised she's even appeared. I thought that she'd stay in her bedroom until Rick and I had gone but, clearly, she's decided to brazen it out. She is, however, staring firmly at the table while eating her muesli. Rick, to keep himself entertained, is reading his favourite obituary column out loud.

'"Many things are new",' he says. '"But nothing will ever change the love I have for you".'

My husband gives me a meaningful glance at that. The bruises round his eyes are worse and the pink plaster on his nose is deeply unattractive. 'This bloke was younger than me when he died.'

I don't mention to Rick that I felt like killing him last night and that his dream of featuring in the obituary column was very nearly realised sooner than he might have expected.

'Here's one. "Sweet are the memories I have kept. Many are the days that I've wept. I love you yet and will never forget, the times we shared and how we cared".' Rick looks up at me again. 'That's nice.'

I think, *Here lies Rick for being a prick and catching our daughter doing something she didn't oughta.* OK, so it may not be Elizabeth Barrett Browning, but I'm currently very stressed. Poetry, even bad poetry, is the last thing on my mind.

'"Time may pass and fade away . . ."'

'Can you stop that please, Rick.'

He folds the newspaper without argument. Two slices of mildly cremated toast shoot out of our rickety toaster, making my nerves jangle. 'I'll get it,' I say, and leap from the table.

It's a good job that I don't have a career in high finance or something, I couldn't cope with the strain. I'm so glad I work at the library where I can at least get some peace.

'Why don't I bring you some books home so that you don't have to resort to the obituary column?' I suggest to Rick.

'I like the obituary column.' Rick looks glumly at his cereal.

What does that say about my husband's state of mind? I turn to Chloe. 'I haven't forgotten that you and I need a little talk,' I tell her. 'And I want you to go out and find another job today. One that doesn't involve you taking your clothes off.'

'But—'

'No buts,' I say. 'Just do it.'

'You're taking his side,' my daughter complains as she shoots a murderous look at her father.

'Yes,' I agree.

Rick gives me a grateful glance, but his gratitude is premature as I haven't let him off the hook yet either.

I sit down at the table again. I've got ten minutes to gather myself together before I go to work. As I'm about to take my first bite of incinerated toast, my mother appears in the doorway. She's looking a little flustered and flushed in the face. The short black kimono that I banished to the bottom of the laundry basket is back in evidence.

'What's wrong?' I want to know.

'Nothing,' she giggles girlishly. 'What was all that fuss in the middle of the night?'

'Nothing,' I answer shortly.

'Why's he all bashed up.' My mother points at Rick.

Chloe and I look at him and wait for Rick to come up with an explanation.

'I had a little accident,' Rick says. 'But I'm fine now, thank you for asking.'

My mother sidles into the kitchen and, frankly, that should worry me as she never sidles anywhere. But because my mind is so fuddled through lack of sleep and general anxiety, I don't even register the fact that this should concern me.

'That's my dressing-gown,' Rick says, mouth dropping open as he points at the ancient towelling robe that should be gracing the back of our bedroom door.

'Yes,' my mum replies. 'Hope you don't mind. Arnold's borrowed it. Just for now.'

'Arnold?' That's me.

When I look up, I see that an elderly gentleman with grey hair and a pencil moustache is hovering behind my mother wearing my husband's dressing gown. He has a genial smile and gives us a pleasant wave.

Even my daughter's jaw has hit the floor. My mother has brought a strange man home with her. He's stayed over in my house. With my mother.

'I didn't want Arnold to go home after our date.' Said Arnold squeezes my mother's hand. 'So he didn't.'

They both titter at that.

'I'd have brought a change of clothes if I'd known I'd get lucky,' Arnold tells us.

Do these promiscuous pensioners have no shame? I have no idea what to say, so I try, 'Did you have a nice time?' Which doesn't go anywhere near to expressing what I'm actually thinking.

'Oh, yes.'

'At Pink Paradise?'

'It's lovely down there.'

'See anyone that you knew?'

'At Pink Paradise?' my mum says. 'Not likely.'

Perhaps it isn't the sort of place that Dad hangs out at and just because he's now gay I shouldn't pigeonhole him.

Similarly, I shouldn't think that my mother is a slapper just because she's had a man that she's only just met in her bed under my roof.

'Sit down, Arnold,' Mum says effusively. 'Make yourself at home.'

'Not too much at home,' Rick mutters, eyeing his dressing-gown jealously.

Arnold smiles at us all, oblivious to the fact that the atmosphere could be cut with a knife.

Then the front door opens and Tom comes through it.

'Nice of you to come home,' Rick says. 'We weren't sure if you still lived here. Your mother's thinking of renting your room out.'

'Leave it out,' Tom says miserably, and slings his backpack on the floor. My son's looking even more dishevelled than normal and it would appear that he's been untroubled by soap since he left here two days ago. His eyes are red-rimmed and he looks like he's joined the sleepless brigade too.

My son's dinner from last night is still wrapped in clingfilm in the fridge.

'Tom,' I say, 'this is Arnold. Grandma's . . .' That title quandary again.

'. . . shag,' Rick supplies beneath his breath.

'Yo, Arnold,' Tom says.

Arnold shakes his hand. 'Very nice to make your acquaintance.'

From my husband: 'What brings you home, son? Need clean pants? Money run out?'

'I've got some bad news,' Tom says, ignoring the pointed questions and flopping down at the table. We're going to have to get more chairs if our family keeps growing.

'You've sold a kidney,' Rick ventures.

'Get a life, Dad,' Tom sighs.

'Well, it's going to have to be pretty bad to compete with some of the stuff that's been going on round here.' Rick shoots a pointed look at Chloe.

'Gabe's dumped me,' he announces. 'No marriage. No wedding. No future.' Tom slumps to the table, head in hands.

I put my arm round him and cuddle him to me. He must be upset as he lets me. 'You're young,' I say, thanking God that's all that's wrong with him. 'There are plenty more fish in the sea.'

'Yeah,' he agrees, 'and Gabe's been swimming with a lot of them.'

I kiss his forehead. 'Let me make you some toast. I bet you've not eaten properly,' I say. 'Tea?'

'Nah.' Tom shakes his head. 'Not hungry. I think I'll just check into my bed.'

'Why not?' Rick says. 'Mum and I'll go out to work. You just relax.'

'Yeah,' Tom says, pushing himself from the table. 'Good idea.' Then he wanders out of the kitchen, saying, 'Yo, Arnold. Yo, Grandma,' on the way.

'Yo,' my mother replies.

'That's sarcasm,' Rick shouts after him.

'That's the lowest form of wit,' Tom shouts back.

'I've got to go to work,' I say. Let me out of here. I'm not sure what's more difficult to stomach – the black looks between Chloe and Rick or the flirty looks between my mother and Arnold.

'Me too,' Rick agrees.

We gather our things and head for the front door together. 'See you later,' I call. Much muttering comes back to me.

I step out into the drive, saying to Rick: 'Is it too much to hope that they've all emigrated by the time we get home?'

Across the road, Stacey Lovejoy is just returning from walking

147

her chihuahua. 'Ricky!' she shouts. 'Ricky, love!' And then she sees me. I'm sure her face falls. 'Oh – hi, Juliet.'

'Wave and get in your car quickly,' my husband instructs.

'I thought you could give me a lift,' I say. 'Chloe will need the car if she's going to look for another job.'

My husband tuts at that. 'You're too soft with that girl.'

I'm too soft with them all, I think. With Chloe. With Tom. With my mother. My father. And my husband too. But maybe one day – and it could be today – I'm just going to get a little tougher.

Chapter 34

Rick was already laying a herringbone pattern with posh Artrandan flooring in the dining room of a large terraced house in the equally posh village of Nash when Hal arrived. The customer had gone for wenge wood complete with metallic border strip. It was too fiddly for Rick's taste – he liked his flooring laid in straight lines, no fuss – but the customer was always right. He only hoped that she'd like it when it was done. Sometimes, finishing a floor like this gave him deep joy, but today, deep joy was proving extremely elusive. Pretending that he was concentrating on the intricate pattern, he avoided looking up at his colleague.

'Morning,' Hal said a touch too brightly.

'Morning,' Rick muttered back.

His friend and workmate whistled self-consciously while he made a fuss of arranging his tools. Eventually, Hal crouched down next to him. 'Fine bit of work.'

'Thanks,' Rick said, admiring his own handiwork.

'So?' Hal cleared his throat. 'How did it go last night?'

'The bit before I discovered my only daughter was a nude dancer or the bit after I got kicked in the face by one of her companions?'

'Sorry, mate,' Hal said. 'I should never have dragged you in there.'

'No, you bloody well shouldn't,' Rick replied, but he allowed himself a smile.

'You have to admit,' Hal continued, relief in his voice, 'it wasn't half funny.'

'That depends on where you were standing.'

'I had a great view from where I was.' Hal laughed at that.

'Don't push it, mate,' Rick warned him. 'It was such a shock to see Chloe like that. I'm not sure I'll ever recover.'

'She's a big girl,' Hal observed.

'Yeah. And now a lot of the less discerning gentlemen in Milton Keynes know that.' Rick sat back on his heels.

The truth was, he was still smarting after the events of last night no matter that he was trying to make light of it. Way back when – as husband, father and provider – he'd been the epicentre of family life, dispensing love and discipline in equal measures to his adoring and respectful children and his doting wife. When had that ended? What had changed? Why was his role now relegated to Chief Shouter and permanent Bad Guy? Why did his children no longer respect him? Why did his wife look at him as if he was a stranger? Rick pulled his attention away from even more depressing thoughts. 'Did you stay long after that?'

'Nah,' Hal said, but as he said it, he looked very shifty. 'I brought a flask this morning. Fancy a brew?'

Rick nodded and he cut a few more pieces while Hal poured out coffee for them both.

'I've got problems of my own,' Hal told him as they stopped for a breather.

'Yeah?' Rick thought that nothing would cheer him up more than hearing of someone else's troubles.

'Shannon's told me that she wants a baby.'

Rick spluttered his coffee.

'I know,' Hal said. 'That was my reaction too.'

'She does realise that you've already got two?'

'I guess that's the problem with shacking up with a younger bird, they've still got a body clock. I just hoped that hers wouldn't start the old tick-tock until I was too old and grey to father another kid.' Hal shook his head, perplexed. 'Mine are complete monsters when they come at the weekend. Do all they can to play us both up. Wouldn't you think that would have put her off?'

'There's so much that young women can do with their lives,' Rick said. 'It was different in our day. You got married, you had kids. No one thought to do anything else. We'd been conditioned to think that way. Now the world is their oyster. You'd think that she'd want to get out there and have a bit of experience before tying herself down.'

'She's a lazy cow,' Hal admitted. 'All she wants is a meal ticket and she thinks that she's got one in me.'

Rick hadn't suspected that it was a meeting of minds. He still wasn't entirely sure why Hal had left his wife and family for a situation that seemed so much worse than the one he'd been in. Melinda, his wife, had always seemed fine – good-looking, good mother, good wife. Although you never knew what went on behind someone else's front door. Whatever little dalliances Hal had, he kept quiet – at least from his wife. They jogged along reasonably well together and there were the kids to consider. Why upset the apple-cart, only to start the same thing all over again with another woman? What was the point in that?

'What am I going to do, mate?'

'What does your life coach suggest?'

Hal sucked air in through his teeth. 'Not seeing the life coach now, mate,' he confessed. 'Got a bit too cosy on her couch one day.' He grimaced. 'That's all I needed.'

If Hal had been a sailor he'd be the one to have a woman in every port.

'I have to put Shannon off. I love her, but there's no way I want any more ankle-biters.'

'You could get a vasectomy.'

Hal shuddered. 'Too drastic. Don't think I could. Would you let someone near your old man with a sharp knife?'

Rick knew how he felt. He was still fully intact himself, being similarly squeamish.

'How can I convince her to wait? All she can see is a little, cuddly bundle of fluff. No one thinks of all the crap that comes with it.'

While he sipped his coffee, Rick thought of Chloe and Tom and what they'd been like as toddlers. They'd been his pride, his life, his own little bundles of fluff. Sometimes he used to feel that his heart would overflow with love for them.

Now look at them: idle blighters, both of them, from a generation that thought life owed them a living. He'd had such hope for them. They'd both been bright all the way through school without ever putting in a huge amount of effort. They'd both shown such promise. Where had it all gone? Now all the kids seemed to want to be were celebrities, with someone else picking up the ticket. How was he ever going to get them out of his house and standing on their own two feet if they didn't get decent jobs and earn enough to buy their own homes? These days the children were teenagers until they were thirty.

'In my opinion,' Hal said sagely, 'having kids is vastly overrated.' And Rick thought that he couldn't agree more.

Chapter 35

'Oh dear!' The exclamation of the elderly gentleman sitting next to me brings me back to the real world. I look at the computer screen. In the library, I'm helping one of our regular pensioners to log onto Friends Reunited on the internet.

'That's not quite right, is it?' He tilts his head sideways and moves in for a closer look.

On the screen, couples in leather gear, with holes cut where holes aren't really appropriate, cavort together. 'Sorry, sorry,' I say. 'That's *Fiends* Reunited. A different site altogether.' How much trouble one little letter innocently omitted can create. I hastily tap in the correct address and note that the gentleman next to me looks rather disappointed.

It's fair to say that my mind isn't on my job this morning. I'm so tired that I could lie down on the library floor, right behind the display of audio-books for loan, and go fast asleep.

The correct site pops up on the screen. 'That's better,' I say to our customer. 'I'll leave you to it.'

I bet the minute my back is turned he'll try to view the fiends instead. It's time for my break and I need to get to the staff room fast for a caffeine hit or else I'll never make it to lunchtime.

Una already has the kettle on when I get there. 'I've made Don go on the desk for us for ten minutes,' she tells me. 'You look knackered this morning. It can't just be because of our late night.'

'You wouldn't believe what my family have managed to pack in

153

since midnight.' I shake my head. 'What am I going to do with them all?'

My friend puts my coffee down on the table. She holds up two Jaffa Cakes for me. 'Don's biscuit stash. I'll have to go out and replace them at lunchtime before he notices.'

I don't think about watching my weight or that one moment on the lips is a month on the hips, I just enjoy the lift the sweet treats give me. If I were on my own, I'd lick the chocolate off the top just for the sheer hell of it.

'In the twelve hours since I last saw you my husband discovered that our daughter was working as a lapdancer, just before being kicked in the face by another one. My mother spent the night shagging a stranger in our spare bedroom and my son has been dumped by his gay lover. Only the dog hasn't disgraced himself.'

'Good old Buster,' Una agrees. 'It's a good job he's no trouble as the other lot are going to send you to an early grave.'

'I'm exhausted with the emotion of it all,' I confess. 'At the moment I feel like packing a very small suitcase and clearing off.'

'Would you take Buster with you?'

'I'd consider it.' We laugh at that. Then I confess, 'I dread going home, wondering what I'm going to find next. Tell me that all is well in your world with Internet Tex.'

Una smiles. 'I'd got another email waiting for me this morning. He seems very keen.'

Don pops his head round the staff-room door and, guiltily, I hide my second Jaffa Cake. 'Visitor for you, Juliet.'

'Back in a mo,' I say to Una.

By the desk in the library, Steven Aubrey is waiting patiently for me. His eyes light up when they see me and I don't think I've had that effect on anyone in years.

'Juliet,' he says, breathlessly. 'I'm sorry to disturb you.'

I steer him over towards the children's section. As it's a weekday, there are only a few mums and toddlers in here. It's only after three-thirty that this part of the library is filled with life and I'm self-conscious that anyone should see me with Steven.

154

'What's wrong?' Already I'm filled with panic.

'Nothing,' he laughs. 'Don't look so worried.'

I try to relax my facial muscles, then realise that they're bruised, so put my hand to my mouth to try to cover at least some of them.

'I just came to see you,' he continues. 'I couldn't wait until next week. Have lunch with me today. I've got a lovely surprise planned.'

I look round nervously. 'I can't possibly ask Una to stand in for me again.'

'I promise that I'll have you back within the hour.'

'I don't know, Steven.' I'm shifting from foot to foot and generally behaving in a very furtive manner. Years ago there was a couple who used to come into the library and meet at lunchtime. It was clear they were both married and not to each other. They behaved like this: looking awkward, guilty, their fingers lingering over the books that they probably never intended to read, touching longingly. All the librarians used to laugh at them – me included – but now I just feel sad that they were compelled to meet like that.

'Please,' he says.

'OK,' I say. I'm too tired to put up a strong resistance. 'Come back at one o'clock.'

'Thank you,' he says. 'I won't be a minute late.' Then he's gone.

This is a very heady situation. All this man wants from me is some of my time. He wants to be with me, to spoil me, not to heap trouble on my head as everyone else seems to do.

Currently, that seems like a very attractive proposition.

Chapter 36

I'm stamping books at the counter when, at ten minutes to one, I see Steven's flash car pull up outside the library.

'Go,' Una instructs. 'Ten minutes isn't going to make any difference one way or the other.'

I finish the book that I'm doing and hand over to her.

'You're a pal,' I say, giving her a kiss on the cheek, and I fly out of the library, wings on my feet.

All kinds of emotions flit through my brain as I slip into the passenger seat. I'm nervous, guilty, shy, elated and excited. The bone-numbing tiredness that has dragged me down all morning suddenly lifts.

'Hi again,' Steven says. Sometimes his confidence melts away too, and he's suddenly shy again, like the teenager I knew so well.

'Hi. Where are we going?'

'Wait and see,' he says as we speed away from the library, leaving the town behind us.

Not five minutes later and we're turning into the driveway of the waterside park. This is the place where Rick was arrested on suspicion of Outraging Public Decency. If Steven has seen my husband's ignominy in the local press then he doesn't mention it – and neither do I. We drive down the quiet lane lined with horse-chestnut trees. It's a very secluded spot. No wonder it's so popular for dubious sexual activities. Then my heart skips a beat. 'What are we doing here?'

Steven gestures at Watermill House at the end of the lane as we drive towards it. It's a magnificent building that I've often admired when Rick and I have brought Buster down here on one of his long walks.

'I live here,' he says. 'I thought I'd mentioned it before. I'm just renting it for now, but there's an option to buy which I'm keen to pursue. I've fallen in love with the place.'

His eyes meet mine and something in them tells me that's not the only thing Steven has fallen in love with on his return.

We pull into the gravel drive and stop outside the triple garage underneath the shade of a glorious copper beech. I gaze around in awe. Watermill House is enormous. I don't know the history, but the front of the house is a traditional building of mellow stone, joined on to a large stoic redbrick construction at the back which clearly used to be a working mill. Someone has spent an inordinate amount of money restoring it to this level of perfection.

Getting out of the car, Steven takes my hand and leads me to the back of the mill.

'You're rattling round here alone?' I ask, as I count the windows. There's got to be at least six bedrooms, maybe more. I think of how cramped the accommodation at my own house has become. When we first moved into number 10, Chadwick Close over twenty years ago, it was my dream home. Rick and I had started off in a tiny terraced house in Silver Street with a back yard the size of a handkerchief. We had just one decent-sized bedroom and a little box room which became Tom's nursery when he was born. When he was five and Chloe was on the way and when property prices weren't insane, we moved up in the world to our current four-bedroomed house complete with large garden. It seemed so vast in comparison that I wondered how we would fill it. I thought that I'd never want to live anywhere else. Now we could do with an extra room downstairs and an en-suite. There's no utility room either and it would be nice to have somewhere to wipe Buster's muddy feet. The hall is always full of dumped handbags and shoes and I'd like to get those out of the way too. Rick says that all we need is for the children to leave home and some days I can see his point.

'I loved this place when I was growing up,' Steven says. 'I used to come down here with Laurence Ashurst and get up to mischief. Remember him?'

I nod. 'He's a presenter now on our local radio station. Very popular.'

'Really.' Steven laughs and it somehow shocks me, how relaxed he sounds when I feel so tightly wound. 'It's the perfect job for him. He always was a chatterbox.'

To one side of the mill house is a large, clear pond. Water lilies float serenely on the surface that's been sprinkled with sunlight, and little sticklebacks dart about beneath them. Dragonflies flit between the yellow flowers. This is pure heaven.

Steven leads me into the back garden of the property. Unlike my own patch, it's manicured to perfection. There are dozens of planters holding pink geraniums, white and blue hydrangeas and standard rosemary bushes. Delicate swathes of lilac clematis grace the old stone walls. Everything I plant, Buster upends or pees on – his only vices. 'This is amazing,' I sigh happily.

'I already have homes in South Africa, Florida and a little villa in the South of France, but this would be a nice addition.'

I bet none of Steven's homes have a grinning selection of multi-coloured gnomes in their garden.

On the terrace – it's too posh to call it a patio – a table has been set with two places. 'I love to cook,' Steven says, 'but I don't get a chance to do it very often. There's nothing better than throwing some good meat or fish on the barbie – one thing I learned from my time out in Africa. So . . . steak or salmon?'

'Salmon would be lovely.'

'Sit,' he instructs as he pops open a bottle of champagne and pours me a glass. 'I'll be two minutes.'

The river runs along the back of the mill, slowly turning the big waterwheel that's been there for generations. There's a pretty arched bridge that crosses the river and leads into meadows beyond – some years there's even a sprinkling of poppies here. The early-afternoon sun is blistering in its intensity. I sit under the umbrella that's fluttering in the breeze and breathe in the air. This is the first time in months that I feel at peace with the world. It's like a little oasis here. Now wonder Steven's champing at the bit to add it to his property portfolio.

True to his word, Steven reappears minutes later, bearing a plate with two succulent pieces of salmon on it; in the other hand, he has a glass bowl filled with a mixed salad. 'There's some rice salad too,' he says, 'but I confess that I bought that from the deli.'

He fires up the barbecue and flicks on the salmon with the expertise of a man who's done this many times before. But then Rick barbecues quite often and he always manages to set something on fire – the grass, the house, himself. Steven looks assured as he checks the fish.

God, I must stop thinking like this. What's wrong with me? Every time I compare Steven to Rick, my husband comes out unfavourably and that just isn't fair. Rick has been a good husband, a good father. I've got nothing to complain about. Apart from the sexual offences and the lapdancing clubs that have recently sneaked into his repertoire, of course.

Steven comes to top up my glass, but I put a hand over the rim. 'Can't have me drunk in charge of romance novels,' I tease.

He crouches beside me and covers my hand with his, then takes it to his lips and kisses it warmly. 'I wish you didn't have to go back this afternoon,' he says, his mouth moving just above my skin. 'I love having you here.'

'It's nice to be here,' I say, and the words catch in my throat.

'Oh Christ,' Steven says. 'Why did I ever let you go? What kind of idiot was I?'

I don't know what to say to that. 'I think the fish might be burning.'

My old love gives me a rueful glance. He pats my hand and then goes to tend to our lunch.

Then I get a pang of regret, unbidden. It's tinged with something which might be envy – a feeling that I've rarely experienced. If I had ended up as Mrs Juliet Aubrey, how different my life might have been. I could have been a lady of leisure, living in a place like this. But women like Una end up in places like this, not women like me.

Chapter 37

The salmon is cooked to perfection as I knew it would be. Steven has made his own salad dressing with basil and walnut oil which is sublime. The conversation has been funny, sparkling. Steven and I have talked about old times, the places we used to go, the people we used to know.

'I often wonder how Mary Williams turned out,' he says. 'She always wanted to be a vet.'

'She did end up running a mobile dog grooming service,' I supply. 'She groomed Buster a few times, but it was quite pricey.' A luxury that we couldn't afford.

Very few of our mutual friends ever moved away from the town. Stony Stratford is the sort of place where people tend to stay. Or if they do go away, then they come back to settle down. I wonder if the latter category applies to Steven. Is he really back for good?

The only downside to our snatched and rather decadent lunchtime meeting is that I've had my eye on the clock throughout as I know that I'm tight for time.

'I have to go in a minute,' I say as I finish my last mouthful. 'This has been lovely. Thank you.'

'Nicer than going to a pub where you're a mass of anxiety.'

'Yes.' I don't tell Steven that my anxiety is down to the fact that he's back at all. I go on: 'With all our reminiscing, I haven't asked how your mum is.'

Steven shakes his head sadly. 'Not good.'

'I'm sorry to hear that.'

'She's had a good innings,' he says. 'There's a lovely nurse comes in to see her twice a day and she's as comfortable as she can be. It's just a matter of time.'

'If there's anything I can do . . .' My words trail away. What can you do for anyone in this situation? To hide the awkwardness, I pick up the plates.

'Leave those where they are,' Steven scolds. 'I don't want you to lift a finger.'

'I'll just put them in the kitchen.' I carry the dishes inside to the cool kitchen with the stone floor that has been perfectly renovated, pushing the image of my own shabby kitchen out of my mind. Steven follows behind with the remnants of the salad bowl.

Having stacked the dishes on the work surface, I turn quickly and bump into Steven. His hands clutch my arms to steady me.

'Oh, sorry.' I'm all of a dither.

On my bare skin his thumb traces a circle. 'You're more beautiful now than you were twenty-five years ago,' he says softly, and pulls me closer to him.

A gulp travels down my throat. 'I don't think so.' Can he not see the bruises on my face where I've foolishly tried to recapture my youth? The girl he was going to marry is well and truly long gone.

'The last Mrs Aubrey was a twenty-nine-year-old Thai woman,' Steven sighs. 'Even while she was beneath me and we were making love, I still thought of your silky soft, white skin.'

Yes, well. There's a lot more of it now, I think. Squashed into size fourteen pants.

'Say that we can do this again,' Steven urges. 'Can you get away one evening? I'd love to make you dinner.'

'Steven,' I say, 'it's lovely to see you again. I've enjoyed our time together. But what we meant to each other is all in the past.' My hammering heart thinks differently. 'This isn't going anywhere. It can't.'

'I don't think you mean that,' my old lover says. 'Why else would you have agreed to come out here?'

Then my mobile phone rings. Perfect timing. It's Tom. He sounds sleepy. 'Can't go on,' he mumbles through tears. 'I can't live without Gabe.'

'Tom, Tom!' I shout. 'Tell me what's wrong. What have you done?'

'Taken tablets, Mum.'

Fear grips me. 'What?' I say. 'What have you taken?'

'Don't know,' he slurs. Then the phone goes dead.

'It's Tom,' I say to Steven. 'He's taken an overdose. I have to get back to the house.'

'I'll take you. Phone an ambulance.'

We run to the car as I punch 999 into my phone and explain to the operator as calmly as I can what's wrong when I really want to scream the place down. My baby could have been dying while I was sitting having an illicit lunch with my one-time lover. The operator promises that a paramedic team will be there as soon as possible.

'Where do you live?' Steven asks as he pulls back onto the main road, showering gravel from the lane in our wake.

'Chadwick Close.' It seems strange that he doesn't even know that about me.

Steven speeds across town heading towards my home and my child who needs me. I feel like tearing my hair out. I know that Tom was convinced that this relationship was The One, but they'd only known each other for such a short time: how can it have affected him like this?

I went to pot when Steven left me, but I'd known him for years. He'd been my only love; we were due to get married. Even at my lowest, did I think of taking my own life? Perhaps I did, but I was too much of a coward to even try it. I wouldn't have wanted people to think badly of me.

Then I call Rick. 'Tom's taken an overdose,' I tell him baldly.

'Oh my God,' he says. 'I'll be right there. Where are you?'

'On my way.' I hang up. 'Go quicker,' I urge Steven and he pushes his foot to the floor.

'Nearly there,' he says.

We screech into Chadwick Close and I point to our house. 'There, there,' I say to Steven. 'That's my house.'

He says nothing as he throws the car to the kerb outside. 'You have to go,' I say, as I jump out of the door. Rick will be here in a minute and I don't want him to find me climbing out of Steven Aubrey's Aston Martin.

'I'll come with you.'

'No, no.' Even now I'm wondering how I would explain what I was doing with him. 'I'll call you.' I'm halfway down the drive. I hope to goodness none of the neighbours are witnessing this.

Steven is out of the car, leaning on the roof. 'I'll go to the library,' he says. 'Tell Una.'

'Thank you.' Fumbling with my door keys I almost drop them and I can feel myself start to cry. If anything happens to Tom, to my son, if I don't get to him in time, then I'll blame myself for ever.

Chapter 38

Racing up the stairs, I shout, 'Tom! Tom!' Buster, barking his head off, chases after me, clearly thinking that it's a wonderful game.

Sure enough, as I'd expected, Tom is in his own room sprawled out on his bed. I go straight across and shake his shoulders. 'Tom! Wake up!'

There's a glass of water on his bedside table and I throw it over his face.

'Huh?' My son rouses.

I wish I had another one as I'd do it again. On the floor by the bed is a bottle of vodka. There's a sizeable puddle around it, so it seems that the majority of it is in the carpet rather than down my son's throat.

'Tom! Tom!' I lift him slightly, even though I don't know if that's the right thing to do. 'What did you take?'

'Ug,' he grunts, and flings a floppy arm out to knock a tub of tablets on the floor to join the vodka.

I scrabble for it and pick up the container with shaking fingers. 'This can't be it,' I sob. 'Tom, tell me what you've taken.'

Searching round the bed, I look for evidence of the tablets that he's swallowed. We don't keep that many drugs in the house as we're a reasonably healthy bunch; so there's not much in the way of painkillers or barbiturates. And, although our drug cache has gone up considerably since my mother arrived, it mainly consists of water tablets and laxatives. I don't think that you can wee or

165

poo yourself to death. So unless Tom has brought drugs in with him, I don't know what he can have swallowed.

'I can't find anything,' I tell him urgently. 'The paramedics will need to know. Were they sleeping tablets? All I can find is this glucosamine sulphate.'

'That's it,' he murmurs weakly.

That pulls me up short. 'You've taken an overdose of glucosamine?'

'Yes,' Tom breathes heavily.

I let my son drop back to the bed and he hits the pillow with an 'Oouff!'

Standing up again, I put my hands on my hips. 'That's to lubricate your joints, Tom,' I point out.

Tom opens one eye.

'Dad takes it for his bad shoulder,' I continue crisply.

The other eye opens.

'I don't think an overdose will kill you. It will just make you very flexible.'

My son is suddenly and instantly awake and sober. He sits up straight. 'You're kidding me?'

'I think *you're* kidding *me*.'

Tom takes the jar from me. 'I've tried to commit suicide with vitamins?'

'I think that strictly they'd be classed as a health supplement, but that's about the size of it.'

'Shit,' my son mumbles. 'It said "high strength" on the front. I thought that would see me off.'

'You didn't think to read the rest of the label?'

Tom shakes his head.

Don't they teach them anything at university? 'Then next time you decide to nearly kill off your mother as well as yourself, I suggest you do your research better.'

My son scratches his head as he does now read the label. '"Excellent for joint health and arthritis".'

'A bit late for that.' I fling open the curtains and, as I'm now not panicking that my child is breathing his last breath, the toxic

166

fug of his room hits me – the smell of festering trainers competing with the stink of rancid laundry and sheets that are in need of changing. The windows are also flung open and as I let the fresh air in I hear the siren of the ambulance at the end of Chadwick Close.

'You can go down and tell them that this is a wild-goose chase,' I chastise. 'Get out of bed. *Now.*'

Tom staggers as he does, but doesn't argue. 'I think I might be a little bit drunk.'

'And you might be a little bit closer to death than you'd imagined when your father gets home.'

Tom's face falls. 'You didn't phone Dad?'

'What did you expect me to do? I thought you were dying.'

'Well, I'm feeling fine now,' he says sheepishly.

'Get to that door,' I say. 'And make sure you apologise. Profusely.'

The paramedics race to the door only to be greeted by the alleged victim mumbling about how sorry he is. I hope that they've charged him for wasting valuable emergency time. But then Rick and I would only end up paying the bill.

Before I can phone Rick, he, too, races up to the house only to meet two very disgruntled paramedics stomping back to their ambulance.

Sighing, I sink onto Tom's bed, wondering when he last changed his linen. I don't come in here these days in a misguided attempt to respect his privacy, but the deal is that he's supposed to respect general standards of public hygiene. One of us isn't keeping the bargain. This is c.difficile central. He's twenty-four years of age and this room looks like it belongs to a stinky fourteen year old. What's happening to us all, I wonder. My ideal image of family life has long since been shattered, but should it really be as bad as this?

Downstairs I hear Rick shouting and Tom, in a rare wise move, isn't shouting back. Buster, tail wagging, starts to lap vodka from the upturned bottle.

'Come here, boy,' I say. 'Don't do that. It's nasty.' Pretty much

167

sums up life *chez Joyce*. The dog comes over and I cuddle him to me, nuzzling the soft fur of his neck for comfort.

I think of my lunch with Steven in the calm sophistication of his garden. Why isn't my life like that all the time? If I'm not to go round the bend or take overdoses of glucosamine sulphate myself, things are going to have to change around here.

Chapter 39

'I have raced across town like a mad thing,' Rick said. He had barely got through the door when he'd started on Tom. 'Only to find that this is all a false alarm.' He knew he was shouting and that, perhaps, it wasn't the best idea but he couldn't stop himself.

'A cry for help,' Tom corrected.

'You're lucky I don't kill you,' Rick retorted. 'What did you think you were doing?'

At that moment his wife came down the stairs. Her face was white and drawn.

'Leave him alone, Rick,' she said wearily. 'This isn't making things any better.'

'Be quiet, Juliet,' he said. 'It's about time both Tom and Chloe started to face the consequences of their actions.'

Juliet held up her hands and walked into the kitchen. He heard the kettle going on, but it was going to take more than a cup of tea to make this right.

'What made you do it?' Rick wanted to know.

Tom fidgeted. 'I found Gabe with another man.'

Maybe he didn't need to know that.

'I was very upset.'

'Life is full of upsets!' Rick said. 'We don't all go round killing ourselves. You've got to get a grip. Go out and get a job then you won't have any time to think about these things.'

'We're not back to that old song,' grunted Tom, raising his eyebrows.

As far as Rick could tell, his son was making a miraculous recovery. Then the house phone rang. Rick snatched up the receiver and barked, 'Hello!'

It was Tom's boyfriend, or ex-boyfriend, on the other end. This was the first time Rick had spoken to Gabe, apart from the morning he'd seen him in his underpants. It just didn't seem right that his son could be so distraught over another man.

'Gabe wants to know how you are,' Rick said. 'Did you tell him you were trying to top yourself?'

Tom looked embarrassed. 'I texted him.'

Rick tutted. 'He's fine,' he said in response to Gabe's question about the current state of Tom's health.

When Gabe had finished speaking, Rick hung up and turned to Tom. 'He says that you're a bigger loser than he thought you were.'

'That's nice.'

'And you were planning to end it all over this man?' Rick shook his head.

His son looked shamefaced. 'Is that all the sympathy I get?'

'Yes,' Rick said. 'Apologise to your mother and then get out of my sight.'

Tom shuffled into the kitchen and Rick heard him mumble an apology to Juliet.

'Promise me that you won't ever do anything like that again,' his wife answered. 'If you're ever in that kind of situation again, just talk to us. Dad and I will understand.'

Rick stifled the snort he wanted to make.

'I'll go and tidy my room,' Tom said.

It made Rick's heart twist as his son sounded like a child again.

'Sorry, Dad,' Tom said, as he came out into the hall.

'Don't do it again,' Rick said gruffly. He high-fived Tom weakly as he passed on his way up the stairs.

'I'm considering a career in the paramedics,' his son said. 'They do a great job.'

Rick bit back the retort he wanted to make and, instead, watched his boy until he disappeared into his bedroom. Then he went into the kitchen, rubbing his face.

Juliet put down a mug of tea. 'Don't think that's going to do it,' Rick said grumpily, but drank it nevertheless. 'Was I too hard on him?'

'Yes,' she said. 'No. No worse than I was. It was a shock and a very stupid thing to do, but I don't like to think of Tom upset.'

'None of them seem to worry about upsetting us though, do they?'

Juliet shakes her head.

'Let's not go back to work,' Rick suggested. 'I'm too strung out to focus on flooring. Hal can manage by himself for once. Let's take Buster and have a long walk through Toombs Meadow – clear the cobwebs.'

'I'll call Una,' Juliet said. 'Tell her I'll see her tomorrow. She'll understand.'

'The Desperate Divorcée will have it all round town by tonight.'

'She won't,' Juliet insisted. 'She's my friend.' She picked up her mobile. 'Una, it's me,' she said. 'Yes, he's fine. I know. I was out of my mind. He'd swallowed glucosamine sulphate, that's all. I know. That's kids for you. I'm not coming back to work this afternoon if that's OK. My nerves are shredded. I'll see you in the morning. I know. Speak to you tomorrow.'

Juliet put her phone on the table. A second later it rang again, making them both frown. 'Yes, he's fine,' she said, when she picked it up. Her cheeks flushed. 'I know. I was out of my mind. He'd swallowed glucosamine sulphate, that's all. I know. That's kids for you. I'll speak to you tomorrow.' Then she hung up.

'Good news travels fast. Who was that?'

'Er, just Una again.'

'But you'd already told her all that.'

'She was just checking. Memory like a sieve.' But Juliet's cheeks reddened further.

'Silly woman,' he said, but something nagged at his brain.

Juliet stood up and smoothed her skirt. 'Do you still want that walk?'

'Yeah. Let's get Buster,' Rick said. 'I need to get out. Leave all this crap behind.'

As they went into the hall to get the dog's lead, the local newspaper was pushed through the letterbox and plopped onto the floor. Juliet picked it up.

She flicked her eyes over the front page and then, without speaking, held up the paper. LAPDANCER SUES LOCAL DOGGING PERVERT FOR ASSAULT, it read.

'Fabulous.' Rick covered his face with his hands, trying to block out the headline.

They'd have to move away, Rick thought. Maybe Australia would be far enough.

Chapter 40

'We never think of taking an afternoon off together,' Rick says as we walk down the path at the back of our house towards Toombs Meadow.

'That's because we're both very busy people.'

'Is that all it is?' my husband asks. He holds my hand as we walk. 'It's not because we've run out of things to say to each other?'

'I don't think so.' The trouble is, at the moment, every conversation we have is about some kind of disaster or another. Do other couples sit down in their living room with a sociable glass of wine at the end of the day and simply chat about unimportant and irrelevant things? Do they discuss philosophy, art, books they've read, plans they might have for the garden that season? All we do is seem to lurch from one crisis to another, communicating in whispered tones or in high-pitched voices. When did we last sit together and talk about nothing in particular?

The sun is still high in the sky. We haven't had rain now for over a week. I must get out into the garden and water the tubs and hanging baskets. The flowers will be parched. So many things to do and so little time. If it wasn't for the fact that we're still paying for Chloe at university, I'd be tempted to go part-time.

'Remember when we used to pack up a picnic and come out here with the kids?'

This part of Stony Stratford hasn't changed much since I was a girl and it was the favourite playground of my own children.

It's a great open space in which to run around and let off some steam. I only wish that I could do that now. The river meanders lazily through the meadows and there's often sheep grazing in here. 'It doesn't seem so very long ago.'

'Now look at the pair of them.' Rick shakes his head. 'Did we bring them up so badly? I thought we did a good job.'

'Me too.' A welcome breeze lifts my hair from my neck. 'We certainly did our best.'

'Perhaps it just wasn't good enough.'

'No.' There's a bench that overlooks the river and we sit on it, watching the water wander through the reeds and the ducks carried along by its current.

'We should celebrate our anniversary,' my husband says decisively.

'It doesn't feel like we've got much to shout about at the moment.'

'We can't just let it slide by. With all the fuss that's been going on at home, it's all but been forgotten.'

I don't remind my husband that he's done his fair share of contributing to the 'fuss'.

'I'd like to treat you to something special too,' Rick adds. 'Is there anything that you'd like?'

I think of what Una would want to have for her twenty-fifth wedding anniversary present, had she made it so far. Diamonds would be on the list, perhaps a trip to an exclusive spa, a weekend in Paris. Many husbands shower their wives with jewellery, or so I believe, but Rick hasn't bought me so much as a pair of earrings in all the years we've been married.

'I know that you need a new dishwasher,' Rick says into my dream of wanton luxury. 'And you've always fancied a greenhouse for the garden.'

I should have known that his thoughts would run along more practical lines than mine. After all, this is the man who bought me a wheelbarrow for my fortieth birthday. It was a very nice wheelbarrow. I was really pleased with it at the time. But it was a wheelbarrow nevertheless. In Una's book that would be grounds for divorce. Maybe Rick should have hidden a little gold bracelet inside it for the sake of marital harmony. He's lucky that I'm so low maintenance.

'Perhaps we should have a little do too. Hire a room out in one of the pubs so that you wouldn't have to do all the cooking.'

'I'm not sure that I'm in the mood for a party at the moment.'

Rick squeezes my hand. 'We are OK, aren't we?'

'Yes,' I say. He gives me a peck on the cheek.

'I do love you,' he says.

'I love you too.' I think of the phone call from Steven and how it made my stomach churn with guilt and excitement and how I haven't even told my husband that my one-time fiancé is back in town. And how I'm not sure that we're OK at all.

Chapter 41

'Why did you give Steven my mobile phone number, you twit?' I ask Una when I see her in the library the next morning. There's a lull in proceedings and we're both leaning on the front counter. Books that need shelving go unattended.

'He was frantic,' she explains. 'He only wanted to find out that everything was OK.'

'You could have told him what had happened,' I point out. 'He rang while Rick was sitting next to me. I was all flustered and didn't know what to say.'

'I didn't think,' she admits. 'I was so worried about you. We both were.'

'I have to tell Rick that Steven's back. This is ridiculous, but it never seems to be the right time. He was jealous of Steven for years when we were first married. Did I tell you that?'

Una shakes her head.

'I never dared to mention his name. With everything else that's going on, I certainly don't want to drag an old boyfriend back into the mix.'

'Maybe you should just stop seeing him,' my friend suggests.

'You were the one who encouraged me to go out with him,' I protest. Then we laugh at that.

'God, listen to us,' I say. 'We sound like a couple of teenagers squabbling over a bloke. I'm a grown woman. I should be able to have lunch with whoever I like. Steven and I have a lot of history

176

together. I don't want to turn my back on him and, to be honest, the hour I spent with him yesterday is helping to preserve my sanity.'

'You haven't told me about that yet.'

'We had a very pleasant lunch. Steven is a wonderful cook and his home is lovely. It's not as if we're pulling into secluded lay-bys and doing the dirty.'

'You can't tell me you haven't thought about it though.'

We giggle again. Don comes out of the office. 'Are you ladies planning on doing any work today?'

'No,' Una says. 'Juliet's fed up. I told you about her son trying to top himself. Have some sympathy.'

'I was sorry to hear that,' our manager says, chastened. I think Una could do worse than date Don as she can wrap him round her little finger. 'Go and have ten minutes in the staff room with a coffee while I look after the desk.'

'Thanks, Don,' Una says, fluttering her false eyelashes.

We retreat to the skanky staff room and to repay Don's kindness Una nicks two of his biscuits to go with our coffee. 'You're a terrible woman,' I tell her.

'I'm not,' she says. 'I'm lovely and to prove that, I've booked us both a make-over tonight straight after work at one of the make-up counters in John Lewis.'

'Oh, Una. That does sound nice. I've always wanted to do that but I've never had the courage to go on my own.'

'We'll only be an hour. I can take you home afterwards or we could go out for a pizza and show off our new faces.'

'Pizza sounds good.' Una never eats pizza. She'll order something involving salad and then leave half of it. 'I'll call Rick and let him know.'

'Thought it might put a few roses back in your cheeks.'

I sip at my coffee. I could do with the caffeine hit but we only have decaff here this week as Una has recently decided that she won't drink anything else and she's decided that we should all do the same. Instead, I pretend that it's giving me a lift. 'What am I going to do about Steven?'

'That's up to you, honey,' Una says. 'He's a very attractive man. I certainly wouldn't say no.'

More giggling.

'It depends whether it's all as innocent as you make out and you have it in control. Or whether you are, in fact, playing with fire.'

And the truth of the matter is that I really don't know.

Chapter 42

Another day. Another laminate floor to lay. In this age of credit crunch and financial squeeze, it seemed that people were still happy to swap their old carpets for shiny new wood-effect flooring. Rick and Hal had never been busier.

There were both taking a welcome ten-minute coffee stop and had stepped out into the garden of the house they were working at to take the air. It was always nice to find a customer who was good at brewing up regularly. As Rick was getting older, this flooring lark was becoming back-breaking work. He put his mug of coffee on the garden wall and massaged his lower back. Stiff as a board – about the only thing that was, these days. He'd have to do something about it. His back, that was.

Hal puffed frantically at a cigarette.

'You're giving those a bit of a battering,' Rick observed.

'Want one?'

Rick shook his head. 'Mug's game.' He'd tried smoking when he was younger but even then the cost of a pack of twenty had been beyond his meagre means and he'd never much liked the taste of it anyway.

'I'd love to give up,' Hal admitted. 'I've been trying those nicotine patches. Bloody useless.'

'Try sticking one over each eye then you won't be able to find your smokes.'

'Very funny,' Hal said, grinding the offending cigarette into their client's patio. Rick would have to remember to clear that up later. 'Can you shoot off at lunchtime to price up a job for me?'

'I wanted to pop into the city,' Rick said. 'I've got something to do.'

'Do it on your way back, mate. This is important.'

'We can't take on any more work, Hal. We're stacked out at the moment.'

'I've got to get some more money in,' his friend said. 'I'll have to see if I can take someone else on. These women are bleeding me dry. I've got to earn twice as much to stand still.'

'I thought Shannon worked?'

'It pays pants. She might be young, but she's got expensive tastes. Nothing but the best for our Shannon.' There was a note of bitterness in his voice. 'Now she's on about quitting so that she can spend time preparing for the baby that I'm apparently going to father.'

'So that's still on the agenda?'

'Not if I get my way.' Hal, oblivious to the fact that he'd just stubbed out a cigarette, lit another one. He dragged on it deeply. 'Let me offer you some advice, my friend. If you ever even think of straying, then you tell Uncle Hal. I'll talk you out of it. Whenever you might be feeling a bit frisky, take a cold shower. Even in these days of inflated energy prices that will cost you round about twenty pence. A divorce lawyer will set you back four hundred and fifty quid an hour. And they'll still seem to be more on the side of your missus than yours.'

'Four hundred and fifty quid?' Rick whistled through his teeth.

'You make sure you treat that woman of yours right. It will be a lot cheaper in the long run.'

And that's what he was going to do. It had been stupid to think that Juliet might like a dishwasher or a greenhouse as their anniversary present – even though greenhouses could be quite pricy. It just wasn't romantic. He'd seen her face fall and had regretted his suggestion as soon as it came out of his stupid unromantic mouth. No, this would be an anniversary that they'd both remember until the day they died. He was going to see to it.

Chapter 43

John Lewis's department store is at the top end of the shopping centre in Milton Keynes. It's a bright, airy place. Una's favourite day out.

Don let us out of the library a few minutes early and now the two of us are sitting on high stools at one of the make-up counters. We both have white protective capes around our necks and, much to my consternation, my hair is scraped back from my face by a tight band. It's not a look I'm keen to share with the general public of Milton Keynes and I wonder why the make-up counters are slap bang in the front of the store rather than tucked away in a little corner at the back that would offer a modicum of privacy. I feel naked sitting here being gawped at by passing strangers.

Una is clearly in her element. I can hear her and the young girl who is doing her make-up enjoying a steady stream of chatter about the latest colours for eye-shadow and lip gloss. I can't do that. Never have been able to. I don't know whether Merry Berry or Silver Sparkle is this season's must-have colour and I'm not sure that I care. Perhaps I should.

My friend is picking out her own colours, getting the girl to try different things. I'm sitting here passively, letting it all happen to me. Maybe I need to take control of my make-up if nothing else in my life.

'You're very bruised around your mouth and eyes,' the girl says suspiciously.

'Over-vigorous Botox and filler,' I explain, at which she tuts.

'I'll use some extra concealer to try to disguise it,' she offers.

'What colours are you using on me?' I ask, not liking how timid I sound. How can I be intimidated by a nineteen-year-old slip of a thing who's wearing three-foot of foundation?

'You're a Classic Beige,' she says, as she dabs some kind of powder on my skin. I want to cough. 'So I'm using neutrals.'

Classic Beige. How depressing. I bet Una isn't Classic Beige. I bet she isn't being daubed with neutrals.

'What's my friend having?'

The girl looks over at my friend's palette. 'Oh, she's an Exotic Bloom.'

Exotic Bloom versus Classic Beige. I know which one I'd rather be. Why can't I have that? I want to ask. Instead, I keep my mouth shut.

An hour later and we're nearly finished. Which is just as well as my patience is virtually exhausted. I'm on the point of pulling my tongue out at all the people who stare at me as they go past. I don't think that I do pampering well.

As the young girl whips off my white cape, out of the corner of my eye I notice a man standing and staring at me from a distance.

'Gorgeous,' he says as he comes closer, and it's a voice that's becoming very familiar to me again. My heart sets up that flutter which alarms me.

'Steven,' I say, as I turn to him. 'I hadn't expected to see you.'

'What are you two lovely ladies doing here?'

'Being beautified,' Una, now by my side, chips in.

'Well, you both look utterly stunning.'

Una's face looks as if it has been sun-kissed. Her cheeks glow, her lips glisten, her eyes glitter. I look matt all over.

'Can I take you both for a coffee?'

'That would be lovely,' Una says, without even looking at me for agreement. 'I know just the place.'

She links her arm through Steven's and steers him out of the shop, tottering on her heels as she does. I trail behind them. Mrs Juliet Classic Beige in the wake of Ms Una Exotic Bloom and Mr Steven Super-Smooth.

Chapter 44

Rick knew that he'd never have enough time during the lunch-hour to do both a quote for another job and pop into the shopping centre. Fortunately, Juliet had phoned to say that she was going out with Una straight after work, which gave him time to do his little errands in peace.

He wanted to take some time to look for a special gift for his wife, for their wedding anniversary – maybe some jewellery, although he didn't know what sort of style that Juliet liked. Then he realised that after all this time as her husband, he really should do. Perhaps she'd like some lingerie or one of those designer handbags that cost an arm and a leg.

While she was out tonight, he'd gone into Marks & Spencer to pick up a ready meal for his dinner that could be microwaved in minutes: a Gastro-Pub sausage and mash creation with pure organic Lincolnshire pork, fluffy Jersey potatoes and rich onion gravy infused with sage. Not just sausage and mash, but M&S sausage and mash. He looked round furtively. This was currently his mother-in-law's favourite pick-up joint and he hoped that she wasn't in here now and was, instead, at home walking Buster as she'd promised.

This was actually quite a civilised time to come shopping. Normally, he tried to steer clear of the shopping centre it was full of mums with prams, screaming kids and teenagers stuffing their faces with McDonald's. He'd never understood the lure of retail

184

therapy, but his kids more than made up for any shortcomings he had in that department by emptying his wallet on a regular basis.

Dinner purchased, Rick trawled the aisles of the centre and looked in the windows of the myriad jewellery shops. Where on earth should he start? Perhaps he should have brought Chloe along with him. His daughter could spend for England and would know exactly what sort of jewellery Juliet would like, and wouldn't be put off by the extortionate price tags. But then he and Chloe still weren't on speaking terms and she'd steadfastly avoided him since the nude lapdancing incident.

Perhaps he could use this evening simply as a reconnoitre, draw up a short-list, drop some hints to Juliet, see if that gave him any clues.

An hour later and the process was starting to lose some of its attraction. All the other shoppers seemed to be laden down with carrier bags, but he'd not yet bought anything bar the microwave supper. To rectify that, Rick stopped at the nearest Costa Coffee and bought a frothy cappuccino to take away. At the serve yourself counter, he sprinkled on some extra chocolate and, while Juliet wasn't there to see, added two sachets of brown sugar to the concoction.

Back out in the shopping centre, Rick sipped the coffee through the tiny mouth-hole in the lid. It was difficult to suck it all up through the frothiness. At this rate, he'd have collapsed lungs before he even got to the coffee beneath. A few doors down from the Costa Coffee was an Ann Summers shop. He stopped and looked in the window which was full of the sort of lingerie that he'd seen scattered around Stacey Lovejoy's home. Perhaps this was where his neighbour did all of her shopping. The pouty mannequin posed in a red lacy basque thing and suspender belt. Personally, Rick liked it. But he knew that Juliet wasn't a crimson lace type of person. His wife's underwear was either white or black and looked vaguely utilitarian. There wasn't a lot of lace in evidence anywhere in her wardrobe.

Stockings. Hmm. Nothing looked sexier on a woman, but Juliet said that no way would he persuade her to truss herself up in a suspender belt – and Rick had to admit they didn't look that comfortable to wear. If the boot was on the other foot, would he torture himself with that get-up? The answer was no.

Rick sucked on the plastic lid of his coffee cup. Nothing came out. This was hopeless; he was going to have to take the lid off if he was to have any hope of getting a drink out of this. He tried to prise the lid off, but it was firmly jammed down. Juliet was always complaining about how hard he put lids on things. She could never open a bottle after he'd used it. Now he could see that she might have a point. Again, he tried to lever it off but the lip was wedged tight. He had another suck, but still nothing. This was ridiculous. All he wanted was a damn coffee, not a wrestling match. Rick decided to have one last tug.

Finally, the lid parted company with the cup. Unfortunately, the lid was the bit that stayed firmly in his hand while his takeaway coffee tumbled to the floor, spilling down the front of his trousers on the way. 'Bloody hell!' Rick shouted, and jumped back, trying to avoid the scalding hot liquid.

He looked down to see that he'd made a poor job of avoidance techniques. There was froth gathered in a place that you really don't want a blob of froth. It look vaguely obscene. Frantically, Rick scrubbed at the froth with the cuff of his shirt. No wonder it wouldn't come up through the minuscule hole in the coffee cup – this stuff was like shaving foam. He rubbed at it again, faster this time.

Out of the corner of his eye he saw an elderly lady drop both of her shopping bags. As Rick turned to see if she was all right, her hands went up to her mouth and she let out a bloodcurdling scream. Heads turned, a few people ran towards her, then Rick saw her point – *at him*.

He looked down to see where she was pointing at and her bony finger was directed at the mound of froth in the groin area of his trousers. Oh no. He looked up and saw the saucy window display in front of him and realised how his innocent rubbing actions might have been misconstrued.

'He was fiddling with himself,' the woman cried. 'I saw him.'

'No, no,' Rick yelled back. He moved towards her to explain, but she cried out again and backed away from him. 'Madam, this is all a terrible mistake.'

How often had he used that same phrase recently?

Not to be placated, the woman launched at him with her handbag, thwacking him about the head and arms. 'You pervert.'

'Ow, ow, ow!' What could he do to stop her killing him? How could he explain that it was just a coincidence that he was outside a sex shop while he was rubbing white stains from his groin area?

Then he saw two burly policemen running down the length of the shopping centre in his direction. This was not taking a turn for the better. What was he to do? He could make a bolt for it, but he'd never outrun these two.

He only hoped that they'd listen to reason. But when they both rugby-tackled him to the ground and slapped cuffs on him without asking his side of the story, he thought that they might not.

Rick sighed inwardly. This was going to mean more trouble. He could see the headline in the local paper now: LAPDANCING AND DOGGING PERVERT ARRESTED FOR OBSCENE OFFENCE AT SEX SHOP. They'd love it. How was he going to explain *this* one to Juliet? There were only so many times that she'd believe he was the innocent and injured party.

He took a deep, calming breath, listening as one of the policemen read him his rights. What was happening to him when he couldn't even drink a cup of coffee without getting arrested?

Chapter 45

Una knocks back her skinny latte in double-quick time. She's been sparkly and entertaining company and, I admit to myself, is much more suited to Steven than I am. He laughed at all of her outrageous tales and jokes while my friend got more and more flirty. Juliet Joyce, the Classic Beige gooseberry.

'Have to dash,' Una says breathlessly as she finishes another story. 'I'll leave you two lovebirds to it.'

'We're not lovebirds,' I hiss to her. 'And we were supposed to be going out for pizza.'

'Steven can take you to dinner,' she offers on behalf of my old friend. 'I'm sure he's not busy.'

'Neither are you,' I remind her.

'Got a date with Tex on the internet.' She winks at me and kisses me on the cheek. 'One day I'll get a real boyfriend.'

Una kisses Steven too. 'Ta-ta!'

And then she trots off. Steven laughs as she leaves. 'She's a lot of fun.'

My friend has abandoned us in a new coffee shop in the Theatre District just across the street from the shopping centre. It's busy and I check round to see that none of my neighbours are in here, but no one's taking any notice of us.

'I didn't set that up on purpose with her,' he assures me.

'You might as well have done.'

'Now that we're here,' he segues smoothly, 'we could have dinner.

I just came up to the shopping centre to buy a few things to make Mother more comfortable. I've no pressing plans.'

'I should get back.' It's one thing having a quiet lunch with Steven, but quite another sneaking behind Rick's back to have dinner with him. That wouldn't be right. 'My husband will be expecting me.'

'Your husband will be expecting you to have dinner with Una.'

'And now I'm not.'

'But you're all dressed up with nowhere to go.'

'I'm not dressed up. I just have posh make-up on.'

'Shame to waste it,' he observes. 'We could go somewhere out of town.'

'Steven,' I say, 'I'm not sure that I can cope with this sneaking around. I don't like it.'

'Why haven't you told Rick about me?'

'It's difficult. With all the things that I've had to deal with recently, we haven't had time to sit and talk about you.' I realise that may not strictly be true, but Steven doesn't need to know my reasons for keeping this to myself. I'm not even sure that *I* understand them.

'I was out of my mind with worry about you yesterday,' Steven admits. 'It was even worse not being able to be there for you or to even speak to you openly on the phone. I realise that I must have called at a bad time.'

'Well,' I say, 'luckily Tom is OK and he realises now how stupid he's been, but he did have us all worried.'

Steven takes my hands and I feel too polite to pull them away. 'I sense that you're having a difficult time at home.'

I laugh. 'That's what families are all about. A few nice bits with lots of difficulty in between.'

'It doesn't have to be like that,' he tells me. 'I could take you away from all this.'

'Isn't that a line from a film?'

'I don't know,' Steven says earnestly, 'but even if it is, I mean it sincerely.'

I think if he could drop to one knee then he would when he says, 'I know I don't deserve a second chance, Juliet, but I'd really like one.'

'Oh, Steven. This is fairytale stuff. I'm a married woman with responsibilities.' Way too many of them, I think. 'Even if I wanted to I couldn't just waltz off into the sunset with you. It would create a lot more problems than it solved.'

'We could overcome anything. Together.'

I want to throw my head back and laugh. How easy Steven makes it sound! Ripping two lives apart and rebuilding a new one. At our age!

'I could never do that,' I say. 'I could never leave Rick. It would kill him. And he's done nothing wrong. He's been a good, reliable and hardworking husband.'

My coffee is now cold, but I finish it anyway. 'I think it would be better if you didn't come into the library again. We've mended our bridges. That's as far as it should go. We're old friends, nothing more.'

'I wish that you could feel the same way as I do.'

'Steven, I loved you so much and I really don't want to tap into those emotions again because that would make life really, really hard for me. So if you do love me, you'll understand that and you'll just let me walk out of here and not contact me again.'

His handsome face is anguished and, do you know, I want to reach out and touch his cheek, to stroke the pain away. 'I don't believe that you don't care.'

'You have to,' I say. 'It's the sensible thing to do.'

'Love isn't always about being sensible.'

'And love isn't always about passion and excitement either. It's about commitment and endurance.' My eyes fill with tears and I bite them down. 'I loved you once, Steven. I loved you so much. Please don't make me do it again.'

Then I stand up and, making my legs go one in front of the other, I leave Steven behind.

Chapter 46

No one was at home when Rick arrived back from the police station. He was getting to be a regular down there. More's the pity. Soon he'd be on first-name terms with the Desk Sergeant and they'd be sending him Christmas cards. Or maybe not.

He was glad to have some time to himself. It was becoming a rare event in this household. Only Buster was there to greet him and there were no unseemly puddles on the floor, so someone must have taken him walkies. Perhaps Rita had done it before disappearing with her latest Meals for One boyfriend.

Maybe he'd take the time to have a nice long shower, wash the all-pervading smell of cappuccino out of his crotch. This time it seemed he'd get off without any kind of prosecution – which he was pleased about, particularly as he hadn't done anything to warrant it. Unless putting your lid too tightly on your coffee became a criminal offence. And, with this government, that wouldn't entirely be a surprise. The hysterical woman with the handbag had agreed not to press charges if he agreed not to press charges for her assaulting him with said handbag. It seemed like a deal to him.

He wondered whether he could avoid having to tell Juliet at all. If he hadn't been charged or anything like that, was she ever likely to find out? Honesty might be the best policy, but he was skating on very thin ice at the moment after the last two incidents. Could he risk a third coming out? Surely Juliet would understand.

But sometimes a hat trick was a good thing and sometimes it was bad, bad news. This was a hat trick of the latter variety.

Rick went upstairs to the bedroom to undress, peeling off his stained trousers and his coffee-splattered shirt with the ruined cuffs. It was a shame the shirt and trousers were his favourites as he was tempted to throw them straight in the bin to try to eradicate any memory of the unfortunate cappuccino/sex shop incident. And, to be absolutely certain, he was never going to walk down that part of the shopping centre again. Every time he saw lacy lingerie in a shop window from now on, he was just going to close his eyes and move on by just as quickly as he could.

Slipping on his dressing-gown, Rick grimaced as he remembered that only the other day, Rita's aging paramour, Arnold or whatever his name was, had been parading himself in it. He ought to have given her gnomes a good kicking for that as a small but satisfying revenge. He still could.

'Yuk,' Rick said to himself as he reluctantly fed his arms into the sleeves. That would be another one for the washing basket.

In the bathroom, he locked the door and turned on the shower to let the water get hot: another thing that needed upgrading in this house. Somewhere hidden in the back of the bathroom cabinet was some luxury shower gel that Juliet tried to keep from Chloe. Rick felt he deserved a bit of pampering after his traumatic experience and he was sure that Juliet wouldn't begrudge him a little drop.

There was a day, long gone, when he used to like to sing in the shower, throw his head back and tickle his tonsils with a tune just for the sheer joy of it. Why was it that he could no longer summon the energy for a shower serenade?

Rooting in the cupboard, he sorted through the mish-mash of bottles, past spare toilet rolls and the various potions and lotions in search of the shower gel. And then he saw something that he hadn't quite expected to see in there. Right at the back, in the far recesses, just short of the cobweb and the slight damp patch, there was a pregnancy test. It was in a pink and blue box and was called *Maybe Baby*. He pulled it out, handling it as if it was an unexploded bomb.

Rick sat on the toilet, seat down, and examined his find. It was clear that it had been opened. The wrapper had gone and the box was a little bit ripped where the contents had been pulled out. He too opened the box and slid out the contents. It was obvious that the test had been used and he tried not to think that it had been wee-ed on. There was the result, clear as day. Weren't these things supposed to be accurate? Rick could feel his heart beating hard in his chest and his mouth had gone suddenly dry.

He checked the pregnancy test once more. No ambiguity there. Not Maybe Baby, but Definitely Baby. It looked like he was going to become a daddy again.

Chapter 47

I get a taxi home from the city centre, cringing at the cost as I pay the driver. It serves me right, I should have left with Una as planned instead of lingering with Steven Aubrey in the coffee-shop.

In the house Rick is sitting at the kitchen table, looking depressed.

'Hello, love,' I say, as I make a beeline straight for the kettle. 'Bad day?'

My husband looks up at me, eyes red-rimmed, and folds his arms in front of him. 'Is there something that you'd like to tell me?'

Instantly, I feel my face flush beneath my shiny new Classic Beige make-up. The new look that Rick hasn't even noticed. I stall for time. 'About what?'

My mind races. Has someone told him that Steven is back in town? Have we been spotted having our cosy lunches together? Was I seen at Watermill House? Or has someone just spied us at the shopping centre? Whatever has happened, Rick's face bears a bleak expression. My heart is pounding in my chest.

Rick unfolds his arms and on the table is a pregnancy test.

'What are you doing with that?'

'I could ask you the same thing, Juliet!'

'Where did you get it?'

'I found it hidden in the back of the bathroom cabinet.'

Not hidden very well then, I think.

'Why didn't you tell me?' my husband asks. 'I had no idea.'

Neither did I. Flopping down in the chair opposite Rick, I put my head in my hands.

'When's it due?' Rick asks.

'I don't know,' I admit with a sigh.

'When were you planning to tell me?' Rick's voice is anguished. 'Have you been to the doctor yet?'

'Me?' My head shoots up at that. I point at the pregnancy test that my husband's guarding. 'You think this is *mine?*'

'Who else would need one?'

'Oh, Rick.' There's only one person that this can belong to. 'This isn't mine. When did we last make love? The baby would have to be an immaculate conception.' I put my hand over his and give my husband a sympathetic look. 'This is Chloe's.'

At that Rick pulls in a sharp intake of breath.

'It isn't me who's pregnant,' I say. 'It's our daughter.'

'She can't be pregnant,' Rick argues. 'She hasn't even got a boyfriend. And there was certainly no evidence of a bump when I saw her in,' his face works with anguish, 'in the nuddy at the lapdancing club.'

My shoulders sag and, instantly, he looks like he regrets bringing that up. Perhaps he wishes now that our daughter was a lapdancer rather than a single mum-to-be.

'Well,' I reiterate, 'it certainly isn't mine. So unless my mother did go for IVF when we weren't looking, then there's only one person's it can be.'

'Oh God,' Rick says. 'Not my little girl?'

I nod in confirmation.

'She's at university,' her shell-shocked father continues. 'What's she going to do? What are *we* going to do?'

'I honestly don't know.' I'm feeling way too calm about this. Shouldn't I be ranting and raving? Shouldn't I be throwing my hands in the air? Shouldn't I be weeping into my handkerchief? Instead, I just feel a deep sense of disappointment. My child is a contemporary woman with all the advantages that entails – shouldn't she have known better than to let this happen to her?

'We'll have to talk to her about it,' I advise. 'We might be jumping the gun. You never know, it could be a mistake. Let's wait until we hear Chloe's side of the story.'

'How could she?' Rick sounds distraught, clearly not enamoured by my plea for rational thinking. 'How could she do this to us, to herself?'

Standing up, I say, 'I'd better put that kettle on.'

'And text your daughter,' Rick says snappily.

Now she's *my* daughter.

'Tell her that her presence is required at home. Immediately.'

Picking up my phone, I write a text requesting that my daughter comes home right away. A minute later my phone buzzes with a return message. *What now?* Chloe wants to know, but I think that's best left unsaid until she gets here.

'The thing I really can't forgive her for,' Rick says, 'is not the fact that she's wasting her life, nor that she's not in a settled relationship. It's not even that she didn't tell us about this, it's the fact that at the tender age of forty-five she's making me a grandad.' He hangs his head. 'That's cruel beyond belief.'

That makes me an impending grandma too and, like Rick, I don't think I'm ready for that either.

Chapter 48

Chloe is crying. We've decamped to the living room. Thankfully, both my mother and my son are nowhere to be seen. Though I dread to think what they're doing.

My daughter is sitting on the sofa and I'm next to her, trying to give some comfort. Buster is snuggled up against her on the other side, looking worried. Rick is pacing the floor, winding us both up.

'I can't get rid of it,' she sobs. 'But how can I keep it?'

'We'll sort something out,' I say, patting her back. 'Don't worry.'

'Oh no,' Rick says sarcastically, 'don't worry. We'll do enough worrying for all of us.'

'Rick, that's not helping.'

'Do you know who the father is?' my husband asks. 'Or are there several candidates?'

'Mum . . .' She turns pleading eyes to me.

'Rick . . .'

'We have to know,' he points out. 'He has to take some responsibility.'

My mind goes back twenty-five years to when we were in much the same situation. It's as if the years peel away. I remember how dreadful it was. How alone I felt, how terrified, how disapproving my mother was, how fingers pointed at me in the street. But times were different then. There's no stigma these days to having a baby while you're single. Rick and I might have been pushed into marriage, but I won't do that to Chloe. God only knows, she wouldn't let me anyway. My daughter is nowhere near as malleable as I was at her age. And I don't think that's a bad thing. If she doesn't want to be involved with the father then I'll support her in that decision too. I want this to be a positive experience for her because no one did that for me.

'Do you know who the father is?' I broach it more gently than my husband.

Chloe nods. 'I think so.'

My daughter 'thinks so'. I close my eyes momentarily. That doesn't sound like a great start. Perhaps Rick was right and there is more than one contender. 'Do you love him?'

My daughter nods again and tries a smile. 'He's someone I've been seeing at uni.'

'*Seeing*?' Rick lets out a Victorian-sounding *pah*! 'It sounds as if you've been doing a lot more than *seeing* him.'

Renewed sobbing from Chloe.

'Rick,' I say calmly, 'can I have a minute with you in the kitchen, please?'

I march out and my husband follows me. In the kitchen, I turn on him.

'Stop this,' I tell him. 'Stop this now. Chloe's pregnant. It's done. Now we have to sort out how we're going to help.'

Rick goes to open his mouth, but I hold up a hand.

'Don't you remember how frightened we were when the same thing happened to us? Is your memory so bad? It was awful, Rick. We had no idea what to do or who to turn to. By some miracle, we managed. But those first few years were hell. They were nothing but struggle.'

'That was different,' Rick says, when I let him get a word in edgeways.

'No, it wasn't. I won't have my daughter go through the same thing. We all make mistakes.' And I know it's a low shot, but I add, 'You should know that more than anyone.'

'I'm sorry,' Rick says. He comes and wraps his arms around me.

'I'm just so scared for her. I thought her life was all mapped out – and now this.'

'We can't control someone else's life. She's a big girl. All we can do is support her decisions even though they might not be the ones we'd choose for her.'

'What shall I do?' my husband asks.

'Go in there and hug her. Tell her that you love her and that we'll support her.' I give him a nudge towards the door.

'I do love her,' Rick says, tears in his eyes. 'I love you too.'

'And I love you.'

'I still don't want to be a grandad,' he says.

'You'll adore it,' I assure him.

'I'm not so sure. But you're probably right.'

I take a second by myself before I follow Rick. The truth is that this baby is going to take some coming-to-terms-with for all of us.

Chapter 49

Rick lay in bed, hands behind his head, staring at the ceiling. This room, like the rest of the house, needed a coat of paint. Moments later, Juliet came in from the bathroom and slipped into bed next to him. Her arm curled round his waist and she inched into his side.

'I think I heard voices in my mum's room. Do you think she's sneaked in another bloke?'

'God forbid.'

'It might be Arnold again.'

'He's not wearing my dressing-gown,' Rick growled.

They nestled together and lay in silence.

'You OK?' Juliet asked.

He nodded. 'Makes you think though, doesn't it?'

'What?' she murmured.

'All this. I'm forty-five, you think you've got masses of time left to achieve all the things you want to do, go to the places you want to see. Something like this makes you realise that you haven't.'

'You're not going to be rushing to read the obituaries again?'

'Might well do,' he admitted.

His wife nudged him in the ribs. 'I don't think it will be as bad as you're expecting.'

'It could be worse,' Rick pointed out.

'It could have been me who was pregnant,' Juliet reminded him. 'How suicidal would you be feeling about that?'

'I don't want any more children,' he admitted. 'Hal and I had a long talk about it the other day. His young lady,' and he used that term loosely, 'apparently, she wants a baby. Hal's only forty and he's dead against it. I wouldn't want that to happen to us. We've done our bit.'

It was bad enough thinking that there might be a baby in the house that wasn't entirely his responsibility. How would it be if Juliet got pregnant now too? A grandma and a new mum at the same time. It wasn't beyond the realms of possibility these days, but that was too freaky.

'I should have a vasectomy,' Rick said.

'You've always been dead set against it.'

'I know, but this has made me realise that I absolutely don't want to go down the baby route again. Let's close that particular door very firmly.'

'If you're sure,' Juliet said. 'We've managed all right all these years.'

'But these "change" babies have a habit of sneaking in.'

'Thanks for that.' He felt Juliet stiffen.

'I'm not suggesting that you're past it,' Rick said hastily. 'Quite the opposite. What if we had a little accident? Where would that leave us?'

'To have a baby, we'd have to be having a sex-life.'

Rick sighed. Then they both froze as a rhythmic thumping came from his mother-in-law's room next door.

'Oh no,' Juliet said. 'That's not what I think it is?'

'Shall I bang on the wall?'

'You'll do no such thing. I don't want her to know that we can hear her *at it*.'

'But we can.'

'I'm going to have to get some earplugs,' his wife huffed. 'This is beyond unbearable.' Then she flicked off her bedside light, turned her back on him and folded her pillow round her head.

Rick studied the ceiling again, trying to block out the pumping noises and the occasional groan. Juliet was right. This was impossible. It seemed as if they were the only people in this household who weren't getting any action.

Chapter 50

'What am I going to do, Una?' My friend is following me round the shelves as I select my books for this morning's Toddler's Tale Time.

'A grandma?' she says, puffing out a surprised breath. 'I'm not sure whether to offer you congratulations or commiserations.'

I look over my shoulder. 'Me neither.'

'But you love kids.'

'Just because I enjoy doing the children's storytime in the library, it doesn't mean that I want my twenty-year-old daughter to abandon her university course to have one.'

'No,' my friend says. 'I can see how that would be a little different.'

'What would you do if it was Danielle?'

'Shoot her,' Una says.

'Don't think I haven't considered it. There are moments when I think that would be the easy option.'

I pull my favourite books off the shelves, the ones that my regular kiddies like the best too. *Ten in the Den, I Know An Old Lady, I Went to the Zoopermarket.*

'How did it go last night?' Una wants to know.

'With the make-over?' My friend hasn't commented on my attempts to recreate the Classic Beige look with thirty-year-old Rimmel remnants.

'No. With Steven.'

'That's it,' I say. 'I can't sneak around with him. I won't do it.

I've told him not to contact me again.' Today, I really could do with sitting in his calm garden, drinking chilled wine, being flattered and fussed over. I block the thought out. It's not going to happen. I have to make sure that it doesn't.

'I knew that I shouldn't have left you two alone,' she tuts.

Slipping my books into the canvas bag I reserve for the purpose, I take up my position on the red stool in the corner. This little nook is all painted in primary colours to make the area attractive for the kids and it's one of my favourite parts of the library. Only five minutes to go and I need to compose myself. Already a few of the children and their parents are arriving.

'Later,' she says, wagging a finger at me. Then Una scuttles off to the desk to take back the books that our mums borrowed last week.

The storytelling area is in the back of the library, away from the draughts of the door. I have my red stool and there's a big rug in front of it with a smiley dinosaur woven into the brightly-coloured pile which the children love.

As the toddlers start to gather, I pull on my glove puppet with the monkey fingers and wiggle them. Already a row of children have been plonked down in front of me and they giggle appreciatively. Just wait five minutes and they'll all be fidgeting or crying.

We always start with a song. 'What do you want to sing today?'

'Twinkle, Twinkle' is proposed by Bea, a little girl in the front row. She's all lisps and smiles with blonde curly hair cascading down her back. Today she's dressed all in pink with flashing lights on her trainers. Chloe was just like her at that age. I can hardly believe now that she's expecting a child of her own. This is going to take some time to absorb.

I normally have about fifteen to twenty regulars. They're dumped on the rug by their mums who then, with very few exceptions, gossip in stage whispers on the sidelines. Sometimes I have to shout to make myself heard above the noise.

I move on to singing 'The Elephant Went Over the Mountain'

with my charges. Will Chloe bring her baby in here, I wonder. Will she be the sort of mum who's keen to do things with her child?

Then I start the stories, accompanied on my part by exciting voices and actions and the monkey-glove puppet. And accompanied, on the children's part, by a series of burps and farts and yawns. Halfway through I usually lose a couple to sleep.

My own mother was terrible with both of my children. She'd never babysit for us – not a chance. Not that Rick and I had the money to go out anywhere. All she did was criticise the way that I brought them up. Whenever I took them to her house, she'd make them sit still and not make a sound. I vow at that moment that I'm going to be the world's best grandma and shower Chloe's baby with love and affection.

I'm competing with the mothers' gossip, my voice having to get louder and louder to be heard above them, so we all sing another song. This time we tackle 'Five Little Monkeys Jumping on the Bed' with varying degrees of success.

Like the parents, there are children that you warm to and children who you feel will grow up to be career criminals and crooked accountants. I wonder what the future will hold for our new little life?

Sometimes it's hard to tell who are the mums and who are the grannies. Will people look at me and think that when I'm with Chloe's baby? We've mums here who are no more than children themselves, pushing prams at the age of fifteen and sixteen, and I suppose I should be grateful that, at least, Chloe is a bit more mature than that. We've an older mother with twins and one with triplets – hard-won babies from gruelling courses of IVF. Again, Chloe has been spared that. Leaving it so late to find the right man and settle down so often means that something which should be the most natural thing in the world becomes a round of hideous drugs and medical check-ups.

Shaking these thoughts from my mind, I launch into our final song. Wherever would we be without 'The Wheels on the Bus?' And that's the end of Toddler's Tale Time for another week.

I give out stickers – pink for the girls, blue for the boys – that say I ♥TO READ. For a change I sometimes have ones that proclaim I ♥MY LIBRARY. Then I put away the books and the monkey glove puppet. The mothers reluctantly wrap up their gossip and load their children into their pushchairs. One little girl comes up and says thank you to me. She's the only one who does so every week. The rest are already on their way. For some stupid reason my eyes fill with tears. That's kids for you, I think, ungrateful little buggers.

Chapter 51

Tonight we're going to meet my father's new boyfriend. Oh, I can hardly bring myself to say those words. Even more of a stunner is that they've invited us to go to Wagamama. Now my dad's eating noodles and using chopsticks. The world has truly gone mad. My mother would faint if she knew. In fact, she'd be more shocked that he was eating oriental food than she would be if she knew of his new sexual orientation.

I still haven't broached the subject with her. But then she's so wrapped up in the aging Arnold and the Meals for One pick-up aisle that she doesn't ever think to ask about my father's welfare. He could be rotting away in his cable-knit cardigan in their old living room for all she cares.

Wagamama is busy and we find my dad and Samuel already waiting for us at one of the communal wooden benches. I'm not sure that this is my style of dining either and Rick definitely didn't want to come here. My husband prefers food that you can eat with a knife and fork. Food that doesn't make slurping sounds.

When I see my dad my heart melts though. He looks so well and is done up in his best shirt – open at the neck! This is the man who wears a tie to mow his lawn. This is the first time I've seen my father do casual in his entire life. And I have to say that it suits him. Samuel is sitting next to him and I don't look too closely, but I swear that they're holding hands underneath the table. I still find it hard to believe that my dad, who has harboured a life-long aversion to 'nancy boys', has become one himself.

'Hello, love,' he says.

'Dad. Samuel.'

I lean across the table and kiss Dad on the cheek, then do the same to Samuel, who flushes. Rick shakes their hands in a particularly manly fashion. We order drinks and I note that my dad has a glass of red wine when he's been a lifelong half a bitter man.

When our food comes, my dad struggles a bit to use the chopsticks.

'Here, Francis. Let me help you, love.' And Samuel leans forward to help him, putting the little wooden sticks into my father's old, bent hands and they giggle together like teenagers.

A lump comes to my throat and I can't help but smile at them. Even Rick relaxes.

'We're thinking of taking a little trip to Italy,' Dad tells me as he slurps his noodles noisily. 'Samuel likes nothing better than to lose himself in Florence.'

Samuel the bookseller smiles his agreement.

I kick Rick under the table in case he thinks of making a joke about that.

'Italy?' I say.

They both nod in confirmation. Again, this is my father who has never, ever been out of this country – unless you count the Isle of Wight. He never liked to venture to foreign climes because they were full of foreigners who ate foreign food. Now look at him.

'I don't think that you've got a passport, Dad.'

'Samuel has filled the form in for me,' he tells me.

Good for Samuel. We tried for years to get my dad to venture further than Eastbourne without success. I'd like to know his secret. And then I think that I wouldn't.

'I'll organise it all, Francis,' Samuel assures him. 'You don't need to worry about a thing.'

My dad beams with pride.

I wonder how different a person my father would have been if he'd married a different woman. Has my mother kept him down all these years? They were both growing old together and had become so set in their ways, so niggardly, so small-minded. Now he's happy and eager to grasp the new world he's discovered is out there. Is this the person he's always been inside? Has it taken a slightly chubby, pleasant gay man to make my dad realise who he really is?

They were the generation who stuck to their marriages through thick and thin. I wonder whether that was the right thing to do. Would Rick and I have turned out to be different people if we hadn't stayed together all these years? Would my husband have fulfilled his dream to travel? Would I have discovered whether I had a dream at all? I toy with my noodles and try to keep my smile in place despite my dark, unsettling thoughts while Samuel tells me what kind of books he prefers to read.

I look at my husband. What if I'd been brave enough to have a baby on my own instead of being rushed into marriage with a man I barely knew? Would I be a different woman now?

'The thing is,' my dad says, 'Samuel and I want to move in together.'

I gasp at the same time as I swallow a noodle, which then goes down the wrong way. I cough and cough and cough until, eventually, Rick comes to the rescue and bangs me on the back. Other diners look in our direction. The people on our communal bench move away from me.

'Juliet,' Dad says in a lowered voice. 'Don't show us up.'

Don't show us up! I'm here with my seventy-two-year-old dad and his new boyfriend who've just announced that they're planning to shack up together and *I'm* the one showing us up?

'You're going to have to tell Mum about this,' I say hoarsely, when I've drunk two glasses of water to clear my throat and I've found the power of speech again.

'I will,' he says cagily. 'Just not yet.'

No, I think. He'll put that one off as long as he possibly can. I know I would. And when he does tell her, I don't want to be anywhere in the vicinity.

Chapter 52

Rick turned over in bed. They'd had a lot to drink tonight with Frank and Samuel, and he knew that he'd suffer for it in the morning. But, odd as the circumstances were, it was good to see the old boy happy again. Happier than he'd ever been, in fact.

He heard the bedroom door creak and footsteps tip-toe across the floor. Unusually, Juliet had put a fair bit of booze away too – no wonder that she was having to get up in the night. But then it was Saturday tomorrow and she had no work to worry about, unlike himself who was stacked to the roof with outstanding jobs and would be putting in a full day. Rick smiled to himself. His wife plumped down on the bed next to him and gave him a nudge as she shifted down.

'Get on your own side,' Rick mumbled sleepily. What on earth was she doing on his bit of the bed? They'd had their allotted sides for twenty-five years. How could she forget now? He smiled to himself. Juliet must have been more tiddly than he thought. Obligingly, he shuffled further into the bed.

His wife snuggled up next to him, twining her arms around him. Her hands roved over his body, hot and eager. Rick smiled again. Definitely three sheets to the wind. He felt her breath on his neck and was surprised when she nipped it gently. That was a bit saucy for Juliet. She hadn't done that sort of thing in years. Then her body pressed against the full length of his, wriggling against him.

Very nice. He'd be taking her to Wagamama again if this was the effect it had on her. Rick reached back and stroked her thigh. No nightie! Very sexy.

Turning towards her, he opened his eyes dreamily. Another pair of eyes looked into his. Even in the darkness he knew that they were the wrong eyes. 'Aargh!' he shouted out, back-pedalling in the bed. 'Who the hell are you?'

The woman sat bolt upright. 'Who are you?'

'I live here,' Rick said, somewhat unnecessarily.

By now Juliet was awake. Rick noted that his wife was still firmly ensconced in her nightdress. She too sat up in bed and flicked on the bedside light. 'Rick?'

In the glare of light, it was quite clear that this woman was not his wife of twenty-five years. She was petite, dark and possibly foreign. Rick blushed to his thinning hair roots to think of how his body had responded to her. But if someone climbed into your bed in the middle of the night when you were half-asleep then it was an easy mistake to make. That was his defence, anyway, should Juliet try to interrogate him.

He turned to his wife in panic. 'This is not my fault. I don't know who she is!'

'Sorry, sorry,' the woman said. 'Big mistake.' She was stark naked and trying to hide behind the duvet cover. It would be fair to assume that she wasn't here to burgle them. 'So sorry.'

'What are you doing here?' Juliet demanded.

The woman smiled sheepishly. 'I'm Silva,' she said. 'I was looking for Tom's room. I must have taken the wrong turn from the bathroom.'

'Tom's room?' Rick and Juliet exchanged a glance.

Silva giggled nervously. 'If you could just point me in the right direction . . .'

'Back down the hall, third door on the right,' Rick instructed.

'Thank you very much,' she said. 'You must be Tom's parents.'

'Yes,' Rick said, as if they were meeting at a cocktail party. 'This is my wife, Juliet. Tom's mum. And I'm his dad, Rick.'

The woman smiled at them again. 'Nice to meet you. I've heard a lot about you.'

They, on the contrary, had heard nothing about her.

Then there was a moment when none of them knew what to do.

'I have to go,' Silva said and, giving them a hint, she looked down at her nakedness beneath the duvet.

'Oh, yes,' Rick said. 'Of course. We'll turn the light out and close our eyes.'

'Thank you,' the woman said. 'I hope to meet you again one day.'

With more clothes on, Rick presumed.

Juliet snapped off the light. Rick closed his eyes and assumed that his wife did the same thing. He heard Silva's feet pitter-patter across the carpet, but he wasn't even tempted to look. The door closed softly behind her.

Both he and his wife opened their eyes. 'Was that the girlfriend of our son who not two days ago was suicidal and gay?'

'Yes,' Juliet muttered. 'That's the one.'

'Bloody hell,' Rick complained. 'What's he doing with a fit bird in his room?'

'I think we can both make a good guess at that,' Juliet grumbled.

'I hope that next week he doesn't bring a sheep home.'

Juliet tutted. 'Let's just go back to sleep.'

'I'm wide awake now,' Rick pointed out. 'It's a bit of a shock when a strange naked woman gets into bed with you.'

'I can imagine.'

He inched towards his wife. 'Don't suppose that you fancy a cuddle?'

'No,' Juliet snapped. 'Just go to sleep.'

Rick sighed and turned onto his back. The only thing that was getting laid in his life was laminate flooring.

Chapter 53

Rick was up and gone to work by the time I woke up this morning. Which was just as well. I have a thumping headache due to the amount of wine we drank with my dad and Samuel, and I'm tired and grumpy due to our disturbed night with Tom's girlfriend trying to mount my husband in our marital bed. Why can't our family life just be quiet and simple? Why do I feel like I'm living in an episode of *The Simpsons*?

When I got up, I gave Buster a good, long walk to try to compensate him for the terrible abuse on the walkies front that he suffers during the week. I wanted to clear my head too, but failed. Now I'm out in the garden, having left Chloe at the kitchen table, nibbling on dry toast and looking green around the gills. Even greener than I am.

I don't get enough time to spend out here. We have a large garden mainly laid to lawn, a hangover from when the kids were small and we had to have room for them to kick a ball around. Now we could do something more exciting, more adult with the space – create an area for entertaining, build in a barbecue – but we don't. It's been a long, hot summer for a change and all my herbaceous borders are looking dry and thirsty. There's not a hosepipe ban in place – not yet – but I'm trying to do my bit for conservation and use water only for topping up the pond and collecting rain from the meagre showers in our two water butts to give to the flowers. Rick isn't a natural gardener. It's not a love we share.

The only time he's happy out here is if he's wielding a chainsaw or has a hedgecutter in his hand.

Buster mooches around, marking his territory, enjoying rediscovering some of the toys that have been lost or forgotten under the bushes. After throwing some food into the pond for the fish, I sit on the wooden bench we bought cheap at B&Q and watch them as they come to the surface to feed, greedy mouths sucking at the little pellets. We have one fish who likes to throw himself out of the pond and lies flapping on the grass until someone rescues him – usually me. It's a good job that we have an amenable dog rather than a cat with honed hunting instincts otherwise the fish wouldn't have lasted this long.

I haven't heard anything from Steven since Thursday night and I guess I shouldn't be surprised at that. Perversely, on one hand I'm pleased that he's decided to drop this silly infatuation with recreating the past and, on the other hand, I'm rather disappointed that he gave up so easily. Perhaps I wasn't worthy of pursuit after all.

While I'm sitting there, staring into space, Tom comes shuffling out barefooted, mug of tea in his hand.

'Hi, Mum.' He sits down next to me and scratches at his messy hair. There's a whiff of the pheromones about him, but when he looks like this I can't imagine what anyone would see in him – man, woman or beast. 'Sorry about last night.'

'Your poor father was terrified.'

'Dad makes a fuss over nothing.'

'A naked woman getting into bed with you in the middle of the night isn't "nothing", Tom,' I chide. 'Plus, I thought that you and women were a thing of the past.'

My son shrugs. 'I've never met a woman like Silva,' he says wistfully. 'This is the real deal, Mum.'

'You haven't known her for five minutes and you did say that about Gabe not three weeks or so ago too.'

'Now I've found what I'm looking for.'

'Oh, Tom,' I say, stroking my boy's hair. 'You're young and should be carefree. Don't think of tying yourself down yet. Have some fun. Find a great career.'

'I'm thinking of photography.'

The only photos I've ever seen Tom take are on his mobile phone of his friends drinking. Not sure how much call there'll be for that out in the big, wide world.

'Anyway,' he says, 'I thought you and Dad would be all for me settling down. You were married younger than I am now.'

'I know. But times were different then. That's what you did. We didn't think to question it. Your generation can do what you like.' I dig him in the ribs. 'You can be gay one week, straight the next.'

He has the grace to laugh at that.

'Silva's great though. She's from Bulgaria. I know that she's older than me . . .'

'Is she?' It was hard to tell in the middle of the night.

'She's thirty-five.'

That's not so old, I think. Ten years' difference isn't too bad.

'And her divorce will be through soon.'

Divorce?

'Her kids are great. You'll love them.'

Kids?

'Her daughter Raya is eight and little Georgi is six.'

'You know, you should be careful about rushing into another relationship. Only a few weeks ago you wanted to marry Gabe. You were suicidal when it was all over. Now you're madly in love with someone else.' Of a different sex, I think.

My son is squirming next to me. He should know by now that Mother is always right.

'This woman is older than you and has children of her own. Are you sure that you really want a ready-made family?'

'I love kids,' Tom insists, though quite where he's had experience of them, I'm not sure. Then he adds, glibly, 'Gabe and I were thinking of adopting a Chinese baby.'

He says it as if they were thinking of buying an old Ford Escort. 'Have you any idea how much responsibility a child is?' I blame

216

all these celebrities who flit round the world gathering their multi-coloured families together like a collection of designer handbags. 'They're not just a lifestyle accessory.'

'I know that,' he bristles.

Chinese baby. I shake my head. Thank goodness *that* one was nipped in the bud. Mind you, I want to tell him not to mention anything about that to Grandma. With her current state of mind, she might decide that she wants one too.

'Do you know that your sister's having a baby?'

'Chloe?'

I nod.

'Really?' Tom digests this information. 'Cool.'

'No,' I say, 'not cool. She'll probably have to give up her university course and come to live back here.'

'It'll be fine,' my son says with a confidence that I wish I could feel. 'You and Dad will sort it.'

And I wonder if that's what our children think of us: no matter how much of a mess they get themselves into, they know that we'll be waiting here to make it all right for them. Is that a good thing, or is it a bad thing? Do they never see us as people who might want lives of our own, who might have unfulfilled ambitions, who might need a little help themselves sometimes?

I stretch as I'm stiffening up through sitting too long on the bench. 'Do you fancy giving your old mum a hand with the gardening for an hour?'

'Can't,' Tom says, as he knocks back his tea. 'Things to do.' And with that, when work threatens, he shoots off.

In answer to my previous questions no, I don't suppose they do.

Chapter 54

My mother is at the kitchen table when I go back inside. She has a green clay beauty mask smeared over her face which is a truly awful sight. Could she not do this in the privacy of the bathroom? It's nearly lunchtime but she's still in her dressing-gown – the inappropriate one – so I can only assume that she had a late breakfast. Now she's sitting painting her nails a vampiric shade of purple, admiring them as she does so. Why can she not shuffle around in slippers and polyester skirts and read *The Lady* magazine like old ladies are supposed to? Why have I been lumbered with this hybrid teen-pensioner?

In the garden, I fiddled about with the borders a bit, but my heart wasn't really into mowing the lawn. I'm hoping that a cup of strong coffee and a few well-aimed digestive biscuits will give me some motivation.

'No Arnold this morning?' I ask.

'He's gone home,' she says, holding out her fingers to blow on them. 'You've just missed him. He was feeling rather tired, so he's going to have a sleep.'

My mother clearly sees no irony in this. I make a coffee, offer my mum one, which she declines, and then join her at the table.

'Heard that Rick found our Chloe pole-vaulting.'

'Pole-dancing, Mum.'

'Oh. I didn't think she was the athletic type.'

From what my husband said, our daughter is far too athletic

for her own good. 'I don't suppose you heard that she's having a baby?'

'No,' my mother says. 'I didn't hear that.' She pauses with the purple paint. 'Pleased?'

'Not especially,' I say. 'I'd love to be a grandmother. One day. Right now I wish she'd finish her university course, have fun, travel the world.'

'All the things you didn't do?'

I nod. 'She's too young to be saddled with a baby.'

'I seem to remember saying the same thing to you.'

'Times were different then.'

My mother shrugs. 'An accident's an accident whenever it happens. All seems the same to me. She'll manage. It's what we women do best. We get on with it. Don't cause a fuss.'

I don't point out to my mum that actually she causes rather a lot of fuss. As I rarely have a heart-to-heart moment with her I don't want to spoil the mood.

'Mum,' I say, 'when did you first realise that you didn't love Dad?'

She doesn't take her eyes off her nails. 'About ten minutes after I married him.'

'No, seriously.'

'I am serious.' Reluctantly, she puts the brush back into her pot of nail polish. 'What's this all about?'

'Nothing.' I try a casual shrug. 'I was just interested.'

'Not thinking that you might have fallen out of love with Rick?'

'Whatever gives you that impression?'

Now it's Mum's turn to shrug. 'He has been behaving like a complete pillock recently . . .'

He wouldn't be the only one, I think.

'. . . thought you might be getting fed up of it.'

I shake my head.

My mother sighs. 'I left your father because he was making me feel catastrophic.'

'Claustrophobic,' I correct.

'I couldn't wait to get out. I'm supposed to be from the

generation who sticks it out through thick and thin. The generation who believe "until death us do part" means just that. Sod that for a lark,' my mum says. 'All I had to look forward to was the grave. Why should you lot have the monopoly on being the easy come, easy go generation?'

'I've never been like that, Mum. Rick and I might have had our ups and downs but we've always ridden the storm. I'm in this for the long haul.'

'Good for you,' she says, but she doesn't sound as if she means it. She can't really think that I should leave Rick, can she?

Well,' she says, 'whoever your father is with now, I wish her every good luck. She's welcome to him.'

I think of Dad and Samuel holding hands and giggling like teenagers. 'You haven't heard any gossip then?' For a place like Stony Stratford, that would be a miracle.

'I did hear some gossip.' My mother leans forward conspiratorially. 'Steven Aubrey's mother is ill and I believe her son's back in town.'

'Really?' I feel myself having a hot flush. That wasn't quite the gossip I'd hinted at.

'I always liked Steven.'

'Was that before or after he jilted me?' I ask before I can stop myself.

'You might have done better if you'd married Steven,' she says.

'That wasn't an option, if you remember.'

'You must have done something to scare him off.' Trust Mum to think that it was all my fault.

'It was a long time ago,' I say, before I'm tempted to tell her a few home truths. 'Anyway, can't stay here chatting. I'd better put some washing in.' And get back into the garden to take out my frustration on the lawnmower.

'I need to wash this mask off,' Mum says, easing herself up. 'Hope it's made me ten years younger.'

Following Mum upstairs, I go into our bedroom, retrieve the laundry basket and take it back to the kitchen. Sorting through

220

the dirty washing I find Rick's favourite trousers and shirt. They're covered in coffee. What has he been doing now? He never mentioned that he'd spilled this all over himself. What a job he's made of it. I'm going to have to get out the Vanish.

In the hall, I hear the local paper being forced through the letterbox and then, eventually, it drops to the mat.

Buster, being a man's best friend, brings it to me. Usually the game is to get it off him before he chews it into a thousand pieces. Today, he drops it at my feet like one of those cute dogs in Pixar films.

I don't know why I read this rubbish. It's just chock-full of adverts these days. There's never anything of interest in it. Unless my husband is on the front page, of course.

Then I pick up the paper. Looks like I spoke too soon. This week it's very interesting indeed. Underneath the heading: LAPDANCING AND DOGGING PERVERT ARRESTED FOR OBSCENE OFFENCE AT SEX SHOP there's a grainy photograph of my dearly beloved looking terrified that seems to have been taken on a mobile phone. He's outside the Ann Summers shop in the city and there's a little old lady hitting him with her handbag.

So Rick is on the front page again. For the third time in as many weeks. Thank goodness my mother didn't see it before me. I can't wait to read this story. What has he been up to now? And why hasn't he told me about it?

I look at the bar of Vanish on the work surface and wonder if this stuff works on husbands.

Chapter 55

Juliet wasn't speaking to him. She'd taken the cappuccino/sex shop incident very badly. Not least because his trousers and shirt were ruined beyond redemption. It was, she said, The Final Straw.

Which was why he hadn't told her about the vasectomy. The waiting list on the NHS was months long and, frankly, after Chloe's shock announcement he couldn't wait until then. There was no way that he could cope with becoming a grandad and a dad at the same time – that would definitely fry his wiring.

Having paid privately, the appointment was for two days later. Mind you, it was, as a result, going to cost him nearly five hundred pounds to emasculate himself. Now he was nervous.

Hal assured him that it would be a doddle. Not that his friend had undergone this procedure, but he had a mate who had, and when Hal had texted him on Rick's behalf, he'd said it had been fine. No worries.

He'd finished work an hour early and, in the waiting room of the private clinic, he flicked through a well-worn gardening magazine while keeping one eye anxiously on the clock. You'd think with the prices they charged in here they might be able to provide a bit of quality reading material or at least something that wasn't three years old. Rick badly needed something to distract him from the finality of his impending operation. *Top Gear* magazine would have been his reading matter of choice. Something chock-full of testosterone, but nothing in danger of giving him a hard-on.

You didn't want that to happen while you were having the snip. It might put the doctor off and he'd cut the wrong bit.

There were two other blokes waiting too who looked as terrified as he did. They were all studiously avoiding making eye-contact. Rick dearly wished that he had discussed this with his wife now, then she'd be here with him holding his hand, uttering soothing words. He'd wanted to, God only knows. But there'd never been the right moment to broach the subject and he was in her bad books again as it was. She might even have had the sense to talk him out of it. Then again, she might not have wanted him to do this . . . and maybe that was the real reason why he hadn't told her of his decision.

Perhaps he should call her now. Come clean. Tell her what he was about to do. He glanced at the sign of a mobile phone with a big red cross on it. Maybe he could nip outside for a minute. She'd be just about to finish work now and could come straight down here and either talk him out of it or hold his hand.

'Mr Richard Joyce.' The nurse stood with her clipboard waiting for him.

Damn. He hoped that she wasn't going to be in on the operation. She was blonde, pretty and young. Why couldn't he have had a raddled old bag of a nurse? Why had someone gone to central casting and ordered a sexy nurse? She gave him a sexy nurse smile.

He stood up, knees shaking, and followed her. Not only was he having second thoughts, but he was having third thoughts. This was rapidly becoming a very bad idea. He and Juliet hardly ever had sex these days. Did their output actually warrant such drastic action?

Too late now. The nurse led him through to a cubicle and instructed him to strip off and put on the surgical gown provided. At his consultation, he'd been told to shave himself 'down below' beforehand, and what a performance that had been at six o'clock in the morning in the bathroom. It's no easy feat shaving your own wedding tackle and he'd blunted two of Juliet's razors. How women did this on a regular basis or willingly, he'd never know.

223

Then the nurse came back for him and led him, like a lamb to the slaughter, through to the small operating theatre.

'Hop on the bed,' she said. Which, being in no position to argue, he did.

Then a woman came through in operating scrubs, her hair covered by a pale blue cap. Despite the outfit, she was even hornier-looking than the nurse. Where did they find these two? The only other place he'd seen this type of nurse was in some of the magazines that Hal had in the back of his van.

'I'm sorry that Mr Wallace is unwell today,' she said to him. 'I'm going to be taking over his list.'

That made Rick feel unwell. A *woman* surgeon? What sane man would let a woman near his favourite friend with a sharp scalpel? Women should be banned from performing vasectomies. It was unnatural.

'OK?' She snapped her gloves more viciously than he would have liked.

A gulp travelled down his throat. 'Fine.'

The operating theatre overlooked the car park and the window blinds were wide open. Couldn't anyone coming here to park their Fiesta or Corsa look right inside and see parts of his anatomy that he'd prefer to keep to himself? They weren't called private parts for nothing. Yet Rick didn't like to mention it in case it made him sound insecure.

The surgeon lifted his gown and felt his testicles. It was hard not to cry out. He felt himself shrivel up – both inside and outside.

'No need to worry, Mr Joyce,' she said in soothing tones. 'I'm just going to give you some local anaesthetic. You'll only feel a little prick.'

And she was quite right, he did.

Chapter 56

Much, much later, Rick was helped off the operating-table and into a wheelchair. Something had not gone according to plan. Not that the lady surgeon had unintentionally slipped with the knife or anything drastic like that, but there'd been a problem with internal bleeding, she'd said. In rather too matter-of-fact a tone for Rick's liking. What it meant was that his testicles were now the size of melons and the colour of the night sky. A particularly dark night.

He'd been told to take two pairs of underpants with him to wear afterwards to support his testicles. Now he felt like he needed possibly sixteen pairs. Or maybe a wheelbarrow like that character from *Viz* magazine, Buster Gonad and His Unfeasibly Large Testicles.

Despite his intention to drive himself home from the operation and break the news to Juliet at some later, more suitable date, preferably over a social glass of wine, it was apparent that she'd have to come out to rescue him. Again. At least this time it wasn't from the police station.

He'd called her, briefly explained the gist of the situation, the revelation of which had been received in stony silence. Now his wife was on her way to collect him. When her little car pulled into the car park, he asked the sexy nurse to wheel him out to meet her.

Juliet's face was dark, set in a mask of disapproval as she came towards him.

'Hello, darling,' he said as brightly as he could manage. 'Thanks for coming out.'

No response. Silently, she helped the sexy nurse to load him into the passenger seat of the car like a helpless baby – a helpless baby with throbbing testicles that were growing in size by the minute. He didn't dare cry out in pain as that would only make the situation worse.

When the nurse had gone, his wife turned to him. The darkness had gone and now she looked like she was going to cry, which made Rick feel even more terrible. 'Why didn't you tell me?'

'I was going to,' Rick said. 'Honestly.'

'We should have discussed it *before* you had it done.'

'I know.' He hung his head. 'But we wouldn't have wanted any more children, would we?'

'We should have talked that through together.'

He didn't like to point out that they hardly had time to exchange two words these days. But he knew that didn't put him in the right. 'I'm sorry.'

'I don't know what's happening to us, Rick. We used to be so close. It was you and me against the world. Now you seem to be on a one-man crusade to destroy us. All these incidents you've been involved in – the dogging, the lapdancing club, the sex shop – they're not like you. And now this.' She wagged a finger at the offending area which was now hurting like stink. Whatever painkillers they'd given him, they just weren't enough.

'I don't know the person you've become.' And it didn't sound as if she liked him very much.

'I'm still me,' Rick insisted.

'But now with a little bit of you missing,' she pointed out. Then she sighed, and it was the most disappointed, weary, frustrated sound he'd ever heard. All that in one small noise. 'Come on, let's get you home.'

And, to exact a small punishment, Juliet drove over every speed bump she could find without slowing down. As a show of contrition, Rick didn't complain once.

Chapter 57

Upstairs in the library, Una and I have a trolley of books each and are pretending to shelve them. I'm clutching Wilbur Smith to my chest. Una has Jeffery Deaver and Tess Gerritsen to make her look as if she's busy.

There's no one else up on this floor yet. It's only just after nine o'clock and the readers of Stony Stratford are not early risers.

'What did you say?' Una wants to know after I tell her my latest news.

'What could I say? It was a done deal by then.'

'Bastard!' she cries.

'Rick's in complete agony,' I tell her, and frankly, there's not a lot of sympathy in my voice. 'He hasn't gone into work today for the first time since I can remember.' My husband is never off sick. Now he's sitting at home, clutching his nether regions and moaning gently to himself. 'How could he do that without telling me?'

'You didn't want any more children, did you?'

'No,' I say. 'I don't know. Possibly. What if something had happened to make me think differently? What if, when Chloe gives birth, it makes me broody again?'

'I think you'll be too busy changing nappies and running round after Chloe to think about being broody,' Una remarks. 'Plus you're forty-five years old. Do you really want to be starting all that business again?'

'My mum's seventy and is talking about having another child.'

'Yes; but your mother's mad.'

That's true too. 'It's just the fact that I was kept completely out of the loop. Has our marriage become so empty that we don't even discuss things as important as that?'

'I suppose it's Rick's equipment to do with as he likes.' I don't mention that Una divorced her husband for less.

'It's a marriage. That's supposed to be joint equipment.' We both laugh at that. 'Oh, Una, what am I going to do with him?' I think the thing that hurts the most is that all the other stupid incidents Rick has been involved in could have been passed off as him being unlucky, in the wrong place at the wrong time – but this vasectomy business, this is Rick's doing and Rick's alone. This can't be blamed on some silly mistake. This was deliberate, intentional and he purposely kept me in the dark about it. It's that I can't forgive him for.

'I take it you've not heard anything from Steven since the other night?'

I shake my head. 'Probably just as well. That's a complication that I can do without right now.'

We slip Wilbur, Jeffery and Tess into their rightful places and then I pick up James Patterson and Ben Elton. Una opts for Martina Cole and Robert Goddard. We continue our chat, safe in the knowledge that Don will never guess we are up here just gossiping.

'I thought I saw you looking longingly at the door yesterday.'

'No,' I say, even though it's a lie. I thought Steven might have popped in just to see how I was. Even though I certainly don't want the complication of having Steven around or sneaking about behind Rick's back – honestly – but for some reason I do miss the attention and, you know, I never realised that I could be so fickle. I shouldn't even be thinking of Steven, but I'm afraid to admit that I am. 'Tell me about Internet Tex instead. That'll cheer me up. Aren't you supposed to be meeting him soon?'

'He sent me through this photograph of him.' Una roots in her pocket. 'I printed it out to show you.'

'Hmm . . .' I say. 'Get a load of *him*.'

Internet Tex is posing without his shirt on, muscles flexed. 'He certainly looks a bit hot.' If a little like a gay pin-up. He's tanned and toned, waxed and oiled.

'I was going to see him next week, but he's had to go out to the Middle East on business.' Una takes the photo back, gives it a kiss. She refolds it and then slips it back into her pocket, giving it a pat for good luck.

'Shame.'

'He's in a real mess,' she tells me. 'Something's happened to his credit card. No one will accept it. I've had to send him my details so that he can settle his hotel bill.'

'What?' Alarm bells ring for me, but clearly not for Una. 'Why can't his company do that?'

'He works for himself.'

'Doesn't he have contacts out there who he can call on?'

'Apparently not,' my friend says.

'What about friends? Why would he ask you?'

'I don't mind helping him out. He said he'll pay me as soon as he's back. It's just a technical hitch.'

'And you trust him?'

Una shrugs. 'He seems sound enough. I've been chatting to him online for a while now. I've had no reason to doubt him so far. He's been as keen as I am to take things slowly.'

'If you're sure.'

'It's just this once,' Una reassures me. 'What do you take me for? I'm not stupid.'

'Be careful, Una.'

Don's head appears at the top of the stairs. 'I'm sure this is all very interesting, ladies, but could I trouble you to do some work today.'

'Sorry, Don,' I say. 'What can we do to make it up to you?'

'Stop stealing my chocolate digestive biscuits.'

That sets Una and me off giggling.

'They say that you should never work with animals and children,'

229

Don mutters as he disappears. 'No one ever mentions middle-aged women.'

'We are *so* not middle-aged!' Una shouts after him.

But we are middle-aged women and as such should have a maturity and wisdom, a peace within ourselves, that somehow seems to be sadly lacking.

Chapter 58

It was three days before Rick's testicles returned to a more normal size and he could walk without looking like John Wayne after a hard day in the saddle. He hadn't been back to work yet and Hal was starting to get bad-tempered about it all, as they were snowed under with jobs. After all, he kept reminding Rick, his mate had had a vasectomy with no problems whatsoever.

Rich had decided that if he could walk down into the town centre and back without feeling like he'd been kicked in the crotch then he was fit enough to go and lay floors tomorrow.

It was a fine, sunny day – just the weather for a walk – and he clipped Buster's lead to his collar so that he could take his faithful friend with him. The dog was about the only person in the Joyce household who was currently speaking to him.

'Come on, Buster, old pal.' And they walked out of Chadwick Close together, trying to skirt past Stacey Lovejoy's house without his neighbour noticing.

If relations between him and Juliet had been better, they could have called into the library to see her, but things were still strained on the domestic harmony front. They'd barely exchanged three civil words since his vasectomy and he'd received scant sympathy for his suffering. It would be a long and rocky road back from this one.

He walked along enjoying the sunshine, not feeling too many twinges in his undercarriage, past Horsefair Green until he reached the High Street. It always pleased him to see that the range of old-fashioned shops were managing to stay open in these difficult times, and he and Juliet shopped here as often as they could. Perhaps he'd get her some of those Belgian chocolates today from the little sweet shop in Stratford Arcade that she liked so much as a peace-offering. Though it might take more than a few well-aimed calories to get back into his wife's good books.

Rick browsed in the charity bookshop, even though he had to tie Buster up outside. Not that he intended to buy a book – with Juliet at the library, there was little point in that – but it was nice to look. Then he popped into the chocolate shop and chose a few of his wife's favourites and a couple that he quite fancied himself. Perhaps he should get some flowers too. But that might be seen as one creep too many.

He pottered further down the High Street. So far, so good in the groin area. Not too much pain. A couple of little twinges, but nothing that he couldn't handle. It was looking like he wouldn't be permanently mutilated which was a blessed relief.

Next he stopped at the newsagents and bought a lottery ticket for tonight's draw. It was a double rollover and worth a stonking twenty million. He was almost tempted to buy two tickets. 'Can you make it a winning ticket, love?' he joked.

Po-faced, the woman muttered, 'No one's ever said that before.'

Normally he wasn't a gambling man – a couple of quid on the lottery draw each week and a bet on the Grand National every year was about as far as it got. And the lottery wasn't really gambling, it was contributing to good causes. Juliet, however, thought it was a complete waste of money. But twenty million! At the moment, even a couple of million would come in very handy. He could buy Tom and Chloe their own houses, a little bungalow for Rita. Then there'd be a round-the-world cruise for him and Juliet for a year or two and they'd wave bye-bye to the lot of them. He slipped the ticket into his pocket wishing for good luck as he did so.

Finally, he thought that he'd treat himself to a coffee at the café in Bull Alley before he headed back to the Close. He planned to have dinner ready for Juliet tonight when she came home – maybe open a decent bottle of wine. Maybe he could bribe her mother and the kids to stay well out of the way. Although there was no chance of romance on the cards tonight, given the current tenderness of his equipment. But it wouldn't hurt to show her that he really did care for her. If he carried on like this he was in danger of losing her, twenty-five years under their belt or not, and he couldn't even bear to think what that would be like. There were times when he felt like just walking away. Didn't everyone? But you only had to look at Hal to realise that it simply wasn't worth it.

He'd loved Juliet from the moment he'd clapped eyes on her. Everyone knew that Steven Aubrey had done the dirty on her and that she'd become something of a recluse since. All he saw was a great-looking girl with a good sense of humour and a vulnerability that tugged at his heart-strings. They'd had their ups and downs, yes, but those had mainly been due to money worries. There'd been a credit crunch in their house for the last twenty-five years, and it was only now that things were starting to get easier for them. Though it was likely that Chloe's new arrival would put the tin hat on that.

Juliet was still a fine woman and he wanted to make sure that she knew that he still loved and appreciated her. He was a lucky bloke and he was well aware of it. He'd be a fool to watch that slip away due to all the stupid things he'd been doing recently.

Decision made. He had a great marriage and he was damn well going to make it to his fortieth wedding anniversary and, if he lasted that long, his fiftieth. It was going to be nothing but a full charm offensive for the next few weeks, or months, however long it took for his wife to regain her faith in him.

Chapter 59

I get home to find my mother at the kitchen table with a face like thunder and crying. It's an odd combination and, as I've had quite a nice day at the library, I'm not sure that I want to find out what the cause of it is.

Rick is also in the kitchen and his face is also bearing its own quota of storm clouds.

'Tell her,' he says, the very second I walk through the door. 'Everyone, *everyone* knows that these are scams!'

'I didn't,' my mother sobs as she glowers.

Hello, Juliet, I say to myself. Had a nice day, love? Everything well in your world? Put your feet up. Let me make you a cuppa. Only Buster seems pleased to see me and wags his tail in appreciation of my entrance even though he's cowering away from the shouting.

Throwing my bag on the floor, I say, 'What now?'

'I thought I'd won.' My mother turns to me. 'How was I to know?'

'Know what?'

'I thought I'd won the Spanish lottery. I got a letter to tell me I had.'

'You and twenty thousand other people.' That's Rick.

'It seemed genuine,' my mum insists. 'They knew my name and everything.'

'And now they know your bank details and *everything*,' my husband snipes.

'Oh, Mum.' I flop down at the table. Something I seem to do a lot of these days. 'You didn't. Please tell me that you didn't.'

'They said I'd won. A million pounds. All I had to do was send my bank details—'

'—including your password,' Rick chips in.

'—and they'd forward it to me.'

'Have you ever bought a ticket for the Spanish lottery?'

'No,' my mother snaps at Rick.

'Maybe that should have given you a hint.'

'There are a lot of very cruel people in the world.' My mother looks pointedly at my husband. 'They shouldn't take advantage of a frail, vulnerable old woman.'

My mother is about as vulnerable as Dr Crippen.

'I've been onto the bank for the last hour,' Rick says. 'I rang them as soon as I found out. The thieves have already withdrawn the money.'

'How much?' I don't know what money my mother has got in her current account. A few hundred pounds, maybe more.

'Eight thousand pounds,' she says weakly.

I'm aghast. 'In your current account?'

'No,' Rick says. 'She gave them the number and password to her savings account.'

'Oh, Mum.' I close my eyes for a moment.

'That's the money for my boob job gone,' she wails miserably.

So every cloud does have a silver lining, I think.

'I've talked to the bank's fraud department. They were actually quite helpful,' Rick tells me. 'They're going to do all they can.'

Putting my arms round my mum, I say, 'Why don't you go and lie down? Don't upset yourself any more. We'll see what the bank can do. All isn't lost yet.'

She allows herself to be helped up from the table and I steer her towards the door. I mouth to Rick, 'Back in a minute.'

I take my mum upstairs and she snivels all the way. 'It'll be all right,' I tell her as I put her in bed.

'You're a good daughter,' she sniffs. 'All things considered.'

Isn't that what's called damning by faint praise? I pull the duvet over her. 'Have a little sleep. You'll feel better in a couple of hours.'

'I hope so,' she mumbles sleepily. 'Arnold's coming to take me out. We're going clubbing in the city.'

From the look on my husband's face as I left him in the kitchen, I think he'd like to do some clubbing of his own.

Shaking my head, I go back downstairs. Rick is stirring a pan on the hob. 'That smells good,' I say with a sigh. 'Special occasion?'

'I thought that we'd have a nice dinner together. Your mother, once again, has managed to take the edge off it.'

'Don't.' Propping myself against a cupboard, I pour out a glass of the wine that Rick's opened. 'What am I going to do with her?'

'We could do with a new patio,' Rick suggests. 'Let's dig it now. We could put her under it.'

'She's my mother.' Though it does sound very tempting.

'She's clinically insane.'

'They say that all women eventually turn into their mothers.'

'Shoot me now,' Rick says.

I laugh.

Rick's eyes meet mine. 'It's good to hear that.'

'There hasn't been much to laugh about recently.'

'I want to change that,' my husband says. 'I want to get back to how we were.' Rick comes to me and slips his arms round my waist. 'I want to make you love me again.'

'I've never stopped loving you.' But I have to admit that I haven't really liked my husband much in the last few weeks. If our marriage is to survive, that has to change too.

Chapter 60

In an all too rare moment of intimacy, Rick and Juliet were curled up together on the couch. Something mellow played on the stereo – Juliet's choice. Not really his taste, since Rick was more of a Van Halen man himself, but even he knew that a bit of 'Jump' was likely to ruin the mood.

They hadn't seen hide nor hair of the children all evening. Chloe was up in her room and Tom had yet to appear from wherever he was. Rita, having finally stopped crying, had gone out with Arnold to who knows where. As long as they were out of the house, he didn't really care where any of them were. Unless, in the case of his darling daughter, it was at a lapdancing club, of course.

'That was a lovely dinner,' Juliet said. He'd made a pasta carbonara – his own sauce with double cream and bacon and lots of garlic. 'I'd forgotten what a good cook you were.'

'I should do it more often.'

'Yes,' she said with a wry smile, 'you should.'

'It's nice to be on our own for once. It doesn't happen enough.'

'I know that having Mum here isn't ideal.'

'It's hell,' Rick told her. 'We always vowed that we wouldn't have our parents living with us. Now it looks like we're going to struggle to get rid of your mother.'

'I feel sorry for her.'

'I don't.' Rick swigged at his wine. 'How can someone be so

stupid as to think that they've won the lottery when they haven't even bought a ticket?'

'You can't expect her to be as streetwise at us,' Juliet reasoned. 'She's seventy. They're the generation that still knew how to trust people.'

Rick sighed. 'Well, let's hope that the bank can do something to sort it out. We've got enough on our plates with Chloe and Tom.'

'It looks like Chloe will have to move back in here with us permanently. I'm not sure that it's worth her returning to university. She'll probably be due just as she's about to take her finals.'

Rick heard himself groan. 'Are we ever going to be on our own?'

'It's not looking likely,' Juliet admitted. 'Not in the foreseeable future.'

'*I* need to win the lottery, never mind your mother.' He checked his pockets, then pulled out the ticket he'd bought that afternoon and waved it at Juliet. 'What time is it? I could be a millionaire right now.'

He glanced at his watch. The mid-week lottery show was just about to start, so he clicked on the television with the remote control. The forty-two-inch plasma screen TV was the only thing that he'd bought for himself in living memory and it was his pride and joy.

Popstar Jamelia appeared on the screen with the cheesy Lotto music playing. The bright logo twirled in the background behind her.

'Stop whatever you're doing and get out those tickets!' Jamelia pointed at the screen. 'We're just about ready to do this week's Lotto draw. So, Alan,' she said to the out-of-vision voice of the lottery, Alan Dedicoat, also known colloquially as 'The Voice of the Balls', 'what's the jackpot this week?'

'The jackpot is an estimated twenty million pounds.'

'Wow!' Jamelia said. 'That's a life-changing amount of money.'

'Yes, and we'd like to offer our congratulations to the five people who shared our last jackpot.'

'Lucky sods,' Rick muttered.

His wife shushed him.

'Tonight we'll be using Topaz and set of balls number eight.' Why did they think people cared about that sort of thing? They just wanted to cut to the chase and get the numbers out, not dress it up as a programme.

Jamelia held up her hands. The lottery machine turned behind her, tumbling the pink, green, yellow and blue balls. 'Let's release the midweek big money balls!'

The lottery numbers rolled out, one by one. Rick used to use the same numbers every week when he'd started doing the lottery, but they hadn't proved to be very fruitful so he'd switched to getting a Lucky Dip ticket instead. Always though, there was the nagging doubt in the back of his mind – what would he do if those numbers ever came up now and he'd ditched them? He'd probably want to hang himself.

'Seven,' Alan Dedicoat said, as a pink ball rolled down the shute to start the Lotto line-up called Millionaires' Row. 'That's the hundred and sixty-first time this has been the Lotto main ball.'

'Ha,' Rick said. 'That's a good start.' Seven was supposed to be a lucky number anyway, wasn't it?

'Number ten,' Alan Dedicoat continued as the next ball rolled out. 'This ball completed Millionaires' Row three weeks ago.' Their house number.

'Good grief. I can't ever remember getting two in a row before.'

'The next ball out is number twenty-one.'

Chloe's birthday. 'Three,' Rick gasped. 'I've won a tenner.'

'It's not exactly going to pay the mortgage off,' Juliet remarked.

'Yeah, but a *tenner*. I haven't had a win in months.'

'Longer,' his wife pointed out. 'You might as well just throw your pound in our pond.'

On the screen the announcer was still in full flow. 'The fourth ball out tonight is number thirty.' Thirtieth of August. Their wedding anniversary and just a few short weeks away.

'Blood and sand!' Rick exclaimed. 'I've got that one too!' Now he was on the edge of his seat. This was the first time ever that

239

he'd had four numbers. What was that worth? Fifty quid? A hundred? Even Juliet had perked up now.

'And the fifth number in tonight's double rollover lottery draw is number thirty-two. Will that give *you* the big win tonight?'

No significance in that whatsoever as far as Rick could ascertain, and yet, there it was in black and white in front of him. He had five numbers. His heart was banging against his chest now. Wouldn't that be ironic, to win with five numbers on the lottery and then have a heart-attack. How much was five numbers worth? He had no idea. But it must be good. Surely it would pay for a decent holiday? Or maybe they could upgrade the car.

He heard himself gulp and he turned to Juliet. 'I've got that one too.'

'No!' He nodded in confirmation as the sixth ball rolled out of the lottery machine. His wife inched up next to him to enable her to see the numbers as well, and she gripped his arm.

'That's five,' he said in an awed whisper. 'We've got five numbers. That must be worth a few bob.' It had to be.

Rick's hands were shaking. He could hardly see the numbers on the ticket. Now there was just the last ball left to go. Even if they'd just got five numbers, they'd be in the money. Rick's mouth felt as if it was full of sand.

With a flourish, The Voice of the Balls announced, 'And the very last Lotto ball tonight that could make *you* a jackpot winner is number forty-two.'

'Omigod. Omigod. Omigod,' Rick said. He stared at the ticket in front of him. He'd got all of the numbers. All six of them. His throat was dry as he shouted out, 'We've won! We've won!'

Jamelia was waving goodbye on the screen, but they were no longer listening to what she had to say.

Juliet was wide-eyed. 'Twenty million?'

'There could be other winners.' He felt breathless with excitement even though he was outwardly calm. It was all he could do to stop himself running round the living room. 'It might not be that much.'

'How will we know?'

'I don't know,' Rick admitted. His legs were shaking now too. 'I think I'm supposed to phone the lottery operator.' Even if there were twenty winners – which was highly unlikely, surely – that would still be a million quid in the bank. Their bank! That would be enough to get Juliet's mother and both of the kids off their hands. If it was twenty million, they'd be going everywhere by private jet from now on. Even down to the local shops! Rick thought that he might fall to the floor and weep.

'This can't be right, Rick. Things like this don't happen to us.'

'Juliet.' He gripped his wife by the arms. 'We've won. I don't know how much, but I can tell you one thing for sure: life will be very different round here from now on. Your mother might not have won the lottery, but *I* have.'

Chapter 61

We lie in bed, but Rick's still fidgeting. I'm buzzing too, but I can mainly put that down to the bottle of champagne we swigged back in celebration of our win. I can't even believe that we had a bottle of champagne to hand to celebrate with. Even the sublime prose of my bedtime book, *A Thousand Splendid Suns*, failed to keep me engaged. This still seems so unreal. I won't believe it until someone has put the cheque in our hands and our picture is in the *Daily Express*, with both of us grinning broadly.

'What will happen when the press get hold of this?' I ask.

'We'll ask for no publicity,' Rick tells me. It sounds as if he's got this all worked out. He props himself up on his elbow and I switch on the bedside light once more. Sleep is clearly not an option tonight. 'I don't think that we should tell anyone. Not a soul. And particularly not your mother, otherwise it will be all round the Women's Institute before you can say "begging letters".'

'Can't I tell anyone?'

'Let's keep a lid on it,' Rick advises. 'Wait until we know how much we've got and what we're going to do with it.'

'OK.' It's going to be hard going to work tomorrow and pretending that nothing's happened. 'You are absolutely sure that we've won?'

'Of course. You saw the numbers come up right next to me. There can be no doubt. Do you want me to try the hotline again?'

I shake my head. There must be some kind of fault with the

phone line, or else there are a million people trying to get through and we've all won twenty quid each because the line has been engaged all night. Rick has tried to get through about two dozen times so far. I look at the clock. Already it's 3 a.m.

'Just try to relax.'

'I don't want to relax,' my husband tells me. 'I want to swing from the chandeliers, run down Chadwick Close in the nip. Do you want to look at the ticket again?'

'Not really.' Rick has put on his tightest pair of underpants – the ones he favoured while recovering from his contentious vasectomy – and has put the precious winning ticket down the front of them. We've never been burgled since we've been here, but Rick is convinced that tonight will be the night. My eyes are gritty through lack of sleep. 'What will we do with all that money?' I ask dreamily.

'Move to a mansion, buy a house for Chloe, Tom and your mum. Get a place in Spain. Treat myself to an Aston Martin. Tell Hal to stuff his job.'

'You wouldn't give up work, would you?'

'You are kidding me?'

'You enjoy your job. So do I.'

'But we won't *have* to work.'

'I'd miss Una.'

'We could pay her to stay at home too and be your friend. You could become one of those ladies who do lunch.'

I wrinkle my nose. 'I'm not sure that I'd like that.' We've never been rich and the thought of all that money seems too daunting. 'Isn't that the mistake all lottery winners make? They give up their jobs, move away from the area that they know and love and then have sad, empty lives.'

'Sad, empty lives with twenty million in the bank? I could cope with that.'

'I don't know . . .'

Rick tuts at me. 'What would you want then?'

I think for a bit and then sigh. 'It would be nice to have a conservatory.'

'Twenty million and all you want is a conservatory?'

'I can't think of anything else.'

'I remember a time when we were in Bournemouth and you had one too many Babychams and cartwheeled along the sand without your knickers on. What happened to that woman? Would she have wanted a conservatory with the world at her feet? Where did she go?'

Suddenly tears prick my eyes. 'I don't know.'

'I'd hate to be one of those losers who wins the lottery and still gets up at five o'clock every morning to work in the same factory because that's what they've done for the last thirty years, the ones who drive around in a knackered old Skoda because they've no imagination to envisage a better life for themselves. I don't want to be like that.' Rick's eyes plead with me. 'I want to set us up with this money, the whole family. Splash out on some luxuries. Have some fun. We'll build that conservatory. But I want to do so much more than that. Please say that you'll support me.'

I snuggle down next to Rick. 'Of course I will.'

'I love you,' he says. 'And I'll love you even more when you're a rich bitch.'

Giggling, we cuddle up together and, for the first time in months and even though Rick's testicles are still tender, we make love. We even move the lottery ticket out of the way and put it on the beside cabinet while we do.

Chapter 62

Rick tried the lottery hotline another dozen times while he was making breakfast. The first thing they'd do with their twenty million quid, he decided, was go out and buy a new toaster – one that actually toasted rather than charred.

'Who's Dad on the phone to every five minutes?' his daughter asked just as he came back into the kitchen. Juliet and he exchanged a furtive glance.

They'd agreed that they'd go about their business as normal while Rick tried to ascertain just how much they'd won. He was going to work with Hal and try to sneak off to make a phone call to the lottery operator as often as he could. Working would take his mind off it too. Juliet would go to the library and stamp books as if nothing untoward had happened. It was going to be hard, Rick thought, as his excitement was rising all the time.

He managed to struggle down a piece of blackened, buttered toast, but that was it; his stomach was too knotted to consider eating anything else. The winning lottery ticket was still safely tucked in his undies, but could he risk leaving it there all day? What if he left it at home and Buster ate it or his mother-in-law used it to scribble her shopping list on and then dropped it in the grocer's? A million disasters could befall it before he could claim his millions. It didn't bear thinking about.

Kissing Juliet goodbye, he said, 'I'll see you later, love.' Then he winked and she smiled back. Everything was going to be all right now – he could feel it in his bones – and he went out to his Walk All Over Me van with a spring in his step. He even waved back jovially when Stacey Lovejoy – in her dressing-gown on the doorstep – shouted, 'Cooee!' at him.

But when he arrived at his job, a big, semi-detached place in the village called Nash, Hal was in a mood. Not a good one. Rick felt himself deflate instantly.

'Four days off for a vasectomy, mate?' his friend complained as a greeting when Rick walked into the living room of the house where Hal was waiting, foot tapping impatiently. 'What's that about?'

'I had some internal bleeding and bruising, Hal.' Rick tried to be patient. He thought of the ticket tucked in his Calvin Kleins and retained his good humour. 'Testicles like bowling balls. It hurt like hell.'

Hal grumbled to himself.

'I'm still not a hundred per cent today,' Rick continued. He didn't explain that that was mainly due to being wide-eyed with excitement all night. Hal could wait to hear about that another day. 'But I'm here, so let's get on with it.'

They had a knacky old carpet to rip up and something tasteful in cream to replace it waiting in the van. It was a job that Rick had done the quote for and they could be out of here by lunchtime and onto the next job if Hal got his finger out.

'If you're sure you're up to it,' the other man sniped.

'Drop it, Hal,' Rick warned. 'I've never been off ill in all the years I've worked for you. Don't begrudge me a few days' recuperation. It bloody hurt, I can tell you.'

'My mate Lee said he was bouncing around like Tigger the next day.'

'Bully for him,' Rick said. 'I was still on eight pairs of underpants and chain painkillers then.' Despite not feeling like it, he then started to get out his tools.

'We're miles behind,' Hal whined. 'I've got jobs coming out of my ears. I'm going to have to work Sunday too, I reckon, and then I'll get it in the neck from Shannon.'

Ah, perhaps that was the real crux of the matter. All was not well on the domestic front *à la Maison Bryson*.

'I'll do Sunday with you,' Rick offered. 'If it will help you out.' He didn't want to leave Hal in the lurch. It wouldn't hurt to work for another couple of weeks. He didn't know how long the money would take to come through once the formalities were completed.

'Don't strain yourself,' Hal muttered. Rick bit his tongue.

'Well, let's get cracking.' His mate still hadn't picked up his tools. Rick tried to sound encouraging. 'We're not going to catch up if you just stand there whingeing. Work *and* grumble if you must.'

Hal bristled. 'Don't tell me how to run my business, mate.'

'Back off, friend,' Rick said. 'I'm not in the mood for this today. I've offered to work extra. The longer we standing here arguing the toss, the further behind we're getting. Are we going to pull this carpet up or not?'

'Who's running this job?' Hal snapped.

'No one at the moment,' Rick pointed out. 'Would you care to do it?'

'Fuck off,' Hal said. 'I've had enough.'

'*You've* had enough?' Rick said. 'I'm the one who's had enough.' Slamming his tools back into his box, he stood up. He didn't need to take this now. He was going to be rich and he didn't have to put up with Hal's rubbish any longer.

'Where do you think you're going?' Now Hal sounded worried – as well he might.

'I'm off home,' Rick announced as he headed for the door. 'You can stuff your job up your arse.'

'I can manage without you,' Hal scoffed. 'You've had an easy ride of this with me.'

'That's a laugh,' Rick retorted. 'I've carried this business while you've carried on with all your fancy women. Ten hours a day I've grafted while you've flitted about here, there and everywhere. You'd have gone bust years ago if it wasn't for me propping you up.'

'I can manage without you, mate.'

'Do just that.' Rick held a hand up to him.

247

'That's it!' Hal yelled. 'Walk away now and we're through. That's the end. Don't come crawling to me.'

'I won't. So long, Hal.'

'Come back!' Hal shouted after him. 'You know you don't mean it.'

But Rick did. Now that he was a Lotto multi-millionaire, he didn't have to take crap from anyone.

Chapter 63

I've been upstairs on the enquiries desk all morning. In that time I've joined up five new people to the library, issued their library cards and made sure that they know where everything is, telling them how to take out a loan from our meagre supply of audio-books and slightly-dated DVDs. I've also shown six people the plans of the new parking scheme due to be implemented next year, causing much grumbling. Two people needed to be shown how to use their computers to log onto the internet and I've also sold three of the lovely birthday cards that we stock which are painted by a local artist and feature relaxing watercolour scenes of places around Stony Stratford.

Perhaps I'll have time to take up painting now that Rick has won the lottery. I can't imagine giving up work full-time. What would I do with myself – apart from discover the art of water-colour painting? I feel privileged to work in the library here and wouldn't really want to leave despite what Rick says about lottery winners who still work being sad losers with no imagination. Some of us are just pretty content with our lot.

I haven't heard anything from Rick yet. He was going to text me if he'd managed to get through to the lottery hotline. Some hotline if it's permanently engaged. My fingernails have been chewed to the quick and the first thing that I'll have to treat myself to is a manicure. Luckily, I haven't seen Una all morning as she's been busy on the reception so I've not been tempted to spill the beans.

Rick has expressly banned me from telling Una, but how can I keep something like this to myself?

Now she pops her head over the banister rail from downstairs. 'Come on,' she says, 'it's gone quiet so we can have our lunch now. Don says he'll hold the fort. Let's take our sandwiches out onto the Green while it's nice.'

So we do just that. It's still blisteringly hot and, of course, the papers are full of global warming this and global warming that.

We sit down on the grass. There are one or two other people here. I recognise a couple of the hairdressers from the place I go to on the High Street and give them a wave.

'What excitement in the Joyce home have I missed?' Una ask as she tucks into her Tupperware container of raw vegetables and what looks like yoghurt. No bread in sight.

I've opted for the tuna mayo on granary route. 'None,' I lie. 'All quiet on the Western Front.'

'I don't believe it,' Una says. 'Is that possible?'

I avoid further questioning by saying, 'What about you? Heard from Internet Tex?'

'Yes. He's back from the Middle East. Safe and sound. Thank goodness.'

'Any sign of your money being returned?'

She nods as she nibbles a carrot. 'This morning. Had a cheque from him.'

'That's good.'

My friend shrugs. 'Tell me about it. I was beginning to worry. Just a bit. You hear such things, don't you?'

'Perhaps he's one of the good guys.'

'We'll have to hook up soon,' she says. 'His emails are getting steadily more steamy. I'm going mad with desire.'

That makes us both giggle. 'If you do arrange to see him, make sure you give me all the details. Better still, take me with you.'

'You've got your own boyfriend, remember?' she teases. 'Hands off mine!'

'You know what I mean, Una. I don't want you going off into the wide blue yonder with some stranger.'

'I won't,' she promises. 'Have you heard anything from Steven?'

'No.' I shake my head. 'I don't suppose I will now. It's probably just as well. He wanted more than I could offer him.'

'Why can't men ever be just friends? Everything comes down to sex in the end.'

'I don't think that we're wired in the same way,' I suggest. 'I'm sure we must have several books on it in the library.'

'Perhaps I should get them out.' Una produces a plastic spoon for her yoghurt. 'Is everything OK with you and Rick now? I know that you've been going through a rough patch.'

I allow myself a secretive little smile. 'Una, if I tell you this you have to swear yourself to secrecy.'

My friend sits up straight. 'What?' Her eyes are wide. 'You and Steven haven't . . . ?'

'No, of course we haven't. What do you take me for?'

'I was just hoping that your morals were as lax as mine,' she grins.

I check round the Green to see that no one's listening – goodness only knows why. 'Promise me that you'll tell no one.'

'I promise,' Una says solemnly. 'God, Juliet, hurry up before I die of suspense.'

'We've won the lottery.'

My friend looks like I slapped her face. 'What?'

'The lottery,' I repeat. 'We've won it.'

'When? How much?' Una is reeling.

'Last night,' I confide. 'I don't know how much yet. Rick's still trying to get through to the hotline.'

'But it's a lot?'

I nod. 'I think so.'

'You lucky cow,' she complains. 'You've got a sexy, secret admirer and now you've won the lottery. Can't you let some of that luck rub off on me?'

'I'll try,' I say. 'Promise me that we'll still be friends whatever happens.'

251

'Of course we will.' Una hugs me, squeezing the life out of me. 'I'm going to have a ball spending your millions for you.' My friend sighs as she lets me go. 'Just think, from now on you can have whatever you like – posh house, flash car, exotic holidays.'

'I don't care about any of those things. I just want to make sure that my family are taken care of.'

'You can certainly do that and still have change to treat yourself to some ridiculously extravagant luxuries.'

'I can, can't I?' That makes me smile some more. The sun shines down on us and I have a feeling that everything's going to be just fine from now on.

Chapter 64

Rick finally got through to the Lotto hotline at five o'clock. His hands were trembling violently; part of it was still to do with his row with Hal, which had really unsettled him, and part of it was down to excitement at the start of his new life.

'Hello, Lotto hotline,' the chirpy voice on the other end of the line said.

Rick had the ticket, now rather crumpled, clutched in his hand. His mouth went dry as he said, 'I've got a winning ticket. For last night's lottery.'

'Congratulations, sir.'

'I've been trying to ring since last night, but the line's been busy.'

'We were experiencing some technical difficulties, sir, and a high volume of calls.'

High volume of calls? Did that mean there were a million other people trying to claim *his* millions?

'Can you read out the numbers for me, sir?'

Rick did as he was told. 'Seven, ten, twenty-one, thirty, thirty-two and forty-two.'

'That's excellent. And can you just read out the date on the ticket for me?'

'Twenty-third of July.'

There was a pause at the end of the phone.

'And you say that was for last night's draw?'

'Yes.'

'I'm sorry, sir.' The chirpy voice sounded a bit more serious now. 'But that was your ticket for *last* week's draw.'

'What?' Rick stared, mesmerised, at the slip of red and white paper in front of him. The letters swam about and merged into one.

'Last night's draw was the thirtieth of July.'

Oh, no. Rick glanced at the date section on his watch. Sure enough, it was now 31 July. The date on his ticket was indeed for last week's draw. 'Wait, wait.' Rick ferreted about in his pocket and there, crumpled in the depths of it was the ticket he'd bought for last night's draw. How could he have been so stupid? So utterly, utterly stupid. 'I've found it,' he said miserably. 'I'd checked the wrong ticket.'

'It's an easy mistake to make, sir.'

If you were a complete pillock.

'Would you like me to check that one for you?'

What were the chances of him winning the jackpot with this ticket? That would be just too much to hope for. 'Yes,' he said weakly. 'That would be kind of you.'

There was tapping at the other end of the phone as he read out the numbers on this, the proper ticket for last night's draw.

'Ooo,' the girl said. 'You are lucky, sir!'

His heart skipped a beat. Could it be . . . ?

'You've won ten pounds.'

A tenner. His dreams of millions dashed against the rocks and he'd won a tenner. It seemed like adding insult to injury.

'Just pop along to your local lottery dealer and they'll happily pay you the cash.'

'Thank you.' Listlessly, he hung up the phone and sank down to the floor. No millions. No houses for the children. No Aston Martin. No holiday home in the Bahamas. No trips by private jet to the Grand Prix in Monaco. Nothing.

And, because of his stupidity, no job either. Rick put his head in his hands. What had he done? Just what had he done? He felt like screaming out loud, but no sound would come. He glanced at his watch again. Juliet would be home soon. And he wondered just how he was going to tell her that, once again, he'd let her down.

Chapter 65

Juliet had cried when he told her. Big, unhappy tears, the like of which she hadn't shed for many years. In fact, he couldn't remember the last time he'd seen her so upset. And it was all his fault for being a fool.

'Let me make you a cup of tea.'

She'd sobbed noisily at the kitchen table while Rick bustled around guiltily and made himself busy rustling up a pot of tea for them both, whilst studiously avoiding her eyes.

'You'll feel better for this,' he said, as he handed over a steaming mug of tea.

'I'm fine,' she sniffed. 'Really.'

He gave her a piece of kitchen roll that he'd ripped off the holder and Juliet had a good blow.

'I could kill myself,' Rick said. 'How could I be such a fool?'

'It doesn't matter,' his wife said bravely.

'And I was calling your mother every shade of idiotic for thinking she'd won the Spanish lottery.'

His wife gave him a wry glance that said something about the pot calling the kettle black. 'At least you haven't lost any money, not like Mum.'

'But I was so *sure* that we'd won.' Rick wrung his hands together. 'So sure.'

'Oh well.' Juliet sighed deeply and the breath shuddered inside her. 'What we've never had we'll never miss.' She started to cry again and it turned Rick's heart inside out. 'I didn't want millions. Just a little extra to help Chloe with the baby would have been nice.'

'I know, I know.' He came and sat next to her and gingerly put his arm round her. Would he have taken it so well if the boot had been on the other foot? Rick doubted it. He'd have been ranting and raving by now. God, he loved Juliet so much. How could he keep doing this to her? And what was even worse was that none of it was intentional. His wife had stood by him through thick and thin, just as she'd promised she would all those years ago.

He wanted to do better for her, be a better husband.

'Don't tell your mum though,' he begged. 'I'll never hear the last of it.'

'Of course I won't,' Juliet promised as she blew her nose into the kitchen roll again.

'Phew.' Rick puffed out a breath. 'I'm really glad that we didn't tell anyone.' He saw Juliet stiffen slightly. 'You didn't, did you?'

'No, no,' she insisted.

He shook his head. 'How stupid would I feel if this got out?'

'I'd better start thinking about something for dinner. Chloe will be home soon and Tom's already told me that he's on a tight turn-around. I'm sure Mum will be going out with Arnold too. Some quick pasta will have to do.'

'That sounds great, love.'

'Not exactly the meal fit for a millionaire.' Her voice was tremulous.

But then he wasn't a millionaire. Even though he had been sure, so absolutely sure.

Juliet pushed herself away from the table.

'You're not too mad with me?' he asked softly.

His wife shook her head. 'We have everything we need, Rick. We've got our health, we've got a nice home. We've got a lovely family.'

'That's questionable.'

Juliet tried a laugh but didn't quite make it. 'And we both have jobs that we enjoy.'

'Ah,' Rick said. 'That might not be entirely correct.'

That stopped his wife in her tracks. She fixed him with a quizzical look.

'When I thought I was going to be a multi-millionaire, I might just have told Hal to stuff his job up his arse.'

Chapter 66

'Who's a lucky girl then?' Mrs Marley winks at me as she hands her books over the counter. Josephine Cox, Freda Lightfoot and Joan Jonker have been keeping her entertained this week.

I look round just to make sure that the elderly lady is addressing me. 'Lucky?'

She winks at me again. 'Mrs Fry told me. I won't say a word.' Then she trots off to the stairs to choose another crop of family sagas for the coming week. What does she know? Has she heard about Chloe's baby from my mother? But would that involve winking? Then it dawns on me. Someone has let the cat out of the bag about our supposed lottery win and it can only be one person.

I abandon the desk and go through to the staff room where Una has her feet up on the table and is sipping tea whilst staring dreamily out of the window, no doubt thinking naughty things about Internet Tex.

'Una,' I say from the doorway. 'You didn't?'

She spins round. 'What?'

'Did you tell someone that Rick and I had won the lottery?'

'Er . . .' she says. 'I might just have mentioned it in the florist's. Only in a vague way.'

'Oh, Una.'

'It's going to get out that you've won sooner or later.'

Slipping into the chair next to her, I mumble: 'Then they'll all know that we've won a tenner.'

259

'*A tenner?*'

I lift my eyes to meet hers and nod in confirmation. 'Ten pounds.'
My friend looks stunned. But no more so than me.

'Rick really messed up this time. He looked at the wrong ticket
for the wrong week. I don't know – something like that. The
numbers he thought he had were for the week before. All we got
is ten pounds.'

'That's grounds for divorce.'

'I'm sure we'll look back at it and laugh. In time.'

'Oh, Juliet.' My friend slips her arm round me. 'What are you
going to do?'

'Nothing,' I tell her. 'Life goes on exactly as it did before.'

Don's head appears round the door. 'Sorry to interrupt this
love-in,' he says. 'Juliet, there's someone at the desk asking for
you.'

'I'm coming too now, Don,' Una says.

'Don't rush your tea break,' our manager insists. 'I don't want
you suing me for sexual harassment.'

I go back to the counter and Steven is standing there, grinning.
He's in jeans and a chocolate-brown shirt and looks amazing. What
do I feel when I see him? It's hard for me to say. Relief, joy, anxiety,
fear and everything else in between. I'm glad that he stayed away
and so glad that he hasn't.

He takes my arm and steers me away from the desk. 'I understand that congratulations are in order.'

'Not you too,' I sigh.

'Is there a problem?'

'There's no lottery win, Steven,' I tell him. 'I assume that's what
you're talking about.'

My ex-fiancé nods.

'It was all a silly mistake.'

'I'm sorry to hear that. You must be devastated.'

Am I? I honestly don't know. If this is the sort of fuss that a
rumour can cause then perhaps we're better off without it.

'Feeling low?'

'A bit.' Money may not make you happy, but it can certainly put a gloss on a few difficulties.

'I'd love to hold you,' Steven whispers.

'There are enough rumours flying about without us starting another one.'

'Have lunch with me,' he pleads. 'I've tried to stay away because you asked me to, but I've missed you so much, Juliet. Just an hour.'

I feel my resolve weakening. 'Steven—'

'Say yes.'

A glass of wine *would* go down a treat right now.

'One little hour. It'll cheer you up no end.'

'Lunch,' I say. 'That's all. Nothing more.'

'That's enough for me,' Steven says.

'I'll see you back here at one o'clock then,' I tell him.

He takes my hands and holds it fleetingly to his lips. 'I can't wait.'

And I know that I may regret this, but, for now, I just want someone to be nice to me.

Chapter 67

Rick told Juliet that he'd call Hal and ask for his job back, but a week later and he still hadn't. But then Hal hadn't been on the phone to him either.

Perhaps it was the right time in his life to be thinking about striking out and doing something else – maybe even running his own business. He could set up in competition with Hal. That would shock him. It would shock Rick too as he wasn't really that kind of vindictive person. Goodness only knows, he'd helped Hal out of enough scrapes over the years; he couldn't turn up the heat on his friend's business now that he was struggling to keep on top of it.

He'd cleared away the breakfast things and tidied the kitchen. Juliet liked that kind of thing and he knew that it was going to be hard work to put this one right. As soon as they'd had breakfast, Chloe and Tom both disappeared. Chloe out of the front door and Tom into his bedroom. Rita took up residence in the lounge watching *Cash in the Attic*, *This Morning* and *Doctors*. That would be her until lunchtime when she might go out to meet Arnold.

Rick thought of all the times when he'd wished that he could finish work, be a man of leisure. All the things he was going to do! Gardening, fishing, maybe take up golf, start running. Now, seven days unemployed, and he had no idea what to do with himself. Even the obituary column was losing its appeal.

'Buster!' Dog-walking would be a good idea. That would give him time to think about what he was going to do to get himself out of this mess rather than moping around the house, getting nagged by his mother-in-law who was monopolising his television with crap programmes, and wondering what his son was doing for all those long and lonely hours in his bedroom.

The faithful hound appeared, wagging his tail, and Rick slipped on his lead and the old dog trotted out of Chadwick Close at his heel. Rick's back was stiffer than it was when he'd been working. He'd always thought that his job made it worse, but perhaps his job had kept him loose. He daren't mention it to Juliet otherwise she'd make him go to Pilates classes or something. The niggling ache was keeping Rick awake at night and she'd already complained about him tossing and turning as he tried to get comfortable. The fact that his brain wouldn't stop whirring didn't help either. Consequently, he was tired all day.

When Rick and Buster reached Toombs Meadow, Stacey Lovejoy was there too with her little chihuahua, Britney.

'Hello, Ricky!' she shouted over at him, waving.

Instead of having his usual heartsink moment when he saw Stacey, Rick's spirits lifted. He'd always wanted peace and quiet at home, but it wasn't actually a lot of fun when you had peace and quiet completely on your own.

The only downside of bumping into his voluptuous neighbour was the fact that he was carrying a little blue plastic bag filled with Buster's poo. As Stacey headed in his direction, he threw the bag of poo into the nearest hedge. He hated dog owners who did that, but sometimes needs must.

His neighbour tottered towards him, Britney barking at her feet. Buster backed away in terror from the snappy chihuahua clad in a pink tracksuit. Rick knew how he felt. Today Stacey was wearing a sort of tight leopardskin all-in-one thing. She wore black leather boots that were laced up to her knees and great big sunglasses that made her look bug-eyed.

'On holiday, Ricky?'

'Not quite.'

She arched one of her over-plucked eyebrows at him.

'Out of work,' he admitted, as they fell into step next to each other.

'Thought I'd seen you around in the day.'

'Slight altercation with the boss. I came off worse.'

Stacey Lovejoy slipped her arm through his. 'A lovely man like you won't stay on the market for long. You'll be fixed up in no time.'

'Hope you're right.' Rick massaged his neck.

'Little stiffness there, Ricky?'

He nodded. 'Back's been dodgy for a while now. Always blamed it on the job, but it's been worse since I've been off.'

Buster was running round his legs, wanting to play. Rick bent down to pick up a stick for him and he threw it overarm as far as he could to give Buster a good run. That was when his neck locked. He felt a sharp twinge and then he couldn't move. Not an inch. His head wouldn't turn either to the right or left without excruciating pain. 'Aargh!' he cried out.

'Oh, Ricky. Let me look.'

Reluctantly, he let Stacey run her fingers over his neck and shoulders. It felt surprisingly good. 'That's nice.'

'I'm a trained massage therapist,' Stacey told him. 'Used to work in a massage parlour. Not one of those skanky ones.' She laughed uproariously at that. 'A proper place with clean towels and all that. You'll have to let me give you a rub-down. I've got healing hands, Ricky. There's many a man told me.'

He didn't have any trouble believing that.

Stacey nudged him in the ribs. 'Come back to my place. The kids are at school. It's nice and quiet. I'll sort you out.'

Juliet would flay him alive. 'I don't think so.'

'What else you got to do, Ricky?' Stacey steered him back towards Chadwick Close, curtailing Buster's walk. 'You can't walk around like that all day. It must be agony, poor lamb.'

It was quite painful.

'I'm sure you'll enjoy it.'

'I'm sure I will.' He didn't like to tell Stacey that wasn't what he was worried about.

Chapter 68

Steven has driven us out to Calverton – a pretty little village just outside Stony Stratford. We can't go very far as I'm restricted for time in my lunch-hour and I don't want Una to get fed up with me being out gallivanting. I notice that she didn't offer to cover for me if I was late back this time. There's a car park just off the main road which borders the River Ouse and we pull in here.

Steven lifts a small picnic basket and a tartan rug out of the back of his car. There's a couple of picnic benches scattered around near the car park, but we eschew those and I follow him as he walks further into the field and finds a secluded spot beneath the shade of a large oak tree. I'm amazed at his ingenuity in finding perfect, romantic spots that are just a few minutes' drive from the library. Surely soon we will exhaust them all. What will we do in the winter, when the weather isn't so amenable? Then I wonder why I am even thinking that far ahead. We can't go on like this. I know we can't.

It's cooler today and the breeze ripples the long grass and creates tiny waves on the river. Weeping willows drape their branches in the gentle current. A herd of golden-brown cows lap the water on the other banks and some of them tentatively dip their toes in. The sky that's been boasting an unbroken Mediterranean blue of late, is softer today and is filled with ice-cream clouds. This is the English countryside at its finest.

I shake out the rug and lay it on the ground while my companion sets about unpacking the picnic.

'There are smoked salmon sandwiches.' Steven looks up at me and smiles. 'I hope you like that.'

'Love it.'

'Some freshly-baked cheese straws.'

'Not by you?'

'No,' he admits, 'by the deli in the High Street. For dessert there's strawberries and cream. And I've packed some Belgian chocolates in ice so that they won't melt.'

'Sounds fabulous.'

'Glass of champagne?'

'Just the one.' I don't think I've ever done so much lunchtime drinking.

'I brought two individual bottles as I'm driving.' He pops the corks and pours them out. Steven is an accomplished host, even in a field.

It makes me smile. Even though the kids are now grown up, my picnics still bear the traces of childhood. I'd never dream of packing smoked salmon sandwiches – peanut butter is my staple picnic food, with bags of crisps and some Morrisons' pork pies if you're lucky. There's usually orange juice rather than champagne. When I'm really pushing the boat out, we might take a flask of tea too.

We stretch out on the rug and enjoy the picnic, gazing out over the river and the fields beyond.

'A penny for them,' Steven says.

'I'm just thinking how different your life is to mine.'

'I might have all the trappings of wealth, Juliet, but that doesn't mean that my life has been necessarily the richer for it. There are things I envy you for.'

I laugh at that. 'I can't imagine what.'

'You have a family, a solid, settled life. I always wanted children, lots of them, but invariably managed to choose women who didn't.'

'Family life isn't all that easy.' Now there's an understatement.

'No, but I would have like to have tried it. With you.' My old love gazes wistfully into the distance. 'What do I have? A stack of money in the bank, property round the world and no one to leave

267

it to. What has it all been for? There isn't a day goes by when I don't wonder how things would have turned out if we had married.'

All the lunches we've had together and yet we've always skirted round the question that I've most wanted answered. 'Why did you leave me that day, Steven? Was the thought of getting married to me so very awful?'

'You know how it was,' he sighs. 'Everything just got on top of me. I wasn't sure that I could be the husband that everyone expected me to be.'

'I never expected anything from you. I just loved you more than anyone I'd ever known.' And in a way, I have to admit, that I've never loved Rick.

Steven and I were, to use that well-worn cliché, soulmates. Despite our tender years there was passion, excitement and the knowledge that we were growing and learning together. We were inseparable. Everyone commented on it. We were so in love. But we were teenagers and we knew nothing else.

'I know. I've never found love like that since. Never even come close,' Steven confesses. 'Though I have had a very good time searching for it.'

We both laugh at that.

'I was young. I was foolish,' he continues. 'What else can I tell you, Juliet? I panicked and ran. I knew that if I did something so horrendous, I wouldn't be able to stay in this town. I'd be pilloried. My parents would have disowned me.'

'I always thought that was the reason, but I never knew. I had no one to talk about it to. I didn't know if there was anyone else.'

Steven shakes his head. 'I think that was part of the reason too. You'd been my only serious girlfriend, my first and only love. I thought there were a lot of women out there who would fit the bill just as well.' He reaches for my hand and I let him take it and lift it to his lips. 'I was very wrong.'

'You can't regret it, Steven. Look at the things you've done.'

'For business,' he says, 'it was probably the best move I could have ever made. If I'd stayed in Stony Stratford, would I have had the vision to be able to see the opportunities available? I have a vineyard in South Africa, a portfolio of property in Cape Town, a boutique hotel in Miami, a range of interests in Asia. Money I can do. Relationships have been more elusive.' Steven swigs at his champagne and stares out over the fields. 'I used to think of you constantly over the years. I'd hear our old song – remember that?'

It was 'Every Breath You Take' by The Police. I still can't listen to it, even now.

'And I'd be right back there with you,' he continues. 'You were the only person who ever really touched my soul. I thought about contacting you over the years, but never quite found the courage. Plus I didn't want the dream to be shattered. When I came back I wondered whether you'd still be the same person. Whether the love I'd imagined was real or whether it was a product of many years of futile longing.'

'Oh, Steven.'

'We still have it, Juliet. Whatever we shared hasn't gone away. Not for me. And I'm sure that you feel it too. I'm so glad that I came back.' Steven kisses my hand again, letting his champagne lips linger on my skin. 'You're still my Juliet.'

But I'm not. I'm older and fatter and married and have two children and am frightened to look closely at my life.

Chapter 69

Buster, uncomplaining, was tied up in Stacey's front garden. Rick, terrified, was now in Stacey's bedroom. It was pink and girly and looked much like Chloe's bedroom had when his daughter had been about fifteen. Chloe, however, had grown out of it. Little fairy lights with feathers attached were draped across the pink, glittery headboard.

'Just take your clothes off, Ricky,' she instructed.

'What?' He felt himself back away from his neighbour. 'All of them?'

This only caused Stacey to giggle. 'I'm not shy.'

No, Rick thought. But I am. 'It's only my neck that's stiff.'

'Sometimes tension in the neck is created by a problem in the lower back,' she assured him. 'You won't get a proper job unless I do all of it.'

Rick hovered at the end of the bed, frozen. He'd never taken his clothes off before in front of another woman, unless you counted the lady surgeon who did his vasectomy – and that was for purely medical reasons. This was more . . . for pleasure. Rick wasn't sure that was the right word. Yet he could hardly class this massage as medical, could he, when the masseuse was wearing leopardskin?

'Want me to help you?' Stacey advanced on him.

'No, no.'

She held out a towel. 'I'll give you two minutes and then I'll be back.'

He stared at her as she retreated. Rick found her as attractive as he did appalling. Hastily, he undressed despite the pain in his neck – still uncertain what he was doing here or why he'd agreed that Stacey Lovejoy could get her hands on him.

When she came back he was perched on the end of her luxuriously squashy bed, towel tucked tightly round his waist, pants still firmly in place.

'There's a good boy,' she said. 'Now lie down on your tummy. I've got some lavender oil here.' His neighbour waved the bottle at him. 'That will make you relax nicely.'

'I'm not tense,' Rick insisted, but Stacey Lovejoy gave him a smile that said she could tell otherwise.

'Over you go,' she said, and encouraged him to lie down. Which he did – very gingerly.

He lay out on her pink duvet cover and, as soon as he was down, Stacey whipped his towel away from him. She slapped him playfully on the bottom before pouring oil all over his back. It felt better than he'd expected it to. Then his neighbour eased down his undies and began to massage his bottom, her hands firm and kneading. Wasn't sure that he was keen on that. Wasn't sure what it had to do with his neck being stiff either. Rick clenched his buttocks.

'Just relax,' Stacey Lovejoy cooed. 'Just relax. Enjoy the sensation of my hands. Feel the warmth in your body.'

Her hands travelled over his back, stroking, rubbing and pressing places that he hadn't realised hurt. It all felt very nice. She then massaged round his shoulders, enveloping him in a cloud of sweet-smelling lavender oil. Oh, that was lovely, Rick thought. Very lovely.

'That nice?' Stacey wanted to know.

'Mmm,' Rick murmured. Try as he might to keep them open, his eyes were starting to roll. He was drifting off, enjoying the rhythmic stroking of Stacey's massage. Now he could understand why men would pay good money for this.

Her hands travelled lower and lower down his back in slow lazy circles. And, to be honest, he didn't remember anything else after that.

Chapter 70

I come out of the doctor's surgery with Chloe. My daughter has already started the pregnancy waddle even though her bump is barely showing. It makes me smile to myself. Only the open top button on her jeans gives any indication that she's not still the slender reed she always has been. I give her waist a squeeze.

'What's that for?' she wants to know.

'Because I love you.'

This is my lunch-hour and I have a dozen different things to fit in before I go back to the library; none of them involve seeing Steven. I've agreed that I'll accompany Chloe to all her pre-natal appointments – the father of the baby living at the other end of the country and still shell-shocked at unexpectedly becoming a daddy. It looks as if I'll be her birthing partner too as the father-to-be hasn't yet expressed an interest in being there and, to be honest, that feels like a real honour for me.

'Happy?' I ask her, as we walk back down the High Street.

'Scared,' she admits. My child turns to me with anxious eyes and slips her arm in mine. 'Suddenly it all seems real.'

You'd better believe it, I think. 'Have you decided what you're going to do about your university course?'

'I'm going to have to give it up,' she says. 'I can't see any other way. I want to be at home with my mum.'

I take some comfort that I must be doing something right if my daughter wants to lean on me now.

'We'll talk to the admin department, see what they suggest. There may be a way round it. This can't be an unusual situation these days.'

'Thanks for being so understanding, Mum.'

'I know what it's like, Chloe. I may be old, but I can just about remember. It's terrifying and exhilarating at the same time.'

'I just wish Dad wasn't so down on me.'

'Give your father time,' I say. 'He'll get used to the idea. You have laid quite a lot on him recently.'

We walk in companionable silence past the greengrocer's, several places selling knick-knacks, a lovely lighting store called Lampwise that I adore and a dozen of the different charity shops that are swallowing up our high streets.

'Is the father of the baby going to stay around?' I ask gently.

'I think so,' Chloe says. 'He and I need to do some more talking about it.'

I don't point out that the best time for talking is before making a baby, but who am I to give out advice?

'You love him?'

My daughter shrugs. 'Yeah.'

'You could sound more enthusiastic.'

'I don't want to consider what it means. Neither of us were ready to settle down.'

'Then take it as it comes,' I suggest. 'There's not much else you can do. You can't force love if it isn't there.'

'I know.'

'Are we going to get to meet this young man anytime soon?'

'I'll arrange for him to come up,' she says. 'What a daunting prospect for him, meeting you lot.'

'You know that we'll do all that we can for you both.'

'I do.' Chloe squeezes my arm. 'You're a great mum.'

We're approaching the bank now where I'm meeting my own mum – the great-grandmother of our impending arrival. Could I class her as a great mum? I don't really think so, but I do know that she did her best for me even though that did fall woefully short at times.

We've got an appointment with the manager to discuss her recent losses on the fake Spanish national lottery. I still haven't told anyone else about Rick's mistake with our own Lotto ticket. He'd never live it down. And my mother would gloat for months.

'Yo, Grandma,' Chloe says as we approach her.

My mother high-fives my daughter. It's draining to live with a seventy-year-old adolescent. Has no one told my mum that seventy is not the new fifteen?

'How'd it go with the doctor, love?'

'Cool,' she tells my mother. 'I've decided if the baby's a boy I'm going to call him Kanye or Peyton, and if it's a girl I thought perhaps Cipriana or Suraya.'

My mum rolls her eyes at me and I shrug.

'Laters,' Chloe says. She kisses me on the cheek and high-fives her grandma for a second time. Then she's off down the street, forgetting to waddle.

'If you were a boy you were going to be called Paul,' Mum observes wryly.

'How times change.' I thought I was being very *avant-garde* with the name Chloe.

Then we go into the bank together and sit and listen to the manager who tells us of their progress in finding my mother's swindled money. Precisely none. They're hopeful, he tells us. We're less so.

Two minutes later, we're back outside. 'I've time for a very quick sandwich,' I tell Mum.

'I'm meeting Arnold,' she says. 'I've only got a few minutes myself.'

'Let's go to *Bon Appétit* then. They're usually quick in there.'

We turn and head back down the High Street in the direction we've just come.

As we hit the main drag of shops, Dad and Samuel come out of the jeweller's. Oh, I do hope they've not been looking at wedding rings. They're on us before I can steer my mother in another direction. She's so busy looking in the window of the Willen Hospice bookshop that she doesn't see my dad until he's right in front of her.

'Oh,' she says, taken aback. 'Frank. It's you.'

'Rita,' is all my dad manages. Samuel straightens up at that.

Mum and Dad gawp at each other. This is the first time they've bumped into one another since my mother packed her bag and left.

Today, Dad is wearing a bow tie and his hair is slicked back in the manner of Noël Coward.

'You're looking well,' Mum says – eventually. Although her tone is more than a little grudging.

Did she hope that Frank would fall apart without her? Far from it! Her former husband has had a lifestyle change, is eating 'foreign muck' and is considering a short cultural trip to Italy. I have told her none of this. Primarily because she hasn't been interested. Mum thinks she's been the only one having fun playing fast and loose. Well, she's wrong.

'Your hair's very red,' Dad says, ever the diplomat.

I wonder how quickly I can usher her away before she clocks Samuel. Even to the untrained eye, Samuel looks gay. My eyes plead with Dad's new partner to hurry him away before Mum can ask any awkward questions. Samuel Scott may have a lot of talents and may have turned around the life of a lonely man who was old before his time, but he clearly can't read minds as he merely smiles kindly back at me.

'Who's this?' Mum points at Samuel.

'This is Samuel Scott,' Dad says with a wide beam.

'I think we should be going, Mum.' I take my mother's elbow, but she shrugs me off.

'What is he?' Mum wants to know, a suspicious glint in her eye. 'Is he your carer?'

She would love it if Dad couldn't manage without her.

'No,' my father says calmly. 'Samuel is my partner.'

'You've gone into business?' Mum huffs. 'At your age!'

Dad and Samuel exchange a perplexed glance. Then my father starts to laugh.

'We'd better be going, Mum.'

'What?'

With that I drag my mother away. 'I'll talk to you later, Dad,' I shout over my shoulder.

I think I just narrowly avoided fisticuffs in the High Street.

Chapter 71

My mother sits in the *Bon Appétit* café still wearing a perplexed look. Our little town is about to be blessed with a Costa Coffee – even things in Stony Stratford move on – but it's not open yet. This is not the most exciting place on earth to have lunch, but needs must. There are a dozen scratched tables with a sundry assortment of ramshackle chairs around them. The menu is stuck somewhere firmly in the 1970s, with jacket potatoes featuring heavily. If I ever give up being a librarian I might consider opening a decent café in the town.

We find a window seat overlooking the High Street which my mother always sees as a small victory. Minutes after we've ordered, our food arrives. It's fresh and the tea is hot. That's the best I can say. It is, however, served on the type of china that you see most often at car boot sales.

Mum attacks her cheese sandwich while observing tightly, 'Your father looked very well.'

'Yes,' I agree non-committally.

'What sort of business has he gone into then?'

My father, the seventy-two-year-old entrepreneur. Even my mum views that as strange. Not quite so strange as the truth though. Maybe this is the time to spill the beans.

'Mum' I say. 'I've got something to tell you.'

'This isn't about Steven Aubrey, is it?' She fixes me with her beady eye. 'Marjorie and Norman Peebles saw you having lunch with him last week.'

That's not good news. I've been seeing Steven a couple of times a week. I know, it's madness. You don't have to tell me that. But he's the only person who provides me with any solace. He's interested in me, in what I have to say. No one else in my family is. He finds me amusing company, attractive even. I have stopped being wallpaper since Steven has been around. And of course I could have told Rick by now — even I have to acknowledge that, as much as I might want to deny it. Call me stupid, reckless even, but something inside me rather liked keeping this all to myself. It was a special secret all for me that no one else knew about. If you don't count Una, of course. Now, it seems, my secret is out.

'It was an innocent lunch, Mother. Nothing more. You can tell Mr and Mrs Peebles that all is well. I've seen Steven a couple of times since he's been back. His mum is ill and I'm just helping out a friend.'

My mother harrumphs at that.

'Think what you like.' But protest as I might, it is about time that I either stopped it or told Rick. 'Anyway, this isn't about me or Steven Aubrey. It's about Dad.'

She raises her eyebrows and waits for me to continue. I take a deep breath before launching into, 'Samuel isn't a *business* kind of partner.'

I can see cogs and gears clicking into place in her brain. 'Oh,' she says eventually. 'Not your father. Not in Stony Stratford.'

All I do is nod.

'What is the world coming to?' my aging parent wants to know – she who picks up men in the Meals For One aisle in Marks & Sparks, she who was planning a boob job and an IVF baby until she was scammed of her money on the fake Spanish lottery.

But who am I to question my mother's rationale? It certainly is a crazy mixed-up world. I have a father who's just finding out who he really is at the age of seventy-two, a daughter who's pregnant but seems uncertain whether she loves the father or not, a son who was gay one week and in love with a foreign divorcée with two children the next, and a husband who's gone completely off the rails and is on the front page of the local newspaper more often than the latest *Big Brother* contestants. Yet how can I question everyone else's skewed morality or sexual proclivities when I myself am skulking around with my ex-lover, pretending that it's all above board when I know in my heart that it's not? As human beings we have a great propensity to delude ourselves.

'Dad's very happy.'

Mum scowls. I don't think that was quite the plan. Dad was supposed to waste away without her – as he very nearly did – not transform himself into a dandy with eclectic tastes and a younger boyfriend. I doubt very much that that was Mum's vision at all.

'Your father's always been *funny*,' she declares. And I don't think she means he could have had a great career as a stand-up comedian.

For the record, my dad has not been *funny* for all of his life. He was a hard-working father and husband who got very little thanks or reward for his endeavours. I for one hope that he finds some joy with Samuel, even though it might be short-lived.

'What am I going to say to everyone?' Mum wants to know. She's more worried about Dad's actions than she is about her own. 'What will they say at the Women's Institute when they find out about your father?'

And find out they will. Let's see what Marjorie and Norman Peebles have to say about that, hey?

'Tricky,' I agree, sucking in my breath. Let her sweat that one. I've got more than enough on my plate.

'It's just not right,' Mum complains. 'It's just not right.'

'Now, Mum,' I say, 'being a homosexual isn't something to be ashamed about. There's no stigma to it nowadays.'

'I know that,' she snaps. 'I'm not some old fuddy-duddy. But your father's got a better boyfriend than me! It's just not right.' She shakes her head. 'Not right at all.'

As my mum is pondering this dilemma, Steven Aubrey comes past the window. His eyes light up as he sees me inside.

I try to pretend that I haven't seen him whilst urging him to walk on by with a subtle inclination of my head. Perhaps Steven misinterprets my signals as, instead of continuing down the street, he swings into the café. Now it's Mum's turn to suck in her breath. Perhaps too she's thinking how well he has aged, how handsome he is, how he looks as if life has been extraordinarily kind to him.

'It's Steven Aubrey,' she stage-whispers to me as the door chimes to show that someone has entered.

'Is it?' I feign ignorance and then turn to find Steven standing behind me. Even Mr Magoo couldn't fail to see the chemistry between us.

His face is the picture of joy whilst mine is the picture of discomfiture.

'Hello,' Steven says. He holds out his hand for me to shake and, as I don't know what else to do, I oblige. 'It's lovely to see you again after all this time.'

'Lovely to see you too.'

'Mrs Britten!' He turns his attention to my mother while she appraises him. 'Not looking a day older than when I last saw you.' Which was on the day of my cancelled wedding, but I hope that she doesn't remember that.

I expect my mother to narrow her eyes and say something pithy but she doesn't. Instead she smiles, goes all girly and sounds breathy when she talks. This is what she must do in the Meals for One aisle.

'Steven,' she coos, 'how wonderful to see you again. You must call me Rita.'

Clearly Steven's brand of urbane charm works on women of all ages. Probably why he's been married so many times. Probably why I feel like a schoolgirl with a crush again when he's around.

'It's so good to be back here,' he says. 'Among old friends.'

My mother flutters her eyelids while I flush to a shade of crimson not often seen other than on a baboon's bottom.

'Let me take you out for lunch.' He addresses me and I can see that my mother is slightly narked to be left out of the invitation. 'We have so much to catch up on after all this time.'

'I'm not sure . . .' How can I warn him that Marjorie and Norman Peebles have already grassed us up?

'Say you will,' Steven begs. 'Persuade her to have lunch with me, Mrs Britten – Rita.'

Now my mum sits a bit more upright. 'I thought you two had already been enjoying cosy lunches?' She fixes both me and Steven with her steely gaze.

'Er . . . well,' I say.

'Gosh, is that the time?' Flustered, Steven checks his watch. 'I'll be in touch. Great to see you both again.'

'Give my love to your mother,' Mum says, mouth still twisted with disapproval.

'Yes,' I say to Steven.

He reaches out to shake my hand again and I know that our fingers linger too long. So does my mother. I'm behaving badly and I just can't seem to get a grip on it.

Steven is out of the café door and heading off down the street without looking back.

'That was nice,' I say, my voice far from normal.

'Humph.' My mother's steady gaze holds my lowered eyes.

I feel like I did when she'd found out that I hadn't done my homework or I hadn't tidied my room or I hadn't come home when I said I would. My mum, as mothers do, knows that I'm lying. But I realise that the repercussions of this will run far deeper.

'You are your father's daughter,' she says. 'I can see that it's not just Frank Britten who has his secrets.'

Chapter 72

Swinging into Chadwick Close, I'm glad to be home at last. My mother and I discussed the Steven 'situation' no further, something for which I'm truly grateful. Even just seeing him now sends my mind into a flat spin. I thought I had this under control – a harmless bit of flirtation with an old flame – but I don't. The old flame still has the capacity to burn like a raging inferno and that's something I hadn't quite bargained for.

After parking in the drive, I go into the house. All I want tonight is to put my feet up, have a long, hot bath if I can get anywhere near the bathroom, and enjoy a glass of wine in front of the television, curled up with my book. I've hardly had any time to read, these past few weeks. I've hardly had time to do anything remotely civilised. The only peace I get is when I'm with Steven, and that's not how it should be. I have to break the habit that's beginning to form so easily. What would my family think of me if they knew? My mother is bound to let the cat out of the bag. She could gossip for England. No secret is safe with her.

In the kitchen, Tom is sitting at the table. 'I'm thinking of going into the police,' he says, and then forms a gun with his hands and pretends to shoot the bread bin and the kettle. Why do men never grow up? Why is my favourite oxymoron 'adult male'?

'The police?' This is Tom's seventeenth different career choice, so far. All of them have come to nothing. Accountant, even though he can't even balance his own chequebook. Pilot, although he doesn't like flying. Photographer, though he only takes photos of his drunken friends with his phone. Landscape gardener, though he has a serious aversion to the lawnmower. I have no idea what my son will end up doing with his life, but I wish he'd decide very soon.

He takes aim at the temperamental toaster. Actually, I'd quite like it if he shot that up. 'I want to be an ace detective like Gene Hunt,' he tells me.

'They'd make you get your hair cut.' I don't know whether they would or not, but this will test my son's dedication.

Tom doesn't look too impressed with that idea and frowns to himself as he runs a hand thoughtfully through his treasured locks. Ah well, back to the drawing board.

'Where's Dad?' I ask.

'Dunno,' Tom says.

'Where's the dog?' I might not be able to guarantee an effusive welcome from my husband, but Buster's a dead cert.

'Tied up outside Stacey Lovejoy's house.'

'He's *what* . . . ?' I sprint to the window, covering the kitchen in three strides. Sure enough, our dog is sitting patiently outside our neighbour's home. 'Didn't it occur to you that's more than likely where Dad is?'

Tom shrugs. Some detective he'll make.

'How long has he been there?' I want to know.

'Dunno,' my son tells me. 'I've been watching telly.'

Perhaps Tom could become a television critic – he'd certainly have a lot of experience for that job.

Standing there, I fume as I see our dog looking longingly at Stacey Lovejoy's door. Well, if no one else is interested in where my husband has got to, then I certainly am.

I get a ridiculous urge to fix my hair and make-up before going over there, but curb my instincts. Instead, I march out of the door to the sound of 'What's for dinner, Mum?' coming from Tom.

I'm trying to stay calm and reasonable as I cross the Close, but can feel my blood pressure rising. I haven't really liked Stacey Lovejoy since she first moved in, and I don't often take against people for no good reason. She's always been too brash, too familiar and way too keen to have Rick round at her house, fixing taps, mending that, always doing something or another. And he flies round there at a moment's notice. If only he was so enthusiastic about all the jobs that are stacking up at home, then perhaps I wouldn't mind.

Is it the way Stacey's fulsome breasts jiggle when she talks or the way she wears tiny vest tops even in February that makes my blood boil? I don't know what it is but we're never destined to be bosom buddies and I resent her trying to lure my husband over to her Barbie pink home at every opportunity.

I'm about two feet away from Buster when he sees me and his tail goes into a frenzy of pleasure. He's so myopic that if he was a human he'd need glasses by now.

'Stay there a minute, boy,' I tell him. 'I want to find out exactly what's going on indoors first before I take you home.'

I ring the doorbell and then hear the tip-tap of Stacey's heels on her laminate floor – laid by my husband – as she comes to open it. When she does, she's wrapped in just a towel and her hair is wet, combed back from her face. On her feet are pink fluffy high-heeled boudoir slippers. My slippers come from Matalan and are built for purpose. My blood pressure ratchets up a notch.

'Is Rick here?' Of course he is. Why am I being so polite? I push past Stacey and into her hall.

Her face is the picture of terror. This woman would not make a good poker player.

'I can explain,' she says, and subconsciously, her eyes travel upwards.

She goes to block my way, but I didn't spend all of my Saturday evenings watching *Gladiator* with my children when they were younger for nothing. I dodge past her before she has a chance to register that I'm heading up her stairs as if I'm pumping up the travelator.

To give credit to Stacey Lovejoy, she's after me in a flash, pathetic slippers or not, pulling at my skirt. 'Wait, Juliet,' she pleads. 'This isn't how it looks.'

285

Her house has the same layout as mine, so I head straight to the master bedroom. Call me suspicious, but I don't imagine that Rick is tinkering about in her bathroom. I can't hear the joyful knock of spanner on pipe.

Throwing open the door, the cloying scent of perfume nearly knocks me out and I'm shocked rigid at the sight that greets me. My husband is face-down and naked on Stacey Lovejoy's bed, with only her pink glittery duvet covering his modesty. He's sleeping soundly, his snores reverberating round the room.

'Rick!' I shout.

At that my husband jumps and opens his eyes. 'What, what? Where am I?'

Oh, that old chestnut. Give me more credit that that.

'Get up and get out of here now.'

He looks down at himself in horror, then at Stacey Lovejoy in her skimpy towel who's at my shoulder looking very stressed.

My husband snatches the duvet round him and holds out a hand. 'Nothing happened here,' he tells me, panic in his voice. 'I promise you.'

'I'm tired of your promises, Rick.' I turn on Stacey. 'And you're a shameless tart.' With that I head off back down the stairs.

Outside and my head's ringing. After the sweet fug of Stacey's bedroom, the fresh air is hurting my lungs. I can hardly believe what I just saw. All of these mad things that my husband has been involved in recently and I've put up with them. And throughout I've believed unequivocally in his innocence. Now I know that I've been taken for a fool. He's been sleeping with Stacey Lovejoy all along, right beneath my nose, and I haven't seen it. I want to be sick, purge all of this pain from my stomach.

He's had it, I think. There's no way back from this. Rick has crossed the line.

'Come on, Buster.' I untie the dog. 'Let's go home. I hope you're still a true and faithful friend.' Because it's patently clear that my husband is not.

Chapter 73

Rick hopped round the bedroom trying to put his trousers back on. 'She'll kill me,' he said. 'You should have told her what happened.'

'I couldn't, Ricky,' Stacey Lovejoy insisted. 'She was like a madwoman. She wouldn't listen to reason.'

Juliet wasn't likely to listen to *him* either. What had he done this time?

'How long have I been asleep?' he wanted to know.

'Hours,' Stacey confessed. 'You were sleeping like a baby and I'd hardly even started your massage. It seemed such a shame to wake you up, poor lamb. You obviously needed the sleep.'

He obviously needed his head testing, agreeing to let Stacey Lovejoy anywhere near his body. Rick had known it would end in tears, he just hadn't realised how many and how soon.

'Why are you dressed like that?' He stuffed his socks in his pocket – better not linger long enough to put those on. The sooner he was out of here the better.

'I spilled oil all over my cat suit, Ricky,' Stacey explained. 'I just had a little shower while you were snoozing. I've got a bit of a leak in there, you know.'

He held up a hand. 'No more leaks, Stacey. You're going to have to make your own plumbing arrangements from now on.' And the same went for electrical failures of any kind or creatures that were too fearsome to deal with or flooring requirements. If he wanted Juliet to forgive him, some other sucker would have to be on call for Stacey's domestic crises from now on. Perhaps he'd recommend Derek at number three. He'd never been that keen on him.

Rick slipped on his shoes, finding the wrong feet in his haste to depart. 'Didn't you think not to answer the door?' He hobbled down the stairs, Stacey in hot pursuit, as he haphazardly buttoned up his shirt. 'You must have known it would be my wife.'

'I lost track of time, Ricky,' she swore. 'I didn't know that Juliet would be home so soon. The minute my hand was on that door, I could have chopped it off.'

Juliet was probably keen to do some chopping off too.

'I only wanted to help.' Stacey looked near to tears.

'I know that.'

'Did you enjoy your massage?'

'I think that's largely irrelevant now but, yes, it was very nice.' What he remembered of it. If only he hadn't been so tired when he started, he might not have been in this mess now.

'It's not easy being a single mum,' she sniffed. 'Sometimes a woman just needs a little male company.'

'Look,' Rick said, 'you're a very lovely woman.' In your own way. 'But for the sake of my marriage, we have to give each other a wide berth. If you see me out walking Buster, please just turn round and go in the other direction.'

'You've been a good friend to me, Ricky,' Stacey said. 'And I haven't had many of those in my life.'

'Oh, Stacey.' Rick felt awful, but this was one misunderstanding too far.

'You're very special to me.'

'I love my wife,' Rick said. And he had to get home to tell her that just as quickly as he could.

Chapter 74

Rick rushed into his house still tucking his shirt into his trousers. Juliet wasn't in the kitchen or in the living room. 'Where's your mother?' he said to Tom.

'Dunno,' his son answered, barely glancing up from the television.

He took the stairs two at a time, racing up to the bedroom. Sitting in front of the dressing-table mirror, his wife stared at her reflection. Her expression was bleak, but at least she wasn't packing a bag. That had to be a good thing, right? Did this mean that she was, once again, going to give him the benefit of the doubt?

'I'm sorry,' Rick blurted out. 'There is a very, very innocent explanation for all of this.'

'Oh, Rick.' His wife turned to him. 'How many times are we going to go through this sort of thing? I used to be able to rely on you. What has happened to you?'

Rick sat down on the edge of the bed as close to Juliet as he could get without touching her. He thought that going straight for the cuddle was a bad, bad idea.

'I bumped into Stacey while I was out walking Buster and I cricked my neck. She insisted that I went back to her place for a massage.'

'She *insisted*?'

'You know what she's like.'

'Yes, I do. And this is supposed to be an *innocent* explanation?'

'Stacey is a trained therapist.'

'Yes, and I'm a tin of dolphin-friendly tuna.' Juliet raked a hand through her hair. 'I can't keep believing the best of you when you carry on like this.'

'She'd no sooner got her hands on me than I fell asleep.' He'd slept like a log, more soundly than he had in ages but, in a rare moment of wisdom, Rick thought it was best not to mention that.

'You were naked in her bed.'

'I still had my pants on,' Rick corrected. 'And I was *fast asleep* in her bed.'

'What had been going on just before that?'

'Nothing,' he assured her. 'Absolutely nothing.'

Juliet looked unconvinced.

'I swear to you.' Rick inched towards his wife. 'I did not have sexual relations with that woman.'

'Hmm,' his wife said, pursing her lips. 'Where have I heard *that* before?'

'Why would I go chasing after Stacey Lovejoy when I have you?'

'Because you can, Rick. She's made it clear since the minute she moved in that she's interested in you and, let's face it, things haven't been right between us for months now.'

Since your mother moved in, he wanted to say, but thought better of it. Instead, he opted for, 'Let's put all this behind us. All of it.'

'I don't feel that I know you any more, Rick.'

Reaching out, he clutched her hands in his and held them tightly. 'I'm still the man you married. Good old Rick.' He tried a smile; Juliet half-responded. 'I'm still in here somewhere. I've just been a bit of a twit lately. But none of it has been my fault, I promise you that.'

'You can't keep blaming everyone else, Rick. Take responsibility yourself.'

'I will. I definitely will.' He slipped his arm round Juliet and he viewed it as a good thing that she didn't shrug him off. 'You *can* rely on me, love. You know that.'

His wife sighed. 'I'm not sure that I can count on anyone or anything these days.'

'Don't say that,' he said. 'It's not like you to be so down.'

'Maybe I have just cause. Maybe I've finally run out of energy.' Juliet stood up. 'I have to go and start dinner.'

'Let me do it. I'll cook tonight.'

'No.' His wife held up a hand. 'I need some time on my own, Rick. To think about things.'

'A glass of wine then,' he suggested. 'I'll pour you a glass of something nice.'

'Just leave it alone. I don't want anything. I don't want to talk.'

'Don't give up on us,' he pleaded with his wife as she headed to the bedroom door. But he wondered whether she already had.

Chapter 75

In the middle of the night I hear an almighty crash from the dining room. I wasn't really asleep, but I'm wide-eyed now. 'Rick.' I shake my husband's shoulder and he mumbles in his sleep. *'Rick!'*

'What?' Now he's awake, rubbing his eyes with his fists.

We'd gone to bed without talking and I can count on one hand the number of times we've done that in our marriage. But now it seems that there's an emergency, so I can't keep up the silence.

'There was a noise,' I whisper. 'In the dining room.'

'It's nothing,' he assures me with a yawn. 'Go back to sleep.'

I click on the bedside light. 'We might have burglars.'

'We've nothing worth stealing. Go back to sleep.'

But then there's another noise from downstairs and my husband sighs. 'I'll go and look.'

There's another crash. I grab Rick's arm. 'You can't go down there by yourself. What if he's armed?'

My husband yawns again. He's clearly not taking this seriously.

'I'll come with you.' I swing my legs out of bed.

'What are *you* going to do if he's armed?' Rick observes. 'Pull a sawn-off shotgun out of your nightie?'

'Don't be ridiculous.'

'You aren't allowed to shoot burglars back these days,' my husband continues sleepily. 'You can only offer them a nice cup of tea so that they're fully refreshed while they steal your loot, otherwise it infringes their human rights.'

If we had any silver they'd have made off with it by now. 'While we're dilly-dallying up here,' I point out, 'they could be loading your plasma screen television into their van.'

That mobilises my husband and he's along the landing in a flash, me hurrying behind him.

'Wait here,' he says, as he starts to creep down the stairs.

'No,' I whisper. 'I'm frightened.'

There's another crash. A chair falling over. They certainly are the world's noisiest burglars.

We're at the bottom of the stairs now. Rick quietly pulls a tartan umbrella out of the stand by the front door.

'An umbrella?'

'Do you have any other suggestions?' Rick wants to know. 'I gave up golf years ago. I told you I should never have sold my clubs.'

My mouth is dry and my heart is pounding in my chest. Rick doesn't look very threatening in his Marks & Spencer pyjama set clutching his umbrella to his chest.

We creep through the kitchen, me holding on to Rick's T-shirt as we do. There are no lights on but the moon is shining brightly through the window. Sometimes I wish I was an insomniac as I love the house at this time of night when everything is peaceful. The nights when we haven't got burglars, of course.

We're at the dining-room doors now. I can see shadows moving through the glass panes. Is there more than one person in there? God, I'd never thought about that. Will we be able to take them on, the two of us?

Rick turns to me. 'After three,' he whispers. 'One. Two. Three.'

He flings open the dining-room doors and then shouts out in horror. I hear a man's voice cry out too.

Jammed up behind Rick, I can see very little so try to peer over his shoulder. 'Don't look,' he says.

So, naturally, I push past him to get a better view.

On the table – my dining-room table – a woman is spreadeagled and naked. My son, who I haven't seen so much of since he was in nappies, is moving above her. Two of the chairs have been knocked over and the fruit bowl, which was in the middle of the table, is upturned on the floor.

'Hi,' Tom says.

'What do you think you're doing?' Rick shouts.

There's really no answer to that.

'Oh, Tom,' I say. 'How could you?'

'Sorry, Mum,' he offers. 'Sorry about the noise. Got a bit carried away.'

I can see that clearly enough.

'Good evening,' the girl says from beneath him. 'It is very nice to see you. I have heard so much about you.'

It's safe to say that we've heard very little about her.

'Clean it up,' Rick says. 'Clean it up now.'

And with that we shut the dining-room doors again. We're both breathing heavily.

'What do you think to that?' Rick's face has gone an unhealthy shade of black.

'I don't know.'

'Was it the same woman as last time?'

'The one who got into bed with us?'

My husband nods, shaken.

'I don't think so. She sounded Italian.'

'What happened to the Bulgarian or whatever she was with the two kids? What's Tom trying to do?' my husband hisses. 'Is he on a one-man mission to foster Anglo-European relations?'

Would I have ever dared to do something like that at my parents' house? Rick and I haven't even had sex on our *own* dining-room table. Maybe we should.

'Let's go back to bed. Not that I'm going to be able to sleep now,' Rick mutters. 'That's another night ruined. Will I ever get any peace in this house?'

I have to say that I feel exactly the same. 'At least it wasn't burglars,' is all that I can offer.

We may pay the bills here, but we seem to have lost control over everything else. I'm weary down to my bones. My joints ache with disappointment.

Rick gives me a tentative squeeze. He knows that I'm still mad with him. The image of him naked in Stacey Lovejoy's bed hasn't gone away. 'You OK?'

I nod. My son was bonking some anonymous woman on the dining-room table. Of course I'm not OK! I want to lie on the floor and weep. I want to weep for the fact that no one cares about me or how I'm feeling. I want to weep for the loss of innocence of my son and my daughter. I want to weep for the breakdown of my family as it crumbles before my very eyes. I want to weep for the love that I lost. And I want to weep because everyone in the world seems to be having a better sex-life than me.

Chapter 76

The next day Steven collects me at lunchtime and takes me back to Watermill House so that we can snatch a brief hour together. 'You sounded very unhappy on the phone,' he tells me.

'It's not been a bed of roses at home recently,' I admit.

We sit on his wrought-iron chairs on the terrace and look out across the beautiful garden towards the river that meanders along the bottom of it.

'What can I do to help?'

'Nothing.' I shake my head as I smile at Steven. How would I manage without these short bursts of sanity in my otherwise mad life? 'Let's walk down by the water for a few minutes. I have to be getting back soon.'

We start out across the lawn, side by side. Steven's garden puts mine to shame even though it's a much larger patch. But I suspect that its faultless maintenance has little to do with Steven. He doesn't strike me as a man who'd be happy rootling around among the hollyhocks in his gardening gloves. The grass is mowed into regimented stripes and, although the garden has a large proportion of wild flowers blooming in its borders to blend in with the surrounding countryside, they are perfectly manicured, tamed. Nothing is left to chance here.

Steven's hand brushes against mine and I don't move it away. Emboldened, my old love takes my fingers in his. Each time we meet our bodies are becoming more comfortable with each other's again, and I think that might be a bad thing.

We walk in silence listening to the water rush into the old mill and babble along in the current of the river. Two swans float serenely by, white and majestic. It tugs at my heart to think that these magnificent creatures mate for life. Just the two, staying together forever to raise their family, battling against the odds of survival.

'I found Rick in bed with one of my neighbours yesterday,' I tell Steven flatly.

'No wonder you're down in the dumps.'

I don't mention the discovery of my son doing the dirty on the dining-room table otherwise he'll think that the whole of my family are sex mad. Which they are. Except me.

'It felt like someone had punched me in the stomach.' Similar to the feeling I had on my wedding day when Steven left me, I think. That's the only other time that I have felt such sickness from emotion.

'My poor love.'

I sit on the grass by the river and Steven joins me. He's still holding my hand and his shoulder is against mine. I'm not sure if he's leaning on me or I on him. But I suspect it may be the latter.

'I love Rick,' I tell him.

'Doesn't sound like he deserves it,' Steven observes.

'No,' I sigh. 'Possibly not.' We have had more than a taxing time recently. 'He swears that it's all a mistake.'

'And are you going to forgive him?'

'I expect so.'

'Juliet,' Steven says, suddenly serious. 'This may be a bad time to raise this, I don't know.' He turns to me. 'We both know where this is leading.'

'Do we?'

'I want to be with you,' he states. 'Permanently. You know that.'

Perhaps I do, but avoiding reality has been rather pleasant.

'We can't spend the rest of our lives snatching the occasional lunch-hour together, holding hands.' He looks down and studies my fingers locked in his. 'Much as I like that.'

We exchange a smile, but there's so much sadness behind it that I find tears spring to my eyes.

'We want to be together,' he says.

Do we?

Steven lets out an unsteady puff of air. 'Where do *you* think this is going?'

'Nowhere,' I hear myself say. 'Rick may or may not have been unfaithful to me, but I can't do it to him.'

'Leave him,' Steven says, just like that. 'Leave him and come to me.'

I laugh at that even though there's nothing remotely funny in Steven's statement.

'I have wasted so many years wishing I could turn back the clock,' he goes on. 'We can't let this opportunity slip through our fingers again.'

Saying nothing, I keep staring at the river and the swans.

'I could give you a life of ease,' my old love continues when I don't speak. 'I have so much money that I don't know what to do with it, Juliet. We could travel the world. I'd love to show you my other homes.'

'Chloe's about to have a baby,' I tell him. 'She needs me here.'

'We can be back here just as often as you want to be. All of my business can be done by phone and email. I have good people looking after my interests in each country.'

I'm discussing this as if it's a real possibility when I know in my heart that it's not.

'You love me,' Steven says, oh so confidently. 'You may not be ready to admit it to yourself yet, but I know that you do. Say that we can be together.'

I shake my head. 'How can we?'

It's beyond my imagination. I can't visualise a life that's any different from the one I lead now. Or perhaps I'm just too scared to. If I could glimpse a different future for me, would I have the courage or be selfish enough to grab it with both hands? Isn't it easier to believe that it simply doesn't exist?

'You need to take me back, Steven,' I say. 'Una will be tearing her hair out.'

We stand up and Steven's hands are on my bare arms and the feel of his skin against my skin makes my mouth go dry. I picture us years ago, two young people who had not a care in the world, arms wrapped around each other, bodies pressed together in a field, deep in golden yellow corn, not so far from here – and the image makes me want to cry out. I never made love with Steven, not fully, and you won't believe how much I regret that at this moment.

'I really hate to do this because I think I might just be in love with you all over again,' I say. 'But I can't see you any more.'

This has to end right here and now. And the sooner I get used to that, the better.

Chapter 77

Rick had spent the morning hoovering and dusting, putting washing in the machine, mopping the kitchen floor. Juliet would like that, surely? Before they'd disappeared he'd chivvied Chloe and Tom into tidying their disgusting bedrooms. Even Rick, who set the bar of his own tidiness reasonably low, could see that they were revolting pits. Now he sprayed the scent of lemon fresh polish through the downstairs rooms just to make sure that his wife noticed his handiwork the minute she came through the front door tonight.

He and Chloe still weren't speaking properly after the lapdancing débâcle and he knew that it was something he would have to address in the coming weeks. He'd wanted to congratulate her on her pregnancy, embrace his forthcoming grandad status, but found himself vacillating between wanting to hold and protect her and, not ten minutes later, wanting to scream at how stupid she was for throwing away everything she'd worked for so young. Until he found his balance, it was best to avoid a confrontation. And, more importantly, he had to get things back on track with Juliet first and foremost.

Rick had taken Buster for his walk this morning, skulking out of Chadwick Close, avoiding Stacey Lovejoy like the plague. He'd taken the dog to the far end of Toombs Meadow away from the usual haunt of the regular dog-walkers. It had made him out of puff but Buster had appreciated the extra length of his daily exercise. Amazingly, and he hardly even dared think this, let alone say

300

it out loud, his neck was completely pain-free. All tension gone. Stacey Lovejoy might be a marriage-breaker but she clearly did have the gift of healing hands. He hadn't told Juliet that and had, in fact, kept his neck at a strange angle over breakfast to try to elicit some sympathy.

In their bedroom, Rick made their bed, changing the sheets for clean ones. Then he decided to polish Juliet's dressing-table – even lifting all of the trinkets lined up on it to make a perfect job. He was replacing them, making a special effort to put them all back in their rightful home when he knocked over the carved wooden box that one of her elderly aunts had brought her back from a cruise holiday in the Caribbean many moons ago. A bunch of receipts fell onto the floor and Rick scrabbled to pick them up. Damn. It had all been going so well until then. How did Juliet file all of these? Were they in date order or just shoved in randomly? Knowing his wife, there would be a system to the keeping of sundry receipts.

Rick started to form the scraps of paper from Budgen, Tesco, John Lewis, etc into a tidy pile, ready to be returned to the box, when one caught his eye. It was for a beauty salon in Swinfens Yard called Face Facts. He didn't know that Juliet had beauty treatments. Goodness only knows, she didn't need them. She was a natural beauty, always had been in his eyes. Unwittingly, his gaze was drawn to the figure at the bottom of the receipt. One thousand pounds. Rick's eyes nearly popped out of his sockets. *One thousand pounds on beauty treatments.* Surely not. Money was tight at the moment. All the utility bills had soared, the council tax had gone up twenty pounds a month, and the phone bill – thanks to his kids yapping to their friends and his mother-in-law gossiping the night away – was always sky-high. They'd need even more money now that they were going to inherit an extra mouth to feed. How could Juliet even contemplate spending that amount of money on facial treatments? How could *anyone* actually spend a thousand pounds on their own face? Botox and fillers, the bill said. Juliet had let herself be injected with poison in the name of beauty? Had she gone mad?

He looked at the date. When had that been? Had he even noticed any difference after she'd blown a grand on her face? That would have earned him several black marks if it had passed without comment. Wait! Wasn't that when she was walking around with all those bruises on her face? She'd spent a thousand pounds and had ended up looking like Ricky Hatton for her pains? He'd have to talk to her about this.

There was no good his wife making him out to be the villain of the piece when she was up to no good either. All the grief she'd given him about his misdemeanours and yet she'd done this without thinking to mention it? Now he was hopping mad.

He had to get out of the house. The scent of the furniture polish was making him feel sick. He'd go into town, have a coffee, calm down and talk to Juliet about this when she came home.

As he came down the stairs, the local paper landed on the doormat. The headline read: DOGGING, LAPDANCING, SEX OFFENCE PERVERT IS LOTTERY LOSER. If this carried on, the newspaper was going to run out of room on its front page.

But worse than that, it seemed that his wife had told everyone about his failed lottery win too, when she'd promised that they'd keep it to themselves. Now he'd be even more of a laughing stock. How could she do this to him when he'd been trying his level best to make amends? It seemed that he and Juliet had a lot of talking to do.

Chapter 78

'So this is really it?' Steven says as we sit in his Aston Martin outside the library. His hands are gripping the steering-wheel. 'All that we once had between us, all that we're just starting to rediscover, you're simply going to let that go?'

'Yes.' I can't bring myself to look at him. 'I have to.'

'Don't make this mistake, Juliet,' Steven says. 'Please don't.'

Steven walked away from me many years ago without a backward glance, I have to remember that and I have to steel myself to do the same.

'This is breaking my heart,' he whispers.

'I'm sorry.' I don't think that I've ever had to deliberately hurt someone before, and it's a situation that I don't like to find myself in. This is so painful that I can hardly bear it. My chest feels tight and my breathing is shallow. 'I'd like us to remain friends.'

'Friends who still see each other for lunch regularly?'

'No.' I shake my head. 'Not that kind of friends.'

'Then what?' Steven sounds cross now, angry, frustrated. 'Am I allowed to say hello to you in the street? Will the library be out of bounds? What kind of friends will we be?'

'The type who think fondly of each other, but who rarely meet.'

I watch the readers go in and out of the library. Some people come in at the same time every single week, regular as clockwork. They like the same books, the same authors. Others are more erratic in their choice of day and selection of reading matter. Mrs Rowley

303

pushes the door open and disappears towards the High Street, tucking her books into her shopper as she does. She likes family dramas – Nora Roberts, Jodi Picoult, Rosie Thomas – and, every now and again, one of Barbara Erskine's mysteries. Mrs Bennett is one of our young mums. Her reading tastes run to more contemporary material – Sheila O'Flanagan, Cecelia Ahern, Jill Mansell. Stories of modern romances gone wrong.

This is my life. This is what my days are made up of. I love the library, the readers, my precious books. Can I imagine myself leaving this behind to globetrot around the world with Steven? I don't think so.

'If I can't be with you, Juliet,' Steven says, 'then I might as well move away. I don't want to be so near to you and yet so far. How can I see you with your family, with your husband, and know that you should be with me?'

'You'll manage,' I say sadly. 'We both will. You've got along just fine without me for all of these years. You can do it again.'

'Think of the fabulous life we could have together,' he urges. 'Promise me. Just think about it.'

Sometimes I have trouble making myself *not* think about it. My head is spinning and I feel sick.

Reaching over, I kiss Steven on the cheek. As I do he turns to me and my mouth finds his lips instead. They're hot, searching and, again, I'm whisked back in time to when those lips were so often on mine.

I break away from him before I lose myself in the sensation forever.

'I love you,' he says bleakly.

'Goodbye, Steven.'

'Don't do this,' he begs.

'Please,' I say. 'This is hard enough as it is. Just let me go.'

With that, I get out of his car, leave his life and run the few steps back to the sanctuary of the library.

Chapter 79

As Rick passed the library, he noticed that there was a sleek Aston Martin parked outside. Oh, the car of his dreams. Rick wondered who that belonged to. Stony Stratford was an affluent little town, but it wasn't every day that you saw an Aston in the neighbourhood. He was tempted to cross the road, ask the bloke who was driving it what it was like. Now that he was a loser on the lottery as well as in love, it was probably the closest he'd ever get to one. But, as he considered it, the car shot off and his opportunity was missed. Rick's heart sank.

He knew that he should pop in and see Juliet while he was here, but he couldn't face it. Rick was still cross, seething, and he needed to calm down before he and his wife addressed some of the issues between them. See what watching daytime TV had done for him? He was even thinking like a talk-show host now.

Instead, he went straight down to *Bon Appétit*, ordered a coffee and sat at a table by the window. Picking up a newspaper that had been abandoned by an earlier customer, he began to leaf through it. Nothing much in there but doom and gloom, he decided – and he'd had enough of that to last him a lifetime.

His coffee arrived and he was just taking his first welcome sip when someone tapped him on the shoulder.

'Rick,' the man said. 'Is that really you?'

Rick turned round in his chair. A tanned, handsome man stood beside him and Rick peered up at him.

'Steven.' The man took his hand. 'Steven Aubrey. It's been a while.'

Steven Aubrey. Bloody hell. It was the bloke who jilted Juliet all those years ago. What on earth was he doing back in town?

Rick stood up. 'I hardly recognised you, mate.' It looked like the years had been kind to Steven Aubrey and, for some reason, it made Rick aware that he was not looking his sartorial best. He was still wearing the scruffy T-shirt and jeans that he'd thrown on for cleaning the house. Steven Aubrey looked like he had other people to do that for him. 'You've been away a long time.'

'Too long,' Steven said, and they laughed at that though Rick wasn't sure why.

'Get a coffee,' Rick said. 'Pull up a chair.'

'Can't stay. I saw you in the window and thought I'd say hello.'

'My God, wait till I tell Juliet that you're back in town.' This was a man they'd argued about incessantly when they'd first married, as Rick always felt that he came up second best to Steven Aubrey though, to be honest, it was nothing that Juliet said or did to make him feel insecure. He was younger then and more foolish – if that was humanly possible, given his recent performance. Now he was man enough to shake hands with the guy, let bygones be bygones. 'I bet she'd love to see you after all this time.'

He wasn't sure that was the truth. Juliet might well run a mile in the other direction, if he knew his wife. Steven Aubrey had seriously messed up her life for a while and, as he was well aware, Juliet wasn't a woman to forgive and forget that easily.

'I've had lunch with her a few times already,' Steven said casually. 'Didn't she mention it?'

Rick felt his mouth go dry. 'No. No, she didn't.'

Steven shrugged. 'I can't imagine why. It's been great catching up with each other.' He laughed easily and tutted at what was clearly a pleasant memory. 'Just like old times. She's still a great lady. You're a lucky guy.'

Was he? Was he a 'lucky guy' when he didn't even know that his wife had been having cosy lunches with her old lover? What was all that about?

The man checked his watch. 'Have to go. See you around, Rick.' He clapped Rick on the back in a genial manner and headed towards the door. 'Make sure that you give all my love to Juliet.'

Rick didn't much like the sound of that but he said, 'Yeah, yeah. See you around.'

Rick watched Steven's back retreat and he fumed quietly. Then he heard the Aston start up and as it purred away, he was sure that Steven Aubrey was behind the wheel.

He drank his coffee again, but now it had gone cold and tasted bitter. Why hadn't Juliet told him that she'd had lunch – 'a few times already' – with Steven Aston Martin Driving Aubrey? Unless, he thought, she didn't want him to know what she was up to.

Chapter 80

We're all round the dining-room table. Which, with hindsight, I think is a bad idea as I still keep getting flashbacks of Tom's bottom bobbing up and down on top of it. I've polished it like mad three times with the Mr Sheen, but I'm not sure the stain of my son having sex here will ever be rubbed away.

I took a lot of trouble with dinner tonight – call it guilt – but I don't know why I bothered. My Mexican chicken dish which I laboured over has not been a great hit.

'It's a bit spicy,' my mother whinges as she pushes pieces of succulent chicken cooked in aubergines, tomatoes and chilli round her plate like a five year old.

I was brought up on a diet of over-boiled sprouts and meat that was roasted to the consistency of tanned leather. Did I ever complain?

'Arnold doesn't like garlic,' she carries on, wrinkling her nose. 'I'm going to be breathing it all over him tonight.'

I so don't want to know that. 'Leave it.' Buster's gagging for my Mexican chicken. He'll finish it off, no trouble. His tail is beating a hopeful tattoo against my leg under the table. 'Go and make yourself some toast.'

'No one's at home to Miss Snappy,' my mother says, but she eats her chicken without any more grumbling.

The thought that I could be having a life that involved a housekeeper, possibly first-class travel to wherever I desired and champagne all the way pushes into my brain and I struggle to push it out.

'Do I look fat?' Chloe wants to know as she also moves more of her meal round her plate than she puts in her mouth.

'You're having a *bay-bee*,' Tom says in a mocking way. 'Of course you look fat.'

'Mum!'

'Tom, don't say that to your sister.' I thought they'd grow out of this bickering by the time they were teenagers and that they'd get along like . . . well, like brother and sister. It seems that I was wrong. The older they get, the worse they're becoming. 'You're blooming,' I tell Chloe.

'That means I'm fat,' she moans, lip pouting.

'You look lovely,' I reassure her. 'But you are going to get bigger, sweetheart. I'm afraid it's inevitable. No one stays size zero when they're having a baby. It's a fact of life. But you'll be back in your jeans before long. Don't worry yourself about it.' I don't like to tell her that she's going to be so exhausted when the baby comes that she won't care whether she's the size of a barrage balloon or not, and that it will possibly continue for the next twenty years, by which time she'll have lost the will to live – just as I have.

I glance over to Rick. He's eating in silence. Perhaps he is also thinking where else in the world he could be rather than here.

'Dinner OK?' I ask.

'Fine,' he says, without looking up. So no compliments there. Tomorrow night it will be back to pasta in a jar of Homepride Cook-in sauce and stuff the lot of them.

I know that my husband and I need to sit down and talk about the Stacey Lovejoy situation, but both of us are currently avoiding it. Can I really blame Rick for taking a bit of solace with our comely neighbour when all he gets is aggro here? Perhaps not. But would he be so understanding about the time I spend with Steven if he knew?

'Can I borrow the car tonight, Mum?' Chloe.

'I want the car tonight.' That's Tom.

'I said it first.'

'I'm going to see Silva.' Is that the Eastern European girlfriend we've yet to meet fully-clothed or the one on the table? I can't remember.

'You're in no position to ask any favours,' Rick growls. 'I'm not even sure why you're still living here.'

'I had a shag on the dining-room table,' Tom puffs. 'It's no biggie.'

'What did he say?' Mum wants to know.

'He said he had a shag on the dining-room table, Gran.' Thank you, my daughter.

My mother's eyes light up. 'Perhaps Arnold and I could give that a go.'

'Over my dead body,' Rick mutters.

'That would work for me too,' my mother says cheerfully.

My husband pushes away from the table. 'I'm done. I'll take Buster for a walk.'

'There's apple crumble for dessert.'

'Maybe later,' he throws over his shoulder. He clicks his fingers for the dog and Buster scuttles after him.

'Now look what you've done,' I say to the rest of the table as Rick departs.

'Dad needs to take a chill pill,' Tom remarks.

'Don't!' They all jump as I raise my voice. 'Don't you dare criticise your father. You have no right.'

Then I slam about collecting the plates from the table, whipping my mother's from under her nose even though it's half-finished. Well, she shouldn't have dallied so long.

In the kitchen I watch Rick as he strides off down Chadwick Close. Moments later, Stacey Lovejoy's front door opens. She comes out with Britney. They're in matching pink outfits. Why would anyone in their right mind want to dress like their chihuahua? Then I think even worse things about her as I watch her totter down the road after my husband.

Chapter 81

Everyone, it seemed, had disappeared when Rick got back from walking the dog. He'd not gone his normal route with Buster just in case Stacey Lovejoy had thought about pouncing on him again. Plus he'd needed longer to walk off his frustration tonight. It wouldn't do to come home while he was still wired.

He put some fresh water in Buster's bowl, fussed with hanging up the lead and then went into the living room. Juliet was curled up on the sofa with a book, glass of wine to hand, Jack Johnson playing in the background. Even that had the potential to annoy him. Rick could have written a bestseller if he'd wanted to. Easy money. Rick Joyce had a few stories he could tell. Jack Johnson – the bloke lived in Hawaii, looked like an aftershave model and was a pop star. Why didn't God spread good fortune around more evenly? Why did some people have it all? Why did others have to be unemployed flooring fitters living with a whining mother-in-law, two stroppy child-adults and a wife who might or might not currently be having an affair with her old boyfriend? At least the dog loved him.

He sat down in the armchair. Juliet looked up. 'Want me to make you a cup of tea?' she asked.

Rick shook his head.

'Glass of wine?'

'No thanks.' His wife sipped at hers. What he actually needed was a double brandy. There was no easy way to broach this and when he did, he knew that there would be no going back.

Rick felt himself swallow as he spoke. 'I didn't know that Steven Aubrey was back in town.'

'Really?' Juliet put down her book. 'Is he? How amazing.'

Her voice sounded wrong. Too bright. Too casual. 'He looked really well.'

'That's great.'

'I saw him today,' Rick said. 'In town. While I was having a coffee.'

'Did he say hello?'

Rick nodded. 'More than that.' He took a deep breath. 'He said that you'd enjoyed several lunches with him.'

The colour drained from his wife's face. 'Steven said that?'

'Yes.'

Juliet sighed. She didn't speak and the silence stretched between them. Then, eventually, 'I didn't know how you'd feel about it.'

'So it's true?'

'Yes.'

'What's he doing back here?'

'His mother's unwell. He wanted to be with her and he's renting Watermill House for a few months. You know the place I mean.'

Rick nodded. An enormous place. He might have known. 'Have you seen a lot of him?' He could hardly comprehend that they were even having this conversation. It was like waking up in the middle of his worst nightmare.

She swung her legs down from the sofa and sat perched on the edge. 'We've been to the pub a few times.'

'Why didn't you tell me?'

More sighing. 'When do we ever get a chance to talk about things with this lot around?' She made a gesture that encompassed the whole house. 'Things that matter to us. I tried to broach the subject, Rick, but the time was never right.'

'Maybe you just didn't try hard enough.'

'We have had rather a lot to contend with just lately.' Juliet was unusually defensive.

'I agree that we've had our share of troubles,' Rick admitted. 'And that I have been a contributory factor to that.'

His wife snorted, which took him aback.

'I found you in someone else's bed yesterday,' she reminded him. 'Don't think about taking the moral high ground with me. I've had a few lunches with Steven and, to be honest, Rick, I think I would have gone mad without them.'

'Do you still have feelings for him?' He'd seen Ricki Lake ask that on her television programme while he'd been off work.

'Yes,' Juliet said. 'I was engaged to him. He broke my heart. You know that. He can't just come back into my life without my experiencing some emotion – but I'm married to *you*.'

'So are you planning any more of these cosy *tête-à-têtes*?'

'No.' Juliet hung her head. 'We've said all that we needed to say to each other. I'm not going to see any more of Steven.'

'I'm glad to hear it.'

'What about Stacey Lovejoy? Seeing as she lives right across the road from us, she's going to be somewhat harder to avoid.'

'The woman's got a silly crush on me,' Rick said. 'I'm doing nothing to encourage it.'

'No more popping round there to fix pipes, mend plugs, check the phone. Have massages.'

'No,' he agreed. 'None of that. I'll keep her at arm's length from now on.'

'Then I'm glad to hear that too.'

Juliet picked up her book again and he noticed that her hands were shaking. He looked at his wife and, for the first time in his life, he didn't trust her. From the way she'd looked at him, he knew that she no longer trusted him either. And if the trust was gone, what else did they have left?

Chapter 82

Una and I lean on the counter. The library is as dead as a doornail today. It's raining stair-rods outside which is keeping the punters away. We have shelved all the books that need shelving, have sent a few faxes, have eaten some of Don's biscuits as he's at a meeting, done all that needs to be done. Now we're twiddling our thumbs and watching the rain stream down the windows. We should probably go upstairs and check that there are no leaks in the roof or any telltale drips that need buckets putting under them, but neither of us move.

'Things are very strained at home,' I tell Una. 'If we had a spare room then I'm sure that Rick would be sleeping in it.'

'That bad?'

I nod, unsure of my voice. 'Rick knows that I've been seeing Steven.'

'Not good,' she says.

'No,' I agree.

'How on earth did he find that out? Did your mum blab?'

I shake my head. 'Steven blabbed.'

'What an idiot,' is Una's assessment.

'Perhaps he did it on purpose to provoke a reaction. He wants me to leave Rick and for us to be together.'

'Does it sound like an attractive proposition?'

I close my eyes and take a moment before answering. 'When I sat there at dinner last night with all of my family bickering and squabbling around me, then yes, I'm afraid to admit that it does.'

'Steven's quite a man.'

'I suppose I've never fully got over him,' I confess. 'It was always unfinished business. Now that he's back it's just thrown everything into complete turmoil again.'

'What did you tell him?'

'I said that I couldn't see him again. That it was over.'

'Good,' my friend says. 'That's the right thing to do.'

'Is it?'

'Yes.' Una casually twiddles her hair round her finger. 'Can I have him now that you've finished with him?' That makes us both laugh.

'I thought things were going well with Internet Tex.'

Una shrugs. 'I think so. He's been so busy that we haven't had time to meet yet, but we've progressed to him phoning me every night.'

'That's nice.'

'He's talking about us going into business together. What do you think?'

'What kind of business?'

'Tex wants to import jewellery into the UK from the Far East and for us to set up an internet shop.'

'Is that wise?'

'He says that he'd like my input into choosing the designs. Tex has sent some images to me by email. They look great. It would mean that we could travel overseas together to source suppliers. I like the sound of that.'

'You'd leave the library?'

Una snorts. 'Like a shot.' She gets the photograph of him out of her handbag and we study it together. Una's expression goes all faraway and dreamy. 'That looks like a man you could trust, right?'

He looks a little too tanned and a little too confident for my liking. 'I don't know. Just be careful. Is there money involved?'

Una bristles slightly. 'He wants me to put ten thousand pounds in.'

I give a low whistle. 'Wow. That sounds like a lot of jewellery.'

'It's just some working capital.'

315

'Do you have that kind of money sitting around?'

My friend shrugs. 'I could cash in some ISAs.'

'I think you should take it very slowly, Una. Meet with him, find out whether you have a relationship or not. This is a big step to take with someone who's essentially a stranger.'

'Have you ever thought that you might just be a little *too* conservative, Juliet?' my friend snaps at me.

I feel stung. She asked for my opinion and I gave it. Now it's clear that she doesn't like my answer.

'This small life might suit you,' my friend continues, 'but it bores me out of my head. I want to get away from Stony Stratford, from the library, from the small-town mentality. All of the things you love about it, I hate.'

Una's venom takes me aback.

'You've been offered the chance to get away, with a wonderful man, start a new life, but you're too set in your ways, too limited in your vision to ever imagine anything else. Well, I'm not.' Una flicks at her hair. 'This might be my big chance to get out of here and I damn well want to grab it with both hands.'

'I didn't know you felt like that,' I say quietly.

'Well, now you do.' Una is breathing heavily.

All the time we've been friends and we've never had a cross word. Now we're squabbling over some dodgy-looking, permatanned, internet gigolo. I don't know what to say. I feel wounded, hurt and at a loss. And I think the worst thing is that some of her words have really struck home.

Chapter 83

Rick had his feet up and was watching *The Jeremy Kyle Show* with Rita when there was a knock at the door. This is what he'd sunk to – morning telly with his mother-in-law. Rick sighed. The sooner he got his act together and found himself another job the better.

He plodded out to the hall, muttering as the bell rang again. When he opened the door, Hal was standing there.

His friend had last night's local newspaper in front of him. The headline DOGGING, LAPDANCING, SEX OFFENCE PERVERT IS LOTTERY LOSER held high.

Rick's heart sank.

'Mate?' Hal said with a big grin.

'I know,' Rick answered dejectedly. 'You'd better come in.'

He led his friend through to the kitchen as he didn't want Rita overhearing this discussion. Rick put the kettle on while Hal leaned on the cupboard next to him.

'Is that why you told me to stuff my job?' his friend and employer wanted to know. 'Did you really think that you'd won the lottery?'

Rick nodded. 'I'd got the wrong week's ticket though.'

Hal chuckled at that. 'So I read in the local rag.'

'I asked Juliet not to tell anyone, but she must have blabbed to someone. I'm guessing the Desperate Divorcée. Next thing I know, I'm a laughing stock.'

'You've got to admit, mate, it's very funny.'

'Not from where I'm standing.'

317

Hal started to laugh properly.

'Let it drop. Twenty million would have come in very handy.'

His friend was guffawing now and Rick, despite himself, started to smile too.

'You plonker,' Hal giggled, holding his sides. 'You total plonker.'

Rick was laughing now. 'You wouldn't find it so funny if I was on a yacht in the Bahamas now, eh?'

'But you're not. You're stuck in Stony Stratford feeling like a twat!'

They laughed together until they cried. When the hilarity died down, Rick gave Hal some kitchen roll and they both dabbed at their tears.

'I needed a good laugh,' Hal said.

'Me too,' Rick admitted. 'Things haven't been so great round here.'

'They're bloody awful at my place too. Shannon's "with child".'

'Pleased?'

'What do you think?'

Rick handed Hal a mug of tea and they chinked them together. 'To the new father.'

'To the lottery loser.' They supped their tea together, then Hal said, 'I have a small peace-offering.' He rooted in his back pocket and pulled out two tickets. 'Who's our favourite football team?'

'Manchester United.'

He waggled the tickets at Rick. 'Man United versus Portsmouth at Wembley Stadium, Jackson's Lager Charity Trophy. Some men would kill for one of these.'

Rick's eyes lit up. 'I'd be one of them.'

'Are you going to be nice to Uncle Hal from now on?'

'It depends what being "nice" involves.'

'Come back and work for me, Rick,' Hal pleaded, all bravado gone. 'It's been crap without you and I know that I've taken the piss recently. All that will stop. Just say that you'll come back.'

'And I get one of the tickets if I do?'

'Oh yes.'

Rick held out his hand and they shook on it. 'It's a deal.'

'I would have let you have the ticket anyway, mate,' Hal admitted. 'I've no other friends since I left Melinda.'

'You're a decent bloke,' Rick told him.

'I'm not,' Hal said. 'I'm a complete tosser who walked out on his wife and kids. And for what? Look at the bloody mess I'm in now. The man who's lost more than he's found.' He laughed again, but this time there was only bitterness in the sound. 'You might not have won the lottery, mate, but you still have your family round you. I never realised how important that was until it was too late.'

Hal's was a salutary tale and Rick realised that he'd come close to losing Juliet over the Stacey Lovejoy and sex-scandal incidents. Well, that was the end of it. He couldn't stand by and let her old boyfriend walk into their lives and waltz off with his wife. Steven Aubrey had blown his chance years ago. Rick wasn't about to do the same. Now was the time to stop the rot and turn this whole thing around.

Chapter 84

Later that afternoon, my dad comes into the library. He has a wicker basket over his arm and a velvet scarf draped jauntily around his neck. His fine grey hair is swept back in what could only be called a bouffant style. I'm watching my father morph into Quentin Crisp right before my very eyes.

Dad shakes the raindrops from the pink umbrella he's carrying and that makes me smile. Pulling his books out of his wicker basket, he places them on the counter. I lean over and kiss him on the cheek.

'All done with these?' I scan in his Wilbur Smith, Peter James, Robert Goddard and John Connolly.

'I enjoyed them. Thanks for putting me onto that John Connolly. I liked his stuff. Nicely written.'

'Want to choose some new ones?'

Dad shakes his head. 'Thanks all the same, love, but I don't get so much time to read now. With Samuel and everything.' A flush comes to his cheeks.

I stop my scanning and look up at my parent. 'Are you happy with him, Dad?'

My father nods. 'He's a very good companion more than anything else. I know you youngsters put a great store by sex—'

I'm not sure that Dad should include me in that.

'—but Samuel makes me laugh and he looks after me. He's teaching me to play chess. I'm glad you like him, love.'

320

'He seems lovely.'

'He is. He's a very caring man. Who'd have thought?' Dad gives a contented chuckle. 'At my age!'

I'm so pleased for my father, but what scares me is that it could take until I'm his age to find out who *I* am.

'I don't see enough of you now,' I tell him. 'Let me see if Una will cover for me for half an hour and we can grab a quick coffee.'

'I'd like that, love. If you can spare the time.'

'I'll ask her.'

My friend is on the top floor, tidying up the rack of audio-books. 'Look at the mess these are in,' she huffs as I approach. Things are still strained between us after her outburst this morning. She bangs about with the CDs and cassettes.

'I want to pop out for a short while to have a coffee with my dad,' I say quietly. 'Is that OK with you?'

'Of course,' she says, and I hear the relief in her voice that we're back on speaking terms. 'You didn't take your lunch-hour today. You're owed it.'

'If you can manage . . .'

'Go on. I'll be fine.'

I scuttle back downstairs, grab my handbag and my own brolly – which is nowhere near as glamorous-looking as my dad's – then I link my arm through his. 'We're on,' I say. 'But we haven't got long.'

'Let's make the most of it then,' he agrees, and together we head out into the rain.

There's a posh restaurant opened up in the High Street. Normally I'd usher Dad into *Bon Appétit*, but I feel this place is more fitting to his new status. The restaurant is decorated with soft heather and silver-grey colours. I'd like to do out my lounge like this, if only I had the nerve. I marvel at the fact that somehow Dad has managed to throw off his old life completely and yet I can't even think about choosing a moderately radical shade of paint for my home.

We make ourselves comfortable on the squashy grey leather sofas and order tea, telling our waiter that we haven't much time. Almost instantly, beautifully presented on a dark wood tray, a pot of English Breakfast tea arrives.

'Shall I be Mum?' I say, and then could nearly bite out my own tongue.

Dad gives me a wry smile.

I pour the tea and we sip in silence, enjoying the companionship. I've always been more comfortable with my dad. Despite the fact he was always slightly set in his ways, he was still better company than Mum. Less self-absorbed. Less judgemental. And we share our passion for books. I'd like to think I've inherited that from him.

'Is everything all right with you?' Dad asks.

'Yes, yes,' I say, swatting away his concern. 'Fine.'

'I thought you looked a little bit . . .' he stops to consider the word carefully. 'Strained.'

'Life is rather difficult at home,' I admit.

'With Rick?'

There's no good pretending with Dad. 'With everyone.'

'It can't be easy living with your mother.'

'No.'

'I should know,' Dad says. 'I did it for long enough.'

'Don't you miss her at all?'

My father shakes his head. 'Already it seems like a different life. I was never very happy with Rita, but we muddled along, made the best of things. Mainly I stayed with her for you.'

'Oh, Dad.'

'Then when you'd left home and were married, it seemed too late to do anything about it. I settled for what I had.'

'I didn't know that. I thought you'd get back together,' I tell him. 'I thought this was just a phase she was going through. You never expect your parents to divorce.'

'We're not technically divorced, love,' he reminds me. 'I'm not sure I see the point of doing all that paperwork at our age. It doesn't seem important.'

I suppose that Mum is entitled to half of the house. But my

parents' home is the world's tiniest place: Dad couldn't downsize from that. Even if they sold it, there wouldn't be enough in the kitty for both of them to buy homes to start all over again. Whatever happens, I can see one of them needing to live with us for the foreseeable future. The thought doesn't fill me with great joy. If only that lottery win of Rick's had been a real one.

'I'm sorry that I've been so wrapped up in myself lately,' Dad says. 'I feel I've neglected you.'

'Don't be silly. Just as long as you're happy.'

'I am. But what about you?'

'Oh, me?' I paste on a bright smile and try not to think how my marriage seems to be coming apart at the seams and my family is going to pot before my eyes. 'I'm right as rain.' We finish our tea and I check my watch. 'Back to work.'

We stand and I help my dad up. He puts his hand on my arm. 'I waited until I was seventy-two to find out who I really am,' he says. 'I'd have never known at all if Rita hadn't upped and left me. I don't want you to do the same. I always put what your mother wanted first, thinking it would give me a quiet life. And I don't think I should have done that.'

'That's what people in families do.' You lose yourself, your own desires to keep the unit together. Isn't that what it's all about?

Dad shrugs as we head together for the door. 'Whatever you do with your life, be happy, love. Don't wait as long as I did to find contentment.'

I think of my husband and I think of my old flame and wonder which way contentment lies.

Chapter 85

Just over half an hour later and I'm back at the library. I've had a good gossip with Dad, which is lovely, and I realise that he's the only one in my family who's not causing me any grief at the moment. Him and dear old half-deaf, half-blind Buster, of course. At the door, I shake the rain from my umbrella and prepare to take up my post again.

I bustle inside, then pull up short. I'm surprised to see Steven standing casually at the desk with Una. She's leaning forward, laughing, displaying an alluring amount of cleavage for a librarian.

'Hey,' he says as I appear, and he stands back from Una.

My friend also straightens herself up, fussing with her hair.

Steven takes my arm and steers me towards the children's section. 'I know that I said I wouldn't come to see you,' he says. 'But I had to.'

'Steven . . .' I begin.

He holds up a hand. 'Hear me out.' My old flame checks round to see that no one else is listening. 'Mum died yesterday.'

'Oh, Steven.' All the barriers I'd tried to erect against him come crashing down in an instant. 'I'm so terribly sorry.'

'It was quite peaceful in the end.' His eyes fill with tears and I want to hug him but I know that this isn't the place.

'I've spent all morning making arrangements for the funeral.' He puffs out a breath. 'I never knew there was so much to organise.'

'If there's anything I can do to ease the burden . . .' I offer.

'Come to the funeral,' he says. 'That's all I ask. Be there for me. I have no one else.'

'Of course I'll come. You know I will.'

'I'll let you have the details later. I've asked everyone to come back to the house afterwards, got caterers in.'

'That will be lovely,' I tell him. My hand strays to his arm. 'Your mother would have liked that.'

'I think she would.'

I hear Una clearing her throat. Glancing over my shoulder, I can see that there's a queue building up at the desk. My friend raises her eyebrows at me. It's obvious that she needs my assistance. 'I hate to do this, Steven, but I have to go and help Una.'

'I understand.' He takes my hand and lowers his voice. 'I tried to stay away. Really I did. But I've missed you so much.'

Then Steven strides towards the door. And I realise that I've missed him too.

Chapter 86

It's nearly a week later when I push open the ancient oak door and enter the Church of St Mary and St Giles. Centred right in the High Street of Stony Stratford, the church has been a landmark of the town for hundreds of years. It's also the place where Steven and I were due to marry all those years ago. I've rarely shown my face in here since then, apart from the odd fête, festival or Christmas service. Now I'm here for Mrs Aubrey's funeral.

It's twelve o'clock and Don has given me a couple of hours of compassionate leave from the library to attend. Many people from the town are here as Steven's mother was a popular and active figure in many of the women's circles until her illness struck her down.

This was Harriet Aubrey's local church and she was a regular every Sunday. I think she was on the flower committee too and, if she was, her companions have done her proud. The church is filled with gorgeous white lilies. Clearly, Steven has given them a generous budget. The inside is bright and airy. Sun shines through the stained-glass windows, throwing pretty rainbow patterns on the stone floor.

Steven is at the front of the church and I don't know what to do. Should I slide into a pew at the back or brazenly go up to him and be by his side? What exactly did he mean when he said he wanted me here? While I'm still pondering my place, Steven turns and sees me. He beckons me to go down to his pew at the front.

Taking a deep breath, I do just that. My heels tap on the flag-stones as I walk to the front and I feel as if all eyes are turning to watch me. I've told Rick that I'm coming here today and he did offer to join me, but then couldn't get the time off work at the last minute. I'm glad that he's back with Hal and I think he is too, even though he still grumbles about him every night.

'Glad that you could make it,' Steven whispers to me. 'Everything OK?'

I nod. 'And you?'

His smile is sad. 'Fine.'

The organist is playing a beautiful hymn. I recognise the tune, but it's so long since I've been in a church that I can't tell you what it is.

As his mother's coffin comes down the aisle to the altar, I feel Steven lean against me, his shoulder brushing mine. I'm worried that he'll take my hand and start the tongues wagging, but he doesn't.

The service is lovely and, afterwards, cars whisk us back to Watermill House where Steven has laid on the most magnificent buffet for the mourners. The sun is shining and the gathering has the jolly air of a party instead of a wake. I think Steven's mother would have approved. She was quite the socialite in the town in her day.

'Harriet was very proud of you,' I tell him as he pours me a glass of chilled white wine. 'Rightly so. She would have appreciated this.'

'I wish I could have done more for her,' he says. 'I *should* have done more instead of gallivanting round the world.'

'She was never lonely here,' I reassure him. 'Your mother had a lot of very good friends. You only have to look at the turn-out today.'

'You're right. No need to beat myself up. But sometimes we do, just because we can.'

We're strolling down the garden now, my favourite place, away from the bustle.

'You shouldn't leave your guests,' I say.

'They can manage without me for five minutes.'

After the recent rain the river is in full flow, but now the sun has returned and sparkles on the water like droplets of crystal. A weeping willow cools its branches in the flow. It's not until we're at the water's edge that Steven speaks.

'I don't need to stay here now,' he says, without looking at me. 'I could be off tomorrow. The lease is due up here in a couple of months. Instead of buying it, I could just let the place go.'

'That would be a shame. It's a beautiful home.'

'But too big for one person rattling around in it.'

'Yes. I can see that.'

Now Steven stops and faces me. 'The offer's still open to come and join me in it.'

I lower my eyes. 'You know I can't do that.'

'Don't days like today remind you just how short life is? How fleeting our time here? I want to spend it being as happy as I can, Juliet. Don't you want that too?'

'Yes,' I say. 'I do.'

'Then leave Rick.' This is the first time he has couched it in such bald terms. 'Leave Rick and come here. You could do it today.'

'I couldn't.'

'Then tomorrow, the day after. I'll wait. I don't care how long it takes, but I want you here. By my side. As my wife. It's your rightful place. I should have seen that years ago.'

'This is a pipe dream, Steven. A lovely fantasy. We can't be together. We've already had this conversation. I can't leave my family.'

'Can't or won't?'

'It amounts to the same thing.'

'But I love you.'

My heart feels like it's ripping apart. 'Sometimes that isn't enough.'

'And sometimes staying where you are through misguided loyalty is the wrong thing to do.'

'I'm married, Steven. That always meant forever to me.'

'I can show you things beyond your wildest dreams. I'll make you the happiest person alive. Don't you want that for yourself?'

'Yes, but . . .'

'I don't want you to get to the end of your life, Juliet, and regret that you never took this chance for happiness.'

With that Steven strides away from me back towards the throng of the gathering. I finish my drink, walk back the house, skirting the party to avoid having to say goodbye, and find one of the cars and a driver to take me back to the library. My head aches and not just from drinking wine at lunchtime.

Is Steven right? Will I regret this in time? Everyone else in my life seems to be doing exactly as they like with no thought of the consequences. Why should I not do that too?

Chapter 87

I sleepwalk my way through the rest of the afternoon at the library, mulling over in my mind what Steven said. My brain tosses it backwards and forwards until I can think no more. Luckily, I'm on the information desk upstairs and every five minutes my emotional turmoil is interrupted by questions from members of the great unwashed general public about the role of the Town Clerk, the plans for the folk festival this year, new library readers wanting tickets and people using the computers. Never have I been so grateful to be rushed off my feet.

When four-thirty comes around, the library has quietened down again and I have a chance to go downstairs. Una is at the counter looking shell-shocked.

'Where did they all come from?' she wants to know. 'I haven't stopped for the last two hours.'

'Me too.' I don't tell her that I'm happy not to have time to think.

'We're completely out of stamps,' she tells me. 'I hadn't realised our stock had got so low. Want to knock off early and go to the post office on your way home?'

'Yes. I'll do that.'

'You look all in,' my friend says, pursing her lips at me. She gives me a hug and I wish she wouldn't as I might just cry. 'Did the funeral go OK? I haven't had a chance to ask you.'

'It was fine. Very nice. As these things go.'

'Was Steven all right?'

'He coped very well.'

'Good.'

I need to get out of here. Grab some fresh air. 'What do we need from the post office?'

'Get a couple of dozen first-class stamps. That should do us for a while.' Una gives me the money out of the petty-cash tin and I slip on my jacket.

'Anything else while I'm out?'

'Perhaps get Don some biscuits. We've scoffed them all again.'

'OK. I'll see you tomorrow.'

'Chin up,' Una says.

'Yes.' But what if I'm tired of keeping my chin up? What if I want to hurl myself to the ground, have a tantrum, tell everyone what I really think of them?

A minute later and I'm out of the library and walking down the High Street towards the post office.

The main one is housed in a small supermarket these days and as I go in the door, I grab a packet of Gypsy Creams for Don as they're my and Una's favourites. But the queues at the till and at the post office counter are horrendous – I notice that there's only one girl serving and she's always slow – so I put the biscuits back and head instead up to the old, decrepit post office that's at the far end of town.

The old post office is scruffy and very few people use it now as the one in the centre is much more convenient, but it's always packed. I probably wouldn't have walked up here myself, but I felt like stretching my legs rather than standing waiting.

The place is filthy dirty and could do with a thorough clean. I don't know how they even stay in business, to be honest. The lino on the floor is cracked and bits of it are missing. There's one of those wire things with a sad selection of greetings cards on it. They're all covered with a fine film of muck.

Thankfully, there's a much shorter queue in here and I take my place in line patiently. Mr Green, the postmaster, is as old as the

hills and is a man who cannot be rushed. In hindsight, it will probably take me just as long to get served here. I get ready to bide
my time. The woman in front of me turns round and smiles at me,
and I recognise her as one of Mum's friends, Mrs Richmond.

'Hello there.'

'Hello, Juliet,' she replies. 'Lovely day.'

'Yes.' And then, before we have a chance to discuss the weather
further, the door bursts open. Probably over-exuberant schoolkids.
Everyone in the queue turns to look at the commotion.

But it isn't schoolkids. Two men in clown masks stand inside the
door. I'd laugh, but it's clear that they don't mean to be funny as
they're both brandishing sawn-off shotguns.

One has a mass of ginger hair. The other is bald with black curls
round his ears. Both have traditional clown faces with wide-eyes
and full red mouths. The ginger one flicks the *Open* sign to *Closed*
and locks the door.

I think I should be frightened, but I'm in a bubble of calm.
Everything is happening in slow motion. This just seems so incon-
gruous, to be caught in an armed raid in sleepy Stony Stratford.
Why would they choose this post office to rob? Do they mean to
be in the bigger, better one in the centre rather than this drab little
outpost?

'Get on the floor!' the bald one shouts. 'And you won't get hurt!'

'Get down! Get down!' the other one joins in. Both are becoming
more agitated now.

Two of the gentlemen and one of the elderly ladies in the queue
crouch down to the floor. Mrs Richmond looks at me. 'Juliet,' she
whispers to me, but still I don't move.

'Lie down!' the ginger clown shouts, waving his gun. 'Hands
above your head!'

I'm still standing up and so is Mrs Richmond. The elderly lady
on the floor reaches up to try to take my hand, but she can't quite
reach it. 'Don't make them angry,' she murmurs.

'You two! Get down!' the bald clown shouts at me and my grey-
haired companion. He points the shotgun in my face. 'Get down!'

'I don't want to get dirty,' I say.

The clowns exchange a puzzled glance.

'If I lie on the floor, I'll get dirty. I've been to a funeral today. This is my best suit.'

'And this is a new mackintosh,' Mrs Richmond says quietly. We all look at her new mac. It's a light beige.

'You wouldn't want to lie on the floor in that,' I tell the gunmen.

'Right then,' the ginger clown says, sounding slightly perplexed. 'Stay there and don't move or I'll blow your fucking head off.'

There's a gasp of terror from the people on the floor. Mrs Richmond and I stay where we are.

'Put the money in the bag,' they say to Mr Green, the postmaster. The bald one throws a brown sack at him. 'Now! Now! Quicker than that!'

Mr Green does as he's told. Which seems quite sensible in the circumstances. When he's stuffed the money in, he hands the full bag to the gunmen.

'Is that it?'

Mr Green nods furiously.

'Stay here,' they shout. 'Don't move! Don't try to follow us! Goddit?'

With that they unlock the door, fumbling as they do, then they burst back out onto the street.

On the floor, the traumatised pensioners don't move. I turn to Mrs Richmond. She's as white as a sheet and looks like she's about to faint.

'OK?'

She nods at me, dazed.

I rush out after the clowns. All I see is them driving away in a car that's the same as Rick's — a Vauxhall Cavalier. I make a mental note of their registration number, committing it to memory. Then I fall to my knees and I'm promptly and heartily sick in the gutter.

Chapter 88

It was good to be back at work. Rick wasn't the sort of person who could amuse himself with daytime television or pottering in the garden. Plus there were the bills to be paid. No, it felt good to be busy again and he was glad that he and Hal had cleared the air between them. His mate had been quite deferential towards him today and he'd also offered him a pay rise. Not much, but every little helped.

Rick stood back and admired his handiwork. Today he and Hal had been laying a laminate floor for a country pub just outside Stony Stratford in the village of Beachampton that had just undergone a major refurb. It was looking good. American oak, one of his favourite colours. Always gave a classy finish. The re-opening was at the weekend and the landlord had invited them both to go along for a celebratory drink.

Hal stood up too. 'Nice job, Ricky-Boy.'

'Yeah.'

The room they'd just finished was on the ground floor at the back of the pub. It was large and square, very airy, and had been painted a shade that would probably be classed as duck-egg blue, if he'd known anything about paint colours.

'This would be a great venue for a party,' Hal remarked. 'I might consider it if I ever get married again.' He laughed at his own joke. In a new spirit of camaraderie, Rick joined in. The chances of Hal getting married again were about the same as Mohamed Al Fayed becoming a knight of the realm.

Then Rick had a light-bulb moment. Hal was right. It would be a great place to have a party and he was thinking of his Silver Wedding anniversary. That's what he could do for Juliet, organise a great party to mark the fact that they'd survived twenty-five years of marriage, maybe whisk her away to Paris for a romantic weekend afterwards. She'd like that.

Tom could do some invitations on the computer – if he could tear himself away from shagging the entire male or female population of Stony Stratford and beyond. Chloe could help him with choosing the buffet and the finer points of party decorations – great, he knew that his daughter's two years of studying media and fashion wouldn't be entirely wasted. And he could rope Rita in for something too. She must have a dozen different friends who could knock up a decent celebration cake for them.

He'd go and find the landlord now, see if he could get it booked in right away. There wasn't much time to lose. Their anniversary was in a couple of weeks' time. Rick could have kicked himself that he hadn't thought of this earlier. But then he could have kicked himself for a lot of things he'd done recently. This party could draw a line under all that had gone before. He rubbed his hands in glee. This was the new start he was looking for.

Chapter 89

The police have only just turned up at the house when Rick arrives home. My husband comes through the front door looking very worried and I wonder if there's some other misdemeanour that he hasn't yet told me about. But, to be fair, he doesn't know that I've been having adventures of my own.

'What's wrong, Officer?' he asks nervously as he comes in, eye still on the patrol car outside.

'They're here about me,' I explain.

'You?' The relief on Rick's face is palpable.

Thanks to my husband, the Joyces are, I fear, in great danger of becoming the Krays of Chadwick Close. 'I think we should go through to the living room.'

I lead and the two youthful policemen and Rick follow. When I've closed the door behind us, I sit down on the sofa and my husband sits next to me. The policemen take the armchairs. They're both boys, younger than Tom.

'You look very pale,' Rick notes as he glances at me.

'There was a robbery at the post office,' I explain with a sigh. 'The old one at the top of the town. I was in the queue at the time.'

'Your wife is a very lucky woman,' the youngest of the two policemen says.

'How's that?'

'The information she gave us earlier has helped us to identify the gang behind this. They're very dangerous men with a high propensity for violence.'

'I gave them the car's registration number,' I tell Rick. 'And the make.' My husband knows that I don't have an advanced knowledge of cars for vehicle identification and duly looks very surprised by this. 'It was the same as yours.'

A happy coincidence for me. Less so for the criminals.

'They've been implicated in a string of robberies,' the officer continues, and are completely ruthless villains.' That sounds like something out of a Guy Ritchie film. 'They recently killed two men and left one for dead.'

'Did they?' My voice is barely audible.

'As I said, you're a very lucky woman.'

'Can we just go over your statement again, Mrs Joyce?' The other policeman flicks open his notebook.

After the robbery, Mr Green the postmaster had called the police. They'd arrived at the post office in minutes. So much for all the complaints about slow response times, etc. They were there right when we needed them. I was still helping to brush down the other people who we'd helped get up from the floor. And it *was* filthy – I was right. After that, I gave all the details I had to the officers who attended and then they let me go.

Despite my bravado at the time, my legs shook as I walked back to my car parked at the library and I had a cup of hot, sweet tea when I got home. I feel a bit sick now thinking about it again. Delayed shock, I expect.

'Can you just take us through the events one more time, please?'

Taking a deep breath, I launch into a description of the post office robbery – telling them about the clowns, the shouting, the fact that I raced after them and managed to get the registration number of their getaway vehicle. All the things I've said before.

'We have,' the policeman checks his notes, 'Mrs Richmond's statement here.'

'Yes.'

'She said that you both refused to lie on the floor when the gunman told you to.'

'Yes,' I say again. 'That's correct. We didn't want to get dirty.'

Everyone's eyebrows shoot up at that, including Rick's.

'It didn't look like it had been mopped for ages,' I offer in my defence. 'Mrs Richmond was wearing a new beige mac.'

'And what was *your* reasoning?' Rick wants to know. His face has darkened somewhat.

'I don't know.' With hindsight it seems not to be the wisest thing to do. Maybe you had to be there.

'I think that's all for now, Mrs Joyce.' Both policemen rise. 'If there's anything else we'll be in touch.'

'Thank you.'

Rick shows them to the door. I curl up on the sofa and hug my knees to my chest. There's a trembling inside me that I can't stop. Then I hear their car drive off and my husband comes back into the living room.

'Do you have a death wish, woman?' he says, eyes wide, voice incredulous. 'Why didn't you do as they told you? What if they'd shot you?'

'I don't know.'

Rick sits next to me again and wraps his arms round me. 'You could have died.'

I could have died. My life could have ended today in the dirt on a post-office floor. And the thought of that makes me shake even more.

Chapter 90

I lie in the bath. It's full to the brim, steaming hot and has a froth of bubbles floating on top. There's a glass of red wine to hand and all of it is failing to soothe me.

There's a knock on the door and Rick's voice asks, 'Everything OK in there?'

We lock the bathroom door in our house. Have done since the children were young. Now it's a habit. Tonight, to my shame, I'm glad that it's keeping Rick out. I just wanted some time to myself. Is that so wrong? Frankly, I'm only able to lie in here for so long because everyone else is out and there's no one banging the door down demanding their turn.

'Fine,' I say in return. But I'm not fine. I'm in a state of shock.

'Just shout if you want anything,' my husband says. I can hear the anxiety in his tone. Perhaps he can hear it in mine.

'I will.'

'I'm worried about you.'

'I'll be down soon,' I reassure him.

'If you're sure.'

'Yes. Positive.'

I listen to Rick's feet tread down the stairs.

Sinking back into the hot water, I scoop the bubbles over me and take a sip of my wine.

I could have died today. How does that make me feel? I'm hit by a wave of emotion, unable to pick one feeling from the deluge of others.

Think of all the things in my life that I'd never have been able to do again if my life had bled away from me. I wouldn't have seen Chloe's baby be born. Rick and I wouldn't have reached our twenty-five-year mark. I'd never see Tom settled. I wouldn't be able to care for my parents in their old age. And I'd never get the chance to hold Steven Aubrey one last time.

Perhaps it shouldn't, but that thought hits me harder than all the others. Then, before I can think what I'm doing, my trembling fingers pick up my mobile phone which is sitting on the floor with the pile of my clothes and I find Steven's number.

'Hello.' The sound of his soft, sexy voice as he answers makes me want to burst into fresh tears, but I bite them back.

I shouldn't be doing this. I know I shouldn't. But I feel as if I'm compelled by a force outside of myself, by fate intervening with its fickle fingers. This conversation could change the course of my life, but I want to have it anyway.

'Hi,' I say, sounding wobbly. 'It's me . . .'

Chapter 91

We're in bed. I put down my book and turn to Rick. 'I'm going to a library conference on Friday,' I say. Which is a lie.

'Oh, right.' He glances up from the newspaper. I hate him reading the paper in bed, but he doesn't do it very often, so I haven't complained. If he's reading the obituary column, then he's wisely reading it to himself. 'You didn't mention it.'

'It only came up today.' About an hour ago when I phoned Steven Aubrey from the bath and plotted how I was going to spend an illicit night with him. I keep the thought to myself. Though I'm amazed that Rick can't hear my heart, which is trying to thump its way out of my chest. 'I'll be staying overnight.'

'Oh.' Now Rick puts down his newspaper and I pick up my book again. 'Why's that?'

'It's in Worcestershire or somewhere. We're doing some team bonding exercises in the evening.'

'Hmm,' is my husband's comment. 'That's nice. I don't remember you ever having to stay away before.'

'Someone must have found some money in their budget. I'll be back on Saturday morning. Probably early.'

'Don't rush back,' Rick says. 'That's the day I'm going up to Wembley with Hal to watch the football. We'll be setting off mid-morning, I think, and I'll be out all day. Mind you,

Uncle Hal's organising it so it will be a miracle if we get there at all.'

'You'll have a great time.'

'Yeah. I'm sure you will too.'

'At a library conference?' I force a laugh.

Taking my bookmark from me, Rick slots it into *A Thousand Splendid Suns* and closes my book, setting it down on the bed. He turns to me, leaning into his pillow.

'What?' Is guilt written large on my face already?

'I'm just thinking,' he says. 'I don't know what I'd do without you.' My husband takes my fingers and toys with them. 'What if something had happened to you today? What if one of those robbers had taken a pot shot at you?'

'They didn't.' My voice contains a bravado I don't feel.

'I want you to promise me, if you ever find yourself caught up in something like that again, that you'll lie low, do exactly what they tell you.'

'Yes,' I say. 'Of course I will.'

'They could have hurt you,' Rick reminds me needlessly. 'Or even worse.'

'I know.' My fingers have started shaking in his. 'I don't really want to talk about this any more.'

'I'm sorry. I just wanted to make sure that you realised how serious this situation was.'

'I'm not stupid.'

'But you behaved recklessly.' Rick gives me a chastising gaze.

And I'm about to do so again, I think.

My husband kisses me, his lips gentle against mine. The last person's lips to kiss mine were Steven's and I feel my face flush with shame at the memory.

'I want to love you and care for you always,' Rick murmurs against my ear. His hands travel to my face and he strokes it, kissing me again. 'Let's make love.'

I inch away from Rick. 'I'm still not feeling great. I have a bit of a headache.'

'Cuddle then?' I can't help but hear the disappointment in his voice.

We slide down in the bed together and Rick pulls the duvet up round me, lovingly. While I lie there rigid, tossing around in my mind what I'm about to do.

Chapter 92

Friday morning came around too quickly for Rick's liking. He was making the toast and one of the slices was propelled across the kitchen like a human cannonball. Rick tutted wearily as Buster caught the blackened bread and hastily chomped it down in three bites before someone thought to wrest it from his jaws. He was just vowing to buy a new all-singing, all-dancing toaster to replace this knackered one when Juliet came downstairs. They were running late and, technically, they both should have left for work by now. But his wife had looked so tired when the alarm went off that he hadn't liked to chivvy her along too forcefully.

'All packed?' he asked.

'Just a small bag. I'm only going for the night,' she said. 'I'm not like Una. I can travel light.'

Rick buttered the toast. 'Is the Desperate Divorcée going with you?'

'Er . . . no, I don't think she is.'

'You don't *think*?' He handed his wife a slice. Buster sat at her feet, tail wagging, waiting for another crumb or two to fall in his direction.

'She's not,' Juliet said. 'I'm sure she's not.'

'And where is this place again?'

'Shropshire.'

'I thought you said Worcestershire.'

'Isn't that the same place?'

344

'I'm worried about you driving yourself,' Rick said. 'You don't even seem to know where you're going.'

'Don's coming in my car,' Juliet told him as she munched her way through her breakfast. 'He knows where it is. I'm leaving it to him.'

He didn't believe Juliet. It was a terrible thing to say and he had no proof that she was lying. But she was being vague, evasive about this, and he wanted to ask her to show him some details – perhaps a leaflet or an email, anything that confirmed that she was actually going to a library conference.

Before he had a chance to question her further, Tom popped his head round the door. 'OK if I bring someone in for breakfast?'

'Male, female? Animal or vegetable?' Rick wanted to know.

'Very funny, Dad.'

If only his son would put as much effort into finding a job as he did seducing people of assorted sexes to bring home with him. Before he could give his agreement or otherwise, a small, dark girl trailed in behind Tom and they sat at the kitchen table. She wore gothic clothing and had scary spiked hair and a pierced nose. Rick didn't think that it was 'dining-room table' woman, but he wasn't about to ask.

'Morning,' Rick said to her.

She held up a peace sign. He felt like giving her one back but with his fingers round the other way. 'If you want toast you can sort yourselves out.' Rick was going to try and enjoy his own breakfast.

Then they heard a key in the lock. 'Is that Chloe?'

Juliet shook her head. 'Looks like my mother.'

'Did you know she was planning to stay out all night?'

'No.'

'Christ,' Rick muttered. 'She's worse than either of the kids.'

Both he and Juliet watched as Rita tried to sneak past the kitchen door without them seeing her.

'Mum!' Juliet shouted, and reluctantly, her mother came into the kitchen.

'Cooee,' she said rather sheepishly. 'Thought you might have gone to work by now.'

'What's that in your arms? A tomato plant?' Rick wanted to know. His mother-in-law was clutching a potted plant to her ample bosom. 'Is it for the garden?'

Her expression accelerated from sheepish to furtive from furtive to rumbled. 'I thought I might keep it in my room.'

'Oh, no,' Rick said. 'Tell me that's not what I think it is.'

The fernlike green leaves looked familiar even though he wasn't much of a horticulturist.

'It's very pretty,' Juliet chipped in, clearly unaware that her mother had been trying to smuggle a cannabis plant up to her room. 'Nice and healthy.'

'It's cannabis, Juliet,' Rick told her.

'Mum?'

'Arnold said it's good for your joints,' Rita countered. 'All his aches and pains have gone since he's had the odd spliff.'

'Rock on, Gran,' Tom laughed.

'Oh, Mother.' Juliet's face was stony.

'Fabulous,' Rick said. 'Now we've got a geriatric drug addict in our midst.'

'Tell me I'm dreaming this,' his wife said.

'I want that thing out of my house now!' Rick pointed at the offending plant.

'It might be your house, but it's my home.' His mother-in-law's jaw set.

'We can make other arrangements to get around that,' Rick suggested.

'Perhaps you should try the odd puff of a joint yourself,' Rita responded tartly. 'Might calm you down a bit.'

Before he could retort, Chloe came into the kitchen.

'Mum,' she wailed, 'I don't feel well.' Then she promptly threw up all over the floor.

'Nice one, sis,' Tom said, wrinkling his nose.

'Morning sickness,' Juliet said briskly. 'Nothing to worry about.'

'I don't want a baby,' Chloe sobbed. 'I'm too young. What am I going to do?'

'Sit down, sweetheart.' Juliet led their daughter to a chair while she grizzled. 'There's nothing to worry about. This is all perfectly natural. Dad will make you a cup of nice, sweet tea while I clean that up. That's all you need.'

Rick opened his mouth to protest and then thought better of it and closed it again. He went and put the kettle on.

'We're out of here,' Tom said, tugging last night's girlfriend by the arm. 'Breakfast at McDonald's is never as stressy as this.'

'I'll be in my room,' Rita said as she crept away. 'If anyone wants me or if anyone cares.'

'I haven't finished with you,' Rick shouted after her as his mother-in-law hurried up the stairs. 'We'll discuss this later.'

'Oh, let her go,' Julie said wearily. 'I've had just about enough today and it's not even nine o'clock yet.'

Rick couldn't blame her. He felt like escaping too. This house was getting too small to contain a joint-smoking granny, a lothario son and a puking, pregnant daughter, and a death-defying wife who said she was going to a library conference, but probably wasn't.

Chapter 93

All day at work, I feel sick. A couple of times I go into the staff toilet and dry retch. Even Una suspects that something's wrong. If it wasn't for Rick's recent vasectomy, she might even suspect me of being in the pudding club too. She'd be even more surprised at the true reason. But after she let the cat out of the bag regarding our non-existent lottery win, then I don't feel that I can confide in her that I plan to spend the night at Steven Aubrey's house, in Steven Aubrey's bed, in Steven Aubrey's arms.

It feels strange to be planning to do something that no other person in the world knows about but me. A thousand times I've nearly picked up my phone to tell Steven that I want to cancel, but then I think of what happened in the post office and how close I could have come to shuffling off this mortal coil, and I know that I want to spend this night with my one-time lover, my ex-fiancé, the man who loves me and adores me and thinks that I'm not just boring Mum, fit for doing the laundry and clearing up sick and walking the dog when no one else will do it. Steven treats me like a woman, a beautiful woman, an object of sexual desire, and he looks at me with hot craving in his eyes. He wants me. He lusts after my body. And I want to know how that feels just one more time.

'What are you doing at the weekend?' Una wants to know.

'Not a lot.' I flush, even though the lie is tripping easily from my tongue. 'Rick's going to the football tomorrow at Wembley. I'll probably do some gardening.'

'Come round and have a cup of tea if you want to. I'll be on the internet for most of the time researching some jewellery sites.'

'Still going ahead with that?'

Una nods. 'Looks like it. Tex is very keen.'

How can I tell her that I think it's ill-advised to get involved financially with a bloke she doesn't know when I'm about to do what I'm about to do?

At five o'clock, we lock up the library and I jump into my Corsa. In the car park, I rest my head on the steering wheel while I work myself up to driving up to Watermill House instead of home to the safety and madness of Chadwick Close.

I could turn away now. Just drive straight home, tell Rick that the conference has been cancelled, and not do this. That would be the simple, sensible thing to do. Starting the car, I swing out of the car park and head for Steven's home.

When I arrive and stop outside the triple garage next to Watermill House, I have another head-on-steering-wheel moment. It's not too late to turn back now. Right now. I could stop this nonsense and go home. Home – where I belong. Then Steven comes out to greet me and there's such excitement, such joy on his face, that – despite all of my misgivings – I get out of the car.

Steven slips his arms round me. 'I'm so glad that you've come. You don't know how much I've wanted this.'

I think I do.

'Maybe you should pull your car round the side, out of sight.'

Shaking my head, I say, 'It'll be OK.'

'Sure?'

I nod, then he leads me to the house, taking my overnight bag from the back seat. Perhaps it would have been better if we'd gone away – to Worcestershire or Shropshire or wherever the hell it is that I'm supposed to be. It seems odd to be planning to stay here, to sleep here, to make love with Steven so close to my own home. I'm sure if I voiced my concerns now then Steven would jump in the Aston Martin and whisk me to a fabulous hotel of my choice without a word of complaint. That's the kind of life

349

I could have with him. Instead, I follow him into Watermill House, saying nothing.

In the kitchen, champagne is chilling in an ice-bucket. There's a pot bubbling on the Aga and an exquisite scent wafting from the oven. My stomach rumbles from hunger and then, for good measure, churns with anxiety.

'Something smells wonderful.'

'Beef Stroganoff with wild rice and a green salad.'

'Lovely. All your own work?'

'Of course. I've laid the table for dinner in the dining room,' Steven says. He's so excited that I could weep. 'Thought we'd be posh while we have the chance.'

I think that I'd have been happier with a tray on my lap as this is only increasing my nerves.

Steven hands me some champagne and he raises his glass to mine. 'To us,' he says.

'To us,' I echo. My mouth is as dry as a desert.

Then he comes to me and holds me close. There's no one here but us, alone in our private bubble. I'm a teenager in love once more. Steven's lips find mine and my head swims even though I've barely sipped my champagne. For one delicious moment, I forget that I shouldn't be here, that I'm a frumpy, middle-aged woman whose makeover branded her a Classic Beige and, most of all, I forget that I'm married to someone else.

Chapter 94

Rick was missing Juliet. This was the first night she'd spent away from him in living memory. In fact, he didn't think she'd ever spent a night away since Chloe was born and she was stranded in the maternity unit overnight and he struggled at home alone with Tom.

He tried to think back to what it had been like when the kids were toddlers and decided that it must have been truly hideous as his mind seemed to have blanked most of it. Isn't that how the body tried to cope with traumatic experiences? He wondered, also, what it would be like to have another toddler in the house very soon. Unlike Juliet, it wasn't something that he was looking forward to.

While his wife was out he'd decided to write out the invitations to their wedding anniversary party – the one he was somehow managing to keep secret so far. Tom had been coerced into doing some invitations on the computer and, to be grudgingly honest, he'd made a great job of them. A photo of Rick and Juliet in the early days graced one side – it was a shame that there were no wedding photographs to draw on, but Juliet's parents had deemed that they'd nothing to celebrate and, consequently, none were taken. The other side contained information about the party and Rick was currently filling in the names of their friends and neighbours, hoping that they'd be able to come along too.

Chloe had been dispatched to buy some helium balloons and other party fripperies and they were now secreted in the back of his Walk All Over Me van. One of Rita's friends was baking a cake and Rick hoped that she didn't have his mother-in-law's propensity for Class C drugs and slip a bit of hash into the mix, otherwise the whole of the party would be in soft focus. He also hoped that they'd all keep their mouths shut too as it was nigh on impossible to keep a secret in this house.

He thought of Juliet and wondered whether he should ring or text her to see how she was, whether she'd managed to find the conference centre in Worcestershire or Shropshire or wherever it was she'd decided that she was going. Rick sat in the living room and looked about him. It had taken them a long time to build up this life, this home, this family. And he was happy with it. He truly was. He knew that now.

The only problem was, he knew that Juliet wasn't really going to a last-minute library conference. It just wasn't happening.

Rick was sure that he knew where his wife really was – and who she was with. The question was, did he want to find out for certain?

Five minutes later, he decided that – for better, for worse – he did. He jumped into the Vauxhall Mid-Life Crisis and made his way over to the northern edge of the town. Rick remembered Juliet telling him that Steven Aubrey was renting Watermill House in Old Stratford and it would mean going to the waterside park he'd vowed to avoid ever since the regrettable 'dogging' incident. Needs must, however. So he headed in that direction and, minutes later, was turning into the secluded lane that led up to the magnificent property. He'd coveted that house many times over the years and now Steven Aubrey had it. He'd coveted an Aston Martin all of his life and Steven Aubrey had one of those as well. There was no damn way he was going to get Juliet too.

His tyres crunched on the gravel as Rick slowly made his way up the drive. He pulled over short of the house, tucking the car behind a tree so that he had a chance to spy on the occupants without them being able to see him. Disheartened, he saw that Juliet's car was, indeed, parked outside.

What to do now? Should he storm in, read the riot act and drag Juliet out, whatever they were up to? It was tempting. But not really his style. It was only when you found yourself in these situations that you had to consider how you'd respond and, invariably, Rick suspected, it wasn't how you anticipated.

Instead of charging in, guns blazing, he sat in the car and just felt very sick. From where he was, he could just about see Steven and Juliet in the dining room at the front of the house. It would have been better if he'd thought to bring along some binoculars. There was a pair in the loft somewhere, but he hadn't seen them for ages; no doubt they were lost in the depths of the sports equipment that had been abandoned there by the kids over the years as they got bored with whatever had been their current fad. Never in a million years had he thought he would use them for anything other than a bit of amateur twitching.

In the dining room, dinner looked like it was going swimmingly. Juliet was laughing in a way he hadn't seen her laugh in years. Did Juliet love Steven Aubrey all over again? It certainly looked like she did. It seemed as if he had lost her for good.

In the car, Rick wanted to close his eyes or, better still, simply drive away and pretend he hadn't seen this at all.

Chapter 95

Dinner is divine. Steven is an accomplished cook, and the glass or two of champagne that I've had has gone right to my head. The room is warm, the lighting soft from the dozens of candles that have been lit in my honour. They cast a soothing glow on the burgundy walls, bringing out the best of the gilt of the picture frames and the gold curtains. I feel cocooned here, safe, protected from the world.

My ex-fiancé and I have laughed about old times, the people we went to school with, the places we used to go. Now we're having coffee, a plate of chocolate mints in the middle of the table. I nibble at one, even though I'm full.

'Do you remember that Roxy Music concert in London?' Steven asks.

'Oh!' I lower my head in shame. 'Not a lot. That was the night we shared a bottle of vodka on the train down to London.'

'And you slept through the whole thing.'

'Even though Bryan Ferry was my idol.'

'I'd saved up all my money from my Saturday job at O'Dell's to pay for the tickets.'

'It was a bit of a disaster.' We giggle together.

'Happy times,' Steven says and then, as we both realise what happens next, the mood changes abruptly. 'Where does Rick think you are tonight?'

I avoid his eyes. 'At a librarians' conference.'

'Come to bed,' Steven says, and he helps me out of my chair, cradling my elbow as I stand, legs shaking.

Taking my hand, he blows out the candles before he leads me from the dining room and up the stairs towards his room. We leave the champagne behind but, frankly, I'm thinking that maybe I haven't had quite enough to drink yet. My mouth is dry, my heart hammering in my chest.

The main landing is galleried and opulent. I haven't seen this part of the house before but it's as beautiful as all the rest. As I expect, Steven's room is particularly splendid.

The wallpaper is duck-egg blue with a pattern of cream flowers. The curtains match perfectly. A glittering chandelier hangs from the ceiling and the furniture is ornate, cream, possibly French in style. I don't know. But Una would.

The focal point is the vast bed with a chocolate leather head-board. It's covered in a quilt of duck-egg blue with chocolate accessories, fluffy Mongolian wool cushions and a folded quilt across the bottom of the bed that's probably chenille. Una would defin-itely approve. Rick would simply be annoyed by the number of cushions that would need moving before he could get near his own pillow if I tried to recreate that look at Chadwick Close. He can't even stand one cushion on the bed. Then I bring myself up short. I must try not to think of my husband right now.

Steven puts his hands on my shoulders and I gasp as the heat of his hands burns right through my blouse to my skin. At what point in a relationship does that stop happening? How long does it take for the strangeness of skin to become familiar? When did Rick's touch stop making me gasp with delight? Was it two years ago, ten? Was it when the children came along? Does that, out of necessity, turn off your gasping reflex? But then I remember that I'm trying not to think of Rick.

My lover is kissing my neck as his hands slide over my breasts. His fingers find the buttons of my blouse and toy with them.

'God, I love you,' Steven whispers against my throat.

I'm having trouble breathing. My lungs are tight and I'm not sure that this is the right response for the situation. It feels more like an asthma attack than the heights of passion.

While Steven continues to work skilfully at my buttons, I can feel myself tensing up. I push him away. A bit harder than I'd intended. 'Champagne,' I gasp. 'Need more champagne.'

'Now?'

Steven, I have to report, looks as if he's having no trouble with the whole arousal thing.

'Yes, yes,' I say, nodding maniacally. 'Now.'

'OK.' My lover shrugs indulgently. 'If the lady wants champagne, she shall have it. I won't be long.' And he kisses me goodbye, a long lingering kiss, before he disappears through the door.

Listening to his footsteps on the stairs, I survey the room. I need to do something to collect my thoughts, but I don't know what. I think about testing the bed, maybe arranging myself seductively, but I just can't bring myself to do it.

While I'm still thinking what to do, I hear Steven coming back. He's whistling happily. Any moment now he'll be at the door. That's when I bolt for the bathroom.

Sure enough, seconds later, I hear his voice. 'Juliet,' he says, 'are you all right?'

'Yes, yes,' I shout from the bathroom. 'I'm fine.'

'I have champagne. I have chocolates.'

'Lovely,' I say. My hands are sweating. 'I'll be out in just a minute.'

'I can't start without you.'

'No.' I can hardly speak. 'I just need a little time.'

'Are you sure that you're OK?'

'Yes, yes.' I pace the bathroom floor. It's gorgeous in here too. Like a bathroom in one of those swanky hotels that are way out of my price range. There's a walk-in shower, thick, fluffy towels, luxurious toiletries that may have been bought just for me. Jasmine and orchid body lotion, vanilla hand soap. It all looks delightful.

Then I catch sight of myself in the mirror. I look pale and drawn. I wear the expression of a terrified woman. Running the tap, I let the cold water play over my wrists. 'This will be fine,' I tell myself.

'This is exactly what you wanted to do. You planned it. You lied to your husband, your family, your friend to be here.'

I splash my face with water as the wrist thing isn't working. I'm getting hotter by the minute and I wonder if I've just picked a really bad time to start the menopause.

If I'm going to get through this then I should think sexy, seductive thoughts. Undoing another button on my blouse, I think that Rick is the only person who I've got naked with for the majority of my adult life. I won't even go for my legs waxed as I'm too self-conscious about baring my body to strangers. I try to remind myself that Steven has seen this all before − warts and all − and he's still mad for it. Admittedly, it's all got a lot more creased and squishy since he last saw it, but my figure's not that bad. Not as great as Una's, but Rick still loves it. Then I try to remind myself that I'm not supposed to think of my husband in this traitorous situation. I stand sideways to the massive mirror and suck in my stomach. If I just don't breathe there should be no problem.

'Juliet.' Steven's voice comes through the door. 'The bubbles are going flat.'

I wonder if that's code for something?

'Are you going to join me anytime tonight?'

'Yes, yes.' I look at myself again in the mirror. Still terrified. Just this once, I think. I'm only going to do this once. And that's it. Never again. So I'd better bloody well enjoy it.

Chapter 96

Rick had seen all he could take. The light had gone from the dining room and was now shining in an upstairs window. Steven's bedroom, he presumed. He saw a shadow moving by the curtain. That was enough. If he was going to confront the lovers, he should have done it earlier. Now he couldn't bring himself to move from the car. Even if he wanted to take a brick and hurl it through the window, all his limbs had gone numb – along with his brain, it seemed.

On autopilot, he started the engine and slipped the Vauxhall into gear. Driving back to Chadwick Close, his head whirred. It was a miracle that he didn't have an accident as he wasn't concentrating on his driving at all. How would he confront Juliet with his newfound knowledge? He was so rubbish at this sort of thing and, thankfully, he'd had precious little reason to do it so far in his marriage.

When he pulled into the drive, he still couldn't get his head round the fact that his wife was with Steven Aubrey on the other side of Stony Stratford being unfaithful to him. That wasn't Juliet at all. What had happened to her? She was a librarian, for heaven's sake. A pillar of the community. She just didn't do that sort of thing.

There was no way that he was going to be able to sleep. Buster would be pressed into service as trusty hound and they'd take a long walk round Toombs Meadow even though it was dark. The chances of him getting mugged were few and far between. But then the thought of his wife having carnal knowledge with another man he'd have considered an equally remote chance.

He looked at the house. What would happen if, God forbid, Juliet wanted to leave him for Steven? They'd have to sell the house, for starters. All that they'd worked for gone up in a puff of smoke. What would the kids do? Her mother? Where would she go? Where would *he* go? What would he do without his wife?

Buster was ecstatic at the prospect of an extra walkies and trotted out of the house, joyful, his less than enthusiastic owner trailing behind. As he passed Stacey Lovejoy's house, he could see her in the living room, standing at the window. The lights were off, but he could see the glow from the television flickering round the room. She waved uncertainly at him as he passed and Rick, equally tentatively, waved back. He sighed to himself. There'd be a welcome in the hillside for him there if he decided to truncate Buster's treat. He could even pop in to see his saucy neighbour on the way back.

Juliet wouldn't know. She was at a librarians' conference and staying overnight. Wasn't that the case? His wife would have no idea if he took the opportunity to play away too. Wasn't the saying that what was good for the goose was good for the gander too?

Buster tugged impatiently at his lead as Rick hesitated outside Stacey Lovejoy's house. But then the other pertinent saying was that two wrongs don't make a right. It was up to him which one he chose to follow.

Chapter 97

'Oh.' When I finally extricate myself from the bathroom, I find that Steven is already in bed. He has a glass of champagne in one hand and nothing on.

'Oh,' he says too.

I think he possibly expected me to emerge wearing some skimpy lingerie or something or, more likely, nothing. But I have to admit that, although I did put on my best pants, they couldn't really be classed as lingerie, not even with a good stretch of the imagination.

Steven was reclining. Now he sits up. 'Is there a problem, Juliet?'

'Yes.'

He slides his legs round and goes to emerge from under the duvet.

'No, no,' I say, waving my hand at him. 'Don't get up.'

Steven does as he's told. 'You *are* planning on joining me?'

'Er . . . no,' I admit. Then I crumple. 'I can't do this, Steven. I'm not a natural adulterer. I'm too married. Too loyal. Too worried about what other people might think.'

'I'm the only person who knows.'

'It was stupid of me to come,' I tell him sadly. 'I thought that I could do it, but I can't. I'm not cut out for deception. I can cope with the odd lunch, because I can pretend it isn't important. But this?' I shrug and gaze round the room at anywhere but Steven. The thrill of clandestine meetings might be fun, but when it comes to getting low down and dirty – what was I thinking of? It's sleazy, sordid and would hurt so many people. I don't think that I want a secret, after all. I want to be honest, straightforward Juliet as I've always been, not this woman who sneaks around telling lies, making out she's some kind of sex siren. 'I can't do it. Not on this scale. I'm sorry.'

Steven goes to get out of bed again.

'Stay there,' I say. 'I'm going. Please stay there.'

'Don't leave like this,' Steven begs. 'Let me get dressed and we can go downstairs and talk about it. We can do this at your pace. Whatever you're comfortable with.'

I'm backing towards the door. 'I have to go home. Rick will be worried.'

'Rick thinks that you're at a librarians' conference,' Steven points out. 'You can't go home. What will you tell him?'

'Er . . .' Hadn't thought about that.

'I'll put some clothes on, make more coffee and we can watch a film. There are a dozen different DVDs down there. We can just have a cuddle on the couch.'

Even that sounds terrifying.

'You can't go anywhere,' Steven reasons. 'You'll have to stay here even if it's in the spare room.'

I can't do that. I have to get out of here now. I know what Steven's like, he'll spend the entire night wearing down my resolve and then I'll give in because I'm weak and feeble and pathetic.

'This was a big mistake,' I say. 'I'm really sorry, Steven. Really I am. But I love my husband and I just can't do this to him.'

With that, I grab my bag and I bolt for the door and am down the stairs, heading out of the house, still listening to Steven shout my name after me.

Chapter 98

I shoot out of the lane leading away from Watermill House as if I'm in *Speed Racer*, just in case Steven is the world's quickest dresser and decides to give chase.

When I'm safely out of harm's way, I pull over in a lay-by and consider my options. Why on earth did I think that rekindling love with my old flame was a good and sensible thing to do? I feel like stabbing myself for my stupidity. Now look at the mess that I'm in, and I didn't even go through with it.

Why couldn't Steven Aubrey have turned out to be balding, chubby and working as a down-at-heel insurance salesman with a dowdy – that word again – wife and four demanding kids in tow? Why couldn't he have found me mumsy, dull and staid instead of seeing the latent sex goddess still lurking inside me? Yeah, and what a femme fatale I turned out to be.

So, what am I to do now? I've drunk too much to be driving at all, so I daren't go far. The last thing I need as a souvenir of tonight, on top of everything else, is a drink driving conviction. Could I go home? I could tell Rick that the conference was dreary, cancelled, hit by a terrorist attack. But would he believe any of that? He'd know. He'd just know.

I could ring Rick now, tell him the truth and ask him to come and collect me before I do myself or anyone else any more harm. My fingers hover over the buttons on my mobile, but I just can't bring myself to press them. Honesty isn't always the best policy and

I know that it would irretrievably damage my marriage if this came out. My husband may be quite understanding – on a good day – but I don't think he'd forgive me this one. Some things, I believe, are best left unsaid. So, this has to stay my secret, whether I want one or not.

Then I realise what I can do. I might be slightly squiffy, but my brain can still function logically – just about. In my handbag, I have the library keys. It may not be the night of comfort and joy that I envisaged in Steven's arms, but it's dry, warm and, even though the sofa in the staff room is skanky, I can stretch out on it well enough. No one will be any the wiser. And I'm sure, given the circumstances, that Don would fully understand my predicament. I can even have a couple of his biscuits for breakfast and be out of there before anyone arrives for work. Don gets in at eight-thirty, so I could set my alarm for eight. Thankfully, I remembered to snatch my overnight bag from Steven's bedroom on the way out, so I have my toiletries and a change of clothes with me. An hour's shopping in Stony Stratford – which I'd have to do anyway – and then I could safely go home without arousing any suspicions, seeing Rick before he heads off for the football match with Hal. And if I can't sleep, then I've got plenty of reading material to choose from. The thought of that gives me a definite lift. Better to spend the night with Bill Bryson or with Jeffery Deaver rather than with Steven.

Now I have a plan, I feel so much better. It's as if my usual, sensible self has suddenly come back. Normal service has been resumed. So I set off, driving really, really slowly and carefully the few miles to the library.

Chapter 99

Rick didn't want to see Juliet when she came home from being with Steven Aubrey – if she came home at all. His wife had called twice already that morning, but he didn't want to speak to her, so he'd let the calls go to voicemail. Nor did he want to face her until he decided what he wanted to do, how he wanted to progress this. Progress it? A rather odd term for tackling something that was likely to turn his life upside down. No, Rick didn't have the stomach for that yet, so he'd organised to go to the match early with Hal as a pathetic blokey avoidance technique.

Now they were having a slap-up cooked breakfast at London Gateway Service Station on the M1 – though eating was the last thing on his mind. Hal's robust appetite more than compensated for Rick's lack of one. Nothing normally put Rick off his food, but then it wasn't every day that his wife committed adultery.

'Ricky-Boy,' his friend complained, shovelling in baked beans as he spoke. 'We're going to be there hours before the gates open at this rate.'

'I wanted to get there early,' Rick said.

'You seem a bit quiet,' Hal noted, though his powers of observation normally weren't so finely tuned.

'Nah, everything's fine.' This wasn't the time to share with Hal what Juliet had been up to. Unlike his friend, Rick preferred to keep things like that private.

'I've got big money riding on this,' Hal said. 'I've put five hundred quid on Man United to win.'

'Five hundred quid? You must have money to burn.'

'*Au contraire*, my good friend. I'm well strapped. This is a desperate measure.'

'We could take on an apprentice,' Rick said, 'if things are that tight. It's not that the work's not there. We could quote for more jobs if we had another pair of hands.'

Hal shook his head, his face suddenly looking drawn and tired. 'It's everything, mate. It's all stacking up. I can tell you, it's no fun running your own business any more. I've got the bank breathing down my neck on one side and two scheming women waiting to bleed me dry on the other.' He laughed to himself without humour. 'What I wouldn't give to be like you and Juliet.'

'Yeah,' Rick said.

'Hang onto that woman,' Hal advised as he finished his mug of tea. 'She's one of a rare breed. Come on then, misery guts. Let's go and see our fine team give Portsmouth a damn good spanking.'

The new Wembley Stadium was awe-inspiring. There was no other word for it. Rick had been gutted when they'd decided to pull down the old Wembley which had given football eighty years of good service, but this colossus that had replaced it was a different beast altogether. It looked like it was ten times the size of the old stadium and its impressive filigree arch – a new addition to the north-west London skyline – dwarfed the twin towers that used to be there.

Hal and Rick walked down Olympic Way jostling along with hundreds of other supporters, heading past the old-fashioned, heroic-style statue of footballing legend Sir Bobby Moore. Inside, the place looked like a swish modern airport, and the friends pushed through the milling crowd as they made their way through to their red plastic seats. Already, the 90,000 seats of the stadium were filling up for what was destined to be a capacity crowd. The age-old, familiar chant of 'Wem-ber-ley!' was being roared out in time-honoured fashion.

'Thanks, Hal,' Rick said as they took their seats. 'This was a great idea.'

'That's what mates are for, Ricky-Boy.'

The new stadium was a vast, saucer-shaped arena. Rick didn't think that he'd ever seen quite so many people in one place. He let the mantra chanting of the crowd wash over him and he simply drank in the heady atmosphere. For a moment he forgot all his problems, what might be going on at home, where Juliet might be and with whom.

Chapter 100

It's about ten o'clock when I decide that it's safe to venture home. My back's stiff after my night on the library sofa, but other than that, I haven't fared too badly. The one thing I'm most relieved at is that my conscience is clear — well, relatively so.

How would I have felt this morning if I'd woken up in Steven's bed? Terrible, I think is the truthful answer. And with more problems than just a dodgy lumbar region and a slight crick in my neck. Despite my aches and pains, I feel a lightness of spirit, as if I've faced a difficult test and have come. through it with flying colours. All I want to do now is see Rick and give him a great big cuddle.

I was up and washed well before eight and out of the library just after, making sure to remove all traces of my night spent there. Heading straight to the *Bon Appétite* café I had a breakfast of toast and honey with a pot of Darjeeling tea. I feel ravenous, as if I could eat a horse.

In the High Street, I bought a few things that we needed at home, hoping against hope that I wouldn't bump into anyone I knew. But at that early hour there were few people to worry about and even fewer shops open — something I hadn't considered in my master-plan. I bought a lovely cake from the deli, one of the few benefits of being out so early that I had the pick of the home baking which has normally all been snapped up by lunchtime. I also picked some Wobbly Bottom Farm cheese — a goat's cheese rolled in sweet pepper – because I know that Rick likes it, and some fat green olives.

Now I swing into Chadwick Close and pull into my drive. Despite the discordant display of Mum's gnomes in the garden, I love this place. This is my home, where I belong. It's pathetic, I know, but I feel like singing.

In the kitchen and Buster barks his joy at my return. No one else is around. 'Hello,' I shout up the stairs.

Nothing.

I unpack the shopping, feeling let down. Here I am, the home-coming heroine of the moment, and no one gives a damn.

Minutes later, Chloe thunders down the stairs. 'Can I take the car?'

'Yes,' I say. 'Where are you going?'

'Love you,' she throws over her shoulder and she's out of the door before I can elicit a proper, grown-up answer. Wait until her own son or daughter is doing the same thing to her and then I'll have my revenge.

Next to appear is Tom. 'Hi, Mum.'

'Hello, love. Do you know where Dad is?'

My son shrugs his slender shoulders. 'Like he'd tell me.'

'You could make an educated guess.'

More shrugging. 'Think he went to Wembley with Hal. He called here at some ungodly hour. They woke me up.'

Wondered why Tom was venturing out of his room before lunchtime. 'I thought they weren't going until later?'

Shoulder communication.

'Any plans for today?'

'Nah,' Tom says. 'Just chilling.'

I often wonder, if you don't do anything at all, how you can chill out from it? By definition, don't you actually have to *do* something to get you hot and bothered in the first place?

'Laters,' Tom says, and disappears.

'Don't you want anything to eat?' I shout after him, to no avail.

Checking my phone, I see that there are no messages from Rick and none from Steven either. The former I'm concerned about, the latter I'm pleased by. I would have liked Steven and me to remain friends, but that clearly wasn't ever going to be on the cards, so it's better if we have no contact whatsoever.

My mum is the last to appear in the kitchen. She's all dolled up, full war paint, inappropriately short skirt, bunions squashed into stilettos.

'You look . . . lovely.' This lying business is becoming so much easier. My mother looks like an adolescent geriatric. A 16–64, Tom would call it. A woman who looks sixteen from the back and sixty-four from the front. Except in this case, Mum looks seventeen from the back and seventy from the front.

'Arnold's taking me out for the day,' she tells me brightly. That'll be her pot-smoking, sex-mad, senile boyfriend. Thought she might have mentioned it earlier, but no.

'Oh,' I say. 'I'm at home alone all day. I thought it would be nice for us to spend some time together. Perhaps have some lunch in the garden while it's fine.'

'No can do.' My mother wrinkles her nose. What's she going to be doing with Arnold that's so much more wonderful than spending time with her only child? 'See you later,' she says as she tip-taps to the door. 'Don't wait up.'

Now what? I have the whole day stretching ahead of me, but I don't know what to do with it. I wish Rick was here. It could have been just the two of us. We could have gone out and had a pub lunch somewhere in the country followed by a long walk to get rid of the carbohydrates. These are the things we should be doing now that we have rare windows of time together.

Chewing my fingernails, I think that I'll just give my husband a call and tell him that I love him.

Finding my mobile phone, I dial Rick's number again. Still, it goes straight to voicemail. If I didn't know better, I'd think that my husband was trying to avoid me.

Chapter 101

I sit in the garden on a deckchair that I wrestle out of the garden shed. It shows how little time I've spent out here this summer when we haven't even dusted down the chairs yet. Buster is at my feet, having a half-hearted chew at the grass, and I've got the new Ian McEwan novel to hand, but I can't settle.

If Rick and I are really going to make a go of rebuilding and strengthening our marriage, then there's someone else who I need to warn off my turf.

Putting down my book, I head back into the house. I have a quick check in the mirror and, deciding that I look OK, head over to Stacey Lovejoy's house. If I was going to have a hope of competing with my love-rival, I'd have raided Chloe's shoe cupboard for something in leopardskin or shiny patent, preferably red rather than my summer sandals with the sensible heels. But I don't think of that until I'm halfway across the road and then it's too late to turn back and rectify my footwear deficiency.

Stacey opens the door as soon as I knock. I don't know if she'd been watching me walk towards her house or whether she was, as a matter of course, lurking behind the door, but the swiftness of my entry takes me by surprise.

'Come in, Juliet,' she says effusively. 'Come on in.'

I would have expected her to keep me at the doorstep, arms folded, and I'm even more taken aback as she sweeps me into her living room.

'The girls are in the city, shopping with my mum. I needed a day to myself. You know what it's like. Bless 'em. I love them to bits but there are days when I'd like to kill them all.'

'Oh, yes.' I can totally empathise with that.

Today Stacey's wearing a hot pink catsuit thing which fits where it touches, and a deep silver belt which gives her the figure of Marilyn Monroe.

'Sit down,' Stacey instructs.

Perching on the edge of her pink leather sofa, I say, 'I won't stay long.'

'Can I get you a drink? Tea? Something stronger?'

'Just a glass of water, please.' My mouth has gone dry even before I've started to address a tricky subject.

'I've got some of that old-fashioned lemonade from the deli in the High Street. It's my favourite. Would you like some of that?'

It's my favourite too. Who'd have thought that Stacey Lovejoy and I would have similar tastes in anything. Now I find three things – lemonade, murderous intentions towards our children and my husband. 'Thank you. That would be lovely.'

In Stacey's living room there's a television that nearly takes up the whole of one wall. Football is playing at the moment. I've never followed the beautiful game myself. Perhaps I should take more of an interest if Rick and I are going to spend the next twenty-five years in domestic harmony together. Wide-angled shots of Wembley Stadium flit across the screen and I realise that they're screening the match that Rick's gone there to watch.

My neighbour comes back with my glass of lemonade. 'Thank you,' I say.

'Are you a football fan?'

'No.' I shake my head. I can't stand it, actually.

'I adore Manchester United,' Stacey tells me. 'Sentimental reasons rather than my love of the game. Had several boyfriends from the reserve team in my younger days. Probably should have stayed with one of them. *Any* of them.' She laughs at that, but there's a nervousness behind it.

371

'Rick's there today.' I point at the screen. 'He's a mad keen Man United fan too.' Perhaps I shouldn't be telling Stacey that. She might see it as something else *they* have in common and take it as a sign.

'Lucky thing.' She gives me a sideways glance.

'It was Rick I came here to talk about.'

Stacey turns the sound down on the television. The roars of 'Wem-berley!' fade away. 'Oh, yeah?'

'We've been going through a bad patch,' I say, hastily adding, 'as all marriages do.'

'Tell me about it,' Stacey says.

'The thing is . . .' I take a deep breath here. 'I want you to stay away from Rick.'

Stacey's mouth drops.

'It's not helping us,' I continue. 'I admit that I'm jealous of you and I don't want him coming here to fix things or to have a massage or to do anything. He's my man and I'd really like it if you left him alone.'

At that, Stacey Lovejoy bursts into tears. Something else that I hadn't anticipated.

'I'm sorry, Juliet,' she sobs. 'I didn't mean for it to come across like that. I love Ricky. He's a top bloke. There's nothing happening between us, I swear. Even when he was nearly buck-naked in my bed, nothing went on. It was just as he told you: I simply wanted to be friends.'

'You don't hit on your neighbours' husbands, Stacey.' Not in Chadwick Close, anyway.

'I'm so rubbish,' Stacey sniffed again. 'No one ever wants anything to do with me. They think I'm loud and my kids are bratty. Your Ricky, he was really kind. I've never had that before.'

Now the girl is really crying hard. 'I like living here,' she sobs. 'I want to get on with everyone, but I don't know how. I never get invited to things. I'm lonely, Juliet. I've got no friends. Men just use me and other women steer clear of me. I'm stuck at home here all day and I don't know what to do with myself. Then I just go and do all the wrong things and frighten off the people who I most want to like me.'

I have a clean tissue in my pocket because I'm that sort of person. I go over to the sofa where Stacey's sitting and hand her the tissue. She blows her nose loudly into the proffered Kleenex.

'Can we start again?' Stacey begs. 'As neighbours and friends? Pretend that I've just moved in and that you might like me?'

'Oh, Stacey,' I say, slipping my arm round her shoulders. She looks so pathetic and sad sitting here in her Barbie home and her Barbie clothes that my heart goes out to her — even though she tried to nick my husband.

Then Stacey's eyes go round like saucers and she reaches for the remote control. 'Oh no,' she says. 'What's happening?'

With the sound up, it's clear that something has gone very wrong at the football match. In Wembley Stadium, the air is thick with smoke. It looks like a fire has broken out at one end of the ground. The match has stopped and the players are being escorted from the pitch. Someone over the Tannoy system is appealing for calm. It looks like most people are ignoring him. The crowd are screaming and pushing as stewards try unsuccessfully to control them and marshal them towards the exits.

'What on earth's going on?'

'This might tell us more.' Stacey flicks to the *News 24* channel.

On the screen, the cool, collected presenter says, 'We're having reports that a bomb has gone off at the stadium and that this is the action of terrorists.'

A red band across the bottom of the screen streams the words: *TERRORIST BOMB AT WEMBLEY STADIUM, TERRORIST BOMB AT WEMBLEY STADIUM, TERRORIST BOMB AT WEMBLEY STADIUM.*

It's then that my insides turn to ice.

Chapter 102

One minute the match was in full swing – he and Hal were roaring Man United on for all they were worth – the next it was utter mayhem. Rick remembered hearing an almighty bang and, for a moment, he thought that it had been from inside him, as if he was having a heart-attack as he'd felt it deep in his chest. It was only when the crowd broke out into screams and shouting that he knew that whatever had happened, it wasn't just to him.

He and Hal were on the floor of the stands and he didn't know how they'd got there. Had the force of the blast blown them over? There was thick smoke in the air and Rick knew that it had to be a bomb. He hoped that he was wrong, but what else could it be?

'All right, mate?' Hal's voice sounded shaky.

'Yeah, yeah,' Rick said. He felt all over his body, but nothing seemed to be hurting. 'You?'

'Yeah,' Hal assured him. His friend was patting himself down too.

There was panic now throughout the stadium. People pushing and shoving, scrabbling to get to exits. Rick wondered how many had been hurt. What about those in the direct path of the bomb? What had happened to them?

From where the smoke was coming from, it looked like the full force had been taken by the other side of the stadium. Christ, it seemed like they'd had a lucky escape.

What was needed was calm and control, but try telling 90,000 frightened people that. Rick and Hal helped each other up. His friend was coughing. Now that the rest of the people in their row were gathering their wits, they were pushing and shoving too, eager to get out, to get away.

'Let's head for the nearest exit.'

'Up there,' Hal said, and together they started to make their way towards the stairs.

As they did, there was another explosion. This time there could be no mistaking the fact that it was a bomb going off. The blast rocked the stand and debris flew around them, pieces of shattered red plastic from the seats, bits of metal and concrete from the stands themselves. Rick and Hal ducked, but not before Rick had been struck on the head by a piece of jagged metal.

He felt the blow, followed by a warm trickle which ran down his forehead and into his left eye.

'Mate,' Hal said. 'You're hit.'

After that, there was a strange ringing in his ears and all he remembered was the floor coming up to meet him.

Chapter 103

Stacey and I sit on the edge of the sofa. My fingers are balled into white fists and my neighbour rests her hands over mine.

'I have to call him,' I say. 'Rick's there. He's right in the middle of it.' With trembling hands, I rummage in my bag for my phone and punch in Rick's number on speed dial. All that comes back is a message saying, *'All networks are currently busy.'*

'I can't get through,' I tell Stacey, my voice rising in panic.

'The networks will have crashed. Everyone will be trying to phone if they've seen this on the telly.'

'What am I going to do?' I turn to my neighbour. 'I should get in the car and go straight down there.' Then I remember that Chloe has the car and I'm stranded.

My neighbour shakes her head. 'You need to sit tight, Juliet.'

'How can I do that?'

'Rick will call you to let you know he's OK just as soon as he can. They've probably thrown a security cordon round it or what-ever they call it. You wouldn't get near the place. We'll just keep phoning and watching what happens on the telly. Don't forget though, that this bloody lot are a bunch of scaremongers.' She casts a disdainful look at the news journalists and talking heads on the programme. 'It's probably nowhere near as bad as it looks.'

Or maybe it's worse and they're only showing selected scenes to the unwitting, telly-viewing public.

When I think of where I was last night, I could kill myself.

376

What if anything happens to Rick? What if he doesn't come home? What if last night should have been the final night we would ever spend together and instead I spent it kipped down on a manky sofa at the library after my aborted attempt at adultery? How would I ever forgive myself?

Please, I pray to whatever God might be listening, *let Rick come back to me. Let us spend the next twenty-five years nagging each other in number ten Chadwick Close, rubbing along together in near-enough to domestic bliss.* I start to cry.

'Oh, darling,' Stacey Lovejoy says, and she wraps her arms around me, cuddling me to her ample bosom. And, despite me not wanting to be clutched to Stacey's chest, it feels surprisingly comforting when I am. 'You have a bloody good cry, girl.'

So I do, my tears soaking into the hot pink catsuit until I've cried all I can.

Whenever you hear anyone speak who's lost a loved one, all they ever say is that they'd like them back one last time just so they could say goodbye properly and tell them that they loved them. That sets me off crying again.

'Sssh, sssh,' Stacey murmurs, soothing me. She rocks me backwards and forwards like a baby, gently patting my back.

I want my husband back. I love him. And, whatever happens, I don't want to have missed my opportunity to tell him that.

Chapter 104

Rick opened his eyes. Hal, inches away, was staring at him. There might have been relief in his eyes.

'All right, Ricky-Boy?'

Gingerly, Rick touched his head and found that there was blood on his finger. It hurt like hell. He tried to sit up, but it made him dizzy. Then he realised that he was on a stretcher, but laid out on the ground. There was noise all around, people rushing back and forth, ambulances with lights turning.

'What happened?'

'You are one lucky fucker,' Hal said with a wobbly laugh. 'You got hit by a flying seat. It nearly took your head off.'

Rick felt at the bloody patch again. It hurt even more now he knew what had caused it. 'Are you OK?'

'Few cuts and bruises, that's all.'

Now that he looked properly, he saw that Hal's face was indeed covered with tiny little cuts that needed cleaning up. 'Looks like you were a luckier fucker than me.' They both laughed at that, but it hurt Rick everywhere to do so. 'I've got to call Juliet.'

He wanted to speak to his wife, hear her voice, have her tell him that everything would be all right. Right now, he didn't care where she'd been or who she'd been with, he just wanted to be at home, his home, with her. What would have happened if he'd copped it in there? How would it have felt never to have seen his wife, his children, even his bloody mother-in-law ever again? There were people coming out on stretchers completely covered with blankets and that didn't look good. Surely with the force of that blast there must be some fatalities. Tonight, someone wouldn't be going home to their loved ones.

Hal waved a phone at him and Rick realised that it was his. 'I've tried, mate. All the networks are stuffed. Not a sausage. Can't even get a text out. I'll keep trying though. You just lie back and relax.'

'Can't we go home?'

'There's no way we can get out just yet. The police are all over the place. We've just got to sit tight for a while. I can get you some water if you want.'

'Yeah,' Rick said, realising that his mouth was bone dry. 'That would be great.'

'The doctor took a look at you and said he'd be back in a minute. That was about half an hour ago.'

'I've been out that long?'

'I guess so,' Hal said. 'They were talking about keeping you in the hospital overnight for observation.'

'Sod that.'

'They're trying to find a bed for you now, I think.'

'I just want to go home. Look at some of these poor sods.' Rick cast a glance at his fellow patients lying on the ground. There was blood everywhere. Every single one of them looked in a worse state than he did. 'Some of these need a bed more than I do. Get me out of this place, Hal.'

His friend looked round. 'OK. But promise me that you'll at least wait for a bandage for your bonce. I don't want you bleeding all over my truck.'

'It's a deal,' Rick said, and sank back to the ground to wait.

'I'll go and see what I can rustle up. You'll be OK for a minute?'

Rick nodded and then watched as his friend weaved his way through the dazed, bruised and bloody crowd.

He wanted Juliet more than anything. Not just now. Not just because of this. But he knew that he wanted her for always.

379

Chapter 105

It's nearly midnight and I'm back at number ten, curled up on the sofa with some hot chocolate. I have a blanket tucked round me even though it's not cold. Stacey Lovejoy insisted. Stacey also insisted on coming home with me and she's the one who's been busy in the kitchen forcing comforting beverages onto me and feeding me toast from our temperamental toaster. She also catered for the rest of the family and even took Buster for his evening walk. My neighbour has been the best type of friend I could have hoped for. She's the one who's got me through the day.

Chloe, Tom and my mother all came back at different times during the evening as they heard about the bomb at Wembley Stadium.

We've watched the television for the rest of the night together and still haven't caught a single glimpse of Rick. It's only when you're intimately involved in something like this that you realise that the news stations show the same shots over and over and over again. What you really want them to do is just go along the rows of walking wounded so that you have some hope of spotting your loved one there.

There's still been no word by phone and every time I try, the networks remain jammed. The bomb is being blamed on terrorists and there's certainly never been anything on this scale in our country before, not even the terrible attacks on the Tube and buses in 2007. Thousands are injured, dozens are dead. All I've done all day is will

Rick to be safe and well. For him not to be one of those sickening statistics. Any minute now, I know that he'll come walking through that door and everything will be all right again.

But it's one o'clock before I hear a car come into the Close and pull up outside the house. 'Rick,' I say, and fly to the door.

As I get there, I hear Rick's key in the lock but wrench open the door before he can use it.

My husband is dirty, dishevelled and his face is all cut. There's a bloodied bandage round his head. He looks completely shell-shocked. But he's standing there, large as life and all in one piece. I burst into tears and so does he.

'It's good to be home,' he says, as I fall into his open arms.

'I thought I'd lost you,' I weep against his neck that smells of smoke and sweat and stale aftershave.

Our eyes meet. 'I thought I'd lost you too.'

And I don't know if Rick had any inkling about Steven, but I hope that my look conveys that it's over, so over.

From now on it's just me and Rick and no one else. I feel as if we've been given a second chance to appreciate just how strong our love for each other really is and, from now on, I want to make every minute count.

'I love you,' Rick says.

'I love you too.'

We're strong. We're invincible. We've survived twenty-five years of marriage. We can do another twenty-five. Just bring it on.

Chapter 106

Rick lay in bed, Juliet curled into his side. It had been a week since the bomb blast and the cut on his head was healing nicely. He was still a bit headachey but, all things considered he had, as Hal so eloquently put it, 'been a lucky fucker'. Twenty people had died in the carnage and many more were seriously injured. Some hadn't lived to fight or to love another day. He was, indeed, very much one of the lucky ones.

'I don't want you going to work today,' Juliet said.

'I should do,' Rick told her. It was eight o'clock and he should be making a move. 'I've been off for a week. Hal doesn't have a great sick-pay scheme and there are bills to pay.'

'Why can't we just stay here curled up together and never go anywhere else ever again?'

Juliet had been like a limpet since he'd returned from Wembley. She could hardly bear to be parted from him, not even for a minute. He didn't think he'd ever known her to be so cuddly and affectionate. It was a lovely feeling to be on the receiving end of it. Don, being very understanding, had given her a week off work – compassionate leave – to look after Rick while he convalesced.

He and Juliet hadn't discussed the situation with Steven Aubrey. This 'incident' had given them both a wake-up call and Rick was sure that whatever had happened between Steven and his wife was over now. Only time would tell, but he felt that this was a fresh start for them both and that they weren't going to waste it.

Tom and Chloe had behaved like model children all week, tiptoeing around, being polite, making cups of tea at appropriate moments. Rick knew that it wouldn't last but he was determined to milk it while he could. He'd even persuaded Tom, without too much effort, to mow the lawn.

The only worrying thing was that his mother-in-law smiled so much at him that it was beginning to be scary. The sooner the status quo was resumed the better really.

Rick's mobile phone rang. 'I bet that's Hal wondering if I'm going to be in work today.'

But when he answered, it wasn't his friend on the phone. It was the police. The charge against him of Outraging Public Decency had been dropped. That was it. Over.

He turned to Juliet. 'The dogging thing,' he said. 'There'll be no further action. I'm in the clear.'

'Oh, that is good news, Rick.'

'Yeah.' Now all he had to sort out was the litigious lapdancer. The woman was still threatening to sue him, but perhaps if he offered her two hundred and fifty quid for a new pair of Perspex shoes in full and final settlement then she'd back down. He could send her a letter today.

'It's no good,' he said. 'Much as I'd like to, I can't lie here all day.'

'Are you sure?' Juliet snuggled in further as she smiled at him.

'I could stay here for half an hour longer,' he conceded.

And they made love, gently and tenderly, even though it was a work day and they were both going to be late.

Chapter 107

'I'm so glad that you're back,' Una says. 'It's been really boring without you.'

We're at the magazine rack by the door sorting out our display. Una has been into the newsagent's to buy some new ones today. As she gets to pick them, cookery and home improvements feature extensively – *Olive, BBC Good Food, Delicious, Ideal Home, Homes and Gardens, Country Gardener*. Though there are a good selection of women's magazines too – *Red, Cosmopolitan, Vogue, Harpers & Queen*. I leaf through the old ones as I go to throw them away. Una is unwrapping the fresh ones and arranging them in the newly-created space. It doesn't take long until they're all dog-eared and torn. You can take out a magazine for a week, but most people just come in and flick through them while they're here.

'How's your hubby now?'

'He's fine.' Thank God. 'Rick's actually gone back to work today, though I think it's a bit too soon.'

'I'm sure you told him to take it easy.'

I nod that I did.

'Everything OK between you two now?' My friend has called round to the house a couple of times while I've been off looking after Rick, but we haven't had a chance to talk properly.

'It's better than OK,' I tell her honestly. 'It feels as if I've fallen in love with Rick all over again.'

'Huh.' My friends looks a bit put out by this. She stacks *Cook*

384

It on the shelf a bit more crisply than she did *Dine With Me!*. 'So what about Steven? Have you given him the flick?'

'Yes,' I say. 'When I thought that I'd lost Rick, I was beside myself and I realised that I just didn't feel the same way about Steven. That was a fantasy, a bit of fun . . .' that's not really the right word, I know '. . . while things were rough between us.'

'And how does Steven feel about this?'

'I'm sure he understands. He hasn't contacted me since . . .' and then I realise that I didn't tell Una about my abortive night with him and I also realise that I don't want to. 'Since I last saw him,' I finish lamely.

'I might nab him for myself now he's back on the market,' she says with a rather edgy giggle.

I throw the last issues of *Grand Designs*, *Grazia*, *Marie Claire* and *Glamour* to the floor ready for the recycling bin. 'All well with Internet Tex?'

'I spent half of the weekend online with him.'

'And what did you do with the other half?' We titter at that too.

Then Una sighs and says, 'To be honest, Juliet, the other half was very boring.'

'Still no nearer to meeting him?'

She shakes her head. Then, as I'm flicking through *Men's Health* before casting it into the 'to be chucked' pile at my feet, the breath in my lungs suddenly stops. I turn to Una.

My friend frowns. 'OK?'

I shake my head. No, it can't be. I look back at the magazine, then I'm sure. Absolutely sure. Holding up the out-of-date copy of *Men's Health*, I show her the page.

Now it's my friend's to gasp. 'Omigod.'

'That's him, isn't it?'

Una nods but is unable to form sentences.

On the page is Internet Tex. His tanned, toned body is topless and he's flexing his muscles, preening at the camera.

Una snatches the magazine from my hands. 'Let me see that again.' She starts to hyperventilate as she reads the text.

The feature is about male models – ranging from the young underwear stud to more mature gentlemen who are more likely to be found demonstrating golf equipment. Guess which category Internet Tex falls into.

Then she turns bleak eyes to me. 'He's a model,' she says. 'He's not an engineer. And he lives in Chicago.' Not South London.

'Do you think you've been talking to someone who has just used his picture?'

My friend nods, stunned. 'I think that's exactly what's happened.'

We pull up two chairs in the corner of the library and study the piece again. I put my arm round my friend and give her a hug.

Una massages her temples. 'I've been taken for an idiot,' she says. 'I haven't told you this but I've been starting to have my suspicions. Every time I suggested we meet, he'd tell me that he was having to go away on business.' My friend looks at me, her eyes filled with tears. 'That cheque he sent me? It bounced.'

'Oh, Una.'

'It was only for a small amount of money, I know. But there have been a few other little sums – a hundred quid here or there.'

This is the first time she's mentioned it to me. Seems we're both keeping secrets where men are concerned. I wonder if we do that when we know what we're about to do is a really bad idea and that a good friend would talk us out of it.

'And he's been pushing me to put money into this internet business,' Una continues shakily. 'Which I suspect is non-existent.'

'I'm glad that you didn't go ahead with it.'

'I could be ten grand down if I'd agreed with his plans. The worrying thing is that I was so taken in by him, Juliet, so sure, I very nearly did it. I was that far away.' Una indicates with her fingers a tiny amount of space. That was very close, indeed.

'Seems that you've had a lucky escape this time.'

Now my friend starts to cry. 'It's horrible being a divorcée,' she sobs. 'I thought I was going to have a wild and exciting life without my staid, boring husband. How could I be so wrong? It was the biggest mistake I ever made, divorcing him.'

'You've just been unlucky,' I tell her.

She shakes her head. 'There are some terrible men out there, preying on women like me – stupid, vulnerable and keen to be with anyone who'll help them hang on to their youth.'

'Oh, Una.' I'm not sure what else to say.

'To think I've been encouraging you to see Steven,' she says. 'That was so wrong of me. Being a divorcée is pants. You stick with Rick. There are very few women that have such a strong marriage as yours. Don't be in a hurry to throw that away.'

'I've already realised that,' I tell her.

'What am I going to do?' Una wails. 'Here's me, I think I've been having a racy affair, and that person doesn't even exist.'

'Next time he emails, you have to ignore him.'

'Just to think,' a tear trickles down Una's cheek, 'I've been pouring out my heart to someone I thought could be my soulmate and he was just trying to scam me for money.'

'I think it goes on a lot.'

'But I never thought that I'd fall for it. I thought I was more streetwise than that. I'm forty-three years old, not some gauche teenager. I should have known better.'

'We all do stupid things.' Una, Rick, me. When I think of how stupid I've been over the last few months, my blood runs cold. Fortunately, Una has only been scammed for a few hundred pounds before she came to her senses. It could have cost me everything.

Chapter 108

'Sure you're up to this, Ricky-Boy?' Hal asked.

'Treat me gently,' Rick said. 'I'm not quite the man I once was.' They lifted the carpet together and walked slowly into the house with it.

'We'll take it at your pace today, mate. Just let me know how you're going.'

They were fitting a new seagrass carpet to the living room of a new-build, ground-floor flat in Buckingham. It wouldn't take them long. Personally, he wouldn't have given seagrass houseroom – the minute you spilled something on it, that was it. Ruined.

'Juliet looked relieved to see you last week.'

'She was out of her mind with worry,' Rick told Hal. 'Every time I move at the minute she's like my shadow. I'm sure Shannon was the same.'

Hal laughed bitterly. 'I wish. The only cuddle I got was from your neighbour when I dropped you off.'

'Stacey?'

His friend nodded. 'Shannon was out clubbing when I got home. Didn't reappear until the next morning. She'd heard nothing about the bomb at Wembley.'

'Nothing?'

'That's the youth of today for you,' Hal said sagely. 'Care about nothing but themselves. The world around them can fall apart and they're not bloody interested. I rattled round the house all night by myself wondering what on earth I was doing.' That laugh again. 'I nearly phoned Melinda.'

'That bad?'

'It was three in the morning and I'd had a skinful. What can I say?'

'Drunken phone calls to exes are always bad news.'

'Not as bad as finding out that you're going to be a father when you don't want to be,' Hal added.

'I know, mate,' Rick said. 'It's not what you wanted.'

'No,' Hal agreed, 'but it looks as if it's what I've got.'

'What are you going to do?'

Hal leaned on the fireplace in the bare flat and stared out of the window. 'I've been thinking, Rick,' he said, a serious note in his voice. 'Say if I disappeared . . .'

'Disappeared?'

'Like went to Australia or somewhere, maybe New Zealand even, where no one could find me, would you take over the business?'

'Me?'

'I don't think I can cope with the pressure. I need to get away. Melinda's got the house and the kids. She could get off her lazy backside and start working again. I'd leave Shannon some money and she could decide whether she wanted to keep the baby or not.'

'That's harsh, Hal.'

'The one thing that last Saturday showed me is that I'm not living the life that I want.'

That was fair enough, Rick supposed. After that, he could see where Hal was coming from. 'You could become a scuba-diving instructor in the Cayman Islands or somewhere.'

'That does, indeed, sound like a very attractive possibility.'

'Do you really mean it, Hal?' Rick asked. 'Would you really turn your back on everything that you know and walk away?'

'If I don't show up one morning, mate, then you'll know that I have. I won't tell you where I've gone so that I don't put you in an awkward position.'

'It's best that you don't tell me any more. I've stopped doing

389

awkward positions now, Hal. They're not good for your health.' Or for your marriage. From now on it was the straight and narrow for Rick. No more late-night car parks, no more lapdancing clubs, no more unseemly incidents outside Ann Summers shops. His sole purpose in life would be to make Juliet happy and proud of him. He was looking forward to it already.

Chapter 109

I'm sitting in the kitchen having a cup of tea. It's the morning of our anniversary and already the postie has been and there is a pile of greetings cards on the table. Judging by the number of cards we've received, we have so many friends and I'm grateful that they've remembered our special day.

Two slices of incinerated toast catapult themselves out of the toaster and across the room. Buster catches one on the fly and then runs to the corner of the room and swallows it whole. He thinks it's a great game and is getting more expert at it the more practise he gets.

'Wait, wait,' Rick says, as I go to stand up in order to replenish the bread and make a second attempt at cremation. 'I told you I had a surprise.' Under his arm there is a sturdy box.

'What can it be?' I ask in mock surprise.

'I thought it was about time,' he says. He places the box which is covered in silver and white paper on the table and I rip it open. Sure enough, there's a new toaster inside. It's stainless steel with multiple settings and the ability to toast not only bread but also muffins and crumpets to varying degrees of golden brown. This is my dream come true.

'I'll plug it in.' Rick bounds across the kitchen with it, wrenches the old toaster out of the way and in seconds has inserted two fresh slices of bread into the new one. 'Aunt Gladys would be horrified.'

Fortunately for us, she died years ago. We can use the shiny replacement toaster with impunity. While I wait for my toast, I start on the cards.

'I wasn't going to tell you,' Rick said, 'but you know that I can't keep secrets.'

I flush a bit at that. It's going to be a long time before I return to my guilt-free status.

'I've organised a party for this evening. At that newly-refurbished pub in Beachampton, The Crown.'

'Rick, that's a lovely idea.'

My husband blushes too. 'I thought we should do something. We couldn't let twenty-five years pass without marking them.'

'But I've got nothing to wear.'

'That's why Una's taking you shopping this afternoon. Now you're supposed to say "what about my hair?"'

'What about my hair?' I oblige.

'You're booked in for an appointment with thingy who normally does your hair at four o'clock. And your nails too.'

'You have been busy.'

'Happy?'

I kiss my husband. 'Very.'

Then my mum comes in. 'Can't you two lovebirds leave each other alone for five minutes?'

My mother has no need to talk. We can hear what she and Arnold get up to in her room. Unfortunately.

She throws a card down on the table, which I duly open. It's a lovely card with 25 on the front in ornate silver lettering. Inside, in Mum's spidery writing it says, *Never thought you'd make it.* Which is probably as near as we're ever going to get to congratulations from my mother.

'I have some good news of my own,' she says, before I can thank her. She waves an official-looking letter at me with a smug smile on her face. 'The bank got my money back for me. All of it.'

'That is good news.'

'Told you so. Is there any tea in the pot?'

'I'll have a look.' As I go towards the teapot, the toaster pings two slices of toast out. 'Wow.' I examine it carefully.

'Done to your perfection, madam?' Rick wants to know.

It's perfectly sun-kissed brown on both sides, a new, improved slice of toast. But it still has a tiny soupçon of burned stuff round the edge of one side to remind us of the old toaster that we managed with for so long.

'It's just right,' I say with a smile. 'I couldn't want for anything more.'

Chapter 110

I'm wearing a sparkly new dress from Coast chosen by Una and paid for by my dear husband. My hair and nails are so groomed that I'd give any WAG a run for her money and it's fair to say that I'm feeling pretty splendid. In my bedroom, I give a twirl and Rick nods his approval.

'Foxy,' he says.

'Can I be forty-five and still foxy?'

'You can in this house.' He slaps my bottom playfully as I bend to pick up my handbag.

I laugh and think that it's so nice that we're having fun together once more. The woman who took off her knickers and cartwheeled on the beach has, I'm pretty sure, put in a tentative appearance again.

We'd got set in our ways, worn down by life and all the stuff around us. Now we're going to move on, go through life with a lighter touch and try not to get bogged down by it all.

This bedroom needs an overhaul. In fact, the whole house does and I think that Rick and I will start on that soon. We should sort this room out first. Make it more romantic. Add some cushions, accessories. I'll check with Una what to do.

My husband is looking very spruce too. He hates wearing a suit and only does so on high days and holidays. This is clearly a high day. 'You look great,' I say. 'Very Hugh Laurie.'

'I thought Hugh Laurie was a nerd.'

'Not now he's in *House*. Now he's hot.'

'Huh.' Rick is impressed with being hot.

Before we set off for the party, Rick kisses me. 'I have one last surprise.' Out of a small, navy-blue box he lifts a diamond bracelet.

'Rick, that's gorgeous!'

'Twenty-five diamonds,' he says shyly. 'I hope you like it.'

'I love it.' I think the last piece of jewellery that Rick bought me was my engagement ring and, although it's much loved, the single diamond in it isn't as big as just one of these little beauties.

Carefully, he clips it to my wrist. It fits perfectly.

'That's it,' he says. 'No more surprises.'

'Not ever?'

Rick's eyes meet mine. 'I think it's best if we just tell each other everything from now on.'

And I know that Rick knows about Steven. I have no idea how, but he does. And I know that he's forgiven me, whatever I've done.

'Rick . . .' I start to explain.

'It doesn't matter now,' he says.

'Nothing happened,' I tell him.

'Then that's even better.' He takes me in his arms and twirls me round. 'Ready to party?'

Chapter III

All our friends are ready and waiting by the time we arrive at The Crown, and a cheer goes up as we enter. Tears fill my eyes. All of the people who are most dear to me are here to celebrate our enduring love. I grab Rick's hand and squeeze it. To think that a few weeks ago we were just planning to ignore the whole thing. I'm so very glad that we didn't.

The room is beautifully decorated with balloons that I believe Chloe is responsible for. At one end is a tall cake which more than makes up for the lack of one at our actual wedding.

There's a disco in full swing and Rick and I are ushered forward to have the first dance. Spandau Ballet's 'True' was our tune. Still is. Rick and I smooch to the sultry crooning of Tony Hadley.

'Remember this?' I ask.

'Wasn't Chloe conceived to this?'

I laugh. 'Chloe and a thousand other babies, I should think.'

'Let's not tell her that,' Rick advises.

It's hard to recall that my middle-aged husband was a trendy young New Romantic when I met him, with fluffed-up hair and ruffled shirts – though he did draw the line at eye-shadow.

When we've finished dancing, we go to find the family. Chloe in a floaty dress is hanging onto the arm of a young man who looks like he might well be a rugby player. Her hand is resting protectively on her stomach. 'This is Mitch,' she says, giggling girlishly.

'Ah.' So this is the father of my grandchild.

'Nice to meet you.' He shakes my hand shyly and I like him instantly. Rick claps him on the back. A good sign.

'We've got some news for you,' my daughter says. 'Mitch has found a job up here for when he graduates. We're going to look for a place to rent together.'

I smile to myself. So, the first one of our brood is going to fly the nest to start one of her own. Kissing Chloe, I say, 'I'm really pleased for you both.'

'We'll still need your help,' she says hurriedly. 'I'm thinking of trying to get a job straight after the baby's born.' My daughter looks adoringly at her boyfriend. 'We'll need the money.'

'There's plenty of time to think about that. I'm just looking forward to getting to know you, Mitch.'

'Likewise, Mrs Joyce,' he says.

Tom's here too – with another woman. He saunters over, bottle of beer in hand. 'Happy anniversary, old girl.'

'Hey, less of that.'

'Ali, this is Mum. Mum, Ali.' And that's it. Ali is pretty, blonde, wouldn't put undue strain on our dining-room table and probably won't last longer than a week.

Nevertheless, I say, 'Lovely to meet you.'

Mum and Arnold are already on the dance floor getting down. No matter how old your parents are, or indeed, how old you are yourself, your folks always embarrass you when they're dancing. Mum gives me a wave and, like a dutiful daughter, I wave back. Next to them, Hal and Stacey Lovejoy are dancing together. Hal seems to be enjoying her spray-on silver trousers and low-cut glittery top. Stacey's girls – all dressed in the children's range from Hustler – run up and they all hold hands and dance together. Perhaps I can have a quiet word with her about her children's clothing now that we're friends and, at the same time, get some advice about sexing up my own. My neighbour and I are starting an aerobics class together at the church hall next week in an effort to get fit. I'm going to have to go out and add some bling to my knacky old exercise gear to keep up with her.

Rick is still getting to know Mitch – probably grilling him about his job and earning potential in typical father style. Chloe will be furious. I see Una and head for my friend. She's with Don and his girlfriend, and Una is out-sparkling them both.

'OK?'

My perky friend nods at me. 'Lovely party.'

'Sorry there aren't any spare men.' Stacey Lovejoy seems to have bagged the only one.

She shrugs. 'Actually, I've started seeing someone.'

'Really? Why didn't you mention it today? You should have brought him with you.'

'Maybe another time,' Una says. 'I might slope off early, if that's OK. I said I'd see him for a drink later.'

'Go for it, girl. Just as long as he's not someone that you've met on the net.'

'No,' Una says. 'I've seen this one in the flesh.'

'You have to tell me all about it on Monday. Everything.'

Then Dad comes up with Samuel in tow. They both kiss my cheek and, out of the corner of my eye, I see that Una is already slipping away.

'Happy anniversary,' Dad says. 'All right, love?'

'I'm having a lovely time,' I tell him.

'We're all sorted for our trip to Florence. Samuel has been teaching me some Italian.'

Samuel grins at me. My dad, talking Italian. I shake my head.

'Florence?' Mum is behind us, hanging onto Arnold. 'Arnold and I are going to Australia.'

It's the first I've heard of this.

'We're buying a camper van and are going to drive across the country. Go native.'

That I would pay to see. I have to say that a camper van across Australia trumps Dad's week in Italy. But I do wonder how long Arnold will last in such close proximity to my mother. I'd kill her within three days.

'I hope you have a great time, Rita,' my dad says, and I can tell that he really means it.

Mum fills up. 'You too, Frank.'

Then Dad puts his arms round her and they give each other a hug. 'Silly old fool,' Mum says. 'You always were very emotional.'

For the record, my dad was never emotional. It's only Samuel who's brought out his softer side.

Then I hear 'Hi Ho Silver Lining' start up, which is one of my favourite songs. 'I think we should all hit the dance floor together, *en famille*,' I say.

'*Come una famiglia*,' Dad chips in.

'What do you reckon?'

We all head to the dance floor, even Rick who hates dancing and yet has done it twice already this evening. Now *that's* what I call true love.

Chapter 112

'So? Come on,' I say. 'Tell me all about your hot date.' It's the Monday after our anniversary party and Una still looks sparkly-eyed. We lean on the reception desk – something that Don hates us doing, but something that he's never managed to cure us of.

'We should talk about your party.' She waves away my question. 'Looks like it was fab.'

'I think everyone enjoyed it,' I tell her. 'I certainly did. My feet are still hurting, I danced so much.'

Then, even though it's only a minute past nine, the doors swing open. My mouth gapes as I see that it's Steven Aubrey coming through them.

'Won't be a minute, Una,' I whisper.

Walking round the desk, I take Steven's arm and steer him towards the children's section.

'Steven,' I say. 'I can only apologise about the other night.'

He goes to speak, but I shush him. I see Una watching us like a hawk in the background. She'll want chapter and verse on this when I'm finished.

'I thought I'd made it clear that it was over between us. Before it even started. I love Rick. It was complete madness to do what I did, but I'm over it now. I'm back on track. And you must do the same, Steven. You have to leave me alone. I'm a married woman and I plan on staying that way.'

'Juliet,' Steven says with a sigh, 'if you let me get a word in edgeways I can explain everything. I know that you'll never think of me in the same way that I think . . . thought . . . of you. That's fine. We both have to move on.'

'That's right,' I agree, relieved that Steven is finally on my wavelength.

'I'm sorry too that we didn't get it together the other night. It would have been fun. For old times' sake.'

'I don't want to talk about that,' I tell him. 'Neither of us must mention it again.'

'That's fine by me,' Steven says.

'Good. Good. Then I'll wish you luck for the future and you must go, Steven.'

That sigh again. 'The other thing I want to explain is that I'm not here to see you, Juliet. I'm here to see Una.'

He smiles over at the desk and my agitated little friend is grinning widely at him.

'Oh.' So that was Una's hot date. Steven. My friend has been seeing Steven Aubrey and she never even mentioned it. I shouldn't be shocked. But I am. I should have seen this coming. But I didn't.

I wonder when it started. Was it before I decided to spend the night with him or after? Good grief, I feel so foolish. My face bursts into flame.

'She's a lovely woman.'

'Yes,' I say tightly. 'Yes, she is.'

'I just wanted to fix up our lunch arrangements,' he says, gesturing towards Una. 'Then I'll be out of your hair.'

'No, no. That's fine. Take as long as you like. I'll be upstairs. Shelving books. Yes. That's what I'll do. Shelve books.' And I want to bite out my own tongue as I'm babbling inanely. So I bolt for the stairs before I can make myself look any more stupid.

Minutes later, when my shaking hands are just finding a home for Jamie Oliver, I hear Una's footsteps on the stairs behind me. Then she clears her throat. 'Juliet.'

I spin round, pretending I was so absorbed that she's taken me by surprise. Is that what it's going to be like now with Una? Can I never be myself with her again?

'I didn't want you to find out like that.'

But I wonder if Steven did.

'Why didn't you tell me?' I ask. 'I would have been pleased for you.' Is that the truth? Is it? Really?

'It all happened so quickly.'

Isn't that the truth?

'We were just swept away by our feelings.'

How jolly nice for you, I want to say. *I spent all my time with Steven fighting my feelings.*

But then Una, I think, deserves some happiness too and she's had precious little of late. Plus she's free, available and, I imagine, very willing. If I'm honest, Steven and Una would probably be well suited to each other. More suited, say, than Steven and me.

'We're very much in love,' Una tells me, and there's a defiant little jut to her chin that I don't like.

It might be awkward working together now. I wonder how much Steven will tell her about our time together. Nothing, I hope. But then he might well be vengeful. I don't know. I only know that I don't want anything to do with either of them now. I want to retreat into my own little world, with my own little family, and love and nurture just them.

'I'm going to be leaving the library,' I say, making my decision on the spot. 'I'll be looking after the baby for Chloe and, well, I think it's time for a change.'

'I won't be here either.' Una folds her arms across her chest, plumping it up. 'I've given my notice in this morning.'

'There's no need for you to do that . . .' If I'm going, then Una can stay. Don won't hold her to it. He's not like that.

'I'm going travelling with Steven,' she adds. 'Round the world. We're starting off in Miami. He has a house there.'

Does she think I don't know this?

'Then we'll probably spend the winter in South Africa. Stay away from all that cold and rain. After all,' and she looks me directly in the eye as she says this, 'there's no reason for either of us to stay here.'

'No,' I say. 'No reason at all.'

'I'd better get back on the desk.' Una flicks her hair in that general direction. 'There's no one there.'

Then she turns and flounces down the stairs. Yes, it's definitely a flounce. And, as I clutch Jamie Oliver to me, it's all I can do to hold back the tears.

Chapter 113

It's a good job that we've got this new toaster as it's working flat out. Rick is on toast duty and is buttering away. I'm just finishing off the sausages, then everything's ready.

We're going to have to move to a bigger house if our family keeps growing at this rate. This morning there are eleven of us for breakfast and we've opened the doors through to the dining room, wedging them back to give us more space, and have pushed the kitchen and dining-room tables together. Otherwise, I would have had to do two sittings.

'OK, guys!' Everyone's chattering away and I have to shout to make myself heard. 'Shall I just dish up?' Much nodding.

'Nothing for me, Mum,' Chloe pipes up. 'I'll just have some dry Ryvita.'

My daughter is still struggling with morning sickness and I'm not sure how she's even tolerating the smell of a cooked breakfast. Mitch is here too. The boyfriend. Their chairs are scooshed close together and my daughter has her feet curled up on his lap, while the compliant father-to-be massages them. He'll have his work cut out with Chloe, I can tell. They're currently looking at flats to rent in the local paper – which, for once, doesn't feature my husband on the front page.

Mitch folds up the paper as I put a plate in front of him. This could be his first meal in this household of many to come. 'Thanks, Mrs Joyce.'

'Juliet,' I say, and he smiles at me before making a grab for the Daddies sauce.

Tom and Ali have also joined us. This one's lasted about three weeks now, which is quite good going for my son. I put their breakfasts down on the table.

'Hey, Mum,' he says, as he picks up a sausage and bites into it. 'Forgot to tell you.' He offers the sausage to Ali and she bites it too – way too suggestively – and then giggles. My son smiles indulgently. 'Ali and I have both got jobs.'

'About bloody time,' Rick says, looking up from his toaster duty.

'We're off to China.'

Didn't quite expect that. It almost creates a hush at the table, except my mother talks through everything.

'Teaching English as a foreign language. In Beijing.'

'When?' I say, still reeling.

'In a couple of weeks,' he says. 'Just got to sort out flights. We've got a twelve-month contract to start with and they give us Chinese lessons, sort us out with a flat and then a teaching placement when we've finished the course.'

My son, who can barely drag himself out of his bedroom, is going off to work in China?

'Does that mean we can rent your room out?' Rick asks.

'Yeah, very funny, Dad.'

'Way to go, big bro',' Chloe says approvingly.

At the other end of the table Mum and Arnold have bought *My Camper Van* magazine and are studying it avidly. The plan for a pensioners' invasion of the outback is still going ahead. 'Where did he say he was going?' Mum wants to know.

'China,' I say, still not quite believing it myself.

'Couldn't stand the food,' is my mother's dismissive view of my son's adventure.

'That's Grandma's way of saying "Well done, Tom, I hope you have a wonderful time",' Rick chips in.

My son grins and Rick winks at him. Rick hasn't exactly been

405

effusive himself, but I know that he'll be proud of Tom for finally doing something constructive with his life.

'*Bella, bella,*' Dad says, casually throwing in a bit of his newly-acquired skill with the Italian language. 'Always knew that you'd make something of yourself, our Tom.'

'Cheers, Gramps,' Tom says, and they high-five each other across the table. 'You'll have to come out and visit us.'

'We might just do that.' He turns to his partner. 'Eh? What do you think, Samuel? I love noodles. Once we've conquered Italy, we could set our sights further afield. What do you reckon?'

'I'd like to do that, Francis.' Samuel Scott has to be the world's most affable man and I'm so glad that my father stumbled across this rather unexpected source of happiness in the latter years of his life. My dad, the man who was once reluctant to venture further than his garden shed, has become an adventurer because of this man. I put my arms round them both and hug them.

'What's that for, love?'

'Just for being you.'

'I'm thinking of going to Gran Canaria for a holiday. Me and the girls. Just for a week or two.' Stacey Lovejoy has also joined us for breakfast as Ikea, Malibu, Levi and Becks are all at the leisure centre swimming this morning. I've grown rather fond of the brash Stacey and her unruly brood, but although I now adore her girls, I'm not sure that I'm quite ready to take on her kids *en masse*. I prefer them in short bursts and, preferably, two at a time. I'm going to need a new best friend now that Una and I won't be seeing each other any more and I could do a lot worse than this kind-hearted and very loud lady. This morning she's wearing a flouncy, low-cut top in citrus yellow which is making the kitchen glow. Arnold is paying rather a lot of attention to it. Just wait until my mother manages to tear herself away from *My Camper Van* and realises what he's up to.

'Gran Canaria?'

'I've got a friend there,' she says somewhat evasively.

Hmm. I wonder. Hal has done a runner, just as he threatened to, and has left the business to Rick. No one is supposed to know where he is, but Hal and our neighbour were getting very peachy with each other at our anniversary party and I wonder idly whether that's where Hal has disappeared to.

'Can you look after the gnomes while we're in Australia?' Mum says to Dad. 'This lot don't respect them.'

'Course I will, Rita. Samuel and I will take them home with us.' Dad pats my mum's knee, which drags Arnold's attention back from Stacey Lovejoy. 'Put the boys back in their proper place.'

I'll swear there are tears in Mum's eyes. Bloody gnomes.

In the background, I see Rick punch the air and mouth, 'Yes!'

So, that's it. Everyone looks like they're pretty much sorted. Even the gnomes. Rick finishes cooking the last two breakfasts.

'Shall I take them to the table?' I say.

'In a second. Just want a quick word first.' And my husband takes my hand and leads me into the hall. He closes the door on the kitchen.

'Yes!' he says again in a stage whisper as he does a victory dance. 'We're getting rid of them all!'

I laugh and say with a sigh, 'You know, the silly thing is that I think I'm going to miss them.'

'You're right.' He shakes his head. 'That *is* silly.'

'It'll be funny, just being the two of us again.'

'Yeah,' Rick muses, stupid grin on his face. 'Hilarious. More hot water than we'll know what to do with. I'll be able to sit on the loo without someone banging on the door. We can run round the house naked.' My husband waggles his eyebrows at me. 'We could even make love on the dining-room table.'

'I rather like the sound of that,' I confess.

'Good.' He takes me in his arms and pulls me close. 'We'll put it on our list of things to do.'

'Your breakfasts are getting cold,' Chloe shouts.

Laughing, we go back into the kitchen. We collect a plate each and then squeeze round the table in the last two seats.

'Everyone OK?' Some nodding, but they're all too busy eating to answer me.

Rick puts his arm round me and kisses my cheek. 'I love you.'

'Pack it in, you two,' Chloe mutters. 'Some of us are eating.'

'I love you too,' I tell him, and I surreptitiously wipe a tear from my eye.

Looking at Rick and all my family around me – who, despite everything we've been through, are still a tight unit bound to each other by blood, affection and loyalty – I feel a contented warmth rush through me. The loving feelings that I thought we'd both lost come flooding back. I realise that love isn't some romantic notion. It isn't all flowers and diamonds and moonlit nights. Love is what you go through together, the troubles that nearly drive you apart, but that ultimately bind you together and make you stronger and stronger.